I0461116

OFFICER JONES

BY DEREK CICCONE

Copyright © Derek Ciccone 2013

All rights reserved.

ISBN reserved

Interior Layout by Cheryl Perez, www.yourepublished.com

All rights are reserved. No part of this book may be reproduced, distributed, or transmitted in any form of by any means, or stored in a database or retrieval system without the prior written permission of the publisher.

This book is a work of fiction. The names, characters, places, and incidents are products of the author's imagination or have been used fictitiously and are not to be constructed as real. Any resemblance to persons, living or dead, actual events, locales or organizations is entirely coincidental.

OTHER BOOKS BY DEREK CICCONE

Painless

The Trials of Max Q

The Truant Officer

Kristmas Collins

PART ONE -

THE LONG STRANGE TRIP HOME

CHAPTER 1

Redmond, Washington

July 4, 1991

The bartender slid a mug of beer in front of him.

Flip Tompkins pulled out a handful of mangled bills and spilled them onto the sticky bar for the tip. He included an extra dollar for looking past the fact he was still eighteen months shy of his twenty-first birthday.

Flip wore a multicolored flannel shirt, tied around his waist, and a T-shirt that saluted his favorite band, Pearl Jam—a local group that was a driving force in the new "grunge rock" craze that had swept through the Seattle area. He even copied the haircut of the band's lead singer, Eddie Vedder, with long, brown bangs that would constantly fall over his eyes.

Instead of attending college like most of his classmates, he'd spent his post-graduation year chasing around local grunge bands like Pearl Jam and Nirvana. His parents were seriously getting on his case about his current slacker status. And they were not thrilled that he'd decided to spend the Fourth going to another concert, instead of the traditional family picnic.

Between sips of beer, Flip glanced at his watch. The plan was to meet his best friend, Tim Kent, for their usual pre-concert party. But Flip couldn't get too wasted, since he had the misfortune of being the designated driver tonight. Tim had lost his driver's license a few years back, so he wasn't an option to drive them. It was a touchy subject.

Flip had hoped that the beer would make Cransky's slightly more tolerable. It was a dive bar in Redmond, a suburban utopia on the north end of Lake Sammamish. Its one saving grace was that it would never be confused with any of the trendy coffee houses and brew factories that were popping up like weeds in the Seattle area. But that didn't make Flip any less fearful that he'd end up like the many "lifers," who had nothing better to do on a holiday, or worse, preferred spending it here. Luckily, the combination of his Walkman and the *rat-a-tat-tat* of the raindrops on the tin roof drowned out most of their mindless conversations.

With all the commotion, few noticed the young man enter the bar. He walked directly to the last remaining seat at the bar, right next to Flip.

The man took off a dripping rain poncho, revealing a tight T-shirt that was tucked into dark blue jeans. Across the chest it read: *USAF: We Fly The Not So Friendly Skies.*

The presence of a non-lifer re-energized Flip, and he introduced himself.

The military man shook Flip's hand with a vice-like grip. "Nice to meet you, Flip—I'm Batman."

Flip first thought he was joking, but the man kept a serious face. So Flip went with the flow, "From the movie or the TV show?"

"It's my pilot moniker in the Air Force."

The guy seemed like he was straight out of *Top Gun,* Flip's favorite movie. "So you got a civilian name, Batman?"

"I would tell you, but then I'd have to kill you," he replied with a grin.

"In that case, Batman it is," Flip said, before swigging down what was left of his beer. He offered to buy the man a drink, but like the superhero he was, he only wanted water.

"What are you listening to?" Batman said, pointing to Flip's headphones.

"Pearl Jam," he answered proudly.

"Never heard of them. I'm a big country fan; Garth Brooks is my favorite. What is Pearl Jam, like hard rock?"

It was Flip's favorite topic—the grunge rock phenomenon. "They're a local band. If you haven't heard of them or Nirvana, then you must not be from around here."

"No, I'm not," Batman replied pleasantly. "Pearl Jam and Nirvana you say?"

"The next big thing. Really down-to-earth music. Totally different from that corporate, big hair, lip-sync stuff from the 80s."

He handed Batman the headphones. The military man placed them over his crew cut and seemed to enjoy the wailing lyrics of Eddie Vedder. Flip saw a possible convert.

"Maybe if you aren't doing anything tonight they're playing in Seattle at RKCNDY," Flip offered. "I'm heading up there with a few friends."

"Funny you should ask. I'm in town for the night and was looking for something to do. I planned on catching a movie at the drive-in—I hear this new Schwarzenegger flick *Terminator 2* is a must see—but with the rain, I thought I'd just call it an early night."

Flip couldn't believe his luck, finding someone at the last minute to take his designated driver duties. "First, we're going to meet my friend Tim. We like to pound a few beers before the concert—it's much better when you got a good buzz going. You can almost feel the lyrics." He hurried another look at his watch, before adding, "Speaking of which, we should be going."

The two men rose off their bar stools. Batman pulled out a credit card and slid it to the bartender with the instructions to pay the remainder of Flip's tab. Flip noticed the name on the card—Kyle Jones—but he'd keep playing along. Once the bill was settled, the two men headed out into the rainy afternoon.

Flip led him to his 1988 Chevy Beretta. The discolored back bumper had a V-like gash and the brake lights were damaged from when he slammed into a guardrail, following a similar pre-concert party last March. He told Batman the story, boasting how he and Tim were able to evade the cops after the accident.

"So you're going to drink and drive?" Batman asked.

"Don't get too drunk, might spill your drink," Flip responded with a chuckle, but grew worried when it wasn't returned. "You don't have a problem with that ... do you?"

"I'm sober, so why don't you let me drive. I heard on the radio that there will be a lot of police traps because of the holiday. If you end up in jail you'll miss the concert."

He had a point, so Flip tossed him the keys and they got in.

Once behind the wheel, Batman turned to Flip and said, "Drinking and driving can be deadly. You should really be more careful."

CHAPTER 2

The rainwater flowed like a river down the windshield. The Air Force pilot gripped the wheel and searched for the wipers. He couldn't believe that he could expertly fly an F-16 with enemy fire closing in on his ass, but was struggling to master this beat-up little Chevy.

It was just another bump along his journey. And he knew that nothing could stop him—he was Batman now. His alter ego that took over when he was carrying out a mission.

Flip provided him a slurred tutorial of the dashboard gadgets, and within a matter of moments they were heading out of the Cransky's parking lot.

"Why are you wearing gloves?" Flip asked.

"I'm used to wearing them from when I'm flying. Kind of a habit, I guess."

"Cool," Flip replied, easily impressed. "So does this make me your wingman?"

"Behind every great pilot is an unflappable wingman. But if you are, you'll need a name."

"I say you call me Robin. That way we'll be Batman and Robin."

He shook his head. "Sorry—already taken. My wingman from Desert Storm goes by Robin. What do you say we call you Pearl Jam?"

He actually saluted him. "Pearl Jam reporting for duty, it's an honor to serve you, Batman."

"The pleasure is all mine, Pearl Jam. Your first order of business can be to provide me the coordinates of where we are to meet Jim."

"Don't mean to correct you, Batman, but it's actually Tim ... with a T."

More specifically, it was Timothy Kent III, and Batman knew exactly who he was. Tim Kent killed his parents.

They had retired to Redmond almost three years ago, just after their only child had left to join the Air Force. Redmond proclaimed itself to be the "bicycle capital of the northwest," and his parents took to cycling through the lush hills like natives. Two years to the day, they spent a steamy Fourth of July evening mountain biking along Wright Street. They never saw Tim Kent speed his brand new Nissan Pathfinder around a corner. Batman's father was killed upon impact. His mother died later that night in a Seattle hospital.

Tim Kent was almost twice the legal limit, following a day of drinking at the lake. He arrived in court with a high-powered attorney purchased by his father, as if it were a graduation gift. Tim spent six months in "juvie" and then walked onto the campus of Gonzaga University with his records sealed. A fresh start that Batman's parents never got.

Batman was stationed in Germany when he received the life-shattering news. At first it seemed random and mindless. But he soon learned that nothing is a coincidence—every action had a reaction that was part of a bigger plan—and this meeting with Flip Tompkins was no different.

As they drove, the two men made idle chitchat about Batman's military exploits in the Gulf War, which he'd recently returned from.

After finishing another beer, Flip rolled down his window and tossed out the empty can. They drove past Redmond Town Center, which was empty due to the holiday. Then the local high school, where Tim Kent allegedly bragged about how he would get off with just a slap on the wrist.

The earlier downpour had tapered to a light mist. Batman knew it was another sign of support. The thinning thunderclouds were symbolic of his personal journey out of the darkness. He upped the vehicle's speed.

"So what brings you to Redmond?" Flip asked.

"My parents live here. I came to visit them." He wasn't completely lying—he'd visited their gravesite earlier that morning.

The conversation returned to the Pearl Jam concert, and music in general. It was more than Batman ever wanted to know about a rock band, but he continued to act as if he were hanging on every word. He didn't bother asking questions about Tim Kent—he knew him better than Tim knew himself. The only relevant fact was that he would soon be dead.

"The cul-de-sac is on McPherron Drive. It's the first right off of Wright Street," Flip provided directions.

It was unnecessary. Batman knew Wright Street. It's where his life changed forever. It's also where he was called to return, seeking closure. "Is that where Tim will be meeting us?"

"Yeah, he's gonna be pissed. I told him we'd meet up like twenty minutes ago," Flip answered, then added, "Sure you don't want a beer?"

Batman felt rage shoot through his veins. "Do you know that over twenty thousand Americans died last year from drunk drivers?"

He sped the car down Wright Street, the needle on the speedometer racing clockwise. "In the state of Washington alone, over half the traffic fatalities were alcohol related. Do you know how many ruined lives could be avoided!?"

Flip looked mystified. Just another pathetic sheep. "Sorry, dude, thought you were cool with it."

As the vehicle tore through a residential neighborhood at sixty-miles-per-hour, Batman pointed to a cassette tape on the floor, marked *Nirvana* in black magic-marker, and returned to a pleasant tone, "Hey, I want to hear that other new band you were talking about, Nirvana or something like that."

The request excited Flip. He began rambling about how it was a rare bootleg tape of the upcoming Nirvana album called Nevermind, which wouldn't officially be out until September. He talked reverently of a singer named Cobain, claiming he was the next John Lennon. Batman doubted it, but even if Flip turned out to be a prophet, like most prophets, he wouldn't be alive to celebrate the accuracy of his prognostications.

The Beretta flew through the suburban streets like a fighter jet with a MiG on its tail, hitting seventy-five on the speedometer. Flip unlatched his seat-belt and reached down to pick up the tape off the floor mat.

Batman viewed the boy as he bent over awkwardly to pick up the cassette. Then he slammed the brake, almost smashing his foot through the pedal. The screeching of the tires drowned out the snapping sound of Flip's neck breaking against the dashboard.

Batman sped the car again—he was now in a trance-like state. He had already gone from zero to fifty when he turned onto McPherron. The cul-de-sac fast approached—the enemy was in sight.

He immediately spotted his target. Tim Kent had a long, chiseled face and his hair was gelled vertically with stylish sideburns. He stood beside his attractive girlfriend, leaning on a canary-colored Volkswagen Rabbit convertible. They were intently locking lips, but the screech of tires caught his attention.

A group of four college-age students stood to his left, guzzling beer from plastic cups. One of them yelled out with laughter, "Sounds like Flip's wasted again!"

The group was the first target. He came at them with such a high speed that their inebriated reflexes didn't have a chance to react. Bodies flew, and screams filled the misty air. Batman knew he wouldn't have to go back to finish the job—the group was clustered, which wasn't a smart military tactic. They didn't know they were at war.

Without a moment to spare, he locked on his target at twelve o'clock, and launched his car directly at Tim Kent.

Batman savored the brief moment—he'd anticipated it for almost two years. It was the one thing that allowed him to continue on with life. Although, he wished he could have found another way. A way in which he could have made Tim Kent beg for forgiveness as he slowly sucked the last breaths from him.

The girlfriend screamed in horror—she would be collateral damage—but Kent remained frozen. The trembling fear in his face would have to be satisfaction enough. Batman was convinced he understood why he was about to die.

The impact shook the Beretta, leaving Batman momentarily disoriented. But he quickly found his "fighter pilot cool." He carefully moved Flip's lifeless body into the driver's seat and surrounded him with his empty beer cans.

"I told you drinking and driving kills," he mocked the dead boy. He then scurried into the rain-drenched pine forest that surrounded the cul-de-sac. He thought this would bring closure, but he would find that he was wrong.

CHAPTER 3

Midtown Manhattan

July 2—present

When you've risked your life in the world's most dangerous places, a long life expectancy isn't so expected. So it wasn't a surprise that I was having a midlife crisis in just my late thirties. The only question was why it took so long.

I sat at a small table on the patio of a trendy midtown restaurant called Norvell's, alone, but not by myself. The relentless machine of Manhattan traffic whisked behind me, filling the summer day with the majestic sounds of honking horns, which someone once described to me as urban bird chirping. The day was a spring-like seventy-two degrees with only a few clouds in the aqua sky, making it hard to imagine that thunderstorms were predicted for later this afternoon.

Across the table sat Lauren Bowden—her glowing blonde hair surrounding her angelic face. She claimed to be eleven years my junior, although my trusty reporter skills told me that her given age wasn't the same one that was on her birth certificate.

Lauren has been what I'd loosely refer to as my girlfriend for the past year. She's also my co-worker at GNZ (Global Newz), an international cable news network, and as long as I'm playing loose with terms, news might be a stretch when describing my industry as of late. It's been taken over by loud, noise-driven sensationalism that my boss, Cliff Sutcliffe, glowingly refers to as newsertainment. The running joke is that GNZ used to spell news with a Z since they were a unique alternative to traditional news, but now it's because much of their on-air talent can't spell. But that wouldn't be my concern for much longer.

Lauren addressed me in her southern accented voice, "John Peter, Norvell's is world famous for its sushi. It's the only real choice. So for the life of me, I can't figure out why you've been staring so intently at that menu."

I had hoped to buy a few more minutes hiding behind the menu. Usually she was too focused on herself to notice my avoidance techniques. Out of options, I was forced to endure a few uncomfortable moments of tedious conversation. But since I didn't get a word in, I'm not sure 'conversation' would be the proper term.

Our waitress arrived just in time to impede the migraine that had begun to percolate behind my right eye. As usual, Lauren waited for me to order for her. But I was drawing a blank.

"What did you say you wanted again?"

"Weren't you listening, John Peter? I said to order two sushis and two glasses of their best cab."

Cab is what I needed, as in the yellow kind with four wheels to flee the scene. I held a long look on Lauren, before switching my glance to our waitress, who wore a no-frills uniform and a pleasant smile. A complete contrast. Her name was Bridget, which I knew because she had been our regular waitress since Lauren decided that Norvell's was going to be *our* restaurant … at least until another eatery became the trendy place to be seen.

"She'll have two orders of sushi—the hosomaki—and two glasses of your best Cabernet. I'll take a cheeseburger and a bottle of your cheapest beer."

Bridget fought back a grin, gathered herself, and asked me which type of cheese I desired on my burger. I made a not very funny joke about holding the cheese on the cheeseburger, which received a giggle. I settled on American cheese. I'd been to so many countries the last twenty years that American seemed exotic.

Lauren flashed me a dirty look for going against her wishes. Or perhaps for evoking the flirtatious giggle from the waitress. The *why* really didn't matter at this point. She then sent an obvious fake smile in Bridget's direction. She'd mastered both looks. *Who says there aren't usable life skills gained from beauty pageants?* Certainly not the former Miss Beaufort County South Carolina who sat across from me.

I ignored Lauren, seeking the refuge of a daydream. But I was jolted back to reality by an angry twang firing at me from pointblank range. "Are you listening to me, John Peter?"

I've always been confused as to why she calls me John Peter, since that's not what JP stands for. "I'm sorry, you were talking about um … well … you know the …"

She flashed me her most displeased look. "I was talking about our trip to visit my parents in Hilton Head this weekend. It's the Fourth of July, if you haven't forgotten."

I racked my brain to think if it were actually possible that I'd agreed to this. I had interviewed rogue dictators and heartless terror-mongers over the years, but I still wasn't sure I was prepared to meet the people who created Lauren Bowden.

"I did?"

She sighed theatrically. "Yes, first we will stop in North Carolina for my big interview with Lamar Thompson, and then to Mommy and Daddy's place. They insisted we stay with them."

It was best not to argue. She would just claim that my forgetfulness was due to jealousy, since she was able to beat me out for the Thompson interview. The truth was, I would have refused it, due to its tabloid nature. In the world according to Lauren, this would be another example of why I'd become a dinosaur in this business, and my career was "in a dreadful decline." Little did she know that this dinosaur was about to become happily extinct.

The interviewee in question, Lamar Thompson, first entered the limelight twenty years ago when he was a high school basketball star out of Columbia, South Carolina. At the time, he was the most celebrated and highly recruited prep basketball player in history. Lamar chose the University of North Carolina, but he never got to play a game.

On an October night of his freshman year at UNC, two weeks prior to the start of basketball season, it all ended for him. In the spirit of being young and stupid, Thompson and a couple of fellow classmates decided to spend their Friday night pulling a prank. They hid in the wooded area alongside a dark, country road in a small town outside of Chapel Hill. When an unsuspecting car drove by, they tossed a lifelike dummy onto its hood, giving the driver the impression of having struck a real person. It was followed by beer-buzzed laughs of insensitive youth and an exhilarating dash for safety.

It eventually led to a high-speed chase with police, which ended with Thompson's car slamming into an oncoming vehicle driven by Marilyn Lacey. The mother of three was killed instantly.

There were two other people in Thompson's car—fellow UNC classmate Brad Lynch, who died from injuries sustained in the crash, and another passenger who survived, but was never identified due to the fact he or she was a juvenile. But when word got out, it really didn't matter who else was involved, because the only name people were talking about was Lamar Thompson … the next great thing.

Lamar's leg was mangled in the accident, ending his promising basketball career. That was the good news for him. The bigger problem was that he was legally drunk, and despite his claims to the contrary, he was identified as the driver. He served five years in the state pen for vehicular manslaughter. The years following were no kinder to him—he was now an unemployed night watchman with a history of substance abuse.

But the reason Lamar Thompson was once again relevant, was his recent assertion that there was a fourth man in the car that night named Craig Kingsbury, and that he was the one who was drunk behind the wheel. The reason this was front-page news, and screwing up my holiday weekend, was that Craig was now Senator Kingsbury, who had just tossed his name into the ring to become the next President of the United States, and many believe the frontrunner.

Lauren grew annoyed with my distracted pause. "John Peter, where *are you* today?"

The question was not where I was, but rather, how the hell did I get here? My old high school journalism teacher, Murray Brown, always preached that journalism went beyond the traditional who, what, where, why, and how. A great journalist tells a story, and to write the ending, one must return to the beginning. And whenever I return to the beginning of my story it always takes me back to Gwen.

CHAPTER 4

I first met Gwen Delaney when her family moved two houses down from ours. We were five years old. From that point on we were inseparable. We went from childhood friends to teenage romance, and then off to Columbia University with plans of one day owning a small-town newspaper and having lots of babies. That was before Saddam Hussein changed everything.

During my freshman year at Columbia, I took an internship at a start-up cable news network called GNZ. The idea of twenty-four hour news was gimmicky at the time, compared to the traditional print journalism that I aspired to. But being the über-achiever that I was, I thought television experience would be a good résumé builder. Little did I know that it would be a career launcher.

Since GNZ was in its infancy, it didn't have the budget of its competitors like CNN. So when war broke out, they offered their one and only intern, JP Warner, the opportunity of assisting their lead international correspondent, Jonathan Horvitz, during the war coverage. This was a dream opportunity for a kid who grew up idolizing war correspondents like Ed Bradley and David Halberstam, and I was all in—I could make up the school work, this was the opportunity of a lifetime, even if my horrified parents didn't see it that way.

As history would have it, Horvitz didn't have the stomach for battle, and ended up hiding under the bed of our Baghdad hotel room, praying to whatever deity would listen. So, three years removed from being able to legally buy a drink, I spent six weeks providing on-camera reports from the front-line.

The Gulf War wasn't much of a fight, as far as military conflicts go, but what it will always be remembered for was that it was the first "TV War." It changed the war correspondent from a brave, noble observer into a television star. Lines were blurred, and some would say it was the beginning of reality TV. Although, nobody is quick to take credit for reality TV.

When I returned home, I learned that I'd become as much of a story as the war itself. I can still recite my first glorious review in the *New York Globe*:

Nobody came out of Desert Storm a bigger star than the youthful JP Warner. With rugged good looks, he appears more like a leading man the likes of Newman or Redford, than the typical news reporter. He comes across as courageous, confident, honest, and outspoken. Some will question his credentials or experience, but nobody can deny he is a star in the making.

I was hooked. During my remaining years at Columbia I worked every free moment I had at GNZ, and then signed on to become an international correspondent the day after I graduated. I wanted Gwen to come with me, but she refused, remaining in New York to report for the *New York Globe*, and spending most of her time writing obituaries. Little did I know that I was writing an obituary for our relationship, as we drifted further and further apart. At one point I actually began to believe our relationship was holding me back. Although, in hindsight, I'm a little fuzzy as to what exactly I was being held back from. Not even when Gwen decided that we need "some time apart," which soon changed to "a lot of time apart," did I ever think that we wouldn't be together one day.

That was, until I received the invitation to Gwen Delaney and Stephen DuBois' wedding. It was the moment JP died and J-News took over completely.

I threw every tortured emotion I had into covering the most dangerous stories in the most treacherous areas of the globe. I was willingly turned into a packaged image of the news warrior, who not only ran toward the danger, but looked good doing it. I wore three days growth on my face to feed the image. Same with my wardrobe, which led to my nickname of J-News, because it was said I looked like I just stepped out of the J-Crew catalog into the war zone.

But I wasn't all style over substance—I took on the toughest stories in places most journalists wouldn't even think to venture. Some, my mother included, claimed I had a death wish. Maybe I did. My youthful idealism was replaced by a hard-edged and arrogant swagger that I'd convinced myself was necessary to survive in such a dangerous business. I wasn't very well liked, but I was respected … at least I thought so.

Then last spring, I walked back onto the campus of Columbia like the conquering hero I believed I was, to be a guest lecturer in my old journalism class. When I finished my ode to myself, a pretty girl with long, raven hair and radiant green eyes rose to ask a question. I was startled by the resemblance; for a moment I actually thought it was her. Then very much like Gwen, she zinged me with a question, asking me if I'd missed being a journalist since my industry had become nothing but loud, ratings driven sensationalism.

It was at that exact moment that my midlife crisis began. And I was forced to face the truth—it wasn't my journalistic roots driving me. And worst of all, somewhere along the way I had become just like Lauren—a self-involved self-promoter who was addicted to publicity.

The reality was that I kept feeding the J-News monster because it was the only thing that could remove Gwen from my daydreams.

CHAPTER 5

Shouts of "John Peter! John Peter!" shocked me back to the present. Unless I was the next contestant on the *Price is Right*, I had no idea why Lauren was shouting at me with such vigor.

"You promised that our lunch wouldn't be interrupted," she chastised.

I found this a little odd coming from someone who'd made three phone calls, sent four texts, and posted a picture of herself on Twitter since we'd arrived. "What are you talking about?"

"Your big slug friend is here."

"What?"

Before Lauren could answer, I felt the gargantuan arms wrapping around my neck, clamping me in a headlock. It could only be one man.

When he released me from his clutches, and my breathing somewhat returned to normal, I looked up to see the smiling man who was once a professional wrestler known as Coldblooded Carter. For longer than I can remember, Jeff Carter has been my scout, confidante, bodyguard, and the man with numerous contacts throughout the world that helped uncover the stories that ratings bonanzas are made of.

"Hope I didn't interrupt you two lovebirds," Carter's booming voice filled the patio.

Lauren looked at him like he was the Ebola Virus. "John Peter and I were discussing our plans for the Fourth of July, and *yes*, you are interrupting."

Carter laughed, further infuriating her. "So what are these big Fourth of July plans, JP?"

Lauren answered for me, "Following my big interview with Lamar Thompson, we are going to spend the holiday with my family in Hilton Head."

Carter faked a look of interest. "Wow! Meeting the parents—this is a big step, JP."

"And Hilton Head society," I added, now also smiling.

Carter flashed his famous sly grin and I could tell he was about to jump off the top rope and drop a flying elbow on her plans.

"Oh, by the way, I forgot to mention that JP won't be able to attend your family gathering. We have business to attend to." He tilted his head toward the ground as if he was mourning the dead.

My ears perked up, suddenly interested in the conversation.

Lauren boiled over. This had happened before. "John Peter," she addressed me like a mother scolding a child.

I shrugged, as if unable to stop the inevitable.

"You have a choice, John Peter—me, or that big slug. If you walk away from this table we're over."

Carter picked me up like a rag doll and slung me over his shoulder. "He's not walking away ... I'm carrying him."

A rumble of laughter erupted from the other patrons. From my perch, I caught a glance of Bridget, who was unable to fight off a smile.

Carter carried me out of the patio area to a chorus of, "John Peter, get back here!"

He finally set me down on the bustling sidewalk outside the restaurant.

"Thanks, I think you saved my life," I said, meaning every word.

Carter laughed. "I have three ex-wives—I can sense when a man needs to get six time-zones away."

CHAPTER 6

We began walking away from Norvell's, looking like the oddest of contrasts.

Even though I stood six-foot tall, Carter still towered over me by half a foot. His head was shaved to the scalp—his only hair above the neck was a goatee that reached two full inches below his chin. He wore his trademark wraparound sunglasses and sleeveless denim jacket.

I, on the other hand, looked like I was preparing for a career on the PGA Tour, wearing a lavender golf shirt and a pair of khakis.

Carter was not one for small talk and got right down to the reason he abruptly ended my lunch, and perhaps my relationship.

He opened his camouflage colored backpack and pulled out a black and white photo of a bearded man wearing the latest in Middle Eastern headgear. "Do you know who this is?"

I halfheartedly examined it. When it didn't ring a bell, I shrugged. "No idea."

"This, my friend, is Az Zahir."

Still nothing.

We reached our subway entrance and descended the crowded, muggy stairwell.

Carter found an unpopulated spot on the swamped subway platform. When the coast was clear, he told me the story of a young man from Chicago named Az Zahir, who was once an engineering student at Northwestern University. He was whisked away from his home in the middle of the night, accused of being a ranking member of Al Muttahedah, and was plotting to do some demolition work on a few of America's favorite buildings and monuments.

Al Muttahedah was a merger of the leading Islamic terrorist groups, who were pooling their resources to try to make a dramatic comeback in the War on Terror. They'd been operating under the radar until I exposed them last year in an investigative report for GNZ. They weren't happy about the sudden spotlight that had been cast on them, and supposedly put a bounty on my head. Carter comforted me, explaining that groups like them are only interested in killing innocent people, and I was anything but innocent.

Our train screeched to a halt with the whistle of air brakes. But prior to boarding, I was approached by a family. They asked if I would take a photo with them, and I happily obliged. Carter didn't share the sentiment. He grabbed me by the collar and pulled me onto the train. Brute force was always his answer to solving a problem, and while it's not always politically correct to say, it's usually an effective method.

We found a spot and grabbed the overhead bars to steady ourselves. Carter's glare repelled anyone who thought of getting within ten feet of us. He showed me the picture again, and this time it clicked.

"I remember now. He was involved in that plot to blow up Soldier Field during the NFC championship game. His parents were on the news every night crying about his civil rights like he was some modern day Rosa Parks. I think they claimed he ordered the tote bag, but they accidentally sent him the suitcase nuke."

"He was such a good Samaritan he won an all-expense paid water-boarding vacation to lovely Guantanamo Bay. But his stay was short, as he cut a deal with the CIA, which released him so that he could re-join his buddies at Al Muttahedah. The CIA wanted to use him as bait to help them assassinate their leader, Mustafa Hakim. I know you'll find this hard to believe, but Az Zahir double-crossed the CIA, and the assassination attempt was foiled. Al Muttahedah was now reportedly hiding out Zahir. His last sighting was in Uzbekistan, almost six months ago. But of course, the US government denies any of this took place."

"Let me guess—they granted us an interview to give them a platform to spew their hatred? We barter propaganda for ratings. Just please tell me we're not going to Uzbekistan. I hate Uzbekistan."

Carter gulped a frustrated sigh, and slowly blew it out. He looked like he wanted to put me in the most painful wrestling hold he could think of. But instead, he pulled out a pen and paper from his backpack and wrote down our destination for me. After I read it, he ate the piece of paper.

CHAPTER 7

When our train hit the 84th Street stop, Carter growled at me, "Okay, I told you my part, now it's your turn."

"My turn?"

"I gave you the details of the mission, now I wanna know what's going on with you."

"I have no idea what you're talking about."

"For starters, this lethargy thing. I just handed you the interview half the industry would sacrifice their first born for, and you're more interested in taking photos with the Cleaver family."

"Lethargy? Don't pull a muscle on the big words, Carter."

He shook his head. "You can try acting like your normal cocky-jerk self, but you're not fooling anyone. I've seen the signs for months. Your mind is somewhere else, and this smiling and being nice to people thing is starting to creep me out."

"Where did you get your psychology degree … Pro Wrestling University?"

"I'm serious."

There are a couple of rules that I live by. One, is to only go so far when messing with a former professional wrestler who still suffers from symptoms of steroid withdrawal. The other I learned from Murray Brown, who drilled into me to always lead with the headline. So I did. "I've decided I'm leaving the business when my contract runs out next month. This will be my last assignment."

He started laughing. "What's wrong, sweetheart—too rough being a rich and famous television star?"

I just stared out the window at the wall of the subway tunnel that was whizzing by. "I don't know. I guess 'the life' sort of caught up with me. I remember a time when I was happy. And believe it or not, I wasn't always considered, how did you so eloquently put it … a cocky jerk?"

I rambled on about the ratings pressure in the news business and no longer having the stomach for the bombs and blood. All could jade the Easter Bunny.

Carter wasn't the "cry on my shoulder" type and asked if I wanted some cheese with my whine. He then gave his version of a pep talk.

"You deal with shady people in shadier places. The minute they see you lose an ounce of swag they'll eat you alive."

"It just wasn't supposed to turn out this way," I continued whining— even if I would never admit it—as we hit our stop at 116th and squeezed out the doors of the subway car. I had to stop and pick up travel items at my residence on the Upper West Side. It was our standard operating procedure, and so ingrained that Carter didn't even discuss the step with me. Perhaps another sign I'd been doing this too long.

I caught Carter rolling his eyes as we climbed the subway stairwell. He slapped on his wraparounds like he couldn't even bear to look at me. We began walking toward my walk-up brownstone. It was no coincidence it was near Columbia University—a place that reminded me of happier times.

"You don't choose life, it chooses you. Do you know how many kids out there would kill to be JP Warner when they grow up?"

"Until they start trying to kill them because they are JP Warner."

"Hey, it could be worse—you almost ended up spending the Fourth with the Bowden family."

His words sent me spiraling back into history. "The Fourth of July used to be one of my favorite days. My family would go to the Samerauk River and watch the fireworks. Gwen and I ..."

"Stop right there," Carter cut me off. "Are you still pining away for this Gwen? I thought that was the liquor talking that night. For chrissake, she probably has six kids and lost her looks somewhere under a pile of plastic kids-toys in the back of her minivan ... at least that happened to all my ex-wives."

"I'm not pining away for anyone," I lied. I'd mentioned Gwen to him the night following the Columbia incident, after having a few too many drinks. We made a deal: I would never bring up such "girly nonsense" ever again, and he would refrain from "knocking some sense" into me.

"It's just the realization that there isn't going to be a happily ever after. You put your dreams on hold, time goes by and one day you realize it's never going to happen. I've made up my mind—this is going to be my last assignment."

He shrugged. "Are you trying to convince me or yourself?"

An awkward silence hung between us as we entered my neighborhood. Lined with the greenery of summer, it was like an oasis in a concrete jungle.

By the time we arrived at my brownstone, the blue sky was just a memory. The wind had picked up and was whipping the tree limbs. It seemed like a symbol of something ... I just wasn't sure what.

We entered the pre-war building, escaping the volatile weather, and I sniffed the comforting fragrance of home. I smiled again—happy with the new life I was heading for, even if Carter wasn't.

"I don't know why you're pining for other chicks when you got a great girl like Lauren Bowden," Carter said with a grin, breaking the tension. "And what's with the John Peter stuff?"

"It shows what type of reporter she is. JP actually stands for John Pierpont. My mother is head of the historical society in Rockfield, Connecticut and ..."

"Is that like one of those cults where they have those rituals with the strange masks and robes?"

"No, that's professional wrestling. She happens to be one of the leading history experts in the state and named my brothers and me after famous people who were born in Connecticut. I'm named after JP Morgan, whose full name was John Pierpont Morgan. My brother Ethan is named after Ethan Allen, the Revolutionary War hero, and Noah is named after Noah Webster. He was the guy, you know, like Webster's Dictionary … that would be a book that contains words, they are the things that …"

Carter shook his head. "I can't believe I'm getting my balls busted by a guy named Pierpont." Then as quickly as the skies darkened outside, he changed the subject, "How's Noah doing?"

"Better," was all I said. It wasn't a place I wanted to go right now.

We entered a mudroom on the garden floor. French doors led to a backyard that looked more rural Connecticut than Manhattan. It looked inviting, but we had business upstairs.

As we began to climb the stairs, a sound stopped us in our tracks. Carter pulled his gun from the waistband of his jeans.

CHAPTER 8

I put up the stop sign.

"It's Christina, the girl who house-sits while I'm away."

"Is she hot?" Carter asked, going quickly from gun-toting to horny, as he often did.

"It's not like that."

"I rest my case—what have you done with JP Warner?"

"First of all, you need to put *both* your guns away. She goes to Fordham and interned at GNZ. Most of her classes are at the Lincoln Center campus, so it's convenient for her to stay here. And in return, she takes care of the place while I'm gone."

We climbed a spiral staircase to the spacious second floor. It featured a twenty-foot ceiling and walls covered with oversized windows that provided a view of the Manhattan skyline. On a normal summer day, light would saturate the room, but the impending storm had now painted the sky black. The room looked as if I didn't spend much time there, which was accurate. It was furnished with just the essentials—a black leather couch, flat-screen plasma TV, and a large desk.

Lauren once tried to decorate the place with what she called an "Old South antebellum motif." When I rebuffed her, she returned with an interior decorator. That's when I decided to have Christina move in to watch the place.

Christina was seated behind my desk, furiously typing on a laptop. She looked up suspiciously. "Hey, JP," her voice jumping three octaves, "they have the new GNZ website up. You should check it out."

It didn't take me long to figure out the reason for her nervousness. Walking out of the bathroom was a college-age kid wearing my evergreen colored bathrobe with the letters *JP* embroidered on the pocket.

My new perspective became a distant memory. When I smelled my own cologne—very expensive cologne—my inner J-News boiled over. The young man in the robe stuck out his hand for me to shake and tried to introduce himself.

Bad move.

"JP, this is my friend Daman. They lost hot water in his dorm, so I let him borrow the shower. He was just …"

"Leaving."

Before Daman could even stutter his way through an apology, Carter's arm reached out and wrapped around his neck. He then escorted—dragged—Daman down the stairs like a rag doll.

I turned my attention back to Christina. "I thought we had one rule—nobody over. There are people who would pay big bucks to get their hands on some of the information I have in here."

"What's your problem?"

"My problem is I let you live free in an apartment that you couldn't afford in three lifetimes. All I had was one rule, and you couldn't follow it!"

"I'm the one doing you a favor, JP, so spare me the guilt trip. Do you know how much it would cost you to have someone look out for this place full time? Not to mention keeping that luna-chick you call your girlfriend out of here. If you want me to leave, I'll leave!"

The front door slammed, briefly stealing my attention—Daman had left the building.

Carter returned, momentarily halting our spat. "I let the kid go," he said as if it truly pained him. He had my bathrobe in his hands, which sparked an unfortunate visual of Daman scampering all the way back to Fordham's Bronx campus in the buff.

"You are the most charitable man I know," I told him.

"I think I'm getting soft."

"Just in your midsection."

"It's warm moments like that I've missed the most since your lobotomy."

I ignored Carter, which he interpreted as a sign to raid my refrigerator. He took out a bottle of Stella, but didn't open it with his teeth, which made me think that maybe he truly was mellowing.

Christina and I resumed our sparring match. But she was a smart kid who knew exactly how far she could push me without getting sent back to Taco Night in the dorm cafeteria. "Listen, JP, I messed up. I'm sorry. It won't happen again."

"You're damn right it won't."

"So where are you guys headed this time?" she attempted to change the subject.

"I can't tell you," I blurted, still in a frenzy, but then something hit me. "How'd you know we're leaving?"

"It's kinda what you do."

"You're going to *kinda* be homeless if you don't give me a straight answer."

She let out a frustrated sigh. "Byron called. Said he'll meet you at your stopover in Germany. How long are you going to be gone?"

"Why, planning a party?"

"Yeah right, JP. I'm taking twelve hours in summer school and have two internships. And whatever social life I did have likely just ended when your henchman assaulted my only friend."

Carter let out his booming laugh, before announcing, "You'll have to excuse JP, he's experiencing a midlife crisis. Being rich and famous is too rough for him. And he's never gotten over some girl from high school, so he's thinking about leaving the business."

"I thought that was between us?" I snapped at him.

"Hey, I was a professional wrestler—you're lucky I didn't scream it into a microphone and then threaten to beat you to a pulp."

Christina joined in his laughter—I think in wrestling they would call this a tag team. She then returned to the computer and said, "Like I tried to tell you before your 'old guy meltdown,' GNZ has an updated website. Do you want to know what they said about you?"

"No," I said and trudged toward my bedroom.

She read it anyway, "JP Warner is GNZ's Senior International Correspondent. Over the last two decades he has covered some of the world's most important news stories, including both Gulf Wars. He also has bravely covered conflicts in the Balkans and the refugee exodus from Kosovo in Albania, Montenegro, and Macedonia. He has showcased his most brilliant moments in major conflicts. JP earned the industry's highest honor for his work as part of GNZ's Bosnia war coverage team. He was one of the first correspondents into Afghanistan post 9/11. JP continues to …"

I was surprised it mentioned anything related to news, especially since Cliff Sutcliffe took over at GNZ. I silently finished packing for another adventure.

Hoping it would be my last.

CHAPTER 9

Frankfort, Germany

July 3

Carter and I flew from JFK to Frankfurt, Germany, where we would pick up the Yugoslavian airline JAT. I was checking my phone messages, when I noticed Byron Jasper heading in our direction.

He was draped in heavy video equipment. But it was no match for the man who was five-feet-nine-inches of pure muscle. Of the three of us, it was fairly easy to figure out who didn't have a gym membership.

"Thanks for the help, Big Ugly," Byron addressed Carter in his usual high-pitched squeal. Byron was the only one who got to call him that without repercussions.

Carter barely turned his weary head in his direction. "I've been carrying you for years, so it's about time you carried your own weight. And besides, you're late—where were you?"

"Tonya had plans that couldn't be broken. I can't just drop everything whenever you wanna jet off to Serbia for a romantic weekend."

"In other words, you weren't allowed to leave until Tonya returned your balls."

Byron laughed at another in a long line of good-natured barbs between the two, before turning his attention to me. When I barely responded to his greeting, he asked, "What's wrong, J-News—upset that your girl stole your Lamar Thompson interview?"

When I took the comment in stride, he turned back Carter. "What did the aliens do with J-News? Those were fighting words I just threw his way."

"You'll have to excuse him—he's having a midlife crisis. Claims he's leaving the business. Maybe you can talk some sense into him … I've given up."

But one look in my eyes told Byron that I was serious, and his tone changed, "Lamar Thompson was a god when I was growing up in South Carolina. Just shows how life can turn in an instant—you gotta do what makes you happy, JP."

Carter shook his head in disgust. That wasn't the 'sense' he had in mind.

But Byron understood where I was coming from. He was an all-American running back at the University of South Carolina, where he came in third in the voting for the Heisman Trophy. He went on to star for the NFL's Arizona Cardinals, until his promising career was put in jeopardy by a gruesome knee injury. The so-called experts said he would never come back from it, but they underestimated him. He was a man who lived for challenges, and as usual, he proved the critics wrong by making All-Pro his first year back.

But at the height of his football career, with a multimillion-dollar contract on the table, Byron walked away. It was his job, not his dream. People were shocked by such a move in an age where greed was king, but those folks obviously didn't know Byron Jasper.

His real passion was to tell the stories of those who couldn't tell them for themselves. He'd caught the bug one off-season when he made a rudimentary documentary, with a hand-held camera, of hurricane survivors in his home state of South Carolina. And then when a teammate named Leonard Harris was killed in a freak accident, he came to realize that life was too short to be putting off his dreams. So he signed up to become a field cameraman for GNZ. The man who once had every eye on him as he streaked to another touchdown, found his real calling behind the camera.

He got off to a rocky start when he was assigned to work for a prickly correspondent named JP Warner. He was the overeager rookie, while I was the perfectionist with no tolerance for mistakes. But Byron took on the challenge, and before long he was considered one of the best in the business. We've now worked together for ten years, and I refuse to work with anyone else.

Byron was also a technology junkie, which helped GNZ remain on the cutting edge of the industry. Due to his contributions, GNZ was one of the first TV news reporters to use the videophone. Since we were usually stationed in remote locations, the videophone was a revolutionary tool. The pictures were often grainy with long delays in communication, but they could take you right to the action, which gave the viewing audience a whole new perspective.

As I boarded the plane for my last assignment, I knew it was time for me to follow Byron's lead, and chase the dream at any cost. I had to be willing to give up J-News. He was right—life really is too short. And in this business, if you lose your passion, life can become even shorter.

CHAPTER 10

Belgrade, Serbia

We arrived in Belgrade tired, but with a second wind of excitement.

Our hotel stay was brief. I could have used about ten hours of sleep, but settled for a forty-five minute power nap. Being my final trip, I'd actually hoped for a little fun—despite the bloodiness of Belgrade we'd witnessed over the years, we'd often had a great time here. Especially the nightlife. After a few cocktails, we would be singing and dancing with the locals, and the traditional Serbian food would actually start tasting decent.

Carter never revealed the details of our mission until absolutely necessary. This was fine with Byron and me, and I think the secrecy made Carter feel like he was some strange combination of James Bond and Dog the Bounty Hunter, which he really seemed to thrive on. The only item he provided in this case was that our guide's name was Milos and for symbolic reasons Zahir wanted to meet on American Independence Day.

We met Milos at what was the biggest event in Belgrade that night—the Euroleague Championship basketball game between the Serbian club team, Partizan, and CSKA Moscow. The arena had an aroma I uniquely related to the Yugoslavian countries—a combination of a musty basement and enough cigarette smoke to cause lung damage. The people of the region have two great loves: basketball and cigarettes.

The place was jammed to capacity a good hour before tipoff, and the smoke hung like cumulus cloud cover. This didn't stop the excitable fans from singing, chanting, and even tossing firecrackers on the court.

Milos was standing in the back row of the arena, looking like a typical American teenager. He wore a replica Lebron James basketball jersey and a pair of jeans. When we approached, Carter and Milos shook hands and made small talk—in English—like long-lost friends.

Milos' baby-face made him appear to be around sixteen, which was saying something in Serbia, where most men had five o'clock shadow on their faces by noon. But Carter insisted he was twenty-five—older than I was when I was avoiding B-1 Bombers in Baghdad during the Gulf War. Carter's sources and guides have an impeccable record, so I never questioned them.

We stood in the back of the arena watching the first half of the game. Paritzan led by ten at halftime and the crowd was worked into a lather. Then without warning, Milos was on the move. And I was pretty sure he wasn't headed to the snack bar. We followed him out of the arena, and then along the Danube River, passing riverboats filled with young Serbs partying to what they affectionately call gypsy music. I guessed it was an acquired taste.

We arrived at a small Hyundai parked in a cobblestone alley. We piled in, and Milos drove a few miles through the crowded city. He parked in another cobblestone alley.

We got out of the car and started out on foot. We walked past the endless brick buildings of Old Belgrade and storefronts advertising in Cyrillic-Script writing. The night was pleasant with a temperature in the seventies, and an oversized moon lit the streets. We'd seen the Belgrade nights lit by bombs, so it was a welcome change.

We arrived at an alleyway where an identical Hyundai sat unoccupied. Once we were safely inside, Milos instructed us that our meeting with Zahir would take place outside of the small Serbian town of Vršac. I was familiar with the place. It was in the middle of nowhere and could only be reached by a treacherous journey. Kind of like a place where an international fugitive might choose to hide out.

The Hyundai drove along a desolate road with no lighting, except for the moon, and even less sign of life. Cell phone reception was nothing but a pipe-dream. A cold rain arrived out of nowhere and temperatures dropped dramatically. Milos explained that the fifty-mile journey would take us almost three hours, due to the conditions. We would have to wait for the tantalizing story.

While I was tired of "the life," I was still energized by the anticipation of the big story. It reminded me of when Byron talked about the end of his football career, when he said he still loved the games, but it was all the hard work and practices that he no longer had the passion for.

Byron displayed his usual nervous energy. He tossed his cookies before most missions, but today he just nervously fiddled with his camera. Nothing ever seemed to bother the unflappable Carter, who sat comfortably in the front seat.

I've often been described as having nerves of steel. But if people could see my insides churning during these moments, they might have a different take. I wore a shearling-lamb suede poncho for the elements, and a few days of stubble for the rugged look. J-News was going to go out in style.

I checked my watch, before casually looking up, expecting another monotonous view of the rugged Serbian countryside. When I did, my eyes bulged.

Carter had already seen it. "Look out!"

The van that had been "innocently" driving ahead of us the last hour, skidded to a sudden stop, blocking the road.

Four men in camouflage suits ran from the sliding door on the side of the van, carrying automatic weapons, and looking like they were willing to use them. But I knew right away that they weren't military. I pegged their language as Arabic, not Yugoslavian. In any language, I knew we were in trouble.

It was all happening too fast. Milos tried to put the car in reverse, but he didn't get far. A round of gunfire shot into the engine of the Hyundai and the radiator fizzed. Milos was hit in his upper chest and he bent over in agony.

The men dragged the four of us out of the vehicle and tossed us on the cold, wet ground. Carter tried to put up a fight, but took a gun handle to his head, knocking him out cold.

Blindfolds were tied around our heads and we were loaded into the back of the van.

I had stayed one story too long.

CHAPTER 11

Outer Banks, North Carolina

Fourth of July

Senator Craig Kingsbury sat in the back of the stretch limo, surrounded by his insufferable father, George Kingsbury, and his annoying press secretary, Joey Lynch. It was the fitting end to the week from hell.

The plan was to spend a long Fourth of July weekend at the Kingsbury's vacation retreat in the Avon Village. They needed to regroup from the sudden return of Lamar Thompson into their lives.

At first, they tried to laugh off the accusations, but kept running into the same sticking point—that they were true. Craig ran his last campaign on the slogan "character and honesty." Right now, honesty was biting him in the ass.

Craig wasn't concerned that the scandal would cost him the presidential election. It was still sixteen months away and he didn't want to win, anyway. His biggest fear was his father pulling him out of the fire one more time and accumulating more debt. The debt paid to George Kingsbury came at a very high interest rate.

He was still on a payment plan for the "incident" at UNC, almost twenty years earlier. The senate seat he never wanted was the biggest punishment so far. The run for the White House was another. But it was still better than doing ten to fifteen in a state pen for vehicular homicide—he was too pretty for prison.

On television or a billboard, Craig appeared to be the ideal political candidate. Boyish good looks accentuated by sandy blond hair that flopped to the side. One prominent magazine billed him as the southern Bobby Kennedy. Craig just hoped the voters would determine he lacked the experience to hold the office of president, and cast their vote for his competitors.

Joey Lynch ended his call and jubilantly provided the latest polling numbers. Still ten points ahead of any other Democrat, even with the mini-scandal, and in a dead heat with the incumbent Republican president.

As usual, his father tempered the enthusiasm by shouting in his hard-of-hearing style, "A lot can happen in sixteen months!"

George was a cranky man of seventy-three, who made no secret that he was living vicariously through his youngest son. The elder children either failed, or worse, turned out to be girls. A Kingsbury would hold the office of president if it killed him to get him there. Craig sighed, thinking of those obnoxious television commercials. *No credit? Bad credit?*

The story broke in a small high school newspaper in South Carolina. Lamar Thompson was being honored as the high school's top athlete in school history. A sixteen-year-old sophomore asked Lamar about the accident that changed his life. Lamar Thompson answered truthfully.

As far as Craig knew, Lamar had never uttered a word about the accident, at least not one that connected Craig to it. He figured King George had threatened him to keep his mouth shut. Or maybe he just thought that nobody would ever believe him. So why did he suddenly decide to talk? Maybe the headlines of Craig joining the presidential campaign opened some old wounds. Or perhaps Thompson saw it as a bargaining chip to shake them down for a nice payday. But if so, why not take the money when it was originally offered? What Craig did know, was that his father was unraveling like never before, which meant it must be the worst-case scenario, which was that Lamar Thompson had decided to talk because he no longer had anything left to lose. You can't threaten a dead man.

The limo followed the police officer in the unmarked SUV down US-64 South—the stealth escort was one of the perks of the Kingsbury power. They were desperate to avoid the slobbering media that smelled the blood in the water. Sand dunes and quiet bodies of water surrounded the road. The only signs of civilization were the vacation homes on stilts that likely wouldn't last through the next hurricane.

They rumbled up NC-12, and King George continued on his soapbox, "I always knew your bad choices would get in the way of our dream."

"This is your dream, Daddy, not mine. It was never my dream."

"You are such a child. Look at yourself, you pathetic little baby. If it wasn't for me, you'd be rotting in jail."

"And my brother would still be alive," Joey piled on.

If Craig had any energy left, he would have reached out and physically wiped the smug look off Joey's face. He had used the death of his brother, Brad Lynch, to extort a career from King George. Brad had been Craig's only true friend involved in the accident—he barely knew Thompson or the freshman kid, who was just another in a long line of hangers-on who had surrounded him throughout his life.

George put up his hand to demand silence. He then made a statement as if he were trying to define hypocritical, "We must worry about going forward and not look back."

Joey had notes. "Lamar Thompson lives not far from here in Kitty Hawk. No wife or kids … at least ones he knows about. Parents are deceased—a grandmother still lives in Columbia. He'll visit her when he's sober enough or needs money. I say we take him out. Make it look like an OD—wouldn't be much of a stretch."

George smacked him in the head, causing Joey to grab his ears in pain. "Can you stop being stupid for a moment? You think the media is harsh now—watch if something happens to this Lamar fella. Any ideas, Craig?"

"What do you want me to say? You're the one who tried to buy him off, not me."

"Do I have to explain to you, son, that payoff is what kept you out of jail?"

"I have been in jail for twenty years."

"Smarten up, boy!" he shouted, before declaring, "Nothing is going to hold back my dreams, especially not some drug addict cullerd boy."

CHAPTER 12

The SUV bounced along the empty beach road that was lit only by eerie moonlight. The Oregon Inlet Bridge appeared in the hazy distance.

The officer pulled to the side of the bridge, just as he had been instructed. Moments later, the Kingsbury limo came to a stop behind him.

The officer got out of his vehicle and calmly walked back to the limo. He knocked on the tinted back window and it rolled down.

He flashed his badge. "Senator Craig Kingsbury, you are under arrest for the murder of Marilyn Lacey."

"Do you know who you're talking to?" Joey Lynch asked. It was the same superior tone he took earlier at the airport while performing a thorough background check on Officer Ron Culver, which delayed their trip by fifteen minutes. But he was now dealing with Officer Jones, not Culver.

Jones shot one bullet into his head with a 9mm Glock. This got everyone's attention.

"Who are you working for?" George Kingsbury demanded, while unceremoniously removing Joey's dead body from his lap.

"George Kingsbury—you are under arrest for the cover-up of the murder of Marilyn Lacey."

The front door of the limo opened and the driver took off, attempting to make an escape over a sand dune.

The officer was in Batman mode now—a trance-like state with pinpoint focus on his prey. He got him in his sights and put one bullet in the back of his head. He collapsed into the sand and lay still. He didn't feel good about it. But this was war, and the driver was collateral damage.

The elder Kingsbury remained defiant. "That was twenty years ago! They were kids—they made a mistake!"

"There's no statute of limitations on justice."

"Please don't shoot me," Craig Kingsbury whimpered.

A grin pursed Batman's thin lips. "I'm not going to shoot you, Senator Kingsbury."

The Senator exhaled with relief. Batman knew it would be short-lived, but he first had to make sure that he fully understood his crimes.

"Did you know almost twenty thousand people died last year in drinking and driving accidents? But they weren't accidents—they were murder, pure and simple. You are a murderer, and Judge Buford isn't around to save you anymore."

"What do you want ... *money*? How much?" George remained indignant.

"It's estimated that there will be over seven hundred traffic fatalities this holiday weekend. Half of those will be alcohol related. Did you try to solve this problem in your time in Washington, Senator—or were you more concerned with covering up your past?"

The officer pulled out a bottle of vodka he stored in his holster. He unscrewed the cap, reached inside the limo, and began jiggling the bottle side-to-side.

"What do you want?" George demanded again.

"This is not about me. This is about you finally learning the lesson that alcohol and cars don't mix."

He casually struck a match and flicked it into the backseat, setting the men on fire. They tried to scramble out of the vehicle, but he coolly shot out the door handles.

Batman watched as the two men tried to escape their burning flesh. They looked as if they were being attacked by a hive of invisible bees. The useless screams and smell of burning flesh was a sight the officer would never forget. Nor did he want to.

He flicked another match into the vehicle, and then another. Within moments, the entire limo was ablaze. It lit up the dark night like ten full moons.

The officer calmly returned to the SUV and left the scene. He drove the gravel-filled beach road, passing villages from Rodante to Buxton. He stopped in Frisco at a convenience store, where he bought a candy bar and a bottle of water.

As he drove toward Hatteras Village, Batman slowly morphed back into Officer Kyle Jones. He left the stolen SUV in the parking lot of the Hatteras Ferry, exchanging it for his red pickup truck, which he drove onto the ferry.

The ferry took him to Ocracoke Island. Upon reaching the island, he made the familiar drive. He passed the marina, noticing the mixture of locals and tourists that had gathered for the Fourth of July festivities. He could see the landmark lighthouse in the distance, feeling as if it were guiding him home like the North Star.

He turned onto his street, and took special notice of the house formally owned by the Not-so-honorable Raymond Buford. He saluted it, thanking Buford for leading him to the information that exposed the evils of the Kingsburys. Buford also introduced him to the identity of Ron Culver, and the messy secret that proved quite valuable in tonight's mission.

He continued down the street until he arrived at his beach house. He parked the pickup truck under the covering and climbed the stairs. Home sweet home.

CHAPTER 13

He opened a window and inhaled the salt air. Then took a moment to listen to the sounds of pounding waves in the distance and the booms of amateur fireworks shows. But now was no time to become complacent—there was much work to be done.

His forehead broke out with beads of sweat, and his stomach felt as if it were being strangled by nerves. This moment was always so overwhelming, yet so satisfying. He grabbed a magic marker and entered the closet of the master bedroom. As he did, he felt the weight of every life that had been taken, and those who were left behind. But it was a burden he was honored to carry on his broad shoulders.

He separated a wall of hanging shirts and removed a piece of wood paneling from the back of the closet, exposing a door handle. He then maneuvered the numbers of the combination lock. The numbers were significant.

He entered an 8 x 8 windowless room that was encapsulated in a steel structure. The door was fourteen-gauge steel mounted in a steel frame and secured by three dead bolts. It swung inward.

The contractor had guaranteed him the room would provide protection from 250mph winds and projectiles traveling at 100mph. Safe rooms were common in beach houses to reduce loss of life and injury during a major storm. His use of the room focused on loss of life, but had very little to do with storm safety.

He walked to the wall that displayed the pictures of Craig and George Kingsbury. He methodically drew an **X** over them with the magic marker. He felt sparks shoot through his body, and he tried to make the pleasure last as long as possible. When he finished, he took a step back, feeling dizzy, and a rare smile leaked from his lips. Another mission completed successfully.

He didn't savor it for long—his attention diverted to the photos still awaiting an **X**. His mood turned melancholy—realizing the job would never be finished. He had so much still to do, and time was rapidly slipping away.

He took one last look at the picture of Craig Kingsbury, which now had a large **X** scrolled across his perfect smile. His eyes wandered to another newspaper article taped to the wall, which had faded to a dull yellowish color. When he locked on the date of the article, it confirmed that it wouldn't be long until the twenty-year anniversary of the event. A reunion would take place in Rockfield, Connecticut, where Kyle Jones was a police officer.

After a couple of deep breaths, he was able to pull himself from the shrine. But before leaving, he tested the alarm—when it was tripped, it was programmed to buzz the medallion that hung around his neck, to indicate that the closet had been penetrated. It was on the same necklace that contained a locket with pictures of lost loved ones. He caressed the necklace, vowing to get them justice, or die trying.

After he secured the lock, he moved to his bedroom and changed out of Officer Culver's police uniform, and into a Rockfield PD T-shirt and shorts. He then made his way to the kitchen. He grabbed a diet soda from the refrigerator and retired to the outside deck.

The humidity felt soothing, and his swirling emotions slowed. He sipped his drink and watched the fireworks over the beach as he dozed off to sleep. His dreams were peaceful.

The next morning, he would fly back to Connecticut and begin the meticulous preparation for his next mission.

CHAPTER 14

Landstuhl, Germany

August 31

Except for the occasional roar of a plane taking off from the adjoining Ramstein Air Force Base, Landstuhl Hospital was a quiet setting amongst the peaceful forests of western Germany. But ever since a certain television reporter was flown in from Belgrade, a large blockade of media had set up camp across the street from the medical center. Since I hadn't been able to leave my hospital room the past six weeks, I was only getting this information from my television.

While my stay had been long, my list of medical maladies was even longer. Concussion, broken eye socket, broken rib, torn knee ligament, and punctured left lung. But the most painful injuries of all were my wounded pride and badly bruised ego. My face was still splattered with dark scabs, although the doctors told me that they were healing, and my face would return to its "TV standard" in no time. I decided not to let them in on the scoop that my television days were over.

Contrary to what my critics often say, my biggest professional nightmare has always been becoming the story. But that's exactly what happened. What the media dubbed ***The Capture of JP Warner!*** was the second biggest story of the summer, only topped by the unsolved murder of Senator Craig Kingsbury.

As the world looked on for twelve long days, we were held captive in a remote eastern section of Serbia, near the Bulgarian border. Perhaps the terms "exclusive interview" and "tortured hostages" got mixed up in translation. Our living quarters were in a small, dilapidated house, where we were chained in sauna-hot, windowless rooms.

The leader was an eerily calm man named Qwaui—one of the top lieutenants of Mustafa Hakim, the top dog of Al Muttahedah. He wore desert camouflage and spent most of his time playing chess with another bearded soldier who was decked out in matching attire.

Zahir, the man we sought for an interview—although, in hindsight, it was clear that they were seeking us—was also present. He wore traditional Islamic garb, and his clean-shaven Western looks from his Chicago days were long gone. He was a loose cannon, often going off on violent tangents about the "infidels," which I brilliantly deduced was us.

I found Zahir's act a little contrived, fearing the quiet Qwaui much more. A deep look into his eyes revealed an unwavering zealotry. I knew there would be no reasoning with him.

To make matters worse, our hosts played the incessant, and usually inaccurate, reports by Lauren Bowden on a small black-and-white television that looked like a relic from the 1970s. Lauren seized the moment to take advantage of my martyrdom, usually referring to me as her "soul-mate" during her reports, and I'm sure to Sutcliffe's delight, often cried crocodile tears into the camera as she begged for my release.

On the twelfth day of captivity, I was summoned before the group and instructed—with machine gun to temple—that I was to deliver a statement to the Western World. The camera rolled and I swallowed hard. Logic said they would kill me anyway, so I should refuse to spread their propaganda and die with a little dignity. It's hard to explain to someone who has never had the cold steel of a gun poking into the back of their neck, but survival instincts kick in, dignity goes out the window, and the only thing I could think of was to survive the next second. For such a natural act, dying doesn't come very naturally.

I completed the anti-American monologue like I was the keynote speaker at an Al Muttahedah convention, and signed off as I had so many times before, "JP Warner ... Global Newz." The camera was shut off and I braced for my throat to be slit.

But nothing happened.

I was still alive, but things were different. There was a distinct change in mood—Qwaui's normally meditative demeanor had vanished. He began pacing like a lion stalking its prey, and barking orders to Zahir in Arabic. We were blindfolded again, and swept us into the Serbian night.

The details of what happened next remain a little foggy. The therapist I'd been assigned at Landstuhl believed that I wanted to suppress them—he was probably right—but no matter how hard I tried, I couldn't remove the familiar screams from my memory bank.

My relationship with the military had always been complex. My job was to uncover information, while they, understandably, wanted to keep things under wrap. So naturally things became strained at times between us. So while they were forced to be nice to me publicly—my capture having turned me into an American hero—they were able to show their disdain in more subtle ways. For example, they claimed that the only room they could find for me was in the "Labor and Delivery" section. For six weeks, my nights and days were filled with the sounds of screaming babies. My nurse, Lieutenant Colonel Knight, told me that I fit in well.

But that didn't compare to the torture of the television, which was left constantly running in my room, playing the GNZ coverage of my demise. If that wasn't bad enough, Lauren was the lead reporter on the story. It was like she had been in my room with me for six weeks. There was no escape.

Today, she stood in the rain outside Landstuhl, doing her best to try to fill up the 24-hour news cycle with another non-story about nothing, but of the most importance, looking good doing it.

"I'm coming to you live from Landstuhl Medical Center in Germany where we have *breaking news*. My sources tell me that GNZ's JP Warner will be discharged today."

This was news to me, although I wouldn't argue if it were the case. But I didn't exactly trust Lauren Bowden's sources.

Then as if she'd angered the heavens, the light mist turned into a downpour. But being a trooper, Lauren continued shouting through the rain, "When JP is released, I'll conduct an exclusive interview with him, seen only on GNZ! If you want to hear JP Warner's first words since bravely escaping from the clutches of Al Muttahedah—turn to GNZ!"

I wasn't planning on giving anyone an interview, and if I did, it certainly wouldn't be with Lauren. But that's not to say I didn't respect the effort. She had made repeated attempts to get in to see me over the past month, only to be repelled by the cranky Lieutenant Colonel Sharon Knight, on the orders of her even crankier patient, JP Warner. It was probably the only thing we agreed on during my stay.

Speaking of the Lieutenant Colonel, she stormed into my room like it was the beaches of Normandy. She was a short, humorless woman who was the chief nurse of the facility. Without asking for any type of consent, she stuck a temperature gauge in my ear, and recorded the results on a chart. I knew the drill, and stuck out my left arm and rolled up the sleeve of my hospital gown. She attached the Velcro blood pressure cuff too tight around my left bicep and pumped.

"Is it true I'm getting out of here today?" I asked.

"You're the smartest man in the world. Why don't you tell me?"

"Seriously."

"That's classified," she said, before moving on to my daily breathing exercises. "Sit up ... take a deep breath ... okay, hold it ... release," she commanded and I obeyed. I had learned my lesson about crossing her.

"Do I at least get a Purple Heart when all this is over?"

"You're lucky you don't get a kick-in-the-ass and a bill."

When she finished recording all the pertinent information, she coldly stated, "You have a visitor."

"Let me guess, the firing squad?"

She didn't rule it out, which concerned me.

But as she left the room, she passed Jeff Carter on his way in. It was like two battleships passing in the night. I let out a sigh of relief at the sight of the one-man rescue team. I hoped he was here to save me again—sling me over his shoulder and carry me home to New York.

"Tell me I'm going home," I pleaded.

"You are," he got right to the point. But before I was able to look up at the pink ceiling of the maternity ward and give thanks skyward, Carter added, "But first we must make a return trip to hell."

Unfortunately, I knew exactly what he meant.

CHAPTER 15

"I'm not ready—I need a couple minutes," I said, overtaken by fright.

Carter shook his head. "There is no amount of time that'll make this any easier. You just gotta tear the scab off."

That was the problem—it wasn't a scab yet. It was still an open wound. A wound that would likely never heal.

"You got two minutes," Carter said. "Do you want me to sing and dance, or do you wanna do small talk?"

"I was hoping for a lap dance."

"I hate to get you all worked up for nothing, but I left my G-string home. So it'll have to be small talk. What's next, Mr. American Hero … book? … Movie? … Talk show circuit?"

I smiled serenely, and I could tell it freaked him out a little. "I just want to go back to Rockfield."

"So what do you plan on doing when you arrive at this glorious field of rocks?"

"Go to the Rockfield Fair."

"Who wouldn't? Just please tell me it has something to do with alcohol and women."

"It's a country fair that's held every year on Labor Day weekend. They have great food, carnival rides, and livestock contests. And it's a showcase for a lot of the newest farming equipment. Since I'm going to start a farm, I need to learn more about that sort of stuff."

Carter burst into laughter. "J-News the farmer, now that I gotta see."

He reached in the back pocket of his faded jeans and pulled out a rolled up *TIME Magazine.* He tossed it softly on my chest. I winced—even the light magazine felt like an anvil.

"So you are telling me you have no plans to capitalize on your hero status?" Carter pushed.

I picked up the magazine and viewed myself on the cover. It was an out-of-focus screen-shot taken from the video Qwaui released to the worldwide media. The picture portrayed me in a way his audience rarely saw me—tired, haggard, and with a look of vulnerability. The caption under his photo read: *With the capture of journalist JP Warner, we ask the question: Has the media gone too far?*

I looked up. "It's nice to read something objective on myself. The news coverage has almost made me believe I'm some sort of hero. We both know the real hero is ..."

And with that, the eight hundred pound gorilla was out of the cage. "How is he? They don't tell me anything."

"How about you find out for yourself?"

Before I had a chance to filibuster, he picked me out of the bed and slammed me into a nearby wheelchair. It felt like every inch of my body had been set on fire.

Carter wheeled me through a maze of hospital corridors. The staff numbered over a thousand, and it seemed as if each and every one of them greeted Carter. He posed for pictures and signed autographs. Military members were some of the biggest fans of Coldblooded Carter. I, on the other hand, received snide glares.

Byron lay motionless in a bed, surrounded by breathing tubes and beeping monitors. We hadn't seen each other since that fateful night—the doctors wouldn't allow it. Byron smiled as wide as he could, but it didn't lessen my guilt, if that was his intention.

Carter had informed me of the grim diagnosis a few weeks back. The paralysis would likely be permanent. But it didn't soften the blow when I saw my fallen friend for the first time.

The reason for the quick getaway that night was that our captors had learned that the CIA had discovered their hideaway and were minutes away from taking them down. The three of us instantly went from bargaining chips to dead weight. Our SUV was sent careening into a ravine, and we were all ejected. I could still hear Byron's screams in my mind from when he was trapped under the vehicle.

"It's okay, man, it's not your fault. It's nobody's fault," Byron said, reading my bleak stare.

We bumped fists—his arms were the only things that he could move. He wore no shirt, revealing that his upper body, while scarred from the crash, was still in magnificent shape. It was impossible to believe a man in such top condition wouldn't walk out of Landstuhl under his own power.

"It was my fault," I forced out the words, my voice shaking. "I'd lost my edge—I should have never gone on that trip."

"Get over yourself, JP—it's not always about you," Byron said. "I'm the lucky one. Do you know how many people leave this place in a coffin? Don't you think that Milos would have loved to have another chance like this?"

"I'm so sorry," I reiterated, almost zombie-like. I pushed out of my wheelchair and wobbled on shaky legs.

Byron looked at me, incredulously. "Listen, man, I got life and life is precious. As long as you're breathing anything's possible. You guys saved my life."

He motioned me to come closer. When I did, Byron grabbed my hospital gown, surprising me with his strength. "Do you understand if you beat yourself up over this I will put you in this hospital … permanently?"

I nodded blankly.

He released his grip. "I'm glad we're understood."

"JP is going home today and going to start a farm," Carter said, attempting to break the tension.

Byron smiled. "You won't give up the life, JP. It's not a job with you—it's who you are."

"The only way I'll ever come back is if you're my cameraman."

"Deal," Byron said with a determined stare.

We had learned never to doubt him.

It would still be weeks before he could leave Landstuhl, but preparations had already begun back in South Carolina. Without his knowledge, Carter and I had contracted to have his home in Charleston converted to the top-of-the-line in handicap accessibility. It would be ready upon his return. We figured that the technology lover would be like a kid on Christmas with all his new gadgets.

Byron mentioned that he couldn't wait to get back home and eat the famous fried chicken from Mama Jasper's, his mother's restaurant. He was also looking forward to getting reacquainted with his longtime girlfriend, Tonya.

We continued the visit until Byron's team of camouflage-attired doctors descended upon his room like the 82nd Airborne, and ushered us out.

"Remember what I said, Warner," Byron got in the last word.

After a final consultation with my doctor, Major Ellison, I was released from Landstuhl. None of the hospital staff seemed sad to see me go.

The media attacked me the moment I was outside the hospital. Carter played interference as I was escorted through the soft rain in a wheelchair. The media got nothing but 'no-comments' from me, and had to settle for a bicep flex from Carter.

We arrived at a C-141 Starlifter that would serve as my ride home. I took one last look at Landstuhl and noted, "What a long strange trip it's been."

"The Grateful Dead?" Carter inquired.

I smiled. "No, grateful to be alive."

PART TWO-

ALL ISN'T "FAIR" IN LOVE & WAR

CHAPTER 16

Glendale, Arizona
Labor Day Weekend—two years prior

He stood outside the small home in Glendale and wiped the sweat from his brow. He told himself it was from the oven-like Arizona night, but for the first time in a long time he felt apprehensive. The voice had been loud and clear, telling him to come here and finish the business between them, but now doubt was creeping in.

He hadn't been back to Arizona since he moved away. And it was even longer since he'd seen Lucy. She was hesitant at first—unsure about meeting her old boyfriend while her husband was away—and she should have listened to that first instinct. If she thought she would just be able to walk away, without him without any repercussions for her for her actions, then she underestimated him once again.

He looked through the window beside the front door, and saw Lucy scurrying around her kitchen, getting ready for their "date." She appeared much the same with her long dark curls and smooth olive skin. She wore the pink sundress, which had always been Kyle's favorite—it looked like she was more excited to see her old flame than she'd let on in their correspondence, he thought.

Wearing latex gloves, he reached into the inside pocket of his blazer and pulled out his Glock. He then rung the bell. When she opened the door, he would take in the immense surprise on her face, and an understanding of what was about to happen, and why, all in a split second. Then he would shoot her right in that sharp tongue that she used to belittle him with.

He gripped the gun as the door swung open. But nobody was there. Then a voice rose up from below, "Are you Kyle? My mom said to tell you she'd be with you in just a minute."

He looked down to see a little girl—a miniature version of Lucy with the same dark curls. He hadn't counted on this. An image of his parents flashed in his mind, followed by the same pain he felt when he lost them. He now understood the source of his apprehension. He misread the voice. He couldn't allow this girl to grow up with that pain.

"I'm sorry, I have the wrong house," he replied in a low voice, and ran as fast as he could up the street, all the way until he reached his rental car.

He drove directly to the airport and boarded the next flight home. He had no fear of being traced—he was using the identity of Grady Benson, who had been Kyle Jones' old Air Force wingman.

He picked up an extra shift on Saturday night. His presence was welcome, due to so many officers being assigned to work the Rockfield Fair during the Labor Day weekend. While on patrol, he tried to make sense of his failed journey. His missions had always been so clear, and brought such a feeling of peace, that this was uncharted territory for him. But he still felt a strong call-to-action hanging over him. Completing his business with Lucy on this anniversary had made sense, but now for the first time since his journey began, he felt unsure.

But later that night, he received a radio message about an accident on the Samerauk Bridge. When he arrived at the scene, he found that it was no accident. And later, in the hospital, as he comforted the mother of the murdered girl, his mission again became clear.

CHAPTER 17

Norfolk, Virginia

September 1—present

The military plane scraped its wheels on the runway, landing me on home soil. A short time later, I stepped onto the tarmac, breathing in the crisp dawn air. I thought of performing the freed-hostage ritual of kissing the ground upon my return, but while that would be right up the attention-grabbing alley of J-News, it was JP who was the one who'd just returned from the European vacation from hell.

I struggled to walk with my cane, which besides a few cuts and bruises was the only visible evidence that I was any the worse for wear. I was met with a relieved smile and hug from my father, Peter Warner. He was thinner than the last time I'd seen him, but still had the same stocky frame and roundish face. It was a look passed on to my brother Ethan, the opposite of the lanky, long-jawed look that my brother Noah and I inherited from my mother's side.

While I can often be a polarizing repellent, my father's natural instinct had always been to pull people together, and he thrived on being the leader. I thought of this as I watched him shake hands with all the military personnel like he was running for office. He did hold political office for twenty-five years as Rockfield's First Selectman. He knew everybody in the town, and everyone knew Peter Warner. He stepped down two years ago when he was diagnosed with prostate cancer, which so far he'd treated like his political opponents—he's winning in a landslide.

My mother, Sandra Warner, was also there, but didn't greet me with the same enthusiasm. She gave me the brief hug of a stranger, followed by deafening silence. Her passive-aggressive protest wasn't very subtle. For years she's questioned why they paid for my Columbia education, only for me to repay them by making a foolish and dangerous career choices. The silent-treatment was a new weapon in this ongoing battle. She was mysteriously absent whenever my father called me at Landstuhl, either babysitting Ethan's kids, or at an event at her historical society—excuses that even Lauren Bowden could have seen through. I understood the grief I'd caused her, but that being said, I really could have used a hug from Mom.

After deplaning, Carter and I bid each other adieu—no hugs, just a manly handshake. I attempted to thank him for all the years by my side in the face of danger, but he mocked my retirement plans with a laugh. "Just get better quick, so we can blow open this Kingsbury case. Go to this Rock place and get that broad from high school out of your head, then you'll be the old JP again."

The "old JP" had a nice ring to it, even if it wasn't what Carter had in mind.

We left Norfolk in a convoy, bypassing the horde of media, and headed northbound on I-95. As the morning sun began to appear in the east, we barreled up the coast, Out of habit, I checked my phone messages. A mistake. There were angry ones from Lauren—something about being contractually obligated to be interviewed by her—ass kissing tangents from Sutcliffe, and one from Christina that breezed over the whole "glad you're not dead" thing, before complaining about the wall of media camped outside the brownstone, trapping her inside. She actually had the nerve to describe it as a "hostage situation." I erased them all in the spirit of a new beginning.

That spirit turned to reality when I saw the wooden sign that read: *Rockfield Connecticut: Incorporated 1756.* With a father who was the town's biggest promoter, and a mother who headed the historical society, I knew all there was to know about Rockfield, both past and present. But I felt like I was seeing it for the first time.

We arrived at a familiar crossroads. Continuing straight on Main Street would take us to the Warner family home. It was the longer route, but also safer. The faster option was the curvy, mountainous drive of Zycko Hill Road, nicknamed Psycho Hill. It was convenient that it rhymed with Zycko, but the name really derived from the infamy associated with the many drivers it had felled over the years, including Noah Warner.

The convoy chose the conservative route. After a few slow miles of country driving, we took a right off Main onto Skyview Drive. The gradual rise of the road provided a breathtaking view of the countryside, which was dotted with farms and church steeples. I observed the children playing along the road, and for a brief moment I felt as if I'd traveled back in time. I could picture playing wiffle ball or kick-the-can with my brother Ethan and our friends, or riding bikes with Gwen. And I could still smell the summer barbecues.

When we arrived at the steep driveway that led to the house my parents had lived in for the past forty years, I was slapped back to reality. The bottom entrance was being guarded by a crowd of media, armed with a small battalion of news vans and satellite trucks. It gave me a flashback to when I returned home after Noah's accident. At that time, I wasn't sure that this place would ever feel the same again. Admitting that I'm wrong had never been my strength, but in this case I'm glad that I was.

The military escort showed no intention of stopping, and the media gave way. I smiled—it was good to be on the other side for once.

"Hey, Warner, suddenly you're camera shy?" shouted a reporter as we sped by. My inner J-News wanted to get out and introduce him to my cane, but JP just kept smiling as the vehicles came to a stop in front of the house.

I took a long look at the cozy A-frame that I grew up in, and then glanced back at the pack of media. I could feel the "JP versus J-News" battle raging inside me, but for the first time I felt that JP might have a chance to win the war.

CHAPTER 18

That afternoon, Rockfield Police Chief Rich Tolland was called over.

No introduction was necessary, since I'd known Rich since kindergarten. But when we greeted each other, I felt like I was meeting him for the first time.

Following the greetings, Rich revealed the main purpose for his visit—me, and the circus I'd brought to town. He'd assigned two officers at the bottom of the driveway to disperse the crowds. He referred to them as "those damn bloodsuckers." He must have then remembered that I was one of those bloodsuckers, because he quickly apologized.

"None taken," I said, choosing not to explain that as of August my bloodsucking days had ended.

My father hadn't grasped the concept that years and distance had turned Rich and me into virtual strangers, and began recounting tales of our childhood. In his eyes, we were still those twelve-year-old kids playing in the backyard. The stories led to the league championship game back in high school, where Rich Tolland—nicknamed The Toll Booth for his large size, and having to pay a price to pass through him—delivered the crunching block that allowed JP Warner to score the winning touchdown.

Rich and I sat politely through story-time, but we both knew it was a different lifetime. I'd been to over two hundred countries since graduation, while Rich lived two houses down from the house he grew up in. If my father didn't mention it, I would never have known that Rich's parents had both passed away, or he married a schoolteacher named Cassie, and they have two adorably chubby children who mirrored their father. Different lifetimes.

Another police officer entered the house. He introduced himself as Officer Jones, and politely stated, "Sorry to interrupt, folks, but I need to steal the Chief—we have some important police business to get to on the other side of town."

There didn't appear to be anything special or unusual about Officer Jones, yet his presence sent a shock wave through me. I studied him as he led Rich to the door.

I was unsure of what to make of my strange reaction, and too tired to try to analyze it. Probably some sort of psychological damage resulting from my capture, that I will be too stubborn to see someone about.

After a quiet dinner, my father got me caught up on all the local gossip, while my mother continued to give me the silent treatment. When I announced that I was headed for bed, she did briefly break her talking-strike to inform me that my old room in the "new house" was made up for me.

"It's good to have you home, son," my father said as I limped off.

I smiled. "It's good to be home."

Mom remained silent.

With the help of my cane, I exited the house and strolled down a lighted path of slate squares. My body creaked, and I felt a thousand years old as I hobbled along—even the soothing sounds of the rushing brook and chirping crickets couldn't ease my pain. The bright moon reflected off the classic colonial known as the "new house," although it had been there for a quarter of a century. My parents built it when Noah came along, believing that our family had outgrown the A-frame. The house was a replica of the Smith-Harris House, now a museum in East Lyme, Connecticut, which was a favorite of my mother. But it never had the same homey feel, and my parents eventually moved back to the cozier A-frame when all the kids had left the nest.

The smell was the first thing to hit me when I entered. It was the smell of my youth. It was the smell of safety. It was the smell of having all your dreams in front of you. And it was as intoxicating as ever.

I was so weary that I wondered if I would make it up the stairs. The most activity I had in the last six weeks was walking down the halls of Landstuhl, and occasional physical therapy sessions that almost made me beg to be sent to Guantanamo.

I hadn't been in my childhood bedroom in years, and I immediately felt as if I were in a time warp. A few boxes that contained my mother's history books were stored there, but besides that, it could have been 1990 all over again. Michael Jordan and Bon Jovi posters still hung on the walls. My Rubik's cube still sat unsolved on my old desk next to a prom picture. Even though I tried to fight off the temptation, my eyes instinctively moved to the ancient picture of Gwen and me, posing in front of the A-Frame on an alluring spring afternoon.

I picked up the picture and studied it. She looked beautiful in a purple, formfitting gown with her long raven hair falling on her bare shoulders. I couldn't help but to chuckle, noticing her glowing orange-ish skin that was the aftermath of Gwen falling asleep in a tanning bed during a misguided attempt to optimize her look for the prom. If someone could look beautiful and radioactive at the same time it was Gwen.

I began coughing, causing a sharp pain to stab through my injured lung, and sending me crashing back to reality. Sadly, I realized Gwen Delaney was just as much in another lifetime as Rich Tolland was. I placed the picture face down on the desk, as if that somehow would hide my regrets.

I viewed the bedroom once more. I was stuck on the idea of my mother treating my old room like a time-capsule. It reminded me of when a family lost a young child and would cling to their memory by not changing anything.

Perhaps she knew death was imminent for her son. I had escaped it for all these years—my number would surely be up soon. And the thing that scared me most was that Mom was usually right.

CHAPTER 19

I fell asleep the second my head hit the pillow. I slept for twenty hours, straight into Tuesday evening. I awoke, ate dinner with my quiet mother and chatty father, before returning to my coma until Wednesday morning. I felt like I hadn't slept in fifteen years, and in some ways, maybe I hadn't.

I spent Wednesday and Thursday hobbling around my parents' property. And following my doctor's order about trying to limit stress and exertion, I chose not to return Lauren's endless phone calls.

By Thursday afternoon I was feeling frisky, so I limped to a wooded area on the edge of the property and cautiously climbed down a sharp slope to the brook. It was the spot where I first kissed Gwen. I thought about exploring the dilapidated tree where we carved our naïve mantra of *true love forever* into the bark, but the pain in my leg reminded me that forever wasn't as long as I thought, and decided against it.

I thought about all the days that had passed since Gwen and I were last down here, and how much I'd changed since that time. Byron's words popped into my head: *It's not what you do, it's who you are, JP.* The reporter in me agreed. But the youthful idealist hidden deep within fought against the notion. I was convinced that the JP Warner who would carve idealistic declarations into tree bark was the real me, and that J-News was just a detour.

I spotted the remnants of a tree-fort that Ethan and I had built when we were kids. I remembered the fight that broke out during its construction, resulting in both of us falling out of the tree. We ran crying to Mom, who would hear none of it, and sent us back outside until we learned how to play nice together. And since Ethan still hadn't phoned his brother after he escaped near-death at the hands of crazed Islamic militants, it appears as if we're still working on it.

By Friday morning I was ready to branch out, and decided to venture into town. But with my father having left for his weekly golf game, and my mother at work, I encountered a major stumbling block—I had no vehicle. So I called Christina. She claimed she was late for a class, but I knew school didn't start until after Labor Day. After a brief battle of wills, she agreed to come to Rockfield to be my chauffeur for the day. Like myself, she was learning that living in that brownstone came with strings attached.

She arrived in style, driving my oversized, sand-colored Humvee that she often enjoyed tearing down Park Avenue in. And not one of those trendy Hummers the yuppies tool around in—this was an authentic military vehicle from Desert Storm that had a few souvenir bullet holes to prove it. It had been my ten-year anniversary gift from GNZ. Between my travel schedule and living part time in Manhattan, I'd never actually purchased a car in my adult life, and had only driven the Humvee on a couple of occasions.

"You're late," I greeted her.

She sent a dirty look in my direction. "Sorry, I had to update the fake JP Warner Twitter account I administer. The funny thing is, I try to play the character even more over-the-top than normal when it comes to your egomania, but people still believe it's the real you. We're almost up to a million followers."

I was about to explain to her that twit is the slang British word for idiot, when she hit me with a surprise. She bull-rushed me and wrapped me with a hug. "I thought you were going to die, JP," she said, her voice cracking with emotion. "And I'm so sorry about Byron."

I was not in the mood to relive the capture, so I deflected, "Why—were you scared you'd have to go back to the dorms?"

"The thought crossed my mind," she said with a wise-ass smile. It signaled a return to normalcy between us, now that the mushy stuff was over.

"How'd summer school go?" I asked

"All A's."

"How's your friend—Dimwit or something like that?"

"It's Daman, and I haven't heard from him in months. Funny how he became less interested in me after your friend tried to execute him. And once word got around, let's just say the boys haven't exactly been knocking down my door."

"And they say capital punishment isn't a deterrent."

"Very funny. Thank goodness those terrorists left your cranky personality intact."

I let it go as I hobbled to the Humvee, which seemed to surprise her.

My directions took us to Main Street. On one side of the road was the high school I graduated from, and where my brother Ethan was currently a history teacher and football coach. It's located next to a campus made up of the town hall, volunteer fire department, police station, and library.

Notables on the south side of the road were the bowling alley, Main Street Tavern, and the Rockfield Village Store. I focused on a weathered colonial that housed both a realtor and the local newspaper called the *Rockfield Gazette*. My teacher and mentor Murray Brown created the newspaper—the one I always dreamed of buying with Gwen, if and when Murray ever decided to hang up the typewriter. But that was before life called, and for better or worse, I answered.

When we passed the high school, Christina noticed the name on the football field. "JP Warner Field? Wow, I'm impressed—did you get to come back like some conquering hero to christen it?"

"They christen ships, not football fields. But no, I've never been there. I was supposed to attend the dedication, but got called to Kosovo at the last moment. My brothers Ethan and Noah stepped in for me."

"Noah's the cute one, right?"

"They say he looks like me."

"In your dreams, old man. Is he single?"

"No," I replied. He might technically have been, but I knew Noah was still emotionally attached to Lisa. He wasn't available.

"When was the last time you were here?" she asked.

I thought hard for a moment. "Three years ago on Christmas. Opened my gifts in the morning and was on a plane to Haiti at noon."

"You haven't seen your family in three years!?"

"I've seen them," I defended. "My parents come down to the city for dinner all the time. And every year I fly the whole family somewhere for a week's vacation during the summer. Last year it was France. Unfortunately, this year I was a little tied up."

"Sounds like an expensive guilt trip."

And a much longer trip than the one they would have made the last few days to check in on me to see if I was still in one piece.

"So did they throw their sugar-daddy a big party when he came home after fighting off the bad guys in Serbia?" Christina asked, before honking at a slow driving elderly couple in front of us.

"No, actually they didn't."

"They probably just want to avoid all the cameras and microphones."

"Maybe," I said, but I knew it ran much deeper. It was time to change the subject. "Turn here!"

CHAPTER 20

Christina jerked the steering wheel to the right and swung the Humvee into the small parking lot of the Rockfield Village Store, almost tipping it over in the process.

"What's this place?" she asked after we skidded to a stop.

"Rumor has it that an old friend of mine works here."

I felt a sharp pain down my leg as I struggled to get out of the vehicle. I stubbornly tried to walk without the cane, but it was a failed experiment. I slowly made it to the front of the store and entered through the same creaky door as the one from my youth. In fact, the whole place looked exactly as it did when I was growing up. Rockfield was one big time-capsule.

I immediately spotted the person I'd come to see. But as usual, he beat me to the draw. "Well, looky here," Murray greeted me from behind the counter. Always an impeccable dresser, he wore red suspenders over his button-downed Oxford.

He was in the neighborhood of eighty, although nobody was really sure—the old journalist never revealed his sources on that one. His hair and mustache had turned much grayer since the last time I'd seen him, but he still had the same youthful twinkle in his eye.

I limped behind the counter to give him a hug. He was always rail-thin, and I could feel the bones in his spine as we embraced.

After releasing, Murray looked me up and down, focusing on my cane. "Looks like I'm still getting around better than you these days, John Pierpont."

His focus then switched to Christina. "John Pierpont keeps getting older, but his girlfriends keep staying the same age."

Christina begged to differ. "I don't know what you've heard but ..."

"Young lady, are you questioning my sources?"

"I think it's time for some new sources, grandpa, because if you think JP and I ..."

"I wouldn't doubt his sources," I cut in with a laugh. "I heard Deep Throat is his bridge partner at the senior center."

Christina, now understanding she was being hustled, flashed the look of a teenager who was embarrassed of her parents.

It seemed like a good time to make the introductions. "Murray, this is my chauffeur and future world renowned journalist, Christina Wilkins. Christina, this is my mentor, and the most over-qualified cashier in history, Murray Brown."

"If I'm his mentor, I didn't do a very good job," Murray remarked.

"So you taught this guy to go off to places that make Hades look like the Club Med?" Christina asked.

"Oh no, young lady. I taught him the art of journalism. I thought he should have stuck with it, but instead he decided to join the circus."

I pointed to the newspaper with the large headline: *Fair Opens Tonight!* "Murray covered the Nixon White House for the *New York Globe*, but always believed that local news most affected people's lives. So he came back here and started the *Gazette*."

Murray smiled at his premature eulogy. "All important politics are local, that is correct. Your father and I didn't agree on a lot, but *that* we agreed on. How is his health doing?"

"I believe he is much more likely to die from boredom than the cancer. You seem to have taken much better to retirement than him."

"I learned that the best way to enjoy retirement is to never retire. I stay involved with the paper's management, and write a Sunday editorial. But I did acquiesce to my wife's demands and hire someone to run the day to day. But it left me with too much idle time on my hands, so I took the job here. If you're going to write about a community, you better know that community, and what better place to learn about the people of Rockfield than the Village Store," he said with a smile, while simultaneously waiting on a customer.

"Once a journalist, always a journalist," I added.

"I agree with that sentiment. But the question is—will you prove your theory correct, and return to your journalistic roots?"

"I'm currently unemployed, so I guess I'm open to anything."

Murray smiled like he was up to something. He usually was. "It's never too late to do what you were born to do. Perhaps you should think about the *Gazette*. We couldn't pay your superstar wages, but we have a great new editor who I think you would work well with. She came from New York, perhaps you may have heard of her."

"What's the name?"

"Gwen," Murray said, unable to hold back a grin.

If his goal was to get my attention, he succeeded. But before I could ask any of the endless questions that were about to cliff dive off my tongue, the doors creaked open and sunlight shot into the dimly lit store. When my eyes adjusted, I recognized Rich Tolland, who acknowledged me with a nod, along with his partner from the day before. And just like our first meeting, I immediately got an uncomfortable feeling as I looked into his eyes. I'd seen that look before.

The officers purchased bottles of water and candy bars. They made brief chitchat with Murray about the upcoming fair, before leaving. My eyes followed Officer Kyle Jones out the door.

Christina brought two peach flavored drinks to the counter, and a newspaper. Feeling nostalgic, I requested a vanilla swirl ice cream cone.

After Murray rang up the damage on an outdated cash register, and we bid each other a cheery goodbye, Christina and I exited into the sun-filled afternoon. I licked my ice cream cone and mentally rang up my own damage. It appeared she too had returned home.

CHAPTER *21*

Rockfield Fair

Labor Day Weekend

The Rockfield Fair festivities didn't start as I'd hoped.

I attended the traditional football game with my parents on Friday night. My father was full of his usual energy and wore the green and gold sweatshirt with large 'R' on the front, as he did to every game during my youth. My mother was bundled up in a sweater and turtleneck on the unseasonably cool night, but she remained anything but warm toward me.

Things with my brother Ethan actually became a little frostier. He's been the head football coach at Rockfield High for ten years, and had numerous league titles to show for it. But when longtime Rockfield principal Wayne Mulville spotted me, he dragged me into the locker-room prior and interrupted Ethan's pre-game speech. Mulville declared that "American hero JP Warner" wanted to say a few words to the team. When I waited for Ethan after the game to explain, I learned that he'd ducked out another entrance like a senior skipping out of study hall.

But I was still looking forward to the official opening on Saturday morning, marked by a parade down Main Street. My father was ready to go with blanket in hand at six in the morning. I struggled with the early departure, but after gulping down three cups of coffee like they were shots of bourbon, I was ready to go. I wanted to avoid being recognized, so I dressed incognito, wearing a baseball cap and dark sunglasses.

I'd never been a fan of parades, but after the events of the past few months I was just glad to be back home, and actually enjoyed sitting on the dew filled grass while watching fire-trucks and marching bands mosey by at a snail's pace. When it concluded, we headed toward the town hall with the rest of the crowd.

First Selectman Maloney stood on a makeshift stage that was covered in patriotic red, white and blue bunting, and delivered the opening speech into a crackling microphone. It was the usual fluffy promotional speech, stolen from my father's playbook. But before he finished, Maloney announced an award to be handed out for the first time this year, in honor of Lisa Spargo. It would be presented to the member of the community who performed the most exemplary work in eradicating drunk driving. He read a laundry list of statistics about alcohol related accidents in the United States, along with a brief history on Lisa. The name Noah Warner was never mentioned.

My father pulled my mother close. I could tell it caught them off guard. A pristine Saturday morning suddenly began raining bad memories.

My father had told me that she still felt guilty that when she'd heard the news of Lisa's death, she'd initially felt relieved that it wasn't Noah who was the one killed. Sounded to me like a normal response of a parent. I was just glad Noah was nowhere to be found. He never rose before noon by choice, so there wasn't much chance of him being here.

Maloney stood in his dark suit, looking like a taller version of the kid I grew up with. The outfit reminded me that he used to wear a suit and tie to school to try to kiss up to our teachers. He called for a moment of silence and bowed his head of slick-backed hair. When the silence ended, he brought Lisa Spargo's mother onto the stage.

She was a dark-haired Italian woman who wore a floral colored sundress and sandals. She looked very much like her attractive daughter had. But even from a distance, I noticed the deep scar of sadness embedded on her face.

After gut-wrenching words about the dreams Lisa would never get to fulfill, and more statistics on drinking and driving fatalities, she presented the award to a local policeman named Kyle Jones.

Officer Jones walked over to Mrs. Spargo and they hugged dramatically for what seemed like minutes. When they released their embrace, the crowd clapped.

I continued to have a bad feeling about Jones. *But why?* There was nothing unusual about his physical appearance—a slender man of average height. He seemed to care about the community, hence the award. I again blamed it on the conspiratorial J-News lingering within me. The transition from reporter to farmer was going to be more difficult than I thought.

CHAPTER 22

After Maloney declared the Rockfield Fair open for business, I followed my mother to the historical society exhibit. I could tell she was shaken up and I wanted to comfort her. I also needed to put an end to this growing gap between us.

I trailed her into the small exhibit tent and began to help her move artifacts. "What are you doing, JP?"

"I thought you could use some help."

"I've been doing this for twenty years, I think I have it down pretty well. Go find your father—he is very proud of your triumphant return and wants to show you off to his constituents."

"Like a prized pony?"

She turned her back on me without a word.

"Are *you* happy I'm back?"

Silence.

"I'm a reporter, Mom, I can tell something is wrong."

She turned in my direction. "No JP, you gave up being a reporter a long time ago. Now you're just a stranger with a death wish. I can't do it anymore, I just can't!"

"Can't do what?"

"I can't attach myself emotionally. I can no longer be your mother."

"You're going to quit being my mom? I think that's against the rules."

"You were a hostage for six weeks, but I've been one for twenty years. You got lucky this time, but eventually I will have to bury you. I can't do it anymore, I have other children and grandchildren who need me, not to mention your father."

The dam broke and she began sobbing uncontrollably. I limped to her and encased her in a hug.

"I'm done with that life, Mom. I promise"

"It's who you are, JP. Between you and Noah, I get scared every time I hear the phone ring."

I wrapped the hug tighter. "I promise you I'm done."

This time she hugged me back, but I felt the doubt in her squeeze.

"Is everything alright here?" my father's voice broke the moment.

My mother wiped the tears from her eyes. "We're fine, Peter. I'm just glad our son is home safe and sound."

"I don't know about sound, but it is good to be home," I said.

"We're glad to have you back, JP. You can stay as long as you need," my father added, before turning excited once again. "Come with me, JP, I want to re-introduce you to an old friend of yours."

For an instant I thought he meant Gwen, and I broke out in a cold sweat. But it turned out to be anything but a friend—it was my old spineless classmate, and my father's successor, Bobby Maloney. Having grown up with Bobby, it was no surprise to me that he didn't have the guts to warn my parents that he was going to drop the Lisa Spargo bomb on them this morning. But before I could even protest, my father was tugging me in Maloney's direction.

The crux of our problem had always been his jealousy of my relationship with Gwen, and while I can't fault anyone for falling for her, I didn't appreciate his constant attempts to undermine me behind my back. And it didn't stop once we graduated high school. While I was off covering the Gulf War, he would travel every weekend to New York from North

Carolina, where he attended college, to "comfort her." Hitting on a guy's girl while he's avoiding missiles in a war zone has to be against some sort of etiquette. And while I'm no psychologist, it seemed to me that his sudden return to Rockfield, in which he sought out my father's former position, reeked of someone not having gotten over the past.

My father gave Maloney heartfelt congratulations on the speech, and he seemed to be eating up the approval. They discussed a couple of local issues for a few minutes until my father spotted a group of his longtime supporters. He excused himself, leaving Maloney and me awkwardly together. There was silence, followed by more silence.

Finally he spoke, "So what do you think your doing, Warner?"

I was surprised by the aggressive tone. "What do you mean, Bobby?"

"It's Robert."

"Who is Robert?"

"I am, dammit. What are you doing in my town?"

"*Your* town?"

"Stop answering a question with a question. What are you doing here?"

"I guess you guys don't have cable in Rockfield yet. I was captured by …"

Maloney looked like he was about to blow a gasket. "I know your story, Warner—the whole goddam world knows your sob story. They can try to make you out to be some sort of hero, but everyone here knows you're nothing but an opportunist. And if you think you're going to waltz in here and take my job, I can assure you that you'll have the fight of your life on your hands."

I began to laugh, but caught myself when I realized he was actually serious. "I was just thinking about starting a little farm. I hear they demonstrate a lot of farm equipment at the fair."

"Nobody in this town wants you here. They don't respect a fraud, so go back to whatever exotic locale you came from."

I flashed him my smuggest smile. The one that had irritated people on all seven continents at one time or another. "I'm just here to enjoy the fair, Mr. First Selectman. And thank you for your kind welcome."

He glared at me, but wouldn't look me directly in the eye—now that's the Bobby Maloney I remember—before storming off.

A certain peace came over me as I limped around the fairgrounds—just me and my cane. Some people stopped me, while others gawked. The Maloney Doctrine, stating that nobody wanted me here, sure didn't seem to be adding up.

I purchased some chicken, along with an expensive cup of suds they tried to pass off as beer. I checked out the lumberjack competition, and then a few art exhibits. The afternoon sun heated up, but a soft wind breezed through, and the smell of pine briefly replaced the aroma of cow shit. I was about to head to the Ferris wheel, my favorite amusement ride, when I heard it.

"John Peter! John Peter!"

It couldn't be.

I turned.

It was.

Moving toward me, awkwardly, sashaying over the mucky grass in her two-inch heels, was Lauren Bowden. Her blonde hair was both magnetic and blinding.

To toss more salt in my wounds, she was escorted by Cliff Sutcliffe, wearing an expensive black suit. He looked like he'd come to pay his last respects to my happiness.

My instinct was to flee the scene, but the cane was now officially a handicap.

"You gotta be kidding me," I muttered.

CHAPTER 23

Lauren pulled her heel out of the muck and looked with disgust at the ruination of her designer shoe. We hadn't spoken since our lunch at Norvell's. Her first words weren't about missing me.

"This place is dreadful, John Peter," she said with a look of nausea.

I pondered escape possibilities. I was captured again. "I think you two are lost—the royal wedding you came dressed for is not here."

The gruesome twosome inched closer. When Sutcliffe got close enough to sting my senses with his heavy cologne, he reached out with his clammy hand and attempted to shake ... but I pulled away. I could tell that Lauren was repelled by the sloppy chicken I held, which saved me from a fake hug—the best investment I'd made in a long time.

"I would go to the ends of the earth for my favorite GNZ employee," Sutcliffe said with a salesy smile. He theatrically sniffed the air. "And I think I have—is that cow shit I smell?"

"I don't know if you forgot to read the fine print on my contract, but as of August I'm no longer a GNZ employee."

It felt good to say it out loud.

"My sources tell me you are thinking of signing on with CNN—please tell me this isn't true, John Peter?" Lauren belted out. She received a dirty look from Sutcliffe for venturing off the script.

"I don't know anything about this CNN stuff, but if your sources said so, then it must be true," I said.

Lauren soaked in the "compliment," as usual not picking up on the sarcasm.

Sutcliffe got their orchestration back on track. He winked at Lauren, before asking if he could talk to me alone. Lauren flashed her big toothy grin, as if she was trying to lock up this year's Razzie award for bad acting.

I tried to walk away, but Sutcliffe was easily able to keep up with me. He attempted to put his arm around me, but I managed to pull away.

We eventually sat down at an empty picnic table. He looked at me as if his job were on the line—it probably was. He reached into a stylish leather briefcase and pulled out a thick bound document, which he laid on the table. It looked like the tax code.

"What do I have to do to get your JP Hancock on this contract?" he asked like a sleazy used-car salesman.

"I told you, Cliff—I'm done. I don't have it in me anymore. I shouldn't have been in Serbia. I almost got Byron killed."

"How is Byron?"

"He's paralyzed."

"I know *that*. I mean can GNZ do anything for him to help him along? He won't take any calls."

Translation: Sutcliffe's bosses were worried about a lawsuit.

"I taught him well then. Can we get to why you're here?"

He smiled. "Nightly studio show in prime-time. You and Lauren—The Warner and Bowden Show! Point counterpoint stuff. Politics ... pop culture ... hell, I don't care if you two spend the hour singing karaoke. It's your show, you'll have complete control."

"Why is Lauren pushing for this? She's already got her own prime-time show."

"Honestly?"

"It would be a nice change of pace."

"We overrated her appeal. What people liked most about her was her relationship with you, and we misread the ratings that spiked during your capture. It was great drama."

"Yeah, a real fiesta. I'm thinking about going back next year, maybe invest in a time-share. Listen, Cliff, I really don't want to spend an hour with Lauren, in a television studio or anywhere."

"If you want Lauren out, then she's out. Between you and me, JP, she's been totally screwing up the whole Kingsbury investigation. The other networks are beating us to the punch on every break in the case. And she couldn't even get an interview with you after your release … and she was sleeping with you!"

"It's easy to hire a bubble-headed beauty queen when the sea is calm and the boat will drive itself. But when the water gets rough you need an experienced captain."

"I don't know what kind of mind-altering stuff they gave you in Spain, but…"

"I was in Serbia."

"Tom-may-to, to-mah-to. I'm talking about news and you're talking about boats."

"GNZ *used* to do news. And they didn't need swimsuit models to deliver it."

"Which is exactly why we need you to come back as News Director. Forget the studio show—this is much bigger. You'll have final call on what we report and who we hire to report it. We are offering you a blank slate to bring GNZ back to where it belongs—tabula rasa."

He reached into his left breast pocket and pulled out an envelope. He handed it to me.

"I know our last offer was insulting. You know how negotiations work, JP. But the contents of this envelope will guarantee you are the highest paid person in the history of the news industry."

I'm sure he figured J-News couldn't turn down that kind of offer. He probably was right. But unfortunately for him he was talking to JP.

I stood and began to limp away. Sutcliffe followed after me.

"I got more, JP."

"That's the thing—I don't."

He remained undeterred, pulling a small plastic doohickey out of his pants pocket and attempting to hand it to me. I again rebuffed him.

"Do you know what this is?" he asked desperately.

"I don't care."

"It's a JP Warner action figure!"

I was speechless—more like frozen in horror. And like someone unable to avoid looking at a gruesome car crash, I accepted the small piece of plastic. The figure wore camouflage and carried a M-16 rifle, depicting me like some sort of GI-Joe superhero reporter.

Once I got my bearings, I tossed the action figure down on the littered fairgrounds next to a garbage can, where I thought it belonged. Sutcliffe desperately scooped the figure off the ground and hurried after me.

"The action figure is just the beginning, JP. We're going to market you like the sizzling hot superstar you are, beyond the scope of news!"

I kept walking without a word. And when it became obvious that I wasn't interested, his tone predictably turned "sore loser." "You'll be back," he grumbled.

"How can you be so sure?"

"Because it's who you are, Warner."

I wish I had a quarter for every time I'd heard that one.

Lauren carefully navigated toward us. She looked at Sutcliffe and immediately knew it was bad news.

"I can't believe you, John Peter," she spat at me like a child who didn't get her way. Her sixth sense was the sense of entitlement.

"When everyone told me not to be seen with you because you were a washed up has-been, I stuck with you. I told them that with a new agent and PR firm, you could be somebody again. Then you get this lucky break of being captured by terrorists and you just throw it all away!"

I didn't know whether to laugh or cry. What I really wanted to do was run, but that wasn't an option. So I said the only thing that made sense to me at that moment, "I'm going on the Ferris wheel. I'll see you guys around."

I turned and limped away to the distant shouts of, "John Peter, get back here! John Peter!"

I went to the nearest garbage can to throw away the envelope. But for some reason I decided to hold on to it.

CHAPTER 24

I'd finally escaped the clutches of Maloney, Bowden and Sutcliffe. I don't think it was a coincidence that my enjoyment level picked up.

I rode the Ferris wheel and ate some more chicken. Despite my attempts at remaining low profile, a few people recognized me. But capturing the spirit of the day, I politely posed for pictures and signed autographs. My father ended any last attempts to meld into the background by dragging me to judge a baking contest.

Eventually I got out on my own again. I soaked in the sunny Saturday and breathed in the barbecue chicken/cow shit odor. It was the smell of peace … the smell of returning home. It took me a long time to get back here and I planned to make it last.

I stopped by numerous farming equipment exhibits, including the FFA from the local high school. I realized that farming might be a lot more difficult than I'd thought. Maybe I'd get back to the original plan of writing for a small newspaper. Gwen returning as editor made it an even more tantalizing thought. I walked around, searching for you-know-who, hoping she was here. But at the same time, scared that she might be.

As the sun began to set behind the large oak trees in the distance, I sat down on a wooden bench to rest my weary body. Shuffleboard and three o'clock dinners couldn't be far behind, I mused. I aimlessly watched people stroll by, and then I spotted a girl I knew. It wasn't Gwen. It was my niece, Ella.

Ella was Ethan's eldest daughter—it was hard to believe she was already ten. Sticking with the family naming tradition, she was named after Ella Grasso, the first woman governor of Connecticut.

There were a lot of whispering and finger points in my direction. I could tell the presence of her television-star uncle made Ella the star of her group of friends. She led the troops toward me, and I was soon surrounded by a group of fourth graders.

Ella played proud spokesman, introducing each wide-eyed friend. I smiled and shook their nervous hands. They spent a few minutes questioning me about my capture. The Q&A session boiled down to fifteen different ways to ask me, "Were you scared?" Which was pretty similar to how the grown-up media works. I answered with heroic cool, but the truth was, *hell yeah I was.*

I sensed it would impress Ella's friends for her famous uncle to call for some one-on-one time. This also fit nicely into my agenda, which was to figure out why her father was avoiding me. The kids scrambled away, but not before making plans to meet Ella at the bumper cars in twenty minutes.

"So how come you guys haven't come over to see me?" I asked.

Ella just shrugged. "I don't know."

I had extracted answers out of those who had refused to talk under torture, but Ella Warner was more difficult to crack. "Are your parents mad at me?"

Shrug. "I don't know."

"Have you guys been busy?"

Shrug. "I don't know."

"What did you think of the game last night?"

"It was awesome," came an excited response. I thought I might be making progress.

"Did your dad say anything about me after the game?"

Shrug. "I don't know."

Back to the drawing board. I knew I needed a more direct source. "So where is your dad?"

Ella turned all the way around twice, viewing the fairgrounds. I couldn't tell if she was looking for her father or trying to make herself dizzy. Then she pointed. "Over there!"

I followed her gaze, which led me to my brother. He was chatting with two burly flat-topped football players. Also present was my sister-in-law, Pam.

"Let's go see your dad," I said to Ella, already limping in his direction.

CHAPTER 25

Ella, on a probable sugar high, left me in the dust.

"Look who I found! Look who I found!"

Ethan's eyes left his daughter and locked on me. I wasn't getting a "happy to see me" vibe.

I led with the headline, "I felt compelled to come over and thank you for all your get-well wishes. Your kindness has been excessive." I was going to clear the air or add another broken bone to my medical résumé. Maybe both.

Ethan told Ella to run along and get some ice cream. Not a good sign. He reached into his faded jeans and pulled out crinkled money and instructed her to take the younger children, Sandy and Eli, with her. He then hastily sent his players on their way.

Pam, sensing the imminent showdown, gave her husband a quick kiss on the cheek, intended to diffuse the situation, and departed with the children. She glanced back twice with a concerned look on her face. Only Ethan and I remained—the battlefield was clear.

He turned to me. "I've been busy, I apologize. I know you're used to the world revolving around you, JP, so it must be a shock to your system to learn that you're not the center of the universe."

"Cut the crap, Ethan. You've been avoiding me like the Bubonic Plague."

"I'm a history teacher, JP. The Bubonic Plague was caused by rats, not egomaniacs who think they can drop in and out of everybody's lives whenever they feel like it."

"I'm sorry you chose a life where the only time you leave the safe confines of Rockfield is on a school bus. I didn't choose it for you."

"Nobody said anything about your job."

"Spare me."

"Spare *you?*" Ethan asked with a look of disbelief. "The key word is *you*. It's always about *you*, JP, isn't it? You couldn't care less that it kills another little piece of Mom every time you run off chasing danger. How about sparing her?"

"I don't have to defend my career to you."

"That's because you aren't the one who has to go over there in the middle of the night. You should have seen her expression when she turned on the news and saw a photo of her son plastered on the screen with a face beaten purple by a bunch of terrorists. And you weren't the one who sat with Dad after he came out of cancer surgery."

"I got him the best care and doctors possible."

"Writing a check isn't the same as being there."

I tried to speak, but Ethan evoked his big-brother rights and talked over me, "And you weren't the one who had to talk Noah down off Samerauk Bridge last year. He was going to kill himself. But did you care? You took us to France, so I guess everything is fine."

I knew Noah was in a bad place, but the depths shocked me. *Kill himself?* I filled with guilt. "I didn't know."

"Because you weren't here."

"I'm not the first child to move away from the nest."

He shook his head like I just wasn't getting it.

"Proximity has nothing to do with it. Just because you take off to God-knows-where doesn't stop Mom and Dad from thinking about you …

worrying about you … contacting you. Their love for you is unconditional. Sometimes I wonder if it works both ways."

"That's not fair."

"You want to talk about fair? Dad gave his heart and soul to this town, and when it came time to dedicate a field, who does the school board vote to name it after?"

I knew where this was headed, but I let him continue venting, "That's right, they named it after JP Warner, a man whose main contribution was getting the hell out as fast as he could and never looking back. You didn't even show up for the ceremony."

"Stop playing this off on Dad," I shot back, angrily. "This is about you and your fragile ego. You chose a life, just like I chose a life, but the only difference is I don't need an award for it."

"What the hell is that supposed to mean?"

We were now face-to-face, a crowd had gathered around us like when a fight was about to break out in junior high. We had become the most popular exhibit.

"Maybe you can get a Mr. Perfect award. The perfect life with the perfect wife. The perfect family man who always does the perfect thing with his perfect kids. When you receive that honor, I promise I'll show up!"

I was getting close to adding missing teeth to my medical résumé.

"Why don't you go do your usual leaving act, JP? It's going to happen sooner or later. There will never be enough attention and spotlight here for you."

"You better get used to me, big brother, because I'm going to be here for a long, long time."

As if she sensed a calamity about to happen, Pam returned with the children. She was a lot like a UN peacekeeping force—good intentions, but not enough firepower to stop anything significant from happening. She hugged me—I was unable to determine if it was a warm greeting, or she was trying to protect me—and then after we traded a couple pleasantries, she invited me to a barbecue at their house on Labor Day.

Ethan turned and began walking away in a huff.

I stood awkwardly with Pam and the children. We made small talk about the weather, and I discussed the impending return to school with my nieces and nephew. Acting as if what just happened didn't happen, seemed like the best way to proceed.

Finally, Pam broke the delusion, "JP, you just have to understand that Ethan puts in all the blood and guts around here. He's done all the dirty work with your mom and dad, and Noah is no picnic, either. Then you walk in like the prodigal son and he gets shoved to the side like yesterday's news. Can you blame him for being a little hurt? He's only human."

I nodded.

"He really is glad to see you. Just give him some time, okay?" she asked with an encouraging smile.

"I will."

"Good. Are you really planning on sticking around?"

Our shouting must have been heard all the way to the ice cream stand. Which meant everybody within shouting distance heard my claim to drop anchor in Rockfield. I doubt anyone believed it.

And words certainly weren't going to change anyone's mind, but they could change the subject, "That was a great game last night, huh?"

Pam looked off into the distance. "There's one of the coaches—why don't you ask him about it?"

CHAPTER 26

I stared at Noah, who was in many ways a spitting image of myself. He just dressed a lot different with his ever-present denim jacket, black boots, and cigarette hanging from his lips. He reminded me of the young Serbs partying on the river.

We made eye contact at long distance, and then he began heading right toward me in a slow jog.

"Dad tells me he's been working two jobs, besides volunteering as a coach, and he's even going back to school," I said to Pam.

"He's made great strides. I worry about him though, especially on *this day*."

"This day?"

"Today is the anniversary of Lisa's ... well, you know ..."

I stared out at my brother as he approached. "Ethan was right ... I should have been here."

Noah arrived with a bear hug for me that sent pain through my broken body. He had a cheek kiss for Pam, and smiles for the children, who declared their love for Uncle Noah, but took issue with the cigarette smell.

Pam excused herself to find Ethan, but first invited Noah to their Labor Day barbecue on Monday.

"I wouldn't miss it, sis," he said with a smile.

It was good to see him smile, especially now knowing what today signified.

"You look a mess," he addressed me.

"You should see the other guy."

"I did … every night on the news, claiming he was gonna kill my big brother if their demands weren't met."

"And he would have, but then he found out how happy everyone would be if he got rid of me."

Noah laughed, before embracing again. This was a much more affectionate Noah than the one I remembered from before the accident.

Our reunion wasn't like old times. Old times, frankly, weren't that memorable in our relationship. We didn't fight like he and Ethan did—we always got along—the problem was that we rarely spent time together. I went off to college when Noah was just in first grade. Maybe because of the wide age gap, he always seemed to be trying to find his identity. I had regrets about not being there for him in the way that Ethan was there to steer me in the right direction, or at least attempt to. Maybe that's why he gripped so tightly to Lisa.

So it was like new times. Times I looked forward to.

We remained standing in the middle of the fairgrounds, rehashing last night's game, and getting me caught up on all the hot-button topics in Rockfield. He also received the first, in what I figured would be many "smoking is bad for you" lectures.

The most interesting part of the conversation was Noah's career plans. As far as I knew, he never had any before. Lisa was his career. He had returned to school to with hopes of becoming a guidance counselor. He wanted to help kids so that they, to use his words, "Don't mess up their lives the way I did."

What we didn't talk about was the accident.

Nobody was closer than Noah and Lisa. They had enough passion to fill up ten rooms, and even though their relationship often played out in an endless cycle of drama, fights, and making up—their love was too strong for anything to keep them apart.

There was an outcry in Rockfield that Noah got off with just a slap on the wrist. There couldn't be anything further from the truth—he received a life sentence. And if it were left up to him, he would have pleaded to anything that got him the death penalty, in order to rejoin Lisa quicker.

Noah looked at his watch. "I gotta take off, JP," he said, before surprising me with another embrace. "But we'll definitely hook up at Ethan's on Monday."

"Hot date?" I asked.

Noah's look intensified. "No, I'm just going to meet an old friend. We haven't talked in a while."

"Are you going to be alright?" I instinctively asked, the big brother in me showing through.

Noah looked back as he walked away. "I'm going to be fine," he said, and smiled mischievously. "And speaking of old friends who haven't talked in awhile—I saw Gwen Delaney walking around here earlier."

I watched him fade into the distance. He turned back momentarily and gave me one more smile and wave. He seemed better, especially compared to the vision of him on that bridge that was now etched in my mind. I looked forward to spending time with him, vowing to do my best to make up for lost years.

Then my mind wandered to Gwen.

CHAPTER 27

I stood as inconspicuously as possible amongst a crowd cheering two fat guys participating in the annual pie-eating contest. It was enough to make me never want to eat again.

After Ethan's stinging words, I had a sudden urge to find my mother so she could work her magic to ease my guilt. I pulled my baseball cap down as far as I could and slipped out of the crowd. I hobbled down a grass corridor between the exhibit tents. And then time froze.

I couldn't help but stare at the raven-haired beauty in the distance. I was paralyzed by a tornado of swirling emotions. History would record our relationship as a complex mix of pure greatness at the highest level and the relentless cloud of what might have been. It was similar to the way my father used to describe Mickey Mantle.

Gwen didn't seem to be afflicted with the same inner turmoil, and began casually strolling toward me. I didn't notice a twitch of hesitation, nor did I sense that this was a life-altering moment for her.

I never wanted to see someone as much and as little at the same time. Her long legs were covered by a knee-length plaid skirt and high black boots, which were more fairground-appropriate than Lauren's heels. Physically, she looked similar to the last time I saw her, but this Gwen carried an aura of sophistication.

A camera hung around her neck, and bounced up and down as she approached—like my heart palpitations. My knees weakened, forcing me to lean on my cane for support.

"JP, I heard you were in town. It's good to see you in one piece after what you went though," she greeted me affably, and offered me a handshake like we were business colleagues.

I just stared at her. I had thought about this moment for a long time, but never really prepared what I'd actually say. In the daydreams the conversation depended upon my mood. Sometimes I would call her every name in the book for moving on without me. Other times we would rush into each other's arms and declare that true love really is forever.

I knew touching her hand would be a mistake, so I didn't. "It's been a long time," was all I could manage to say.

"Yeah, it's been a while. It must be a few years now."

Must be a few years? The words ripped at me. Her casualness in the wake of such a historic event—our last meeting, well over a decade ago now—was like a knife to my lungs. Could she possibly not have our last meeting burned in her mind, as I had?

We started making chitchat about mundane subjects. This didn't add up, as in no reunion fantasy of mine was it ever blasé. And as the shock of our sudden meeting began to wear off, I started to grow irritated. I searched for any clue that she carried the same devastating scar from our relationship, but found none.

As we continued beating the humdrum, she caught me staring at her ring finger.

"Stephen and I got divorced two years ago, to answer your question," she said.

Just the mention of his name brought out my inner J-News. "I never know whether to give condolences or congratulations when people get divorced."

"It was a tough time for both of us. Everyone goes into marriage thinking it will last forever."

It shouldn't have been that tough. In fact, it should have been the easiest decision she ever made ... since she was supposed to still be in love with me. I never let myself think that she actually loved the guy, or dreamt of spending her life with him. I'd convinced myself that she'd married him out of spite or youthful naiveté, and she eventually realized where her heart stood on the issue. Maybe it would have been best to never see her again and maintain my delusions. But it was too late for that, and I could no longer hold back.

"I'm relieved it was just divorce. I thought he might have died of old age. What was he like, a hundred when you married him?"

Her face turned beet-red—I had hit a nerve.

"The guy I dated before Stephen was an immature child, so it was nice to be with a grownup, no matter how it ended," she said, her eyes wandering to my cane. "I guess the more things change the more they stay the same."

The small dash of anger in her words provided me the hope I needed to continue on. I knew, or at least hoped, that there was no way our once epic tale of love could turn into handshakes and bland discussions of the weather. I needed there to be an emotional connection, even if it came in the form of hatred or regret.

I followed Gwen's eyes—still a radiant green—to my cane. My stare appeared to make her uncomfortable, forcing her to look away as she spoke, an edge in her voice, "It was good to see you, JP. I assume you're just on a stopover between exotic countries. So have a safe trip."

I continued staring at her. I couldn't stop.

"What?" she finally asked with irritation.

I said nothing. I couldn't.

"Shouldn't you be getting back to that news model who has set journalism back a couple of centuries? I think she's still trolling around somewhere in her supermodel heels."

My smile came to life. "How did you know Lauren was here today?"

Gwen was now flustered, but recovered nicely. "I'm a journalist, remember? You know, like you used to be."

"Used to be?"

"Yeah, back before you became a bad example of reality TV."

Reality TV was a low blow. Our relationship had officially hit rock bottom.

"You mean that same time right before you kicked me to the curb, and ran off and married Grandpa Warbucks."

She crossed her arms around her chest like the temperature had suddenly dropped fifty degrees. I remembered it as her trademark move when we fought. "Oh *please*, you were the one who needed to go off and *see the world*. You can try to write history all you want, JP, but it'll never change the outcome."

The cards were now on the table. I ran off to parts unknown and shut her out of my life. Gwen married someone else. But as much as I might want to rewrite a better ending, she was correct about one thing—it wouldn't change anything.

"Just tell me something, Gwen."

"And that is?"

"When those terrorists took me hostage, were you rooting for me or them?"

"Knowing you, JP, you probably staged the whole thing for a publicity stunt. Are you sure you even need that cane?"

She kicked the cane away with her boot, causing me to helplessly fall to the ground. The cane scattered to my right and my baseball cap flew off. A new rock bottom had been established.

She immediately knew she'd stepped over the line. She likely wanted to get things off her chest, not commit assault and battery. And she was sharp enough to realize that it wasn't a smart move to beat up a handicapped American hero in a public place. Small town gossip could be relentless.

I remained on the ground, playing the empathy card to the hilt. Nothing else was working. Gwen gathered my cap and cane, and reached down to help me up, which I stubbornly refused.

I rolled onto my strong side and maneuvered to a kneeling position, before pushing myself to my feet. I begrudgingly accepted the cap and cane without as much as a thank you.

After dusting myself off, I said, "One of my best friends was paralyzed, and our guide was killed on that so-called publicity stunt."

"I'm sorry, JP ... I didn't know ... I was totally out of line."

This time I accepted her apology, but wasn't ready to talk about Byron. I had become an expert at holding stuff in to let it boil and fester. I called it intestinal fortitude, while Christina referred to it as the first warning sign of my inevitable stroke. So I did what I do so well—I changed the subject.

"It's good to know I still bring out the best in you," I said, testing the rough waters with a grin.

That's when I noticed a slight smile escape from Gwen's lips. It was the smile I had longed to see for all those years.

CHAPTER 28

The moment was fleeting.

Seemingly appearing out of nowhere, a uniformed Rockfield police officer came up behind Gwen. I was still feeling the effect of the smile, and playfully said, "Thank you for you concern, officer, but I don't plan to press charges."

When I took a closer look, I realized it was Jones. The man was everywhere. A small, dark-haired boy rode piggyback on his shoulders. He set the child down and they slapped smiling high-fives. The boy ran to Gwen and hugged her, before rambling on about his ride on the roller coaster.

Jones put his arm around Gwen, marking his territory. "So who brings out the best in my girl?"

Gwen made the introduction. She referred to me as her "childhood friend" and simply called him Kyle. No mention of the BF word, even if it was implied. We awkwardly shook hands, before informing her that we'd already met.

"Congratulations on your award," I said, trying to buy some time to wake up from my worst nightmare—maybe that was the reason for the bad vibes. I looked into Jones' eyes as I said it. Once again they gave me an eerie feeling. I pulled away from the gaze and tried to look at Gwen, but she subtly turned away.

Jones looked back at me like he was sizing up his competition. "You are Noah Warner's brother, correct? I'm sorry, when I was at the house the other day, I didn't put two and two together."

"Some would say he's my brother."

"It's too bad," Jones said, shaking his head while eying the ground.

I predicted his condolences about the accident, and mentally prepared my reply.

He stared at me so hard it actually gave me a chill, then said, "It sickens me that your brother murdered that innocent girl."

The comment hit me like burning shrapnel. "That's a family matter."

"It's the community's business when someone chooses to drink and drive. It's no different than if a sex offender moved into the community."

I strained as hard as I could to convince myself to take the high road. I really did. But Gwen's *boyfriend* calling my brother a *murderer* was just too much to take.

"Everybody makes mistakes. For example, your parents had you."

Jones flushed, his beady eyes narrowing to angry slits. The subject seemed personal.

Gwen stepped in between us—the frightened child in her arms—trying to play peacemaker. "Doesn't your shift start in a few minutes, Kyle?"

"Duty calls," he said, forcing something resembling a smile. He gave Gwen a peck on the lips, which made me cringe. He then exchanged another high-five with the boy. "I'll see you later, Tommy."

"Bye, Kyle," Tommy replied, waving at Officer Jones as he walked away. The boy then shifted gears—now pleading with Gwen to purchase a candy apple. Gwen agreed in motherly fashion, but warned him to return immediately after the purchase. Dollar bills seemed to magically appear in her hand. The boy gleefully grabbed them and ran to the concession stand.

Awkward silence filled the air, until I couldn't take it anymore, "Kyle seems like a really great guy." I didn't even attempt to sell the statement as sincere.

"I'm sorry for the comments about your brother. He's seen some bad tragedies from drinking and driving in his job, and he's become quite close with the Spargo family. I'm sure he didn't mean anything by it."

I nodded, although I believed Officer Jones had meant every word of it, and most likely had held back due to Gwen's presence.

My attention went to Tommy, taking special notice of the striking resemblance between Gwen and the boy. It was just starting to sink in that Gwen had a son. Just one of the many dynamics that I didn't factor in during my daydreams about recapturing the past.

"I didn't know you had a child," I said. I wasn't sure why this surprised me—Gwen was in her late thirties and had been married for years. It was logical.

"Not sure why you *would* know," she said.

I remained quiet. This wasn't exactly how I pictured this moment.

"What's wrong? No wisecrack about how surprised you are such an old guy like Stephen could *rise* to the occasion. Then flash that annoying smug smile of yours and quip 'no pun intended.'"

She couldn't jar me out of my serious mode. "How's Tommy handling the divorce?" I remembered when Gwen's parents divorced and how traumatic that was for her.

Gwen couldn't hold back a smile, which confused me. "I'm just messing with you, JP."

"I'm not sure I understand."

"Stephen and I never had children. Tommy's not my son—he's my brother."

I tried to do the genealogy arithmetic in my head, but I was never very good at math.

Gwen seemed to be reveling in my perplexed look. "My father re-married—a woman much younger than him. They had Tommy, she bailed, and then my father had a heart attack."

My confusion quickly switched to concern. I'd always had a close relationship with Mr. Delaney. "Is he ..."

"He pulled through, and has improved a lot this past year, but he needs a lot of help with Tommy. I temporarily moved back to Rockfield when Stephen and I split up, but temporary is a lot longer than it used to be."

I was relieved that Mr. Delaney survived. But the stronger pangs of relief were because Gwen hadn't started our family without me. I needed a whole team of therapists.

"So how's your mother doing?" I asked.

"She's good. Lives out in Tucson. Has a male companion, which I guess is a way to say boyfriend when you are over sixty. And yes, JP, you are still her favorite, which she subtly reminds me every time she sends me the latest newspaper clipping about your adventures."

I was just about to smile, until Gwen added, "I guess mother doesn't always know best."

The return of Tommy was welcomed. If nothing else, he could fill in the awkward pauses. He pointed his candy apple toward the bustling carnival area, and exclaimed, "Can we go on the Ferris wheel, Gwen?"

I could tell that Gwen saw it as an excuse to get out while she was ahead, or at least not losing. "Of course, Tommy."

Tommy flashed a satisfied look, took a big bite of his candy apple, and pointed at me. "Can the guy with the stick come?"

Gwen looked up at me, then at her younger brother.

She looked conflicted.

So I spoke for her, "I'd love to, Tommy."

CHAPTER 29

The Saturday prior to Labor Day, two years to the day, was a day permanently scarred into the memory bank of Noah Warner.

It was the night part of him died. The biggest part. He had made remarkable progress over the past year, to the point where he was able to tell the story of that night to a local reporter. She promised him that she wouldn't release it until he was ready. He was close, but not there yet.

Noah left the fair in his Jeep—a Warner family hand-me-down that every member has taken ownership of at one time or another over the last twenty years. It was a lot different from the flashy convertible Mustang he drove up until the accident. He was glad to see JP, and hoped to spend time with him while he was in town. But this was not a day that Noah could be happy.

He soon arrived at his destination—The Rockfield Cemetery. He parked the Jeep and swallowed hard. Indescribable feelings surfaced. He grabbed the single red rose off the passenger side seat and slipped his denim jacket on over his black T-shirt. As the sun sunk behind the trees, the crisp feel of fall was in the air. The same as it was two years ago.

He walked the path to Lisa's resting spot. He wore out the grass the first year. The second year had mostly been special occasions and anniversaries.

Lisa would understand. She was the only person ever to truly understand him.

He stood before her headstone and read it again, still trying to connect it to reality. *Lisa Spargo—a beautiful shooting star that brightened the world.* Noah knelt down and placed the rose in front of the grave. He forced the words, "Hey Leese, sorry it's been a while. I missed you." He tried to keep it together, but he never could. He didn't even acknowledge the tears, or attempt to wipe them away.

He'd met Lisa the first day of seventh grade. The Spargos had moved to Rockfield from Boston. Lisa was the sassy, big city schoolgirl who seemed light years older than the rest of the students. Noah was the small town rebel who would go to any length to impress her. The connection was instant.

It seemed like just yesterday they were roaming the halls of Rockfield High. Lisa in her tight jeans, her curls bouncing with each confident strut— Noah in his denim jacket, the one he wore if it were ninety degrees or fifty below zero. Rebellious youth who looked like they popped out of a James Dean flick, riding around in Noah's Mustang as if they owned the world.

It wasn't always fun and games, but they loved each other so hard it hurt, and that was all that mattered. Their toughest stretch was the years after graduation. Lisa went off to college in Boston, while Noah didn't have much interest in school, and remained in Rockfield. When he wasn't getting into trouble, he worked as a bartender at Main Street Tavern. Her parents never approved of Noah, and encouraged her to cut her ties with him. But it would take more than distance and disapproving parents to keep them apart. All leading up to the moment that Noah asked her to marry him, two years ago to the day.

Day turned to dusk, and then to night. Noah continued to sit on the wet grass in front of Lisa's marble headstone and talk to her. He wanted to hold her in his arms again so bad that he would make any deal with the devil just for a few precious seconds.

He gave updates on her parents and siblings—the ones who blamed him for her death, but he still loved them, for no other reason than Lisa loved them.

He tried to keep the topics to happy memories and the positive strides in his life. He told her about JP returning safely. Then he reminisced about the time he tried to use his famous brother to impress her when they first met. Lisa wasn't much into the news, and had no idea who JP was, but she became a fan when she met him during one of his rare visits. Lisa knew that Noah looked up to JP, and that was good enough for her.

He held the most important surprise for last—his return to school. He didn't want to tell her during earlier visits, for fear he would get her hopes up if he wasn't able to stick it out. He could almost feel her pride when he told her.

The part she'd be most impressed with was that he was going back because he wanted to—not for her. It would take him years, but without her, it seemed like he had too much time on his hands, anyway.

Noah eventually drained all of his emotions. He again apologized for his recent absence, vowing to make a quicker return next time. He could almost hear her playfully say, "You better, Warner, if you know what's good for you!" Accompanied by that infectious smile that made him melt.

Noah's pilgrimage wasn't over. It was important for him to go to "the spot." He put the top up on the Jeep and was on his way—to make a return trip to hell.

Noah took Zycko because he needed to follow the same path they took on that night. Last year it was a route to the end—a dead end—as he'd planned to join her. This year he just wanted to pay tribute to his eternal soul mate and try to make some sense of the whole thing.

Zycko Hill was dark and menacing, just as it had been that night. Noah replayed it, second by second, as if he were viewing each moment in slow motion. He passed the entrance to the nature preserve, known as The Natty.

It was a protected area beside the Samerauk River, best known for being the hangout for Rockfield's youth. It was also the place where he'd asked Lisa to marry him.

He twisted the Jeep around another curve, passing the blinding bright lights of a pickup truck coming in the other direction. Noah remained in a hazy state, re-living the accident.

Just before they crossed the small one-lane bridge, the giddy newly engaged couple looked at each other and Lisa mouthed, "I love you." They both smiled.

Then out of nowhere, the light rain turned into a downpour. The wipers struggled to clear the windshield. Lisa urged him to slow down.

Noah listened, but the rain intensified. Just after crossing the bridge, the car began to hydroplane. Noah slammed the brakes, but it only made it worse. No matter what he did he couldn't stop the car from sliding. Noah cursed and Lisa screamed.

With a massive jolt, the Mustang slammed into a large oak tree. The passenger-side door took the worst of the collision, and of more importance to Noah—Lisa. She couldn't get out, as the door was jammed against the tree, branches shooting through the shattered window.

Noah maneuvered her out through the driver's side door and examined her from head to toe. She was shaken, but not a scratch on her pretty face. It was a miracle.

Lisa encouraged Noah to call the police and report the accident. He briefly argued with her, wanting to sober up a little from their celebratory champagne. Lisa assured him that the conditions, and not alcohol, caused the crash. Noah gave in and made the call.

They stood in the rain, waiting for the authorities to arrive. Noah complained about the twisted metal of what used to be his car, while Lisa kept reminding him they were lucky to be alive, and still had a wedding to plan.

As they waited, Lisa mentioned that she felt cold. Noah went to bring her his denim coat, but before he could get to her, she collapsed.

He called 911, this time in a panic. It seemed like days passed before he could hear the ambulance siren echoing off the river. They rushed Lisa to the hospital.

Noah thought it was some sort of cruel joke when the doctor told him that Lisa was dead. "She's fine! Not even a scratch!" he kept yelling. He was too distressed to hear the explanation from the doctor that the impact with the tree caused massive internal bleeding and there wasn't anything that could be done for her.

Later that night, he was arrested and charged with driving under the influence, along with vehicular manslaughter. The nightmare had begun.

CHAPTER 30

The sound of Lisa's scream woke Noah from the nightmare. He spotted a pair of headlights following too close behind him. He was in no mood for such a trivial annoyance on *this night*.

As Samerauk Bridge came into his field of vision, lights flashed behind him.

"Cop?" Noah muttered, unable to think of any violation he might have committed. In his brasher days he would have made a run for it. But he cooperated, pulling off to the side of the road just before the bridge.

Noah took a glance into his rear-view mirror. He recognized Kyle Jones exiting the cruiser and walking slowly toward the Jeep. Jones was known to have a special dislike for drunk drivers, which had put Noah in his crosshairs. He'd heard rumors about Jones planting evidence and doctoring Breathalyzers. It wasn't their first encounter, but he had a bad feeling about this one.

Noah rolled down his window, and a gust of wind blew through the Jeep. "Can I help you, officer?"

Jones smiled, but didn't look happy. "Please step out of the vehicle, Mr. Warner."

Noah began to argue, "I wasn't doing anything wrong, Jones. I don't …"

The officer took matters into his own hands. He opened the door, and in one fluid motion, grabbed Noah by his jacket and tossed him to the ground.

When Noah tried to get to his feet, Jones took his nightstick and pounded it into his knee. Noah collapsed back to the ground in agony.

Jones pounced on top of him, pushing his face into the pavement. He forcefully twisted Noah's arms behind him and handcuffed him. He pulled him to his feet, pushing him face-first against the hood of the car, and grinding his nose into the still-warm metal.

"What the hell are you doing, Jones?"

The officer remained calm, almost trance-like. "You are under the arrest for the murder of Lisa Spargo."

Noah had watched enough TV to know you couldn't be charged for the same crime twice. He tried to reason with him.

Jones would hear none of it, again jamming Noah's face into the hood of the car.

"You took an innocent life, and now you must pay with your own."

"You're crazy."

"I'm crazy?" he asked with condemnation. "Crazy is murderers like yourself being allowed to drive the streets."

"You will never get away with this," Noah shouted as loud as he could. The only response was his voice echoing back at him.

Jones' expression never changed. "I remove the evildoers one at a time. If they couldn't connect me to the death of Senator Kingsbury, with every law enforcement official in this country working on it, I truly doubt I'll be connected to the suicide of a small-time punk like yourself." His nightstick landed another blow to Noah's back with a hollow thud.

Noah gritted his teeth. Only the intense pain distracted him from grasping Jones' insane claim of killing a US senator. "My brother will never let you get away with this."

Jones laughed. "JP Warner is too wrapped up in his own vanity. He will only be concerned how good he looks in the suit he wears to your funeral."

"He will know I didn't kill myself."

"It wouldn't be the first time you attempted to take your own life. The way I see it, on the anniversary of your murderous act, and ravaged by guilt, you couldn't bear to live another day without your beloved Lisa. And this year you found the guts to go through with it."

The mention of Lisa's name shot a warm energy through him. Noah wanted to live. He kicked his leg back like a mule, knocking Jones to the ground. He began running away over the bridge, his hands still cuffed behind his back.

CHAPTER 31

With Tommy present, Gwen and I remained on our best behavior. We weren't exactly swapping old stories and falling into uncontrollable laughter, but she hadn't shoved me to the ground in over an hour, so I considered that progress. But a tense awkwardness still hung in the air. There was too much clutter between us to let down our shields—hurt feelings or wounded pride could surface at any moment.

As nightfall arrived, Gwen dropped Tommy off with his father. Despite having been briefed, I was still surprised at how frail Mr. Delaney looked. I remembered him as the strapping carpenter with the year-round tan from working outside, muscles bulging everywhere. I always wanted to be Mr. Delaney when I grew up. Maybe I still did.

He greeted me like the long lost son and told me how happy that Gwen had finally got rid of the old guy with the funny French name, so that his daughter and me could rightfully be together once again. He didn't actually say that, but he did give me a warm greeting.

Gwen kissed her father goodbye, and I'm pretty sure I heard her whisper in his ear, "Don't get your hopes up, Dad, it's not gonna happen."

Without Tommy's presence, Gwen and I returned to silence.

Silence has never been my thing, so I broke it, "I missed this."

"This?"

"The whole thing—the town, the people, the atmosphere."

"The smell of cows?"

"I missed *you*."

I caught her blushing, but she quickly covered it with the stony look of ambivalence. "What do you want?"

I was still surprised I said it. I didn't mean to, but my mouth always had a mind of its own. "What do you mean? I thought it was a simple statement."

"Everything you do is scripted, so obviously you said that because you want something."

When my critics called me scripted and self-serving, I always brushed it off. But coming from Gwen, it felt like a gut-punch. It was like the girl from Columbia all over again ... only worse.

I covered the hurt with a grin. "What I want, Gwen, is to win you a stuffed animal for old times sake. I'll bet Policeman Kyle never won you a stuffed animal at the fair."

Gwen took a deep breath, before turning to face me. "Listen, JP, this was fun and all tonight. And I'll even admit it brought back some good memories. But I must be going—Sunday is my big day at the paper."

She tried to shake my hand. When I refused, she gave me a "your loss" shrug, and said, "Take care, JP. And when you make your next trip to East Dangerous, please try not to get yourself killed. It was actually good to see you again."

She walked away. But she wasn't walking out of his life again without a fight. "Do you want to know what I really want, Gwen?"

"You had your chance," she said, her step never slowing.

"I want a job."

"That I can't help you with."

"Sure you can, I know you're running the *Gazette*. Murray told me."

"We're not hiring."

"Don't make me go to Murray—you know he'll hire me."

That made her stop. She pirouetted back toward me, looking annoyed. "Except that he gave me the last word on staffing in my contract. Like I said, we're not hiring, but even if we were, we would hire someone who would stick around more than a couple of weeks before he went off to something *bigger and better*."

"I told you, I'm here for good."

She turned and began walking away again as if to say she wouldn't even dignify the statement with an answer—this time her strut had finality to it. She kept getting farther away—like a dream of mine where she keeps getting smaller and smaller, and there is nothing I can do to stop it.

Without turning, she bellowed back at me, "We're not interested in your services at the time, Mr. Warner, but thank you for your interest."

"I don't know why not—I was just offered the highest salary of anyone in the history of the news business today. I think that would be quite a coup for the *Gazette.*"

"You use the term *news business* loosely. We can't afford you!"

"I'll work for free."

"We can't afford that much."

"I'll pay *you*."

I knew her stubborn pride wouldn't allow her to accept the Gross National Product of Japan to hire me, but I kept shouting, and receiving many strange looks from the fair-goers.

"I'll give you exclusive rights to my first interview since the hostage crisis. All the major networks would kill for it."

"That's the thing that makes you great, JP. Most people waste so much time trying to conceal their inflated opinions of themselves. But not you."

"You'll sell more papers than you will the next three years combined!"

The *Gazette* was in constant financial trouble—what small town paper wasn't? Hell, most major newspapers were. But I knew she wasn't going to cave in.

All I could do was watch her long legs glide away. I continued watching as she reached into her purse and pulled out a cell phone. *Calling Jones? A late night dinner after he gets off his shift? And then arrest me for harassing his girl?*

My stomach sank.

She pushed her long hair behind her ear, and answered a call. Maybe Jones was calling her. Whatever was said, it stopped her in her tracks—a jolting stop. She dropped the phone back in her purse and began jogging back in my direction. Her face filled with dread.

I had often dreamed of Gwen desperately running toward me, but I got the feeling this time there would be no leaping into each other's arms and kissing like there was no tomorrow.

When she reached me, she said, "It's your brother, JP—it's Noah."

PART THREE -

NOAH'S ARK

CHAPTER 32

Gilbert, Arizona

Labor Day Weekend—1995

"Are you almost ready?" shouted Lucy Enriquez.

Kyle took another glance in the mirror, playing with his short-cropped hair. He was admittedly pretty average in all regards, from his looks to his medium height, and he certainly wasn't one of those charmers who could captivate a room with his personality. So he was as surprised as most that he was able to attract such a desirable girlfriend as Lucy, even if she wasn't always a ray of sunshine.

When he stepped into the foyer, he immediately stopped in his tracks. Lucy looked annoyed, as usual, but also beautiful. He was drawn to the dark curls that fell onto her tanned shoulders like she just appeared out of a shampoo commercial. At work, where she was his commanding officer, she always wore a ponytail and little makeup, along with the stiff blue and gold police uniform. It had nothing on this sizzling pink number she was wearing for the picnic.

"Wow," was all he could say.

She smiled. "Don't even think you can charm your way out of making us late, Kyle Jones."

After spending most of his life in the military, he'd never been late for anything. But since becoming a "civilian," and meeting Lucy, his outlook had changed on a lot of things.

"Should I see if Grady wants to join us tonight?" he asked, already bracing for the answer.

Her smile suddenly disappeared, and she looked like she was fighting back every urge to lash out. It reminded him of Mount St. Helens, a dormant volcano three hours from Seattle, where he went on the anniversary of his parents' death to spread their ashes, as was their request. He knew that Lucy could erupt at any moment.

"It's not bad enough that you pay his rent—now you're going to subsidize a night out for him?"

"Shh … he's in the next room."

"I really don't care, Kyle!" her voice raised. "He sits on the couch all day watching that stupid murder trial, hoping you'll feel sorry for him and keep supporting his free ride!"

"He's been sick, Lucy, and he's had some tough luck."

When Kyle left the Air Force, law enforcement felt like a natural transition. As an "army brat" who'd lived everywhere from Germany to Lake Cumberland, Kentucky, he welcomed putting down roots in Gilbert, which was near Luke Air Force Base, his last stop in the military. It provided a stability he thought he'd never find again after the deaths of his parents.

But post-military life had been a struggle for Grady. He was lethargic and sick all the time, and blamed it on a mysterious illness the media was calling Gulf War Syndrome. This was completely different from the Grady Benson that Kyle remembered from their Air Force days. Back then, he was one of the most brash and daring pilots that Kyle had ever known. And when he wasn't flying, Grady spent his time on the ski slopes and rollerblading around the base.

But that man had vanished. This Grady would sit on the couch, watching endless hours of the OJ Simpson murder trial. He talked about the players as if they were his friends—Kato, Marcia, Johnnie, and Judge Ito.

Grady had bounced from menial job to menial job. Each one that didn't work out seemed to sap more energy from him, adding to his bitterness. But the bigger issue for Kyle was the strain Grady placed on his relationship with Lucy. And when she sighed again—this time like a dragon exhaling fire—Kyle knew he was on unsteady ground. He'd found out the hard way that three sighs meant no sex for a week.

"He's been to all those doctors and they haven't found one thing wrong with him. Not one thing!"

"Come on, Lucy," Kyle pleaded. He tried to put his arm around her, but she pulled away. "Please keep it down—he's in the next room."

Her voice rose again in defiance. "Tell me why you put up with it?"

"You don't understand—we have fought the same battles."

"I *understand* that he can't hold a job, and sits on his ass all day while you pay the rent."

"By battles, I don't just mean the war."

Lucy took a deep breath to fight off her frustration, and attempted a calmer approach, "Kyle—it's tragic what happened, but it would be cheaper for you to hire a whole team of psychiatrists for him, than letting him slack his way through life on your dime."

Lucy would never comprehend their bond. He and Grady were only children who lost their parents within a year of each other, both under tragic circumstances. Kyle still couldn't grasp the irony of his own parents' death. After surviving all the years living the dangerous fighter pilot life, including numerous combat missions, they had retired to a tranquil community "on the lake," only to have their lives taken in an instant.

Kyle had faced those who were responsible for taking them away, and convinced himself that he'd gotten the closure he needed to move on with his life. He thought he'd put it behind him, but lately he felt the emotions bubbling underneath the surface … like his own version of Mount St. Helens.

Lucy stared at him, which made him feel like an enemy MiG was locked on his soul, ready to fire. But she showed restraint this time, choosing to ease off the trigger. "Fine, see if he wants to go," she said, flashing Kyle a peace treaty smile.

Maybe she did understand after all.

CHAPTER 33

With a zombie-like click of the remote, Grady Benson turned up the volume on the TV. Did they really think he couldn't hear them through the thin stucco walls? Or maybe they no longer cared. It was the same conversation, anyway—Lucy aggressively vilified him (faking Gulf War Syndrome) while Kyle did his best to defend him (members of the Dead Parents Society). But Kyle was no match for her, and she would eventually make him believe he got his way, when in reality, she was toying with him.

Out of the corner of his eye, he viewed Kyle hesitantly enter the living room. "Lucy and I are going to the GPD picnic. But we're going to hit that new bar The Ostrich after, if you're interested in meeting up. Might be fun … like the old days."

Grady forced himself to peel his eyes away from the television. "I'm kind of engrossed in this show. But thanks for asking."

"What are you watching? I thought the OJ trial took the weekends off," Kyle made some charity conversation.

"It's an investigative report on GNZ about a judge in North Carolina named Raymond Buford. He doesn't believe in laws against drinking and driving, and recently let off a man named Craig Steele, who then mowed down an innocent family."

Kyle predictably began to squirm—he believed in the concept of closure, and used it to rationalize the emotional pain of his parents' death. Grady was convinced that the only thing closure would accomplish would be to build up the pain inside him. And when it eventually came out, and it would, it wasn't going to be pretty.

But as expected, Kyle found his inner closure, and attempted to change the subject. He pointed at the reporter on the television. "I can't stand that JP Warner—he's such a phony."

Grady disagreed. "I actually think he is the most brilliant journalist alive."

Kyle looked surprised. "I remember you telling me that JP Warner was an insufferable glory-hound who was all about himself, and not the story."

"I did say that when he arrogantly refused to cover the Simpson trial, thinking it was beneath him. But this recent investigation series on dirty judges has changed my mind. Maybe if more reports like this were done, many tragic accidents could be averted."

He knew the mention of tragic accidents would get Kyle to leave him in peace. He'd rather numb the pain than find a cure for the disease. And it did. Grady didn't even hear Kyle and Lucy leave for the evening, as he remained glued to the television.

He couldn't get his mind off the investigative report—he envied reporters like Warner who could shed light on injustice, and in doing so, stop future tragedies. Wasn't that what he and Kyle vowed to do—Batman and Robin?

Well past midnight, Kyle and Lucy returned home, stumbling drunk. They were singing a loud duet of the theme song from the television show *Friends* that was on top of the charts.

"I'll be there for you! I'll be there for you!" they continued to belt out in loud, drunken voices, before tumbling to the floor.

Lucy laughed hysterically as she unsuccessfully tried to pick herself up off the ground. Her inebriated personality was friendlier, and spoke to Grady as if they were long lost friends. "Kyle was swerving all over the road," she explained, placing her hands on an imaginary steering wheel, and continuing to laugh like a hyena.

Kyle joined her laughter. "I told Lucy I saw three lanes," he stopped and looked at Lucy—who lay next to him on the floor—and they broke into giggles at their inside joke. "She told me to use the one in the middle."

The domineering Lucy spoke over him, "Kyle got pulled over at the corner of Alma School and Ray Road."

"Good thing it was one of our buddies from the force or I woulda been screwed. The rookies were the only ones on duty tonight because of the picnic, so what were they gonna do ... arrest me?"

Grady's eyes narrowed with confusion. "They knew you were drunk, but let you continue to drive?"

Lucy walked to Grady and patted him on the shoulder. "It's okay—they were our friends—it was one of those *wink wink* things." She tried to wink her left eye, but it more resembled a seizure.

Grady calmly walked to the phone and began to dial.

"What are you doing?" Kyle asked.

"I'm calling the police, I have to report this. I'm sorry, but you could have killed someone."

"We *are* the police—we should arrest you for being a freeloader!" Lucy fired back. She had sobered enough to remember that she despised him.

She lunged at Grady. He responded by forcefully shoving her to the ground.

Kyle discovered the spine that had been missing since he found closure. But his punch was slow and telegraphed. Grady saw it all the way, blocked it with raised hands, then clutched Kyle by the throat and jammed him against the wall, shaking paintings of Arizona sunsets.

Kyle tried to squirm, to no avail. For months, Grady had lacked the energy to pick himself off the couch, but now suddenly had the strength of two men. He glared into Kyle's eyes and felt a powerful chill throughout his being. He knew he was looking into the eyes of evil.

He let go of Kyle's neck, and he fell to the ground in a heap beside his girlfriend. Grady quietly walked to his room and shut his door, leaving stunned looks on Lucy and Kyle's faces.

He couldn't shake the darkness he saw in Kyle. But he also saw the future with clarity—a future in which he'd have to be the one to stop Officer Kyle Jones.

CHAPTER 34

Rockfield, Connecticut

Saturday Night—Labor Day Weekend—present

We took off without a word. Gwen moved briskly, while I limped through the pain as fast as I could. We arrived at her vehicle—a white van that advertised the *Rockfield Gazette* on the side—and sped off.

Gwen had no answers to my incessant questions, but something told me it was related to this being *this day,* and that scared me. Gwen explained that she got the tip from Jones. He was the first officer to arrive at the scene. I wasn't surprised.

Three police cars blocked the bridge, their flashing lights blinding. A sick feeling attacked my stomach like nothing I'd ever felt before. I'd witnessed more than my share of death and knew what it looked like. I saw the stretcher covered in the black tarp.

As Gwen slowed the van, I hopped out before it came to a full stop, almost falling in the process. But I felt no pain shoot through my brittle body—I was completely numb. I stormed past police who tried to hold me back.

I walked to the tarp and pulled it back. My world immediately spun out of control. Staring back at me was Noah. His face was full of abrasions and the calm look of death. I instantly knew that any peace I'd rediscovered had vanished. Maybe forever.

I lightly stroked Noah's face. I reached behind his head, feeling a big gash in the back of the skull so wide my finger slid into it like the grip on a bowling ball. I pulled the bloodied face close to mine and kissed his forehead.

My gut wrenched, thinking of my mother's reaction. Throughout my career, I'd always been able to maintain some semblance of composure, no matter the situation. But I felt like I'd lost all control of my emotions.

I snapped my head to Jones. "What the hell happened?"

He remained calm. Too calm for my taste. "I'm sorry, Mr. Warner, I know this must be hard for you. But please let us complete our investigation, and then we can properly inform your family of the cause of your brother's death."

The cause of my brother's death. The words stung.

I glared fiercely back at him. "Perhaps you should take the cotton out of your ears, officer. What the hell happened to my brother?"

Jones looked to Rich Tolland to see if it was all right for him to talk. Rich nodded his block-shaped head.

"I was patrolling the area at approximately 0200 hours. When I came upon Samerauk Bridge, I saw a male standing on top of the guardrail. I got out of the patrol car and shouted for him to get down. At that point, I made the identification of Noah Warner. He was in what I would describe as a trance, and shouting, 'I miss you, I miss you' over and over again. I tried to talk him down for minutes. When I continued to receive no response, I returned to my car to radio for help. Before I could make the call, he leaped off the bridge."

"Did you just say my brother took his own life?"

He lowered his head. "I'm afraid so, Mr. Warner."

"So are you going to tell me what really happened?"

Jones eyes remained steely and calm. He didn't even blink once. "I know such news is hard to accept for any family."

"Especially when some dumb cop is lying through his teeth."

Gwen tried to play peacemaker, and pulled me into an embrace. I wasn't sure if it was to comfort me or to keep me from killing her boyfriend. As she pulled me closer, I was hit with the memory of her being with my family at the hospital when Noah was born. The image was now vivid in my mind. I could see Gwen holding Noah, who looked like a loaf of bread draped in a blanket.

"I'm so sorry, JP," she whispered in a shaken voice. "But there is nothing you can do here. Let's get out of here before you do something you'll regret."

Her words weren't what I wanted to hear, so I turned to Rich Tolland. "Where the hell are the crime scene investigators? And what about all that fancy yellow tape you guys like to hang up?"

He gave me a look of pity, which further infuriated me. "JP, there's no evidence of any crime here. For goodness sake, we had to pull him off the same bridge last year. It was self inflicted."

"He didn't commit suicide, so I think you need to start looking to other theories."

I saw a slight crack in Jones' normally cool demeanor. "What makes you so sure?" he asked.

"For starters, we had plans tomorrow. People who plan on killing themselves don't make plans. But I think the real question is how can *you* be so sure?"

"Because I was here."

"Exactly," I said, jabbing my finger in his direction. "You know what happened here, officer, and I will get to the bottom of it if it's the last thing I do!"

Gwen stepped in again, and knowing I couldn't be reasoned with, she physically moved me out of harm's way back towards the van.

As she did, my eyes never left Officer Jones.

CHAPTER 35

The evidence was clear. On the anniversary of the death of his soul mate, Noah Warner went to the darkest of places. Faced with nothing but lonely years ahead, he made a pilgrimage to the place where the accident took place, just as he had the year before. But this time he didn't back down, and threw himself over the bridge onto the rocks below.

Over the years, with the success or failure of a story hanging precariously in the balance, and sometimes life and death, I'd learned about trusting instincts and hunches. And in this instance, every bone in my body screamed out that Noah did not commit suicide.

The living don't kill themselves. People that are already dead do. The ones who are just matter taking up space, with their breaths being nothing but window dressing. Our conversation from the fair replayed in my mind. I didn't have a doubt—Noah was one of the living. Now I had to figure out a way to prove it.

Chief Tolland, along with his sidekick Bobby Maloney came to my parents' house late last night to deliver the grim news. Gwen and I showed up a few minutes later to witness my father unsuccessfully trying to console my mother. At the break of dawn, Ethan and Pam arrived. It was the day everyone had feared for two years, and now it was the reality we would have to live with for the rest of our lives.

I sneaked away to my quarters and went immediately to my laptop. I had access to numerous files through my lengthy list of connections and could get information on almost any person on the planet. But even with this access, I still didn't learn a lot about Kyle Jones.

He had lived the life of the typical military child. Born in Germany, but spent time in San Diego, North Carolina, and Lake Cumberland, Kentucky before he was in middle school. The military background made it more understandable as to why he'd described the incident in military time, which I had found odd at the time.

Jones followed his parents' footsteps into the Air Force, a career that culminated with him piloting a jet fighter in the Gulf War. Other than the combat service, his military career was bland but honorable. He left in the mid-1990s—his last stop was Luke Air Force Base in Arizona.

Following his military service, he joined the police force in Gilbert, Arizona. His next stop was the Outer Banks of North Carolina, where his only job of note was giving flying lessons to the locals. Then he must have rediscovered his love for wearing a uniform, because he accepted a job of police officer in Rockfield, Connecticut, where he had a stellar record … except for the fact that he might have killed my brother.

If my instincts were correct, and Jones was responsible for Noah's death, the question was why. The obvious connection was that Noah was responsible for Lisa Spargo's death, and he had grown close to the family. I recalled the angry words he had for me about Noah and the accident. But I needed more than that. I knew how this looked—I was a distraught family member who wasn't thinking straight, and when you throw in the Gwen factor, it would also look like I was motivated by jealousy.

My lack of sleep had me running on fumes and I was struggling to concentrate. But anytime I began to nod off, my thoughts always returned to the moment where I held Noah's lifeless head in my hands.

A mid-morning phone call to his old boss, Gilbert Police Chief Steve Dahl, didn't provide any significant clues. According to Dahl, Jones was a model police officer who was still missed in Gilbert all these years later. "If I had me fifteen officers like Kyle Jones I'd be on to something," he exulted.

When I questioned as to why Jones left, Dahl recalled the conversation where Jones told him of his desire for a new start. He'd just broke up with his girlfriend and always grew restless being in one place for too long. Dahl speculated that it was the Air Force in him.

"Do you know why he chose North Carolina?" I asked.

"I really don't know, but he always complained about the brutal summers in Arizona, and mentioned he hoped to go someplace where the seasons change. He always talked about his love for the water, so it makes sense that he headed for the beach."

Dahl mentioned that he'd "lost touch" with Jones after his move, but they'd reconnected briefly when he was thinking about returning to police work. They traded a few emails, Jones asking if he could use him as a reference, and he gave Jones a glowing review to Chief Tolland. He hadn't spoken to him since his return to Rockfield, but Jones had sent him a 'thank you' note for the reference, and they exchanged Christmas cards each year since.

My explanation for the call was that I was doing an article for the *Rockfield Gazette* on Jones having received the *Lisa Spargo Memorial Award*. Dahl wasn't surprised that Jones would win an award, but when I pressed him about Jones' devotion to drinking and driving, he couldn't recall any such compelling interest when Jones was in Arizona. But added, "Kyle was always trying to help the community, so maybe he was affected by a specific case."

Not only was I not getting anywhere, but was actually making a case that Gwen would be better off with Jones. The guy was a Boy Scout.

My questions soon turned more personal in nature and Dahl became suspicious. When I asked how I could reach the ex-girlfriend whom he'd broken up with prior to his move from Arizona, I crossed the line. Dahl began to answer, giving her first name as Lucy, but then his police instincts took over. He stopped in mid-sentence without providing a last name.

When I pushed, he turned testy. "Why are you so interested in his love life?"

I stumbled through an obvious lie. My lack of sleep dulled my usually sharp answers. Dahl demanded a number of my superior at the paper. I gave him Murray's name, but couldn't remember his phone number, which made me seem even more suspect. The next sound I heard was the click of the phone.

At that point, I tried to get some much-needed sleep, but my dreams kept reliving my last conversation with Noah.

I gotta take off JP, but we will definitely hook up at Ethan's on Monday.
Hot date?

No, I'm just going to meet an old friend. We haven't talked in a while.

I woke up in a cold sweat, realizing that I wouldn't be able to sleep until I got justice for my brother.

I would do my own investigation of Jones. The police department was too close to it to see straight, and Gwen was obviously fooled by him. I paused in thought; still unable to believe Gwen could be with this guy. I doubted I could accept anybody she dated, but this one really didn't add up.

Then a sad truth hit me. One that I had been aware of since our encounter at the fair, but I didn't want to admit it—Gwen Delaney wasn't the person I once knew.

CHAPTER 36

While wandering around the Rockfield Fair on Saturday afternoon, in one of the few moments I wasn't fighting with someone, I ran into an old friend from high school named Adrian Herbert. He invited me to watch the opening week of NFL football at Main Street Tavern with him and some of the old gang, and gave me his phone number. He said it would be like old times, although I couldn't remember ever watching football with Herbie. I doubted I'd take him up on the offer at the time, but I gave him lip service about keeping it in mind. And following Noah's death, I suddenly had the urge to meet up with the boys and swap some stories. Preferably about a certain police officer.

Main Street Tavern was a wooden firetrap that was a favorite watering hole of the locals. A small but raucous crowd was always present on fall Sundays to watch NFL games, including some of my old high school football buddies.

They proceeded to greet me warmly, along with providing condolences for the loss of Noah. I spotted my old teammates, Vic Cervino and Steve Lackety. We used to get together once a year for a reunion of our league championship team, but the reunions became fewer and fewer, before dwindling to non-existent about ten years ago.

I knew it must look strange that I'd be here, just twelve hours after my brother committed suicide, but nobody questioned my presence.

Before I could get into the topic of Kyle Jones, there were old football stories to be told. They had grown into Greek mythology over the years, and what they lacked in truth, they made up in grandiosity. Between stories, I continued buying rounds of beer for the boys until one o'clock; when the game between the Main Street Tavern favorite, New England Patriots, and the Miami Dolphins began.

When halftime arrived, it was time to talk Officer Jones. I was counting on the alcohol removing all inhibitions, and assisting in some honest dialogue.

Herbie was the first to take issue with him, "I'll tell you what that guy did. He came to our softball party—he was dating the sister of one of the guys on the team, who worked at the bowling alley—hung out with us and acted like our best friend. Then he left and hid down the street and nailed half the squad with a dee-wee."

"But you guys *were* breaking the law by driving drunk," I played devil's advocate.

"I'm not saying we were right, but if Jones really wanted to stop people from driving drunk, he could have taken people's keys or arranged rides when he was at the party. He wanted credit for making the bust."

I noticed a bunch of nodding heads. A man named Lucas caught my interest. He identified himself as being a former member of the Rockfield Police force, who had worked with Jones, but left for a job in the private sector. "The guy is obsessed. Something is not right with him," he remarked.

The bartender, Wally, who was also the tavern owner, chimed in, "He's not allowed in here anymore. He used to wait in the parking lot in an unmarked car and follow my customers home."

"You should do one of your investigative reports on that bastard," Vic Cervino shouted out with a mouthful of salsa chips.

I smiled. "I would if I had something good on him. So far, nothing you told me is against the law. And those he arrested certainly were breaking it. Sounds like he might just be doing his job a little too well."

The former cop, Lucas, spoke up again, "I've witnessed him break the law."

"How come you didn't report it?"

He laughed as if I were naïve. "If I accused the department's fair-haired superstar of doctoring Breathalyzer results, or that he pulled people over without just cause, it would have been spun that I was not committed to reducing crime. Besides, with all due respect to Noah, the fact he got off with what appeared to be a slap on the wrist put a bull's-eye on Rockfield. Maloney, like any public official looking to get re-elected, made drinking and driving his top priority, and Jones became his poster boy for this pursuit. Even if Tolland wanted to do something about Jones, Maloney would overrule him, especially after the money began rolling in from the ADDs."

"The ADDs?"

"The against drunk driving organizations. They do good work, don't get me wrong. They've played the biggest role in cutting fatalities. But sometimes when money gets involved, people tend to turn their heads at the means, as long as they get to the ends."

Sounded like the Maloney I knew.

Halftime would be ending soon, so I had to move fast. A guy named Scott Busby, who owned a local hardware store, provided me with the incriminating story I was waiting for.

"Jones had heard a rumor that I'd driven home from here, three sheets to the wind. I don't know where he heard that, but I was home the whole night watching the Yankees game. I put down a six-pack and chomped on a bag of potato chips. I got a knock on the door and when I answered, it was Jones. He dragged me down to the station, where they charged me with drunk driving."

"And he got away with it?" I asked.

"Yeah, they gave me a Breathalyzer, which of course I failed because I was drinking … *in my house!* It was Jones' word against mine. The judge basically called me a liar at my sentencing."

Herbie asked, "Hey JP, what's your beef with Jones—did he pull you over?"

Before I had a chance to answer, Lackety cut in with a knowing smile, "I hear that Jones has been dating Gwen Delaney. I'll bet that's the problem."

This led to hearty laughter at my expense.

"The woman from the paper?" the bartender asked, obviously new to the town.

Lackety butted in again, "She could put me in her story anytime, if you know what I mean."

Unfortunately, everyone did.

Herbie cleared it up for anyone who didn't know the story of JP and Gwen, providing the *Cliff Notes* version of the past thirty years. It was not a happy ending and I cringed with embarrassment, but kept my mind focused on the task at hand.

"So that's your issue with Jones," the bartender said. "That punk stole your girl. He's bad news!"

Everyone at Main Street Tavern agreed, raising their beer-filled mugs in salute. I shrugged, acting as if I was busted, even though I knew *my girl* left by her own choice a long time ago. "What can I say, I guess I still have a thing for her."

The second half began, diverting attention back to the screen. I remained until the game ended. Herbie offered me a ride home, but he was sloppy drunk, courtesy of myself, as were most of them. So I called cabs for everyone on my dime. "Hey, you never know if Jones is out there," I explained.

Once I made sure everyone was safely getting a ride, I autographed a few things for Wally, and in return, he gave me a lift home.

The house was empty. There was a note on the kitchen counter from my mother. It read in matter-of-fact language that she was making funeral arrangements. It was like she was describing a trip to the grocery store—as if by keeping a sense of normalcy, she wouldn't have to acknowledge the truth.

I was glad she was keeping busy, but knew that one day it would hit her like a ton of bricks. One thing I learned the hard way is that it's impossible to run away forever. I vowed to be here for her when the storm hit.

Leaving was not what I did, it was what I used to do.

CHAPTER 37

Monday was Labor Day. It was also the day of Noah's wake at the Laconia Funeral Home on Main Street. I didn't attend.

The whole point of the wake and funeral is to lay someone to rest, and in my opinion, Noah couldn't properly rest until justice was served.

I bummed a ride from Herbie to the local police barracks, and it wasn't to invite them to a Labor Day barbecue. I wanted an update on their investigation into Noah's death, even though I knew none was planned. Rich Tolland didn't seem thrilled by my appearance, but he tried to play nice with me. It was the best strategy to make me disappear.

"I'll do what I can, JP," he told me.

I knew the answer was a load of crap, but I wasn't ready to pick a fight with the police department ... yet. I thanked him and left. I needed more ammunition to fight city hall. I did get a copy of the police report, but it was the same fiction they tried to sell me that night—a distraught Noah jumped to his death from Samerauk Bridge as the courageous Officer Jones tried to save him, blah, blah, blah.

I was supposed to spend Labor Day at Ethan and Pam's picnic, catching up with Noah, but instead I spent it researching his death. I couldn't handle being in the house, standing on the same floors where Noah crawled around as a baby, or deal with the endless stream of well-wishers who kept stopping by. But most of all, I couldn't face my mother right now.

On Tuesday, my first call was to Christina. She put up a mild fight, since it was the first day of classes, but like myself, she was always drawn to the action. I wouldn't go into details as to why she was summoned, but instructed her to bring Hoseman.

I had covered the death of an American woman in Rome a few years back. She was a newlywed who'd accidentally fallen to her death, while making some wild marital bliss with her new hubby on their hotel balcony. But the more I studied the "grieving" husband, I grew convinced that her death was no accident. So to prove my theory, I worked with a local fire department in Rome to create a fire hose to simulate the woman and re-enact her tragic fall. The husband is now serving a life sentence in an Italian prison, and I got to keep Hoseman as a souvenir.

Christina greeted me with heartfelt condolences, but then our conversation returned to normalcy. "A hose that looks like a woman, JP—not getting any up here in Sticksville?"

I struggled into the vehicle without a response. I then instructed her to drive us up Zycko Hill to Samerauk Bridge.

"So are you going to ever tell me why I had to drive all the way out here to the middle of nowhere, and miss the first day of classes?"

"We're going to solve a murder," I said without further detail, as she parked the Humvee just before the bridge. It was the exact place where Noah had left the Cherokee.

I hopped out with anticipation. But intense pain shot through my body, a reminder of my current condition. I gritted my teeth and went to the back of the vehicle, leaning heavily on my cane. Christina opened the hatchback.

She took her time, which annoyed me, "C'mon, I don't have all day."

"I had a late night. So how about a little more gratitude and a little less attitude," she snapped back.

I glared at her, causing her to back off. I think she realized today wasn't the best day to push her luck. We dragged the heavy hose out of the back of the Humvee.

I headed straight for the four-foot high guardrail on the side of the bridge, where Noah allegedly spent his last moments. Christina followed, draped in hose like she were being attacked by a giant Boa. "Are you going to help me with this?"

Ignoring her, I dropped my cane on the road and climbed up on top of the guardrail.

Christina peeked out from under the heavy hose. "Are you trying to have your mother bury two children in one week?"

She had a point, but logic never stopped me before, and I didn't plan to let it start getting in my way now. "Based on the police report, Noah would've had to be up here for at least the three to five minutes that Jones estimated he spent trying to talk him out of jumping. It's very hard to maintain your balance for that long. And remember, it had begun to rain. It's possible he could have, but not probable."

It was also possible that Noah was recreating the scene from a year ago and lost his balance. But I doubted that, and why would Jones lie about it and say he jumped?

Christina struggled to hand me the end of the hose that was knotted like a balloon animal to simulate the woman in Rome. I wrapped it in one of Noah's denim jackets, and placed his favorite Red Sox cap over the wig. Since the Warners were born and bred New York Yankees fans, I never understood my little brother's devotion to the hated Red Sox. My best guess is that it had to do with the "rebel without a cause" image he embraced, which I was sympathetic of, but never fully comprehended.

I secured the hose and held it next to me, as if it were Noah, while I balanced myself. It was like a twisted version of *Weekend at Bernie's*.

"See that rock there? That's where they said Noah landed."

Christina followed my point to a jagged rock formation at the bottom at the river's edge.

"I'm going to prove that it was impossible to fall in that direction without a good amount of force."

"They said he jumped, wouldn't that have the same result as a shove?"

"It's impossible to get the proper footing up here to jump with that much force, and even more so when wet. A jump would end a similar distance from the rail as an accidental fall. If you don't believe me, maybe you can come up here and test it out."

"Very funny. I wouldn't want my hard head to damage the rocks."

"I guess I'll have to settle for you securing your end of the hose as tightly as possible, while I toss it off."

She sat down in the road, gripping the end of the hose between her clenched legs like she were the anchor in a tug-o-war, and held on for dear life.

When I sent Hoseman over, the simulated arms flailed and the wig blew in the wind. It looked like a bungee jumper. It hit the rocks thirty feet below and bounced in a lifelike style. The Red Sox hat flew off, landing softly on a small rock. I decided I would leave it there as a tribute.

Christina ran to the edge of the bridge, still holding the other end of the hose. Working together, we pulled it up slowly.

"So what did you see?" she asked.

"I saw that there was no possible way Noah wasn't forced off the bridge in some fashion, especially since he was much heavier than the dummy. I also saw, by the way the hose bounced, the impact wounds on both his right side and on the back of the head were impossible to achieve by jumping. I think he was killed earlier, and then he was thrown over to make it look like a suicide. I'm betting that Jones' nightstick caused those wounds."

If so, I knew that weapon was long gone.

"But it was just a hose, JP," Christina questioned. "And it's not like it was made to Noah's exact measurements."

"I'm not saying it's a smoking gun. All I proved is the need for a full investigation to answer the questions."

We performed the same test five more times. Like a mad scientist, I used different levels of force and dropped it at different angles. Then after about forty-five minutes of tossing and hoisting Hoseman over the side of Samerauk Bridge, a police car appeared with lights flashing, but no sirens.

A uniformed police officer, along with his female partner, stepped out of the car. He formally introduced himself as Officer Williams, and his partner as Officer O'Rourke.

"Mr. Warner, you are going to have to come with us," he stated.

"What charge?"

"Chief Tolland wants to talk to you. If you want us to come up with charges such as suspicion of stealing a fire hose, we will."

"So let me get this straight—in Rockfield it's illegal to toss a fire hose over the side of the bridge, but it's perfectly fine to throw my brother over?"

"I'm sorry about Noah. I went to school with him and he was a good guy. I'm just the messenger here," said Officer Williams.

I looked forward to a discussion with Rich Tolland, especially after what I just learned. "I tell you what, officers. If you make my life a little easier by helping me load my hose into my vehicle, then I'll make your life easier by getting into the back of your squad car without a fuss."

Williams and his partner must have seen this as a peaceful solution to a potentially volatile situation. They helped Christina finish hoisting Hoseman from its final swan dive, and loaded it into the Humvee.

I turned to Christina. "See how small town politics work. You wash my back and I'll wash yours. Look the other way and accept my money and one day you get to be mayor. It's no different in Rockfield than it is in Kabul or with tribes in Pakistan."

The police officers didn't appear to be amused, but neither did they seem overly offended. Like most people I've encountered, they just wanted to get rid of me.

CHAPTER 38

I walked through the police station, flanked by Officers Williams and O'Rourke. My arrival stopped all police business and the whispers began. I was used to the attention, but the difference in this case was that I wasn't reveling in it.

I limped directly into Rich's office. The first thing I noticed was an attractive woman talking to him. She was dressed in a business blazer, mid-length skirt, and heels.

What are you doing here?" Gwen asked with surprise.

"I killed a hose … what are *you* doing here?'

"I was just …"

"Here to see your boyfriend?"

Her face crinkled with annoyance. "If you mean am I meeting Kyle for lunch, then yes, that's why I'm here."

"Good thinking, you never want to cover up a crime on an empty stomach."

"JP, I understand you're hurt. I won't say I know how you feel, because I never could. But your family has always been like my second family, even if we haven't been in touch in recent years. So I feel like I lost a family member. At the same time, it wasn't anybody's fault. Everyone did all they could do to try to save him."

"Don't patronize me, Gwen. You know he didn't kill himself."

She looked like she wanted to send me to the ground again, but held her emotions in check this time. "I'm sorry about your brother," she said quickly, before turning to Chief Tolland. "Thank you for your time, Rich."

She dashed out of the office as if she were trying to outrun her emotions.

Rich stood before me, looking angry, and I didn't believe it was related to my spat with Gwen. As if this wasn't going bad enough, Bobby Maloney strolled into the office. Rich slammed the heavy wooden door of his office, and closed the shades on the glass partition, walling off the gossipy audience.

Rich's face had turned a shade of scarlet, just as I remembered it as a kid whenever he became angered or flustered. But there was a new confidence to him that concerned me. "Sit down, JP."

"I swear the hose committed suicide. I turned to go call for help and the hose was shouting, 'I miss you' over and over again, before it just jumped off the bridge."

"Sit down!" Rich repeated, this time rattling the framed photos hanging on the wall.

I followed orders. "So what's this all about?"

He spoke in a measured tone, "JP, what happened to your brother was a tragedy, and sincere condolences go out to you and your family from both myself and the entire police department. But what I will not put up with is you trying to publicly show up or denigrate my department. If I find any evidence to contradict the findings in your brother's death, I will open a full investigation. But I'd appreciate you working with us, instead of this public grandstanding."

Maloney couldn't fight off the temptation to add his two cents, "I think you're looking to capitalize on your brother's death for your own publicity, which we all know you're addicted to."

I rose out of the chair, raising my cane as a weapon.

Maloney inched back with a look of terror on his face. A large yellow streak formed on the back of his dark suit jacket. He knew I wouldn't lose a second of sleep if I bashed his head in. For once, he was right. After you've faced an AK-47 pointed at your head, silver spooned kids from the suburbs didn't exactly evoke fear. Especially one who once missed our Little League game because he sprained a finger during a piano lesson.

Rich regained command. "JP, my suggestion to you is to mourn your brother, console your parents, and be with your family. All this nonsense is going to do is tarnish your brother's legacy."

"I got a better idea. How about an investigative report on GNZ about what a dangerous cop Kyle Jones is, and how you enable his abuse of power?"

Maloney interjected again, "Jones is an excellent officer with a spotless record. You pull a stunt like that and we'll file our lawsuit before the report is over. Go ahead, Warner, we need money to improve roads and schools."

"He's a vigilante," I shot back. "He's forgotten that his job is to protect and serve. I have one guy on record who says he broke into his home and arrested him on suspicion of DUI."

"The allegations made by Scott Busby were completely unsubstantiated," Rich returned fire. "I wish all my officers had such an exemplary record."

"He knows what happened to Noah, and when I prove it, you two clowns are going down with him."

Maloney looked ready to fight—as long as The Toll Booth was there to protect him—but Rich kept things professional. "JP, if you are intent on accusing an award winning officer of being involved in the death of your brother, you can file an official complaint before you leave. But unlike the way your business works these days, we still need things like proof and evidence, neither of which you have."

"I didn't say he killed him, but the tests I performed today proved it wasn't a suicide. Everybody's record is spotless until they find the bodies in the basement. You better open an investigation, or I'll bring your whole department down."

"Is that a threat?" Maloney asked.

I stared angrily at him. "It's a promise, Bobby."

Rich shook his head. "Ever since we were kids it's always been about you, JP. But this one isn't about you, it's about Noah."

We finally agreed on something. I struggled to my feet. "Consider my complaint filed."

Having put my cards on the table, I limped out of the office as fast as I could. When I entered the parking lot, I spotted Jones beside a police cruiser. He was holding the passenger-side door open for Gwen to step in.

"If they won't get to the truth, Jones—I will," I shouted in his direction.

"JP!" Gwen blurted, shocked at my outburst. I wondered if she felt responsible for contributing to this lunatic I'd become.

Jones whispered something to her and shut her door. If he planned on playing knight, I hoped for his sake he wore his shining armor underneath his uniform.

He approached me and spoke in a low voice, "My girlfriend and I are just trying to go to lunch. So please be a gentleman and leave us alone."

"Cut the act, Jones. You know what happened to my brother and I'm going to get to the truth."

We engaged in a battle of smug looks, before he said softly, "Your brother did the honorable thing. He committed an act of evil and decided to fall on his own sword. It was common courtesy, which I see doesn't run in the family. I actually felt respect for him when he jumped."

"I'm sure he'd be honored that such an *award winning* officer thought so highly of him."

"Now you should follow your brother's lead and do the right thing, which is to leave this town before you cause any more trouble."

I couldn't help but to stare into his eyes. It confirmed what I already knew. I turned away and headed to the waiting Humvee. I thought of what

Noah would have wanted me to do in this situation. So to honor him, I gave Jones the finger.

My adrenaline practically lifted me into the vehicle.

"Who was that?" Christina asked as she peeled out of the police parking lot.

"The man who killed my brother."

Her mouth hung open. "You think a cop killed Noah? Do you have any proof?"

"I'm working on it."

She noticed a strange grin escape from my trembling lips. "Why are you smiling?"

"I like to get under people's skin."

"You must smile a lot then."

CHAPTER 39

Noah's funeral was held at the Rockfield Congregational Church on Wednesday.

My parents had been active members for years. My father was the obvious choice to give the eulogy. He delivered more in his years as first selectman than I could remember. But he couldn't bring himself to eulogize Noah. He asked me if I would do the honors. I respectfully declined, but offered Ethan as the more logical choice. It was the first thing that made sense to me since I'd returned.

Ethan always did the tough work around here, and why should this time be any different?

Following the packed ceremony, the mourners congregated back at our house on Skyview to "celebrate" the way too short life of Noah Warner. I stood by my lonesome in my best suit. It likely cost more than the funeral. I greeted guests and discussed Noah with many old friends of my family. Sadly, I didn't recognize many of them without an embarrassing reintroduction. Ethan was right—I didn't know Noah the way I should have.

As I stood on one side of the living room, I made long distance eye contact with Gwen. She wore a funeral-appropriate, ankle length black dress that was buttoned in the back. Her long hair was tied up in a bun. One accessory she wasn't wearing on her arm was her boyfriend, Kyle Jones. She was smart enough to know his presence would have only tempted a confrontation. I knew a hug or smile from Gwen was the only tonic on the planet that could lift my spirits, but there was little chance of that.

I was approached by a friendly face that needed no reintroduction.

"I'm sorry, kiddo," Murray said with a friendly pat on the back.

"He didn't commit suicide, Murray."

"Is that the journalist in you talking or the grieving brother who doesn't want to accept the truth?"

"I know what I sound like, but there are too many holes. I talked to Noah hours before and he made plans for later in the weekend. He was in good spirits … best I've seen him in a long time."

"It doesn't mean those feelings didn't change. It was an anniversary of a horrible day, and he did drive to the spot on his own. Not to mention, they had to counsel him off the same bridge a year ago."

"The wounds don't match the fall. I think he was dead before he went over."

Murray smiled strangely. "Is that what you learned from that amateurish forensic study you performed at the bridge with your young companion?"

"How'd you know about that?" The second the words left my lips I realized what a stupid question it was. I was talking to Murray Brown.

"Your research was good, although a little too confrontational for my taste—not surprising after your many years in the television arena. Do you have a suspect in mind?"

"A local police officer," I whispered as loud as I could into Murray's hearing aid.

"And what was Officer Jones' motive?"

"I'm not completely sure, but he's obsessed with drinking and driving. I talked to a few townsfolk who relayed numerous instances in which Jones violated their rights to make DUI cases."

"Anything in his past that might have sparked him to action?"

"His parents died suddenly, in some sort of accident."

"Was it alcohol related?"

"Hard to say. There was an out of court settlement, but no details were revealed. And there are no arrest records I can find. All the records were sealed."

"And all that would provide is a motive. What you need is evidence that he murdered your brother. What else did you find in his background?"

"Not much. Lived the military 'brat' life as a kid, before following his parents into the Air Force. Nothing special about his service, other than he served in the Gulf War."

"As did you, John Pierpont, if I remember correctly. Even if journalists aren't given medals for their courage."

"Post military, he went into police work in Gilbert, Arizona. I talked to a Chief Dahl, who was his commanding officer, and it sounds like Jones was a perfect employee. He left on his own terms, moved to North Carolina, where he bought a plane, probably with the settlement from his parents' death, and gave flying lessons. Then one day he must have gotten the police bug back because he packed up and moved to Rockfield."

"I guess the question is *why* he came here."

"He seems to make a habit of picking up and moving very suddenly. Maybe he's running from something."

"I get the impression that Officer Jones is running toward something."

I pondered the interesting thought.

"Wife, child, family?" Murray continued.

"Just a mention of an old girlfriend who I only have the first name of. He's an only child, with no living relatives as far as I've been able to find."

"This profile you paint doesn't resemble the obsessive, prickly police officer that I've met on a few occasions."

I sighed. "The guy's record is totally clean."

"As they like to say, records are made to be broken. I broke a dish years ago and just recently found a piece of it in a pesky crevice in my kitchen. Sometimes you have to look under the surface to find the pieces of the broken record."

His attention traveled across the room to Gwen, who was in the middle of saying her farewells to my parents. When she hurried toward the door, Murray pleasantly smiled at her and she returned a quick wave.

"I think you should take the lead of a true journalist," he said, his eyes never leaving Gwen. "I wonder why she seems to be in such a rush."

He didn't have to ask me twice. I gave Murray a quick goodbye and headed after her.

As I made my way through the crowd of mourners, Ethan interrupted my path. "First you don't show up for the wake, and now you are bailing on the funeral. Typical JP."

"C'mon, Ethan, I gotta go."

"I guess we shouldn't have expected anything different from you."

"I'm the only one here doing something for Noah. Funerals are about the living—justice honors the dead."

Ethan rolled his eyes. "The only thing you're honoring is your own glory. And you're using Noah to do it."

"See it any way you want, Ethan—you always do," I raised my voice, catching the attention of a few onlookers. Their sad looks turned to interested ones.

"Too bad you didn't pay this much attention to him when he was alive."

I stood silent for a moment, before saying, "I agree with you. And I'll have to live with that the rest of my life. Maybe it's the guilt talking, but I need to do this for him."

Ethan took a deep breath, knowing he was fighting a losing battle. But then surprised me, "Can I do anything to help?"

We traded glances, and I realized he had his own doubts about Noah's death.

I reached into the breast pocket of his jacket and took out his keys. "Yeah, I need your car."

Before Ethan could protest, I'd pushed passed him.

CHAPTER 40

I tore out onto Skyview, struggling at first, not having driven a car since Lauren and I took a regrettable trip to the Hamptons last Memorial Day weekend. The pain in my leg throbbed, but just the thought of those six hours stuck on the Long Island Expressway with her reminded me of an important lesson—things can always get worse. By the time I passed through Main Street I'd located my inner Dale Earnhardt, but still no sign of Gwen. I dashed onto Zycko Hill, following a hunch.

I found her van hidden in the woods, just inside the entrance of the nature preserve—not sure what type of amateur she thought she was dealing with. The Natty was a place where Gwen and I had some of our most memorable moments. I got the idea that this meeting might also be memorable, but perhaps not in the good way.

I looked into the vehicle and saw her black funeral dress neatly folded on the seat. I also noticed a bicycle pump tucked under the seat. Whatever she was doing, she didn't want anybody to know. I figured she'd changed into some rock climbing gear and biked. *What are you up to, Gwen?*

I drove the minivan up to Samerauk Bridge and parked. I removed my suit jacket, and searched the vehicle. I found nothing useful, except a pair of football cleats. Mixing the cleats with an expensive suit was admittedly an outfit that J-News wouldn't be caught dead in, but all JP cared about was making his way to Gwen. Without a flashlight, I descended the sharp, rocky incline.

Gwen was attempting to balance herself—her legs straddled on two adjacent rocks at the river's edge. As I'd suspected, she had changed into a sweater and blue jeans with hiking boots. When I got close enough for her to hear the rhythmic tapping of my cane on the rocks, she turned with fright.

"So are you trying to cover the tracks of your boyfriend?" I went on the offensive.

Her look turned annoyed. "You scared me, JP. What do you think you're doing here?"

"I might ask you the same. Except I know what you're doing."

"And what would that be?"

"Working with your boyfriend to cover up his crime. You might as well come clean—I'll get to the bottom of it sooner or later. And if I was a betting man, I'd put my money on sooner."

Gwen laughed. "With the way you're going about it, JP, it looks to me like you might want to hold off on placing that bet. I'm pretty sure whatever answers you're looking for, I've already found them. So don't worry your pretty little head over it."

A brief silence filled the night, except for the sounds of the rushing river in the background. Despite my bravado, I was no less confused about her purpose than when I arrived. But I had a theory—one that made me smile. "Are you investigating your own boyfriend?

She shook her head. "It's hard to find answers, JP, when you don't even know what the question is."

"Why don't you fill me in."

"The most important question is: what were you thinking when you put that outfit together? Was Brooks Brothers having a sale on athletic cleats?"

"Maybe I should give your boyfriend a call so we can sort this out. I hear he likes to hang out by the bridge at night."

"He's not my boyfriend," she blurted, then caught herself.

If my relief happened in a forest without anyone around to hear it, would I still be relieved? The answer was, *oh yeah.*

"So you're pretending to date this guy to get a story, Miss Ethics and Morals?"

"Shouldn't you be at your brother's funeral?"

"Are you trying to get rid of me?"

"Leaving is one thing you'll never need help with, JP. Now I need to get back to work."

"Let me save you some time—Noah didn't kill himself."

"Tossing a hose over a bridge isn't research, it's a childish prank."

"What do you know about this guy, Gwen?"

She continued to sift through rocks. "Did I just hear the great JP Warner actually ask little ole me for information?"

I moved closer, struggling to balance the plastic cleats on the rocks. Somehow, I arrived safely at the river's edge and sat next to her on an adjoining rock. When I took a closer look, I saw the vulnerable girl from our younger days.

After a moment of awkward silence, she asked, "Have you ever heard of Casey Leeds?"

CHAPTER 41

"About a year and a half ago, a rash of suspicious fires hit Rockfield. And what really raised people's eyebrows, was that a local fireman named Casey Leeds was showing up before anyone to save the day," Gwen began.

"Hero syndrome?"

"That's what the police thought, so they had Leeds tailed."

"Let me guess, the cop who tailed him was none other than Kyle Jones."

She nodded. "And he must have been willing to work holidays, because Jones called in on the Fourth of July, claiming that he'd witnessed Leeds set an old farm ablaze on the north side of town. Sure enough, Leeds was the first one to arrive at the scene, seemingly to save the day. Within minutes, half the Rockfield police force arrived."

"I'm presuming this didn't turn out good for Casey."

"He'd somehow wrestled away the gun from a trained police officer before backup got there, and was holding Jones hostage. Casey refused to drop the weapon, and was making frantic claims that a mysterious caller had been informing him about the fires—that he was the only one who could save the children inside. He sounded just like a man holding a police officer at gunpoint should ... crazy.

"The police gave Casey his last warning to drop the weapon. But he didn't trust anyone at that point. Jones then pointed toward the burning farmhouse, yelled, 'fire!' and dropped to the ground

"Casey was a fun-loving gregarious man, but he wasn't the sharpest tool in the shed. He thought that Jones was referring to the burning farmhouse. By the time Casey figured out that 'fire' was a cue for them to shoot, he was riddled in bullets."

I began throwing out questions as fast as they popped into my head. Who was the caller? How exactly did Leeds get Jones' gun? Why couldn't he let the police go in to save the children?

"The whole thing was fishy to me, too," Gwen said. "Especially since there were no children who resided at the residence. So I started checking around. His sister, Mary Leeds, was the one person he confided in. Over time, I gained her trust enough that she talked to me off the record. She told me that the caller initially threatened to expose a secret in Casey's past if he didn't follow orders. The caller continued setting the fires, providing him the chance to redeem himself from his 'sin' if he saved the children inside the burning homes. But if he didn't save the children himself, or if he told anyone about the phone calls, the caller would continue to set fires, but this time wouldn't inform him, and the children would die. So Casey thought he had no choice, and made Mary promise that she wouldn't tell a soul."

"His sin?"

"He never revealed it to Mary, so I continued searching. I found a source in the First Selectman's Office who told me of an incident from years ago, long before I returned to town. There was a house fire on Grayson Drive. When the call came in, Casey was at Main Street Tavern. By this point, he'd long forgot the difference between drunk and sober, and sped to the firehouse. He drove the large hook-and-ladder truck, his usual role. On the way to the fire Casey drove off the road, rendering the vehicle useless. The rest of the fire trucks made it safely. All of the family members were rescued, except one—a seven-year-old girl died of smoke inhalation."

"Did Casey's accident cause the girl to die?"

"Probably not. But the fact that Casey was over the legal limit when he crashed the fire truck was covered up by the fire department. By the time the truth came to light, Maloney had replaced your father in office, and he didn't operate with the same integrity.

"After Noah's trial, Maloney had used the lingering negative publicity surrounding the perceived light sentence to reinvent himself into the drunk driving warrior. It became priority number one around here, and the money started to role in from the ADDs and other similar organizations. Problem was, he'd learned about the Leeds incident prior to Noah's trial, and chose to keep it covered up—my source told me he rationalized that it would have hurt the public confidence if people believed the firefighters were driving around drunk, especially since the incident had happened years ago. So if the Leeds incident came out after Noah's trial, then so would the questions as to why Maloney didn't do something about it, and at best he would have looked like a total fraud.

"Until Noah's death, I didn't know that we were dealing with a vigilante-style serial killer," she went on, "or that drunk driving was the common thread. I considered Leeds and the fires to be an isolated incident. If I could have put it together earlier, then maybe I could have warned Noah he was in danger."

I was now pacing the river edge, thinking aloud, stating what was now obvious, "Jones was the caller, and the redemption referred to the fire truck accident—the accident that both Leeds and Maloney hoped would be buried forever … and the secret that Jones obviously stumbled upon. I'll bet that Jones offered to be the one to follow Leeds, and made it look like he was a team player willing to do the dirty work. No cop I've ever met likes stakeout duty."

"And being first to arrive, gave him time to drop his gun without witnesses. And knowing that Casey was at his wits' end, he was betting that he'd do something irrational … like pick up the gun and take him hostage.

By being taken hostage, Kyle would be absolved from any blame in the shooting."

Gwen had begun to shiver. The temperature had plummeted. "Since you were offered the highest salary in the news business, maybe you can tell me why Kyle Jones is so obsessed with those who drink and drive?"

"I'm actually just an unemployed farmer living with his parents."

"I'll be sure to temper my expectations."

I shrugged. "I've checked a few items in his past, but I've come up empty."

I didn't waste time running any of my initial theories or research by her. With her direct access to Jones, she was already two steps ahead of me on all fronts. Problem was, I got the feeling that Jones was about a mile ahead of both of us.

A sound startled us—a scurrying through the brush. Gwen's eyes cut through the darkness, as if expecting Jones to leap out at us. But I knew that wasn't his style—everything he did was meticulously plotted. It was likely some sort of wild animal, which I found strangely comforting.

"Let's get out of here," Gwen said. It was the first thing we'd agreed on in a long time.

Instead of dropping me off at my car, she took me to the house she shared with her father and Tommy, off River Lane.

We went inside and Gwen disappeared into a bedroom. She returned with a printout and handed it to me.

"It's an exclusive interview Noah gave to me about a month ago. He opened up about the accident. I promised him I wouldn't print it until he was ready. I figured you should see it."

I sat at the kitchen table and began reading my brother's words. After a few pages, my emotions grabbed me so tightly I thought Carter had me in a chokehold.

I looked up at Gwen, tears in my eyes. "He wanted to live."

"I know."

"We need to work together to bring Jones down."

"We? You don't seem like the team player type, JP."

I didn't like the insinuation—never had. "Why don't you call Byron Jasper and Jeff Carter and ask them if I'm a team player? Ask them if they trusted me in their foxhole with our lives on the line?"

"I did," she said with a grin, always taking joy in one-upping me. "They said you would die for them, JP Warner, and they wouldn't trust their lives to anybody else."

I recovered from my surprise with a smile. "So I guess we'll be working together ... just like old times."

Gwen matched my smile. "They also told me not to take any crap from you."

We were about to sail out into uncharted waters in Noah's Ark, and Gwen was the captain—these were definitely new times.

PART FOUR-

BATMAN & ROBIN

CHAPTER 42

Gilbert, Arizona

Day after Labor Day—1995

Kyle Jones finished putting on his police uniform. His military background had rendered him meticulous—Lucy called it anal-retentive—about the look of his uniform. He checked himself one last time in the full-length mirror, passing the inspection. He took a deep breath, not looking forward to what he had to do next.

He couldn't sleep the last few nights. Grady's words had awoken something in him, something that he thought he had put behind him years ago. He knew he must rededicate himself to the vow that he and Grady had made—seeking justice for those who were unable to help themselves.

But even with this epiphany, Grady's assault on Lucy crossed so many lines that he knew their relationship would never recover, and he had no choice but to evict him. Batman and Robin would be no longer.

He walked into the sun-filled kitchen to find Grady sitting at the breakfast table, slurping cereal and reading the morning edition of the *Arizona Republic*.

Grady looked up from his cereal with an apologetic look. They both began talking. Then simultaneously stopped and then began to talk again at the same time.

"You first," Kyle finally said, once again putting off the inevitable.

"I just want to say how sorry I am about the other night. I had no right to attack you and Lucy like that. I was wrong."

The apology was nice, but not enough. "Listen, Grady, I think it might be best if you found another place to live. Lucy feels uncomfortable around you after what happened."

"I totally understand," he said. "I've already started looking for a new place, but would you mind if I came back to shower when I have a job interview, and perhaps keep some clothes here? I promise I'll call ahead to make sure Lucy isn't here if I come by. I really don't trust the people at the shelter."

"Shelter?" Kyle asked with surprise.

Grady returned his attention to the classified ads. "Yeah, I checked out one in Tempe yesterday. Hopefully I'll land a job soon, so it'll only be temporary."

"You're looking for a job?"

"I heard what you guys were saying about me the other night before you left."

"I'm sorry about that, Grady."

"Don't be. You were right. It's time for me to stop making excuses for myself. Today is the first day of the rest of my life," he said, proudly holding up the classified ads full of his ink circles. "There's a lot of opportunity out there and I plan on going after it."

Kyle sat down across from him. "That's good to hear. If you want to drop by to clean up when you have an interview, it's fine by me."

Grady smiled. "Thanks, Kyle."

Kyle studied him. It was more like the Grady he knew. Even his slouching posture was gone.

"Sometimes when I have a difficult project in front of me, I like to keep a journal, so I can keep track of my goals and then mark things off when I accomplish a task. I find it very helpful," Kyle offered.

"I'll keep that in mind—I appreciate the advice."

Kyle looked at his watch, noticing that he was running late. But just before he turned to head for the door, Grady set the paper on the breakfast table. Staring back at them was a front-page photo of Leonard Harris of the Arizona Cardinals. He was flashing a big smile at the news that he only received probation for the vehicular homicide of two Arizona State coeds, despite his blood alcohol level being well past the legal limit. It had been the biggest story in the Valley for the past year.

Kyle felt like the headline was mocking him. He was lucky he didn't kill any innocent people the other night. He and Grady looked at each other, and it was as if they were reading the other's mind. Sending a bat signal.

Kyle began to head toward the door. He knew it was another reminder that he needed to recommit himself to justice. As he did, Grady called out, "Kyle?"

He turned, "Yeah?"

"We'll always be Batman and Robin, right?"

Kyle nodded, feeling their bond rekindling. "Always—Batman and Robin."

CHAPTER 43

He was Batman now. The mission was clear—written out in a bold headline on the front page of the newspaper. He could no longer deny his destiny. He must get justice for those two girls.

The accident took place in December of last year. Harris had been the star of the game, getting three sacks as the Cardinals beat their rival, the Dallas Cowboys, on Monday Night Football.

After the game, he joined a couple teammates, who hopped from bar to bar on the festive Mill Avenue, accepting numerous free drinks from strangers. Harris finally felt like the star he was always supposed to be. He partied until two in the morning, before leaving in his Porsche 911 Carrera.

The two girls had gone out to celebrate their final night of the semester at nearby Arizona State University. Finals had just ended and Kelly and Laura were booked on flights home the next day—Kelly to Wisconsin, Laura to Boston—but they wouldn't make it. They never saw the black Porsche that sped out of nowhere as they attempted to cross University Drive.

As part of his probation, Harris was given court ordered alcohol rehabilitation. With the unique access available to a police officer, Batman was able to discover the location of the rehab class. It was in an unmarked storefront in a North Scottsdale strip mall, located between a Subway and an Osco Drug.

The meeting was open to all comers. Batman, outfitted in US Air Force T-shirt and jeans, walked inside the windowless room. Metal folding chairs were set up in a semicircle—it looked like a school classroom, with a desk and blackboard facing the "students." He sat next to the large black man dressed in a running suit.

A middle-aged woman was the instructor. She wore glasses and a blue sundress. Her reptilian skin told a story of many unprotected years in the Arizona sun. She began predictably, "My name is Barbara and I'm an alcoholic."

After the class gave her the expected applause, she pointed to the two new members—the more famous one being Leonard Harris. "I see we have two new members today. Please make them feel part of the group."

There were about ten other people in the class, and they all clapped.

Harris slumped in his chair. He seemed to want to be anywhere else but here. Perhaps he could switch places with Kelly and Laura, Batman thought, wondering if he'd prefer their accommodations at the Motel Six-feet-under.

So he took the lead. "My name is Batman and I'm an alcoholic," he said. He received the applause of the class, along with a few chuckles at the superhero moniker, which cut the tension.

It seemed to inspire Harris. He followed Batman's lead, stood, and looked around the room. He remained frozen for a good minute, before sitting back down, and mumbling, "I can't do this."

Barbara comforted, "It's alright. It would be perfectly fine if you just want to sit and listen today."

Harris began to cry. "It doesn't matter what I do. Nothing I do will bring those girls back. Nothing—you hear me ... *nothing*!"

Batman put his arm around the bulging shoulders of Leonard Harris. "It's okay. When I got back from the war, I came down with Gulf War Syndrome. I had no job skills, and my girlfriend left me. I was sick and tired of being sick and tired—so I began drinking. My life became all about getting the next drink. I had no job, no friends, no life. One night I put a pistol in my mouth and just as I was about to pull the trigger it came to me."

The story was complete fiction, based on others he'd gone to war with, but it captured Harris' attention. "What came to you?" he asked in a soft voice. It was as if they were the only two souls in the room.

"How important life is. The knowledge that we have to live every day to its fullest, and anything less is unacceptable."

Tears began to stream down Harris' face once again. "No matter what I do, I can't bring them back. I stole their lives!"

Batman moved closer to Harris and hugged him. "In that case, it will never be good enough to live your life to the fullest. You must also live *their lives* to the fullest. That's why you need to get better, so you can live for them."

The passionate speech closed the deal. He wiped the tears and rose to his feet. "My name is Leonard and I'm an alcoholic," he said in a firm voice. The group clapped.

Batman walked out of the meeting, feeling satisfied with his first encounter with Harris, having laid the groundwork of trust.

He put on dark sunglasses to hide his eyes from the triple digit temperatures of early September in Scottsdale. The sky was painted aqua, with just two noticeable clouds. They crisscrossed to form an 'X', looking like vapor trail from a missile. It was as if the heavens approved of his work.

He strolled across the sizzling blacktop of the parking lot toward his vehicle. He wouldn't have to chase Leonard Harris. He would come to him— it was a fait accompli. And if there was any doubt in his mind, it was erased when he heard Harris' voice.

"Hey Batman … wait up."

CHAPTER 44

Rockfield, Connecticut

September 28—present

Outside the New York Public Library there are two iconic marble statues of lions. Their names are Patience and Fortitude. It wouldn't be very hard to figure out which one is my favorite.

It had been three weeks since Noah's death. Patience wasn't getting me any closer to justice, so it was time for the roar of fortitude.

I walked into the restaurant of the Hastings Inn, an elegant dining spot on the north side of town, which fit in with Rockfield's general disdain for the 21st Century. My father once tried to bring a McDonald's to town, which sparked the locals to form an Attica-like uprising. Murray referred to my father in the *Gazette* as "Mayor McCheese." He received only 85% of the vote in the next election, his all time low.

As a tuxedo-clad waiter walked me past a crackling fire to my table, my eyes locked on Gwen. She wore a sequined dress held up by spaghetti straps. The slit up the leg was almost too much for me to take.

Somehow her date was not clinging to her every breath, allowing us to trade a quick glance. Officer Jones was focused on the burly man at the bar who was slinging back shots like they were water, and spouting lewd remarks in a drunken slur.

Suddenly the man at the bar turned in my direction and shouted, "Just the man I wanted to see!"

He hopped off the bar stool, almost falling in the process, and rushed me like an angry bull.

"Carter … ugh … how've you been?"

"Don't give me that shit, Warner." He was actually slobbering—and poked a strong finger into my chest that was going to leave a mark.

"We risked our lives for you, and now you're throwing us out like yesterday's trash. You told me you were leaving the business, but now I hear you used our capture to get a better offer—leaving Byron and me behind!"

"That's not how it happened. I've meant to call, but I just …"

"Are you denying the offer to become the highest paid person in the news industry?"

When I didn't respond, Carter gave a two-handed shove into my chest and I fell to the ground. The uppity dinner theater crowd gasped.

I used my cane to prop myself up, but as soon as I reached my feet, Carter sent a too-close-for-comfort punch glancing past my chin. I fell to the floor again. He stood over me and glared menacingly. "Get up! You're not so tough when you have to face the music, are you?"

I stumbled to my feet and attempted to hit him with my cane. He grabbed it from me and tossed it away. He then picked me up. A shocked look came over my face—this wasn't in the script.

He carried me to the mahogany bar and sent me for a ride, as if the bar top was a bowling alley, my body knocking over drinks and plates before I crash-landed on the hard floor.

"Had enough?" Carter shouted.

I had. These fake fights sure felt real.

He obviously hadn't. Once more he raised me over his head.

"I thought you promised no body-slams?" I spoke softly into his ear.

"We gotta make it look good," he whispered back.

"If we make it look any better, I'll be dead."

More shrieks and clamors filled the room. The panicked patrons scattered—and Carter sent me flying.

I crashed violently onto a table, landing on top of a half-eaten baked potato with sour cream. A sharp fork scratched my back.

"Agh," I screamed out.

He put me in a headlock, and said for my ears only, "I take back what I said—that Gwen is a prime piece of ass."

I let fly a "for real" elbow back into Carter's midsection that knocked the wind out of him. I'd awoken the grizzly—not a smart move. He let out a primal scream and picked me up like a rag doll. I sensed that the "no body-slam" rule was off. He tossed me to the floor, knocking me dizzy.

Before I could begin to beg for mercy, Jones became involved. Although, a little late for my taste. He couldn't help himself, which is what we were banking on—hero syndrome. He flashed a badge and began rattling off different types of assaults Carter had committed.

Carter laughed at the off-duty police officer and stormed out the front door. A few moments later, I could hear the screech of the Coldblooded Cruiser leaving the parking lot.

Jones informed Gwen that "duty called" and he must leave. She begged him to stay, but the thought of a potential drunk driver on the road was too much for Jones. How any man could leave her in that dress was a mystery of Area 51 proportions to me.

He kissed Gwen on the cheek and promised to make it up to her. She acted upset and looked away.

Jones put his hand on her chin and lifted it to meet his eyes. "I promise, Gwen. But I have a job to do. You understood that when you met me."

I wanted to puke.

She returned a cold, "I guess," and looked away again.

He kissed her on the cheek. "I'll call you tomorrow," he said, before rushing away.

Once the coast was clear, Gwen turned her attention to the injured guy on the floor. She knelt beside me while I continued to writhe in pain.

"Are you okay, JP?"

Despite my pain, I had to admit that things were starting to look up.

CHAPTER 45

Carter was dragged into Chief Tolland's office by his arresting officer, Kyle Jones. When the cuffs were removed, Tolland instructed him to take a seat across from his desk, and for Jones to close the door.

After leaving the restaurant, Carter had taken off in the Coldblooded Cruiser—a luxury tour bus that was the closest thing Carter had to an official residence. Back in the day, the Cruiser was a destination of debauchery for his groupies and followers that made Vegas seem like a trip to the monastery. But he had matured greatly since those days, he thought to himself, as he placed his feet up on the chief's desk and listened to the many charges against him—disturbing the peace, assaulting JP Warner, and taking a thirty-five foot bus for a drunken joyride through town.

Jones had a superior look on his face that Carter wanted to rip off. In fact, he wanted to remove his entire head. But as he attempted to get up to confront him, he winced in pain. He would have to take care of Jones in a battle of wits, instead of his preferred method—a battle of fists.

Tolland demanded he remove his feet from his desk. He almost equaled Carter in size, and commanded respect, reminding him of his military father. JP had spoken highly of him. The two men glared at each other, before Tolland asked, "What do you have to say for yourself?"

"First of all, I'm not sure when knocking the snot out of JP Warner became a crime. Who in this room hasn't wanted to do that? You should be sending me flowers."

"I don't know how you conduct yourself in other places, Mr. Carter, but Rockfield is not the Wild West, or worse, an arena for professional wrestling. We don't take the law into our own hands in this town."

Carter shot a look at Jones. "Oh, you don't?"

Jones looked ready for round two, but this was Tolland's show. "We can debate the merits of your assault in a court of law, but drinking and driving is much less subjective, once you've received a Breathalyzer test."

"I am not, and never was drunk. I have been falsely accused."

This finally sent Jones over the edge. "Stop the lies! I saw you consume at least eight drinks in under an hour."

"How do you know what I was drinking?"

"People in the next state knew what you were drinking."

"You're just mad because that hot number you were with was checking me out."

"Enough!" Tolland roared. "Jones, you sit. Mr. Carter, Officer O'Rourke will now take you for your Breathalyzer."

Carter was not going to make it easy on them—he needed to stall for time. He declared any physical or eye tests at the scene inadmissible, claiming he wasn't made aware of his right to refuse. He added that he wouldn't take further sobriety tests without a confidential call to his attorney. His claims were legally accurate, and Tolland knew it. Unlike Jones, he didn't play by his own rules.

Once Carter's requests were met, he continued to stall, requesting a sample of his breath be preserved for independent testing. He also demanded to be released for an independent blood test following the completion of the necessary paperwork. It made him seem like a guilty man looking to get off on a technicality, and as a bonus, it looked as if Officer Jones might blow a gasket.

When he ran out of material, Carter headed off for his test. He returned fifteen minutes later with the results. They ran the test twice. Both times Jeff Carter registered a zero point zero. He had no alcohol in his system.

Carter smirked. "I guess I'll be on my way."

Jones was livid. He pointed an angry finger in Betsy O'Rourke's direction, accusing her of doctoring the test, and made the claim that she had altered the test because she'd succumbed to Carter's charm.

Tolland admonished Jones, declaring that he had no proof that the test wasn't properly administered, or that Carter had any charm. He then turned his attention to the accused. "Not so fast, Mr. Carter, I'm going to hold you on the assault charge."

Before he could pretend to argue, a knock rattled the door. They looked up to see Officer Williams, who informed the room that the bus had been towed to police headquarters and searched. He held two objects in his hands. "Chief, we found this camera in the bus. We think it possibly taped the entire arrest."

"Oh yeah, I forgot to tell you guys—I've been working on a documentary for GNZ about my life. I'll bet it caught the whole thing ... looks like I'm *busted*."

Jones squirmed in his chair, causing Carter to grin from ear to ear. He placed his feet back on the desk and announced, "This should be good—I love reality TV. Can somebody make some popcorn?"

Tolland cleared the room of everyone except Jones and Carter, closed the blinds, and played the video on his computer.

It began with Carter driving the bus, noticing a police car in full pursuit from behind. He looked into a camera and recited the alphabet to prove his sobriety. He missed the "Q" and "R", but he appeared sober. He just didn't know the alphabet.

The camera angle then changed to outside the bus, where Officer Jones approached the driver's side after the bus had pulled over. Jones demanded that Carter step out of the vehicle. Carter responded with, "If you want a ride, try putting a jackhammer up your ass."

Jones didn't look happy at the comment, but it didn't make what he did next any less shocking. He pulled out his gun and shot out the window of the bus, glass shattering everywhere.

This time Carter took the threat seriously, and exited the bus with his hands up. After Jones handcuffed him, he began mercilessly punching Carter in the ribs. He fell to the ground, where Jones sent vicious kicks into his midsection.

Tolland had witnessed enough and angrily ejected the disc from the computer.

Carter grimaced as he re-lived the worst ambush he'd been involved with since an unfortunate encounter with his old nemesis Rowdy Roddy on Piper's Pit. But he still found joy in his victory.

"I thought this wasn't the Wild West and you play by the rules here. Or worse … professional wrestling."

CHAPTER 46

The Hastings Inn shrunk in the rear-view mirror as Gwen and I drove off in the *Rockfield Gazette* van.

Jones lived in a remote north section of town not far from the restaurant. The drive would only take five minutes. I sat in the passenger seat, unable to take my eyes away from Gwen's long legs as she alternated between gas-pedal and brake.

Her attention was split between the road and the cut just above my left eyebrow. She reached her hand over to gently wipe a spot of blood, and asked again, "Are you okay, JP?"

"I'm fine," I responded curtly.

"What's wrong? This was your idea, if you remember."

"Nothing," I said. But I think jealousy had gotten the better of me. When I saw her in the restaurant with Jones, images filled my head of Stephen DuBois taking Gwen Delaney to swanky Manhattan restaurants, while I ducked bombs in some war torn country nobody ever heard of.

"I've known you since you were five years old, JP—I can tell when something is bothering you."

I decided to evade. The more things change ... "What do you guys talk about on a date?"

She smiled. "We don't talk, JP. We're at that great stage of the relationship where it's just *sex, sex, sex.*"

I suddenly understood the term "acid reflux."

Our arrival saved me a response. Gwen turned off her lights as we drove up Evergreen Street. We then came upon a long, sloping gravel driveway.

She stopped the car in the middle of the dark, lonely road and explained the battle plan. "About fifty feet down the driveway it splits like a fork. The left leads to Kyle's house, but we will take the right to his neighbors' home, the Walkers. They are on vacation, so we will park at their house and walk through the wooded area separating the homes"

We continued down the driveway—the only sound coming from the small rocks being kicked up by the van's tires.

When we arrived at the Walkers', Gwen parked the car and hastily searched the backseat. She cursed herself for leaving her jacket in Jones' car when he'd brought her to the restaurant. I had driven the van to Hastings. We stepped out into the night, feeling the cool chill of autumn. I offered her my jacket, but she refused, proving we still had enough stubborn pride between us to fill a small country.

I leaned on my cane, trying to catch my breath. I looked at Gwen. Actually, I hadn't stopped looking at her. "I can't believe he went for the bait."

She looked at me with surprise. "What do you mean you can't believe it? You said you were a hundred percent certain."

"I was, but I didn't factor in you wearing that dress."

She blushed, but recovered to remind me, "That's nice of you to say, JP. It's one of my favorites—Stephen bought it for me for my birthday one year."

Suddenly I found the dress less appealing. With no time to waste, we moved into the wooded area. Gwen took the lead, knocking away thin tree branches that were camouflaged by the dark night.

I watched her glide through the light forest—no small feat in stilettos—gracefully moving tree limbs out of the way. She bounced over an embankment, but then disappeared like a trap door had opened beneath her.

I ran as fast as my injured leg would allow. When I arrived at the top of the embankment, I looked down to see that Gwen had gone "ass over tea kettle" into a patch of poison ivy. My fright dissipated and I began to laugh.

"Shut up!"

"I didn't say anything," I said with a guilty smile, reaching out my hand to her.

She refused, choosing to struggle to her feet. She almost regained balance when her shoes slipped again on the wet ivy. I instinctively reached out and caught her.

It felt like no time had passed since the last time I'd held her in my arms. I remembered it vividly—it took place in the small closet on the Upper West Side that Gwen referred to as her apartment, after I'd returned from Bosnia. This is where I had longed to be since that day.

"Thanks," Gwen said in a hushed tone, and pulled away. Just like that, the moment faded away. "We better hurry," she urged.

You wait for a moment for fifteen years and it only lasts five seconds. But that's life in a nutshell—a few monumental moments, surrounded by a lot of mundane time where we wait for the next fleeting moment of grandeur.

I placed my suit jacket over her bare shoulders. This time she didn't fight me.

We evaded one last branch and arrived at a manicured lawn that led to the back of Jones' abode. It was a modest one-story, ranch-style house. All lights were off and it appeared deserted. It seemed like a place where a large attack dog would let out an angry stream of barking at intruders, but none did.

Gwen moved to a screened-in porch area. Just outside of it was a barbecue, which she frisked through, only to come up empty. "Dammit!"

"What is it?"

"I talked to a girl named Holly who briefly dated Kyle. She works at the bowling alley here in Rockfield. It never got serious, but she did come here on a couple of occasions and told me the extra key was hidden in the barbecue."

"Did she give you any inside information on Jones?"

"According to her, he was weird."

"That's not a real scoop."

"Agreed. A real scoop would be finding a way in."

"When I get in a tight spot, I think of what Carter would do and then I scale it down to something I'll get less years in prison for."

"Breaking and entering into a police officer's house is going to get us locked up for a long time, either way."

She had a point, but I'd made a career of tuning out the voice of reason, and this time would be no different. My eyes adjusted to the dark as I searched for an opening.

"So what would Carter do?" she asked.

"He would set an explosive device on that window over there," I said, pointing at the window closest to the screened-in porch.

"Your friend is a piece of work."

"He's the most loyal man I know. He'd die for me."

"If he doesn't kill you first. What's the scaled down version?"

"See that window? I think it's cracked open just enough that one of us could fit through."

Gwen volunteered. "Give me a boost and I think I can get in."

"I was thinking about going."

"I'm younger than you, JP. This is not a job for a decrepit old man."

"Only by six months, three days, and four hours."

She smiled. "I'm impressed … but I'm still going."

There was no time to argue. And pride aside, she was likely the only one of us who would fit. I anchored myself with my cane and after removing her shoes, Gwen climbed on my shoulders. I boosted her up and she tried to squeeze through the window.

She was three-quarters of the way in as I held tightly to her ankles. She slithered a little more and I started to lose my grip. I held on as tightly as possible, but it was no use. She broke away from my grip and disappeared through the window with a scream, followed by a loud thud. Then everything went silent.

The silence was frightening. I had no idea how far the drop was, or if the paranoid Jones had some type of booby trap set up. I visualized an oversized bear trap with sharp metal claws.

"Gwen? Gwen? Are you okay?" I shouted in my loudest whisper.

No response.

My stomach sank.

"Gwen!"

CHAPTER 47

An hour went by.

It was actually more like a minute, but it seemed like an hour. I started to panic. I had to get in. Calling 911 wasn't exactly an option.

But then around the corner of the house, Gwen appeared like an angel. She looked unscathed, and said, "I opened the front door, let's go."

She wore gloves and provided me a pair. I had no idea where she stored them in that dress. I handed her the shoes that she'd removed.

"Are you okay?" I asked with concern.

"No thanks to you dropping me, I am."

I followed her around to the front entrance. The place was cold and sterile, I thought as we entered, and the only detectable odor was from the recent use of a fireplace.

We entered the living room. It contained two chairs and a couch. A small coffee table sat empty in front of the couch. No magazines, notes, junk, or anything. It was as bland as Kyle Jones' physical appearance.

"Look what you've been missing out on," I remarked.

"A little too clean for my taste."

"A little too clean is making me suspicious."

"JP, we already are suspicious. That's why we broke into his house. We need to find something that connects him to Noah's death."

I walked a circle from living room to dining room, through the kitchen and back to the living room. I checked for cameras, listening devices, and anything that someone like Jones might put in his house because he was paranoid. A handy news-industry survival skill that I had picked up over the years.

I found nothing.

Gwen headed down a hallway, stopping to look at photographs hanging on the wall. "Do you find it odd, JP, that every picture and memento he has is related to his time in Rockfield. No old friends, family—it's as if his life started the day he arrived here."

"Not really," I said. "He's an only child who moved around, so he likely doesn't have a lot of longstanding relationships. And as far as his parents, he probably doesn't want a daily reminder of their death. We haven't found any cracks in his timeline—he had a good record in the military, his boss in Arizona thinks he's the Second Coming, and if he had something to hide in North Carolina, then why did he keep his house there?"

She nodded, but my words didn't seem to convince her, so I stole Murray's theory, "I think he might be running toward something, not away from it."

I entered the first bedroom on the right. It was neat and antiseptic, just like all the other rooms. A single bed, a laptop computer sitting on a desk, and a twenty-inch television in front of the bed.

Gwen followed me in, and went directly to his closet—dry-cleaned police uniforms on one side, casual wear like jeans, flannel shirts, and sweaters on the other. On the floor, hidden behind a folded ironing-board and a pile of heavy winter sweaters, were three cardboard boxes. Gwen knelt down and began going through them as I looked on.

It contained the history Gwen sought. A lot of awards and certificates dating back to Little League, including those noting his military and police achievements. He was so anal that he actually saved his schoolwork from the many schools he'd attended, spanning the globe from Germany to San Diego to Kentucky. Nothing incriminating.

Gwen appeared to discover something and summoned me over. She handed me a copy of the picture of Jones' parents. I took a close look at them—they appeared to be out on a houseboat at some unidentified lake. "I told you he doesn't want to deal with it every day. Those memories are best kept in a box in the closet."

Gwen handed me more photos. They were from the Air Force days. Most were group shots—a bunch of cocky Top Gun wannabe pilots hamming for the camera. It made the military seem more like spring break than the blood and guts of war that I had witnessed firsthand.

She handed me more shots of Jones, posing in his Gilbert, Arizona police uniform, along with some assorted ones from his time in North Carolina, posing by a small airplane.

Gwen continued to dig, locating a photo titled "Batman & Robin." This was another Air Force photo, but this one was specifically of Jones and another man. The photo was signed: *Batman & Robin—Wingmen Forever!* It was dated January 28, 1991. She handed them to me.

Both men, dressed in their sand-colored flight suits, were young, vibrant, and didn't seem to have a care in the world. They stood beside their aircraft, arms draped around each other, either about to embark on another successful mission, or perhaps just victoriously returning from one. Jones seemed to be having a more difficult time with the desert sun, his skin was blotched and blistered, while his buddy had a bronze tan.

"Do you think you can find out who this wingman guy is? He might know something about Kyle that we're missing."

"The only military contacts I have left are the kind who would like to use me for target practice. Maybe Carter can help with that. He's like a cult hero with the troops."

Gwen quickly changed the subject, handing me another photo. "Check this out."

I studied a photo of Jones standing beside an attractive girl with curly dark hair. It was titled: *Lucy's Birthday*. "I'm guessing this is the Lucy that the police chief in Gilbert mentioned. And I must say, for a strange anal-retentive murderer, he does pretty well with the ladies."

I'd love to have a conversation with this Lucy, but without a last name, and only a photograph, she'd be difficult to locate. I looked for a copy machine, but couldn't locate one. It would be too risky to take the photo, so I took a picture of it with my phone. It would have to do. I did the same with the photo of *Batman & Robin*.

We knew we didn't have much time left, so we did one final sweep.

In his desk I found the usual identification markers, such as his social security card and his pilot license from both North Carolina and Connecticut. Unfortunately, there was no diary where he confessed to killing my brother. Gwen found a pile of old VHS tapes with my name marked on them in magic marker, and according to the label, they contained some of my most famous stories for GNZ. Looks like he was returning the favor by doing a little research on me.

All interesting finds, but nothing worth risking a long prison term for. "Hurry and put that stuff back, Gwen, I want to check out the basement before we go."

CHAPTER 48

We cautiously descended the steps. My leg began to flare up with pain and I lagged behind. When I got to the bottom, I thought I'd walked into a Batman convention. Gadgets, posters, dolls.

"Can you shed any light on this?" Gwen asked.

"I think he might like Batman," I said, feeling nostalgic. "I remember watching the Batman television show with you and we had to have my mom come in the room to read all the words that flashed on the screen during the climactic fight scenes. *POW, BAM, KABOOM.*"

Gwen smiled. "If I remember correctly, I learned to read before you and put a stop to that."

"Are you ever not competitive?"

"I can't believe you're talking."

She wandered to the wall and read the inscription out loud. It was a poem, entitled *Batman: The Dark Knight.*

I repeated the words in my mind. *He battles crime, his victims bleed* stuck with me. I thought of Noah.

My cell phone startled us. It was Carter. "I just left the police station. And so did Jones, so you might want to think about getting out of there."

"What happened to stalling?" I asked, motioning Gwen to hurry up the staircase.

"Once I showed them a video of your boy assaulting me, they got rid of me as soon as possible."

"I owe you one. I'll give you first shot at Jones when we nail him."

"It's only going to take one. I'm going to kill that little punk."

"Deal."

We bolted up the stairs and out of the house, fairly confident nothing was out of place and no evidence of our break-in was left behind. I trailed her into the woods, using my cane to fight off branches and prickers. My adrenaline warmed the cold night.

We arrived at the van, huffing and puffing. At least I was, Gwen appeared ready to run a 5K. She started the vehicle and we peeled out of the driveway like we were driving the getaway car at a bank robbery. As we turned onto Evergreen, it seemed we were home free, and I let out a sigh of relief.

But that's when we saw the flashing aerial lights of a police car. We both knew who it was.

I braced as Jones stepped toward the van. Gwen rolled down her window.

"Are you lost ma'am?" he said with a plastic, obviously forced smile.

What a comedian.

He looked to the passenger side and didn't exactly look happy to see me. "Good evening, Mr. Warner. I'm glad to see that you're still in one piece after such a brutal assault."

I doubted that he was. "Thank you, officer. I never like getting my ass kicked on an empty stomach."

Jones turned back to Gwen. "I thought you were going home?"

"After the fight, I brought JP up to the emergency room at New Milford Hospital. But it was the typical Friday night zoo and the wait was like three hours. He said he was feeling better, so I was bringing him home."

Jones looked at me. "I didn't know you lived around here?"

Gwen thought fast once again. "We were headed there. But first I wanted to stop by and see that you were okay. I doubted you'd be here, but I wanted to at least leave you a note. It was actually an IOU for another dinner. I really hope we can do it again soon, but I also wanted you to know that I understand the sacrifices you have to make for your job."

She reached into her purse and pulled out a note in an envelope and handed it to Jones. He read the note and appeared satisfied. She had thought of everything.

"I didn't want you to think I was one of those clingy girlfriends, so I decided against leaving it. I guess I'm kind of a wimp." She smiled at him.

"I'm glad you gave it to me," Jones said with a creepy smile, and reached toward her. She jumped back—a natural reaction, but one that might make him suspicious … if he wasn't already. Jones picked a pine needle off of her dress. I looked down and noticed that we were both covered in pine needles. She made up a lame story about stopping at my parents' house so I could pick up my health insurance information, before heading to the hospital. "The place is practically in the middle of the woods, and with his parents at the football game, there were no lights on. I ran right smack into a pine tree."

"I've been to the Warner house, and it is very remote. I hope that you're alright."

"I'm better than the tree." She laughed nervously once again, and then attempted to change the subject, "I thought you'd be working all night, Kyle. Maybe it's not too late to have that dinner."

"I'm tired, Gwen, and I've had a rough night. So we'll have to take a rain-check," he held up his IOU as proof of a future date. "But we're still on for our trip next week, right?"

"Of course. I've been looking forward to it for weeks."

"That's good to hear, Gwen. And it looks like I might have some unexpected vacation time coming to me. I'll call you tomorrow—drive safe."

Before returning to the police car, he handed Gwen the jacket she'd left on the way to the restaurant. He also flashed me a quick look to kill. I couldn't figure out if his point of contention was my close proximity to Gwen, or if he wanted me to back off my investigation into Noah's murder. Or maybe he was concerned we might have broken into his home and touched his Batman action figures. I contemplated the possibilities as I watched him walk back to his vehicle.

The minute he was gone, Gwen blurted, "He knows."

"He just thinks we were doing it in the woods."

"The way he looked at me—he knew."

"He knows *what*? That we broke into his house? That we're having a steamy affair? That we found out he longs for some kinky three-way with you and Batman?"

"He's starting to scare me, JP."

"Starting? You're not really going on vacation with him."

"I can't back out now. Besides, it's a much better plan than this charade."

"It wasn't a question, Gwen—you're not going."

A lecture commenced about my right to have any opinion about her life, due to circumstances from years ago.

"C'mon, Gwen. That was like three lifetimes ago."

"Those who don't remember the past are condemned to repeat it."

I leaned back, defeated, and rubbed my temples. I remembered from the past that this was an argument I'd never win, and I wasn't going to repeat it.

CHAPTER 49

Ocracoke Island, North Carolina

October 1st

The small Piper propeller plane made a perfect landing on the small airstrip on Ocracoke Island. The only access to the small island off the coast of North Carolina was by sea or air.

Kyle Jones helped Gwen out of the plane like a perfect gentleman. She stood on the runway in her white buttoned down shirt tucked into mauve jeans that she wore with sandals. She breathed in the warm, salty air. "Plan Gwen" was under way.

She was always more subtle than JP, which showed in their ideas on how to solve the case. They were in agreement that they believed Jones was a murderous vigilante who killed Noah. But that's where the consensus ended. Gwen doubted JP's breaking and entering plan would be productive, and it wasn't. It only led to more questions. High risk/low reward.

She knew the only way to connect the dots was to find the motive behind Jones' obsession, and the only way to do that was one on one, like a real reporter.

A couple areas of interest were Jones' parents, whose death led to the settlement that helped him afford the home in Ocracoke, and the plane that delivered them here. The other was Kyle's wingman from the photo. JP was working with Carter to get access to Air Force records to try to discover his identity, but Gwen thought her time alone with Kyle would be more fruitful in that search. The other point of emphasis was the girlfriend from Arizona named Lucy.

Jones' extensive Batman collection fascinated her, and she'd researched the Batman tales since the break-in. Bruce Wayne and his parents were returning home from the theater after watching *The Mask of Zorro,* when Bruce witnessed his parents shot to death by a mugger in a dark alleyway. Bruce vowed to dedicate his life to fighting crime in the dark night. He did so with a relentless obsession and a burning passion to punish all criminals, disguised as a mythical figure called Batman. On some levels, it seemed to parallel Jones' pursuit. But for all she knew, he could be just a Batman fan like millions of others around the world. She had her work cut out for her.

Jones put his arm around her and walked her across the small runway to a waiting taxicab. He held the door for her with a smile. He was very much like many zealots she had interviewed in the course of her work. Calm, smiling, and charming most of the time. But when their zealotry was questioned, even slightly, they would lash out.

He made no mention about the one-week suspension he'd received from the force. Her source told her that it was related to an incident where he was caught on video roughing up a DUI suspect, which Tolland had tried to keep quiet—although, it sounded more like the work of Maloney. Officially, Jones was on vacation. Her source was Jeff Carter.

She never pushed the issue. The last thing they wanted was to shine a light on Jones. He would have gone on high alert, and the odds of connecting him to Noah's murder would decrease.

They entered the cab that advertised low rates to "all island airports," even though there was only one. He instructed the driver to take them to a restaurant called The Back Porch. The familiarity of the island seemed to put him into a comfort zone. Gwen played the passive girlfriend, allowing him to feel in charge.

The taxi sputtered as it pulled away. Jones lightly set his hand on her leg. "You have been so quiet."

Gwen came out of her daze, sporting a nervous smile. "I just have a fear of flying. I feel better now that we're safely on the ground."

"It's completely safe, Gwen. I used to fly with people shooting at me … now that's when someone should have a fear of flying," he said with a grin.

Gwen went into reporter mode. "I guess you were like one of those guys in *Top Gun*. I had the biggest crush on Tom Cruise."

He appeared annoyed by the question. "We were Air Force—*Top Gun* pilots are Navy."

Jones could spot a drunk driver three counties away, but couldn't notice a sense of humor if it smacked him across his skull.

"Did you still get to have one of those cool pilot nicknames like Maverick or Ice Man?"

"I was Batman."

"Did you have one of those co-pilots like Goose?"

"It's a wingman—not a co-pilot. He was Robin … we were Batman and Robin."

"Well, I'm glad we had a couple superheroes keeping us free and safe. That must be an amazing bond, I can't even imagine the connection."

"What do you mean?"

"Wingmen. You put your lives on the line for each other every time you went up in that plane. It must connect you for life. Do you and Robin stay in touch?"

"I haven't seen him since I left Arizona. We had a falling out—a girl came between us."

"I'm sorry. Maybe I can arrange a reunion." She smiled. "Your new girlfriend wouldn't make you choose. If you give me his name …"

He put his arm around her. "I'm just concentrating on who I'm with right now. I'm very happy." He kissed her on the cheek and she fought against her natural squirm.

"Then I'm going to concentrate on getting to know my brave pilot even better. Did you get the name because you were a big Batman fan? I used to religiously watch the TV show when I was a kid."

He seemed to travel down memory lane. Gwen wondered what skeletons he passed on his trip.

"I got it because just when it looked like the bad guys would get away, I'd spring out of the darkness to save the day. Just like Batman. Plus, I flew in a swooping style like a bat."

"For what it's worth, Kyle, I think you are a lot like Batman. Always taking the law into your own hands to get the bad guys, so that Rockfield is a safer place. When I was a little girl I always dreamed of marrying a cowboy. You are a modern day cowboy."

Jones' mood switched on the dime. "I never take the law into my own hands! I'm a police officer. I took an oath to follow the law and that is what I do."

Gwen took it as a sign to back off the conversation. As he brooded, she gazed out the window of the taxi, taking in the view of Ocracoke. It was a quaint island with pristine beaches. It looked like it came straight out of a travel brochure.

A few miles later they entered the most populated section of the island that surrounded Silver Lake—motels, grocery stores, and gift shops seemed to appear out of nowhere. People filled the streets, walking and biking like they were in a fitness infomercial. Her attention was grabbed by the Ocracoke Lighthouse, which stood over the village as if it were guarding it from intrusion.

Jones noticed her interest. "The lighthouse was built in 1823 and can be seen as far as twenty miles out at sea. If you'd like, we can take a tour during your visit."

She forced a smile. "I'd love to Kyle."

So you can toss me off it like you tossed Noah off the bridge?

CHAPTER 50

Gwen reached into her overnight bag and pulled out a camera. As the taxi stopped at a sandy intersection, she snapped photos of the lighthouse. "This place is wonderful, Kyle. What inspired you to move here?"

"We came here on vacation a few times when my parents were stationed in North Carolina. When I left Arizona, I was at a crossroads—unsure what I wanted to do with the rest of my life. Ocracoke had always provided me with peace, so I figured it would be a good place to sort things out. I fell in love so much with the homey atmosphere that I bought a house on the beach and vowed I'd only leave if I could find a place that matched the small town feel. That's why, when I decided to return to police work, I chose Rockfield over other offers. You should see the small store that's docked in the harbor. It's practically the floating version of the Rockfield Village Store."

"What made you return to police work?"

"I enjoyed my life here, but I'd always felt a calling to stopping the bad guys, so to speak."

His answers sounded like cover stories to Gwen. His preparedness didn't surprise her, and his intelligence wasn't to be underestimated.

The cab driver pulled into the small parking lot of The Back Porch and dropped them off. The wait was short, and they were soon seated at a patio table—a light breeze blew, filling Gwen's senses with the aroma of the ocean. She thought that this really would be a fantastic vacation spot under different circumstances. Jones took control, ordering for her—a fillet of flounder dredged in nuts, and an iced tea.

When the waiter left, Gwen instinctively rolled up her sleeve to scratch her itching arm.

He reached across the table and grabbed her hand.

"What are you doing?" she asked, nervously.

"You shouldn't itch that—it will only make it worse."

Gwen stared back, thinking there was no way he could ever have known how she got it. But there was something about the look in his eyes that scared her.

"You're right, Kyle. But sometimes it itches so much it's hard not to."

"Life is all about self discipline, Gwen."

She nodded subserviently.

"So where did you get poison ivy?" he asked.

The question caught her off guard. "Um … I'm really not sure. I must have gone somewhere I shouldn't have." She fixated on the oozing red bubbles spread across her forearm.

"I guess there are always consequences for going where we shouldn't go."

Gwen needed to regain control of the conversation. She reached into her bag and pulled out her camera. She focused it on Jones, and took a photo of him as he sipped his drink.

"What are you doing?" he asked, flustered.

"I think I'm going to do a story on you for the *Gazette*. Rockfield's superhero policeman relaxing on vacation."

His face angered. "I thought you came here to be with me. But obviously you only care about your career."

"All I want to do is get to know the real you—as would Rockfield. You never talk about your past … your family … your hopes and dreams. I'm your girlfriend, but you treat me like a reporter," she said loud enough to purposefully make a scene. She hoped the patrons staring in their direction would remember this moment when she went missing.

Jones got his emotions under control. "I'm sorry, Gwen. It just takes me a long time to trust someone."

"I'm sorry too. I guess the journalist in me gets the best of me sometimes. I know it can be a little overbearing."

The waiter arrived with their food, interrupting the tense moment. They ate in silence, allowing Gwen to gather her thoughts. And since he'd brought up the topic, she thought she'd continue with the theme.

"You know how you said you don't trust people easily, Kyle?"

"Yes."

"Well, I don't either ... so I've been debating whether I should tell you what I know about a certain subject. Can I trust you, Kyle?"

He perked up. "Of course, Gwen ... of course."

"Okay," she said, acting as if she were in the midst of an internal debate. "I got a call from a source the other day. The Casey Leeds case from a few years ago ... no I shouldn't tell you ... I'm sorry."

Jones looked to be on the verge of springing out of his seat. "No, please tell me, Gwen. Maybe I can help."

She feigned hesitance. "Okay, but this is only between us ... promise?"

"Of course."

"My sources have indicated that Leeds was set up by a member of your department."

His face turned pale as a ghost. He took several sips of iced tea, which seemed to help him recover. "Go on, who did they say was involved?"

"No, I shouldn't. I've already told you too much."

"Gwen, if there's a dirty cop on the force I have a right to know about it. I work with these people. My life could be in danger. Leeds took me hostage—I'm involved, whether I want to be or not."

She paused to let him twist in the wind some more, before adding, "My source claimed it was Betsy O'Rourke." She flashed a look of buyer's remorse. "Are you sure this will remain just between us? At least until I have enough to go forward with it."

"You have my word," he said, looking relieved. He reached into his pocket and pulled out Gwen's missing diamond earring. "If I wasn't trustworthy I'd have already sold this on eBay."

She looked stunned. "Where did you get that?"

"It must have fallen off in my car on our way to the restaurant the other night."

Gwen looked at the earring and then at Jones. It was like trying to read a book with no words. She felt the hairs on the back of her neck stand up.

"Thank you, I do trust you," she said, no longer feeling in control.

CHAPTER 51

Gwen spent the rest of the afternoon strolling around the island under a splendid, sun-filled sky with her pretend, murderer boyfriend. Not exactly every girl's dream. When he would grab onto her hand she felt chills down her spine, and not the romantic kind.

They journeyed in and out of the many specialty shops, galleries, and historic island cottages that surrounded Silver Lake. Gwen stopped to take photos of the sailboats that were scattered throughout the protected cove.

They eventually reached the less populated northern beaches. The day began to ease into night, dropping the temperatures. Gwen suddenly felt very alone, and very vulnerable.

Jones stopped in his tracks, surprising her. He pointed at a typical beach house, and announced, "There it is."

"There what is?"

"My house. Come on in, I want to show it to you."

She held back, and he noticed. "What's wrong?"

"I just think it's strange that you've never invited me into your house in Rockfield, but now you want to show me inside your beach home."

"Like I said, it takes me awhile to let someone in. In this case, literally," he said with a disarming smile.

She knew when she agreed to come, at some point she'd have to be alone with him in his house. Still, it reminded her of that moment in every horror movie where you're pleading with the character not to enter the house with the killer.

"We'll just be a few minutes so that we can change to go sailing—the lake is beautiful at night, and really it wouldn't be proper to change on the beach," he added.

The fact that the lake was a much smarter place to kill her, rather than in the house, strangely made her feel better about entering. The sailing was another story—she pondered how dark it would be at night on the water. *An easy place to get rid of a body.* But she'd come this far and couldn't turn back now.

"That sounds great, Kyle," she mustered up enthusiasm as she followed him toward the weathered beach house. They walked underneath the stilts that held the place up, into a garage area. She noticed a red pickup truck already hooked to a small sailboat.

They climbed a rickety wooden staircase, arriving at a small deck with peeling green paint, and entered through a sliding glass door. Jones took off his docksiders to avoid tracking sand into the house. Gwen followed his lead and removed her sandals. The first thing she noticed was a similar sterility as inside his Rockfield home.

Jones played gracious host, offering a glass of water, which she declined, and then showed her to the bathroom, as she requested. He clicked on a radio and a twangy Tim McGraw song filled the house.

Gwen tossed water on her face and stared into the mirror. *C'mon, Gwen, you can do this*, she muttered. Like the Little Engine that Could (get herself killed), she found the resolve. She strolled back into the small living room and plopped down on the couch. In front of her on a coffee table sat a newspaper called the *Ocracoker*. She noticed the date on the paper was from last summer.

She skimmed the front-page story entitled: *Kingsbury Suspect Cleared.* The suspect was a local police officer named Ron Culver, who was in charge of providing a secretive security escort for the Kingsburys that night. Gwen's skim turned disinterested and she gently set the paper back on the coffee table.

Jones noticed her reading the old paper, and explained, "That was from the last time I was here. I like to leave a paper or magazine so it feels more lived-in when I return."

Gwen nodded, remembering when Stephen first moved out of their apartment, and she used to leave the television on so it seemed like someone was home when she returned from work.

"I can't believe they haven't solved this case yet. What's it been, three months?" she said, pointing at the paper.

"It took place on the Fourth of July. Biggest fireworks these parts have ever seen."

"How close to here did it occur?"

"It happened on the Oregon Inlet Bridge. About twenty miles north of Hatteras, which is where people pick up the ferry to come to Ocracoke."

Gwen forced a smile. "I guess they need Officer Jones to come down here to solve it for them."

He didn't appear to be listening. He was staring intently at his watch, as if time was suddenly critical. "We better hurry, Gwen. You can change in that room over there."

His urgency struck her as strange. The whole day he wouldn't let her get an arm's length from him, yet now he showed an eagerness to get rid of her. She knew that whatever the reason, the only way she would find answers would be to play along until he was in a more vulnerable and weakened state. She stood with her overnight bag, which contained the tools she hoped would do the weakening, and entered the bedroom.

She pulled a fuchsia-colored string bikini out of her bag, thinking that it was more string than bikini. All was fair in love and war, and this certainly wasn't the former.

CHAPTER 52

When he stepped into the master bedroom he became Batman. He overloaded with anticipation and began to sweat profusely. He opened a window and the breeze cooled him.

He was convinced that Gwen had no idea that he was aware of her betrayal when he found her earring in his yard, in a patch of poison ivy. *Leave me a note? Do I seem that stupid, Gwen?* But it was to his advantage to keep it that way. He also knew he had a weak spot for her that he'd never had for anyone before. He would have to fight off the temptation. It would be his toughest test in completing his mission.

He walked into the closet and parted the clothing. His necklace began to vibrate—his warning system working perfectly.

Once he completed the code for the combination lock, he opened the heavy door and strutted into the musty room. He flipped a light switch and the room filled with dim light. He took a plastic, three-ring binder from a small bookcase. As he held the sacred book, his hands began to shake. He waited for the shaking to cease, and then added his new entries into the binder, which told the cautionary tale of Noah Warner.

He understood that he'd be hailed as a hero in future years, which was why it was so important to chronicle his journey. But until that day of acceptance, he faced the reality of having to do his work in the dark, just as Batman had.

He moved to the pictures on the wall, once again feeling the heavy burden of responsibility. He removed the cap of this black pen and proceeded to mark a large **X** over the photograph of Noah Warner. He did it in slow motion to prolong the ecstasy.

But there was only a brief moment to savor the accomplishment. There was so much more work to be done, and he immediately focused on his next mission. It would be less than two weeks from today, on October 10.

He knelt down in ritualistic fashion, as he always did during the "Crossing Off Ceremony." He thought of the Spargo family and wished they could have shared this moment with him.

A knock on the bedroom door stunned him back to reality, followed by the sound of Gwen's voice, "Kyle, are you in here?"

He wiped the tears off his face and raced out of the storm room. But before he did, he grabbed a small box. It would give Gwen the surprise of her life. What was left of it, anyway.

CHAPTER 53

Carter removed his wraparound sunglasses to view the sign before him: *Hatteras Ferry*.

JP sat in the passenger seat, asking questions like a nervous mother. "Are you sure you got the directions to his house? ... Are you sure you don't want me to come with you? ... Do you want to go over the plan one more time?"

"Thanks, Mom."

"This isn't funny, her life could be at stake."

Carter couldn't contain his laughter. "I haven't seen you this in love with a woman in ... well, actually, I've never seen you this in love with a woman."

"She's out there all alone with a murderer. I'd do this for anybody."

"Whatever you say, boss."

Carter thought that Plan Gwen would achieve similar results as JP's genius idea to break into Jones' house. So he offered what he thought was a better solution, which would be to just kill Jones and hide the body. But he got outvoted—confirming his belief that democracy was overrated.

JP added his own amendment to Gwen's plan, sending Carter as her personal bodyguard to shadow her. A change that Gwen knew nothing about, and if they wanted to continue to live, it was best it remain that way. It was clear to Carter that Cupid's crossbow had delivered a direct hit so far up JP's ass that he couldn't think straight.

They'd departed Connecticut over twenty-four hours ago with the cover-story of going to visit Byron. They were pretty sure Gwen bought it. They stopped Friday evening in Washington DC, before continuing on the next morning.

"Let's go over the plan one more time," JP said.

Carter sighed. "I got it. Take the ferry over and hitch a ride to the village. Spy on Gwen and her boyfriend until Sunday. Then we meet up Monday night over there." He pointed at the small, replica sloop pirate ship that was anchored to the dock. It had been converted into a restaurant/bar called Sloopy Joe's.

"Are you sure you don't want me to go with you?"

"Never been more sure about anything in my life. Besides, they'll probably spend the whole weekend cozying up in his bedroom." Carter took pleasure in his friend's wince, then mercifully—for JP—changed the subject, "I can't believe you've never been to Charleston."

"I think it's the only place on the planet I haven't been to. I'm looking forward to my first Mama Jasper's meal. Although, I'm not sure it could ever live up to the hype that Byron has bestowed on it."

"Like myself, Mama Jasper's is one of the few things in this world that lives up to the hype." Carter began to drool just thinking about it. "And so does Charleston. My dad, rest his soul, used to take me down there all the time—a lot of military history in those parts. We used to always go to Fort Sumter, and tour the aircraft carrier the Yorktown."

JP slid over to the driver's side, while Carter exited the vehicle into a drenching Saturday sun and the smell of low tide.

"And be inconspicuous," JP yelled last instructions.

"Is that a fancy French word for Carter gets to kill someone?"

"No, stay hidden—camouflaged—concealed."

"In other words, don't let Gwen find out, or our balls will be on the chopping block."

"Just make sure she is safe, okay?"

He gave JP a thumbs-up sign and headed for the ferry docking station. JP backed up the Humvee, beginning his journey to Charleston so that Byron could babysit him. Carter thought he should take a detour and head straight to the loony bin.

Carter hid behind the ticket booth as he waited for the ferry, playing a hunch. The first ferry came and went, but he remained. Moments later, his instincts proved correct. When the man came around the corner, Carter drove his forearm into his larynx, dropping him to the pavement. "Where do you think you're going?"

JP looked dazed. He tried to talk, but nothing came out.

Carter picked him up by his hair. "Maybe my directions weren't clear—my bad—Charleston is the other way."

JP returned to the Humvee. This time Carter was sure he was on his way.

The Hatteras Ferry took forty-five minutes to arrive on Ocracoke. Once on the island, Carter found a taxi to take him to the village. They drove along a two-lane road lined with dunes and marshland grasses.

According to the driver, the hub of activity was in the Silver Lake Village. That's where Carter began his reconnaissance mission, and worked his way to the north shore beach, where Jones owned a home.

He doubted Gwen was in danger. He knew a few things about men and women, one of which was that a man doesn't kill a woman like Gwen Delaney as long as he thinks she's his. It's when the man finds out his woman is with another man that she's in trouble. He got the feeling that Gwen was smart enough to realize that.

He also doubted Jones was stupid enough to bring a journalist into his home if he had incriminating evidence spread out on the coffee table. So he was skeptical as to whether he would find anything inside. But the other thing he knew, was that hot women make guys do stupid things. So anything was possible.

Carter waited at a distance for someone to show. He'd never bought into the whole 'patience was a virtue' thing—he thought it was a waste of time, literally. He was tempted to open up one of the Coronas he had brought along, knowing this job had death-by-boredom written all over it.

As dusk settled over the island, Jones finally showed up with Gwen. They arrived by foot from the beach, walked under the house, and ascended stairs to a front entrance.

Carter smiled. Let the games begin.

CHAPTER 54

When Jones opened the door, his eyes popped out of his head—mission accomplished. Score one for the over thirty crowd, Gwen thought. Actually the *way over* thirty crowd.

She'd been suspicious of the long silence coming from his room. The reporter in her knew he was up to something, while intuition told her it would be an ideal time to catch him off guard. So she stepped into his room.

"Wow," was all he was able to stammer. But while she'd like to take all the credit for his nervousness, she believed it had begun before her entrance.

Gwen gritted her teeth and played the sex kitten. "I thought I'd give you a little surprise for our boat trip. I hope you like it."

He wiped the sweat from his forehead. "I like it, but where's the rest of it?"

She walked up to him and gave him a kiss on the cheek that she held for a couple extra seconds. "I'll take that as a compliment. Now I think you owe me a romantic night on the lake."

Before he could protest, she was pulling him toward the door.

Once outside, the cool night air made her re-think wearing just the bikini. Fortunately, she'd brought along her lucky Columbia sweatshirt—she could use all the good luck she could get—and slipped it on. The bikini was no longer visible, but she felt it was still quite vivid in the mind of Kyle Jones. She had softened him up, and now it was time to get answers.

They drove in his pickup truck, pulling the boat. Gwen nuzzled up next to him, which made her feel queasy. The salty breeze swirled through the open window of the truck. Part of her wanted the wind to whisk her away like Dorothy.

Jones launched the sailboat from a commercial marina. Not a soul in sight, which further frayed Gwen's nerves. He navigated the dark harbor until he found a spot to drop anchor. No other boats were in the area and she was questioning her wisdom, along with her sanity. But the show must go on. "This is beautiful, Kyle—absolutely beautiful!"

"A lot of history in these waters."

"Really, like what?" she acted enthused.

"We are over the exact spot that legend says the pirate Blackbeard was sent to his death."

Gwen had heard of Blackbeard, but she was no expert, as most of her knowledge had come from those Johnny Depp movies.

He continued, "He was beheaded by Lieutenant Robert Maynard of the Royal Navy. Some people think he still lives on the bottom of the lake, and haunts it."

Gwen fought off thoughts of Jones using similar methods to rid himself of his victims. "I'm so happy, Kyle. To be in such a beautiful spot with the man I love. Thank you for such a great day."

He turned serious. "Are you sure I'm the only man in your life?"

"What do you mean?"

"I'm talking about JP Warner."

"JP and I are just friends."

"What about when I saw the two of you off the other night in your van? I checked with the hospital and nobody on the staff could validate that you were there that night. I'm not stupid, Gwen!"

"He's been going through a rough time. He was captured by terrorists, lost his brother, and then received a public beating by a former colleague. He needed a friend. I've known him since he was five years old—please don't make me choose between you."

Jones grew more agitated. He rose to his feet, almost losing his balance on the bobbing boat. "I just get really jealous when I see you with him. I wish you wouldn't see him."

Gwen stood and walked carefully to him. She'd never felt so vulnerable in her life. "Kyle, you are the man in my life. JP is the past. He's the one who should be jealous of you, not the other way around."

He peered at Gwen with a chilling look.

"What about your old girlfriend in Arizona? What was her name—Lucy something-or-other? Maybe I should be the jealous one."

"How do you know about Lucy?"

"You told me about her," she replied, trying to sound casual.

"I never told you about Lucy."

"How else would I ever know about some old girlfriend of yours? I'm a good reporter, but not *that* good. I don't even know her last name."

"Are you prying into my past, Gwen?"

"No different than you checking with the hospital about me. But if you have nothing to hide, then why are you so upset? I thought you said I could trust you, Kyle? I went out on a limb to tell you about Betsy O'Rourke being involved in the Leeds case."

He took a deep breath. "You can, Gwen ... I'm sorry. I just have never felt this way about a woman before, and I guess it makes me a little crazy."

A little?

"Not even Holly from the bowling alley?"

"Not the way I feel about you."

"Then why can't you just say you love me, Kyle Jones? Do you love me?"

"Of course."

"Say it."

"Say what?"

"Say you love me. I need to hear the words."

A strange look came over his face. Most of his looks were either placid or creepy, but this one she never saw before. "I'll do better than that." He reached into his pocket and pulled out the small jewelry box. He then knelt down on the boat deck. "Gwen Delaney, will you marry me?"

She stood silent, but horrified. *She sure didn't count on this.* She didn't know what to do—she had to say something.

As she attempted to stutter an answer, she was rescued by the ring of her phone.

"Don't answer it," Jones pleaded.

Gwen was torn and nervous. "It might be about Tommy," she said and took the call. On the other end was JP. He'd saved her again.

Gwen spoke into the phone, "I'm fine, thanks for asking … we're out on a boat on Silver Lake … in Ocracoke Island where Kyle lives … I'm fine, just a little tired … I'm in the middle of something, can I call you back? … Okay … talk to you later."

She ended the call, and looked at Jones. "It was my father."

He angrily shut the ring box. "Don't lie to me, Gwen. That was *him.*" He rose from his kneeling position and turned his back to her.

Gwen moved over to him, struggling with her footing on the bobbing boat. She rested her hand tenderly on his shoulder. "You are right, Kyle, it was JP. But that doesn't change how I feel about you. Maybe it was just a sign from above that we're not ready for marriage."

He pushed her hand away. His shoulders slumped as he moved to the anchor and began to hoist it.

"Come on, Kyle—it's such a beautiful night."

"We must go," he said, still refusing to look at her.

"Back to your house?"

"No, back to Rockfield. I just have to pick up a few things at the house and then we can leave."

"Please don't be angry with me, Kyle. Let's stay."

"Don't talk to me, Gwen," he said in a hurt voice.

CHAPTER 55

After about thirty minutes, the "lovebirds" came out of the house. Gwen wore a string bikini that made the trip worth it for Carter. But then she put on a baggy sweatshirt. There was always a catch.

They left the house in his pickup truck with sailboat trailing behind. Carter knew if he planned to kill her on the water, there was nothing he could do about it. So he stayed behind to check out the insides of the beach house.

He wasn't sure how he would get in. That was, until he noticed that Jones did him a favor by cracking open his bedroom window. The sloppiness didn't seem to match JP's scouting report on Jones. Perhaps that bikini was messing with his mind.

He scaled the outside of the house, using a paracord climbing-rope he always kept in his backpack. He normally used it to tie people up, both enemies and girlfriends, more so than climbing. Also in the pack were his videophone, a gun (in case Jones came back), and a few bottles of beer (in case he didn't).

Within ten minutes, he was standing in the master bedroom. He noticed nothing out of the ordinary, so he walked out to the main area of the house. Nothing unusual—just as he thought. He did a sweep of the bathroom, along with the other bedrooms. He only found Gwen's bag, and her clothes folded neatly on the bed.

Carter was convinced the house was clean. He also knew that if they went sailing, they'd be gone for a while. He had time. He popped open a bottle of Corona with his teeth and sat on a chair in the living room. Part of him hoped Jones would return, so he could gain some payback for their last meeting. The thought made him grin.

When he finished the beer, he decided to move on to his next mission—to find out if Ocracoke had any strip clubs—and returned to the master bedroom with plans to exit out of the same window he entered.

As he walked through the bedroom, something pulled him toward the closet area. A sixth sense that had developed from his many years spent in the danger zone.

He stepped in the closet and moved the clothes out of the way, expecting to find someone hiding. Maybe Jones had a partner in crime. But what he found was a door with a complicated lock scheme. A piece of wood paneling was missing—obviously Jones wanted to keep this room secret. Which begged the question: why would he put so much effort into securing the room, yet leave it cracked open? He was pretty sure the credit should go to Gwen's bikini.

Carter entered the room. It was small, eight by eight, and dark. He found a light switch and flipped it on. The photos on the wall illuminated. Some he knew, some he didn't. The **Xs** drawn over the faces weren't subtle.

Carter continued to scan the photos and remembered JP telling about the unlucky fireman named Casey Leeds. Another picture was a friend of a friend, which puzzled him. *Didn't he die in a freak accident in front of numerous witnesses?*

The picture of Senator Craig Kingsbury with his face crossed out dropped his mouth. But then his logical side kicked in, and he grew skeptical. It was unlikely a small town cop could get so close to a US senator. *He must have been celebrating their deaths with his hit list, but involvement in some wasn't possible.*

He walked to a cork bulletin board. It was full of push-pinned newspaper articles about the members from Jones' wall of fame. Some were old and had turned a shade of yellow. The most recent were a *New York Times* article on the demise of Craig Kingsbury and the *Rockfield Gazette* story on the death of Noah Warner.

The article refocused Carter on Noah's photo. He was captivated by the resemblance to JP. He could smell the fresh smell of magic marker and his anger boiled once more.

The only piece of furniture in the room was a cheap, plastic bookshelf. On it sat a three-ringed binder. Carter placed his backpack next to the bookshelf and picked up the binder. He opened it and began to read. It was quite a page-turner, to say the least.

Any doubts of Jones' involvement evaporated. It detailed each murder in horrific detail, outlining his deepest thoughts, perverted reasons, and sickening joy of the acts. Unless Jones was writing fiction, he was more than some small town menace—he was on his way to becoming one of the most notorious murderers in history!

Carter turned to the section describing the death of Noah:

It was my duty. It was my destiny. I honor the great master who sent me to Rockfield, having confidence that I would be the one who could eliminate an evil force like Noah Warner. I was invigorated when he fought. It made it extra special that he wanted to live. I would have killed him the previous year, but he wanted to die last year.

Carter decided he would wait until Jones returned and rip his head from his body. But when he set the binder down, his sixth sense perked up again.

Then everything went dark.

CHAPTER 56

Batman remained stoic as he applied the sharp snap of the stick to the back of the behemoth's neck. He dropped to the floor like a wounded Woolly Mammoth, barely conscious. Two more blows put him out cold.

Taking no chances, he placed masking tape over his mouth, and handcuffed his arms behind his back.

He reverently caressed his vibrating necklace. Once again it didn't let him down. But he was angry with himself for not securing the room—too drawn by the temptation of Gwen. He vowed that would be the last time he would fail that test.

"Kyle, are you okay? What was that noise?" his temptress called from the kitchen.

He thought for a second. Was she working with Carter? Did she use her seductiveness to lure him away from the house so that her partner could search it? She did plead with him to stay out on the boat.

He would get his answers. And when he did, he would take pleasure in adding her to the wall with an X slashed through her pretty face. But for now he saw how she could be very helpful to him.

He didn't have time to rid the world of Carter. He would have to return for that. When he gave him one last kick in the ribs, the unconscious giant didn't even flinch. This time he made sure the room was secure and headed toward the living room.

"It was nothing—are you ready to go? The taxi is here," he told Gwen in an emotionless voice.

"Kyle—I am so sorry—please, let's stay."

He refused to even look at her. They walked out to a waiting cab in silence. Within half an hour, they were on a flight heading back to Rockfield.

CHAPTER 57

Charleston, South Carolina

October 2

I drove the Humvee along the cobblestone streets of Charleston, passing horse drawn carriages and stately mansions. I finally gave up the idea of finding parking along the street and entered a parking garage north of Broad Street.

With help of my cane, I headed by foot toward the Waterfront Battery Park on an idyllic seventy-five degree October day.

From the quaint alleyways to the majestic steeples, Charleston gave off the historic feel of another era. I passed a pineapple-shaped fountain that welcomed me to the park. My steps were slowed by apprehension, spotting the white gazebo where I was to meet Byron.

The sight of him trapped in a wheelchair tainted the perfect day for me. It just didn't look right. And I was struck by the irony of the strongest man I knew, both physically and mentally, constricted by a chair.

Behind the chair was his mother, known affectionately as Mama Jasper. Standing to Byron's left was his long time girlfriend, Tonya. It didn't surprise me she stood by him in such a troubling time. It would have surprised me if she hadn't. Not only was she beautiful—often mistaken for Tyra Banks—but also one of the most loyal and supportive people I've met. It's not easy to find someone who understands the crazy business that we chose. Byron found a good one.

Mama Jasper was a large woman, but she wore her weight proudly. She was the first to spot me and gave me an enthusiastic "over here" wave. I felt a fleeting sense of relief to see the friendly smiles. When I reached the group, Mama Jasper gave me a big hug that knocked the breath out of me. Tonya followed with a much gentler one.

The last embrace came from Byron. Attempting to get my arms around a man strapped to a chair was an awkward movement, but even more so for me, since I knew I was the one responsible for him being in that chair.

Because he always thought of others first, he first said, "I'm so sorry about Noah."

I nodded a thank you, but was unable to shake my feeling of guilt, which Byron picked up on. "Do you remember what we talked about in the hospital?"

"I just wish it happened to me instead of you."

Byron laughed so hard I thought he was going to tip over. "JP, God only gives people what they can handle. You couldn't handle this."

He was right.

"Besides, I can still beat you one-on-one. When you can beat me on the basketball court, *then* I'll be handicapped."

Everyone laughed, except Mama Jasper. Overcome by emotion, she was busy wiping tears from her cheeks.

"Thank you so much, JP, for what you and Carter did with the renovations. I don't know how I can ever repay you," she said in a deep voice, seasoned with a southern accent.

I tried to speak, but she wrapped me in another affectionate hug, crushing my diaphragm. "You don't have to repay me," I replied the best I could.

"Maybe not, JP Warner, but you ain't leaving Charleston without gettin' a meal at Mama Jasper's ... on the house."

Byron had bought the restaurant for her—her dream—when he signed his first NFL contract, allowing her to leave her job as a seamstress. I kept saying for years that I would make a trip there, but instead, I found myself eating with her son in places like Beirut and Sarajevo.

Tonya, with her gentle style, pulled Mama Jasper away. "What do you say, Mama, that we leave the boys alone and go do some shopping?"

She agreed, but not before delivering last words, "I expect you two at Mama Jasper's at six o'clock sharp."

We nodded our heads like obedient children and watched the two women walk away.

Always the reporter, I had noticed the large rock on Tonya's finger. "Is there something you're not telling me, my friend?"

"I don't know what you are talking about."

"Are you getting married?"

"I almost forgot that I was talking to the great J-News. Yes, we got engaged the night before we left for Serbia," Byron said, unable to hold back a grin. "I would have told you on our trip, but those terrorists tied my gag a little tight."

We slapped hands—it was the best two crippled men could do to celebrate.

"I'm taking the plunge," Byron said, as I took the pushing position behind him. "I guess I couldn't run away anymore." He tapped the sides of the metal wheelchair to make his point, and then snorted a laugh.

I was too conflicted to see the humor. I was glad he couldn't see my face, and notice the tear roll down my cheek. After collecting myself, I asked, "So what did Mama say when you told her?"

"When the hugging ended, she said it's about time."

"I'm happy for you two, and *it is* about time. She's beautiful, smart, and loyal. There are like six of them in the world."

"Is Gwen Delaney one of the six?"

I wasn't going to touch that one. "Somebody's been talking to Carter. Let's get out of here."

I handed Byron my cane and pushed him toward the waterfront. "Don't you need it?" he asked.

"Not as much as I thought."

We traveled alongside the calm waters of Charleston Harbor, made our way through the battery, and began to move up Meeting Street. We stopped for a moment to admire Calhoun Mansion, one of Byron's personal favorites.

We returned to South Battery Street and went east two blocks, passing one old mansion after another. We stopped for a moment so I could rest my still-healing lungs. I used the time to dial Gwen's number, but once again received no answer. I still couldn't believe she was out on the lake with that lunatic, and not having heard from her since our brief call last night, she was making me more nuts than usual.

As we made a right on Church Street, Byron spoke excitedly about the foundation he started to try to cure spinal cord injuries. By the time we passed Catfish Row, I was convinced that he would.

"If anyone can it will be you, Byron."

He shook his head. "No JP, I will play a role, but you should have seen these brilliant doctors I talked to yesterday. They're getting close!"

"But I'm sure, like anything else, it'll cost money. I'd like to help out with the fundraising."

"Appreciate it, but on one condition."

"You're putting conditions on my money?"

"The condition is that you let me help solve your brother's murder."

The request sobered me. "If I can think of anything, you know I'll call you. A lot depends on ..."

"What Carter and your girl find in Ocracoke?" Byron cut me off. "I can hear the anxiety in your voice, JP."

"I'm just worried about her. It was a crazy idea to try to bait him. Jones has killed before, and you know as well as I do, if you kill once then you'll kill twice. She's lost her mind."

"Just a dumb enough plan to sound like something JP Warner would have come up with."

I had no argument for that one. "This guy Jones is a mystery. I feel like the answers are right in front of my face, but I just can't see them."

"Sometimes you just need a fresh set of eyes, which I can provide. And JP ..."

"Yeah?"

"She's going to be fine."

I sure hoped so. "It's almost six. We better get to your mother's restaurant."

"Or we won't be fine."

As I began to push him toward Mama Jasper's, he added, "And one more thing."

"Which is?"

"If I ever catch you shedding a tear on my behalf again, I'm going to give you a reason to cry."

I nodded.

While holding back a tear.

CHAPTER 58

I pushed Byron toward Mama Jasper's, which sat on a popular congregating spot along the busy Meeting Street.

"So why did you decide to call it Rubber-Band Foundation?" I asked him.

"My old teammate Leonard Harris with the Cardinals. After he was in the accident that killed those girls, he dedicated his life to them. His philosophy was that since he was responsible for taking their lives, it was his duty to live their lives for them in a symbolic way.

"He wasn't a perfect man by any standard, but well-intentioned. He wore a rubber band as a symbol of the accident. The elastic reminded him of how fragile life was and how it could snap at anytime. I think that's a good symbol for our organization," Byron said, snapping the red rubber band around his wrist. It broke, which made his point.

We entered Mama Jasper's to the aroma of she-crab soup mixed with sizzling fried chicken. My senses were in overload, reminding me that I hadn't eaten since yesterday.

Mama Jasper's was a converted warehouse. It was a casual, but elegant restaurant that still had the feel of a small diner. Mama met us at the doorway with a smile. Her smile was Byron's smile, and it swelled with pride. She paraded us through the restaurant as if we were foreign dignitaries. Byron shook hands with numerous patrons like he was running for office. Many he knew, some he didn't, but everybody knew him. I continued to be ignored, but gained instant credibility by the company I was keeping. The Jaspers were like Charleston nobility, and Byron was a rock star here.

The walls were lined with grand oil paintings of Charleston history, with an emphasis on the black history of the region. The highlight of my tour was a rare meeting with the chef, which according to Byron, was the highest honor given by Mama. It was like I was knighted. Sir JP and Sir Byron were then seated in the large VIP room in the back. Tonya was there waiting for him.

"Are you tired, baby?" she greeted him.

"Why would I be tired? JP did all the pushing."

I moved toward the wall, where I could get a closer look at the large framed team photos of Byron's football teams, displayed chronologically. This was the unofficial Byron Jasper Hall of Fame.

The team photos ranged from when he was in Pee Wee League to his last season with the Cardinals. The early photos were taken in black and white film. I got a kick out of the size of Byron's afro in the photos from high school. In college he met Tonya and the hair got cut off.

I casually studied each one until I came upon the photo from 1995. I was drawn to a particular man in the photo. He wasn't in uniform, so perhaps he was one of the many coaches or trainers. I realized that of all the people who looked at that photo over the years, probably none of them noticed the nondescript man hidden within a group of professional football players.

At first I didn't believe what my eyes were telling me. So I took a closer look. Byron and Tonya stopped their lovey-dovey conversation and focused their attention in my direction. I'm sure I looked strange putting my face right up to the photo.

"You need glasses, man?" Byron called out.

I took a step back, feeling dizzy. I looked under the picture where the names were listed from left to right. I traced my index finger across the line of typed names until I got to the man. *Grady Benson.*

"Are you okay, JP?" Tonya asked.

My mind was spinning so fast that it sounded like she was miles away. "Byron get over here."

"Can't exactly walk, man."

"Get over here!"

He wheeled over to my side. "What's going on?"

"Who is Grady Benson?"

"Grady Benson?"

I impatiently pointed at the man in question, jabbing the photo.

It rung a bell. "Oh, *that guy.* Remember when I told you about how Leonard was trying to turn his life around after the accident?"

"Yeah?"

"Leonard convinced the Cardinals he needed to travel with his 'spiritual adviser,' who was Benson. He gave him credit for turning his life around." Byron rolled his eyes. "Listen, I said he was a good dude, not a sane one. Anyway, Leonard led the league in sacks that year, so the Cardinals bent over backwards to please him. They gave this Benson guy a job with some made up title like Assistant Equipment Manager or something like that. Personally, I think he was some crackpot trying to take Leonard's money. He was always attracting those types."

"The accident where the two girls died was alcohol related, right?"

Byron looked quizzically at me. "You know that. What's the deal, JP?"

"Was Benson present the night Leonard Harris died?"

"I'm not sure, but my guess would be yes. They were inseparable. What's going on, JP?"

I turned back to the photo. "That's him," I mumbled.

"You're worrying me, man. What are you talking about?"

I looked down at Byron in his chair. "I thought Kyle Jones killed my brother, but he didn't."

"I'm completely lost."

I reached down and kissed Byron on the top of the head. "Remember when you said you wanted to help with the case. Well, you just solved it."

I buzzed with energy. "I gotta go," I said and quickly headed toward the door.

Mama Jasper simultaneously walked into the room and this time I gave her a big bear hug.

"Oh no you don't, JP Warner," she belted out.

But there was no stopping me. I was already halfway out the door.

"Don't forget your cane," Byron shouted.

I turned my head back to him, but never stopped. "You keep it—you'll need it for when you take those first steps."

Byron looked at the cane and then up at me. He just shook his head in disbelief.

PART FIVE-

KEEPIN' UP WITH THE JONES'

CHAPTER 59

Gilbert, Arizona

Memorial Day—1998

Kyle Jones entered the frigid air of his Arizona home, a major contrast from the triple-digit temperatures outside. He took a last look at the almost empty living room—just a few boxes remained.

He picked up the remaining items and headed out to the truck. The heat grabbed him and he felt momentarily lightheaded. The experts said it would be a summer dominated by home runs, heat waves, and a presidential sex scandal. McGwire already was pushing twenty homers, and the temperatures had hit triple-digits by Memorial Day. As for the sex scandal, Kyle hadn't got any action since breaking up with Lucy, so he wasn't about to begrudge someone who was.

The decision to move was not an easy one. He liked living in Gilbert, and enjoyed his work on the police force. But ever since his breakup with Lucy he felt less connected. And perhaps all the moving he did throughout his childhood had gotten in his blood.

He didn't have any specific plans, which was a major change from the structured life he'd lived. But he'd saved most of the money from the settlement that resulted from his parents' death, so he had some time to find his way. He would start by visiting them at Mount St. Helens, where their ashes were scattered. They always gave him good advice throughout his young life, and thought he might benefit from being in their presence once again. He would then travel to Lake Cumberland, Kentucky, where the accident occurred. It was his most favorite place in the world growing up, as it was for his parents, which was why they chose to retire there after leaving the Air Force. It was also the place where they were taken from him, and he felt he needed to make a final visit before moving on for good.

When he told Grady of his plans, Kyle was surprised by the unemotional response. He was a little hurt, actually, especially since he'd helped Grady get back on his feet. Not to mention the many years they'd spent together. Kyle offered to leave him six months' rent to allow time for him to find a new roommate, but he declined.

Kyle entered the house for the final time. He wrote Grady a note, in which he promised he'd send a forwarding address and phone number when he settled somewhere. It was not the way Kyle wanted to say goodbye, but Grady was gone again—speaking at another safety conference, which had become his passion since Leonard Harris' death. And a not-so-subtle reminder to Kyle that he should have done more to get justice for his own parents.

When he finished the note, Kyle entered his bedroom—the only things left to pack were a few items of clothing. He opened his suitcase and began taking shirts off hangers—neatly folding them, of course—and placing them in his bag.

On another trip to the closet, he found a few shirts belonging to Grady. They often traded clothing over the years. Their looks and builds were so similar that one of their squad leaders at Luke AFB used to always mix them up. Kyle didn't really see the resemblance, but nobody ever debated that their personalities were complete opposites.

Kyle carried the borrowed shirts into Grady's room and hung them in the closet. When he looked down, he noticed the journal that Grady began keeping after his suggestion to do so.

He knew he shouldn't read it, but was caught in one of those debates with the angel on one shoulder and the devil on the other. Grady was such a mystery to Kyle, and even after all their years together, he sometimes felt like he didn't really know him.

July 4, 1991

Timothy Kent was in my sights. I had waited for two years for this moment, but there is no statute of limitations on justice. Not only did Kent kill my parents, but he would now be responsible for the death of his girlfriend, and the Tompkins kid, who would play the role of lead suspect. The part I enjoyed most was the brief moment before the car split him in half. It was the look on his face. The look that told me he now understood his crime and that his punishment, while final, was also just.

Kyle urgently flipped the pages forward until another passage caught his eye.

July 4, 1996

My mission was clear. As I stood on the houseboat, I struggled to keep a straight face as Leonard Harris told me about how he'd changed his life. But I knew that like the leopard, evil couldn't change its spots. His alleged metamorphosis was just a trick to fool the public, and perhaps himself. It was no surprise to me when his hedonistic tendencies betrayed him during his final party. It was the same behavior that had led to him taking the lives of those two girls.

Kyle trembled and began to sweat, despite the high-powered air conditioning. Thoughts of calling the police entered his mind, as did the idea of running to his truck and hightailing it out of town. But he couldn't pull himself away from the macabre tale.

I stifled a laugh while the divers frantically searched for him, as if there was a chance Leonard was still alive. My heart raced, but at the same time I felt at peace. I could almost feel Kelly and Laura thanking me from heaven. It was truly the moment I was put on the planet for. I wish every day that my parents were still walking the earth, but that would be selfish of me. Because it was their tragic death that woke me to my destiny. From now to the end, I will mark July 4, 1989 with a sacrifice in their honor every Fourth of July.

Kyle's head spun out of control. Could this be some sort of delusion, or was it fiction? How could this be? Grady was weird, no question … but a killer? He backtracked pages and was drawn to another passage.

September 4, 1995

I have not written in this journal in over four years, but the actions of my roommate, Kyle Jones, and his girlfriend last night has caused my return. Ironically, it was Kyle who suggested I keep a journal, but what he didn't know is that he'd sparked me to return to a dormant one.

I thought the sacrifice of Timothy Kent would end the nightmares. But I learned in the last few days that it was just the beginning. The first sign came while watching a television program on a judge in North Carolina named Raymond Buford. Buford chose to defend the indefensible—drunk drivers. The second sign was Kyle arriving home after committing this very same act, with full knowledge of how my parents were killed. I looked into his eyes that night and saw that he'd gone to the dark side. From protector to enabler, betraying the vow we made to fight for justice.

Even though they didn't participate in the direct murder of another, the crimes of Buford and Kyle Jones were worse—using their position of power to circumvent the enforcement of the drinking and driving laws. Laws that are too light, anyway. My mission, I now know, is to rid the world of this evil. Those like Buford and Jones must be stopped.

Kyle read it again. *Must be stopped.* A lump formed inside his throat. Then a thin metal necklace wrapped around his neck. It was pulled back with strength and vengeance.

Kyle looked back to see Grady Benson in a trance-like state, his hands shaking as he squeezed the last breaths out of him.

CHAPTER 60

Kyle Jones collapsed to the ground, the journal landing beside him.

Batman had wanted to kill him on the Fourth of July, but Kyle's unscheduled plan to relocate had forced his hand. He always took out his prey on the anniversary of their misdeeds, so that the day would never be forgotten. He also made an annual sacrifice to his parents on the anniversary of their murder—July 4—a date he saved for the most heinous of the predators. There was much plotting and planning, sometimes for years. So this improvisation didn't feel right, even if it ended in proper fashion.

Batman knelt beside Jones' lifeless body. He caressed the silver necklace that he used to end his wretched life. It featured a locket that held photos of his parents. He had never felt so close to them.

Batman struggled to control his emotions, as there was not a minute to waste. The first move was to resolve the renter situation. He wrote a letter to the landlord, indicating that both Grady and Kyle had re-enlisted in the Air Force and would be leaving immediately. He included six months' rent and suggested the landlord keep the security deposit for the short notice. He signed Kyle's signature, which he had become quite adept at, and was sure they would never hear from the happy landlord ever again.

He rolled up Kyle's body in a rug and packed it into the back of the pickup truck. Then did a final sweep of the house—luckily the orderly Kyle had done a brilliant job of packing. The place was spotless. After loading the final items, Batman took a seat behind the wheel, put on his aviator sunglasses, and headed toward his next mission.

He would take on the identity of Kyle Jones from this point forward. He knew it wasn't a coincidence that he'd been placed so close to a police officer who was so similar in look and build. He was chosen, as was Kyle, but he chose not to heed the call.

As he drove across America, he couldn't stop thinking of the day that began this journey. It was July 4, 1989, and he was stationed in Germany. He tagged along with a few other members of his squadron to a viewing of the top rated US movie at the time, *Batman.*

He now knew it was a sign. Later that day he was called into his commander's office and told of his parents' murder. Just like Bruce Wayne, he would dedicate his life to fighting crime so nobody else had to go through what he did. He accepted his destiny, but understood that it would be a long and lonely road.

That didn't mean he didn't have help along the way. Having access to a police officer like Kyle Jones allowed him to more easily research his targets, like providing him the location of Leonard Harris' court ordered rehab. He had taken on Kyle's identity on numerous occasions, including when he bought Flip Tompkins his final beer with the credit card he'd gotten in Kyle's name. It might have been suspicious if Tompkins' death hadn't been ruled an accident.

Now he would become Kyle Jones full time. He had all the essentials— social security card, credit cards, driver's license. And access to Kyle's savings, which had been enhanced by the blood money he accepted from his parents' death. It should have been his first clue as to Kyle choosing to fight against him.

The photo identification was passable, but he planned on updating it when he arrived at his destination. He would get photos taken in Kyle's police uniform that was packed in the cab of the truck.

He also brought along Kyle's past—a box filled with numerous photos, including a picture of "Batman and Robin" in Iraq during Desert Storm that he signed for Kyle. *Wingmen Forever.* Although, he was painfully aware that nothing was forever.

One photo he wanted to toss to the side of the road, was one in which he and Lucy were standing together in the backyard, straining smiles as Kyle took their photo. But he had no choice but to take it with. He looked forward to the day he would remove her from this world.

He drove through the night, too excited to sleep until he landed on Ocracoke Island. The landing spot was not a coincidence. He knew Raymond Buford owned a vacation getaway on the island. He'd researched the judge extensively over the past year, gathering vital information, which he knew would make him easy prey.

One of his first acts in Ocracoke was to purchase a sailboat. He took it out on Silver Lake his first night on the island. He thought that since his old friend Kyle was so into military history, he would be disposed of in the same way that the Lieutenant Naval Commander Maynard dealt with Blackbeard.

It was unlikely that the body would ever be found, but if it was, it would be decomposed beyond recognition. Not that anyone would be looking for Kyle Jones, anyway, since he wasn't considered missing. But even if the body were discovered well preserved, murder by strangulation would be hard to prove. The only hope for investigators would be small hemorrhages under the skin, or a broken bone. He wasn't worried by such a long shot.

The next day he met with a realtor. She explained that it was the perfect time to buy, since the recent hurricanes had brought the prices down. But she assured him that government agencies would provide funding for a secure storm-proof room.

The third house he saw was the one he had to have. It was one of the typical beach houses seen along the Carolina coastline. The realtor was surprised he would be so interested in a house on the less glamorous north shore. It wasn't so much where it was, but who's home it was near.

The man now known as Kyle Jones first made contact with his new neighbor Judge Raymond Buford while walking alone on the tranquil beach, two days after he purchased his home. Buford was standoffish at first. But when he hinted at his true intent, Buford became friendlier.

During his intensive research, he'd uncovered a secret that the macho, Civil War loving judge went to great lengths to keep from the world—that his vacation home on Ocracoke was purchased to pursue the company of young men, away from the watchful eyes of his wife and colleagues.

The timing was perfect, as Buford had just come off a breakup with a police officer named Ron Culver. Benson earned the judge's trust, to the point that he revealed his role in a cover-up of a crime so revolting that Benson vowed to bring all involved to justice. And when he did, the date of the crime would be marked each year by future generations, as a warning to those who choose to prey on the innocent.

The date was October 10.

CHAPTER 61

Outer Banks, North Carolina

October 3—present

For the fifteen-gazillionth time since I left Charleston, I called Christina. This time she picked up.

"This better be good," she answered.

"Where the hell have you been?"

"Is this a booty call?"

"If you don't tell me where you were I'm gonna kick your booty out on the street."

She sighed. "I was at the library studying, and had my cell off. I have a big test tomorrow … can you get to the point?"

"I need you to find out every bit of information you can on a Grady Benson. All I know about him is he worked for the Arizona Cardinals in the mid-nineties, and he had a relationship with a player named Leonard Harris. I also need anything you can find that connects him with Jones—so far, I know they were in the Air Force together."

"Who is this guy?" Christina asked, suddenly interested—the future reporter in her shining through.

"He killed my brother."

"I thought that Jones dude killed your brother?"

"I was wrong."

A long silence came from her end of the line. "Christina?"

Silence

"Christina?"

"Sorry, I had to pick myself off the floor. It must be early because I thought I heard JP Warner say he was wrong."

"Just get me the information and call me ... please."

"And where exactly would I be calling?"

"I'm heading to North Carolina to pick up Carter."

"Oh yeah. I forgot you two Neanderthals are still on your *JP is a Jealous Idiot* tour. You should print up some T-shirts."

"I don't have time for this. Just get me the information."

Christina was smart enough to realize being a pushover in this situation might lead to more early morning calls. She was going to make me work for it. "I always thought you were just a typical pissed off old guy, JP. But now I understand."

"Understand what?"

"How much stuff you have bottled up inside you. Just tell Gwen you love her and get it over with. The whole overprotective, stalking, passive-aggressive thing you're trying to pull off is not big with the ladies."

She then got the last word by hanging up on me. She was getting better at this.

CHAPTER 62

I continued to drive through the wee hours of the morning. My mind had been on Benson since I'd left Charleston, but now my thoughts were only with Gwen. Our last contact was on Saturday night when she claimed to be out on the lake with him. I got no answer all day Sunday. I would have called in the FBI, CIA, and military to locate her, but I'd burned too many bridges to expect a helping hand. And Carter—her supposed bodyguard—was employing his usual avoidance tactics. He was really starting to piss me off.

I entered the Outer Banks at just after five in the morning. The sun began to rise over the Atlantic, cutting through the morning fog. My stomach growled; still craving the Mama Jasper's dinner that I'd missed out on. I drove straight to Sloopy Joe's, which was where I was supposed to meet Carter in about fourteen hours. But with my Grady Benson discovery, the game plan had changed.

I purchased a copy of the *Ocracoker* from a metal box outside, before "walking the plank" to enter. Once inside, I took a seat in a corner booth and opened my paper. The front page featured a story on the still-unsolved murder of Senator Craig Kingsbury. It might have been the biggest story in the Outer Banks since the Wright Brothers' first flight. I was just glad that there were no stories about an unidentified woman being fished out of the lake.

I ordered a plate of pancakes and did some people-watching, while plotting my next move. I eavesdropped on a group of older men in the booth beside me who were talking proudly about what they deemed a safer time— World War II. The ring of my phone interrupted my thoughts.

"Oh my god, JP!" Christina screamed from the other end. "I have his military file in front of me, which includes his official photo. Jones is Benson!"

"How about telling me something I don't know," I replied with disinterest. But truth be told, I was impressed that she was able to get his file. I had come up empty with my military sources.

"Grady Benson is forty-two years old. Born and raised in a suburb of San Diego. He's an only child. Following high school he joined the Air Force, and flew bombing missions during the first Gulf War. About this time, his father took a job with Boeing in the Seattle area. His parents were killed … can you guess how?"

Nothing new, except he was a few years older than I thought. "Let me take a wild stab—drunk driving?"

"Well done, JP. As strange as it is to say, that's the good news. The bad news is the driver was a juvenile, so his records are sealed."

"Whoever he was, I'll bet he's dead. Keep working to see if you can get a name. What was the date of the accident?"

I could hear Christina typing away. "I know it was 1989, let me check on the month." She quickly found it. "July 4."

I tried to locate a pattern. Leeds was killed on the Fourth of July, but Noah was September. It was still not a connected dot.

"When was Leonard Harris killed?"

After some more typing, she said, "Leonard Harris died on July 4, 1996. People sure seem to be accident prone on Independence Day."

"Was Benson present when Harris died?"

"I'm a college student with access to my landlord's computer, and a couple of data networks, not an intelligence officer."

"When life gives you lemons ..."

"Ask for the salt and tequila."

"What I really need to know is when did Benson become Jones, and is there a real Kyle Jones out there who's had his identity stolen?"

Christina emailed a copy of the Air Force photos. When I viewed them on my phone, I understood why Kyle Jones would be the perfect target for Benson. They had similar looks and backgrounds. My best guess was they met in the Air Force, and Christina soon confirmed my theory.

"Benson and Jones were together at a couple of stops along the way, and flew together in the Gulf War. Their last stop together in the military was at Luke Air Force Base in Arizona, where they were stationed for a couple of years. After being discharged, Jones became a police officer in the neighboring town of Gilbert and rented a house on Ash Street."

"I know all about Jones," I said impatiently. "I need more about Benson. And is there any way to connect them besides their military service?"

"I'm looking at some phone and electric bills from the late 90s. Guess who also lived in the house on Ash?"

I smiled. "Benson."

"And they say you are washed up."

"Excuse me?"

"Hey, don't shoot the messenger."

"When did they move out?"

"Neither of them was the owner of the home, so I assume they were renting. The owner sold the house back in 2003. The final bills from either Benson or Jones—electric, phone, cable—connected to the Ash residence was June of 1998. Coincidentally, Kyle Jones bought a house on Ocracoke Island in North Carolina later that same month."

"Have you found any record of Grady Benson after he moved out?"

"He's totally off the grid, so I think it would be safe to assume that Benson stole Jones' identity, and then got rid of the real Kyle Jones,"

Christina said, but then thought for a moment. "Or do you think they are working in tandem?"

I'd never thought about that possibility. Jones did seem to be everywhere, and moved with the speed of two men. But I chose to concentrate on what we did know.

We now had visual proof that Benson was Jones, and could make a reasonable assumption that the real Kyle Jones was no longer, but had no proof of such. It was also confirmed that Benson's parents were killed by a drunk driver, which would provide his motive. A nice start, but there were many more questions, and to answer them I would have to follow the Murray philosophy—return to the beginning of the story to figure out the ending.

CHAPTER 63

I loaded the Humvee onto the Hatteras Dock ferry for the forty-minute trip to Ocracoke. The morning looked brilliant, but out on the choppy water a brisk wind was knifing through me. The warm sunlight on my face was the lone thing keeping it bearable. I caught my reflection in the window of a neighboring vehicle, and I barely recognized myself—I looked like I hadn't slept in a month. But there was no time to rest until I got to Gwen.

I tried to reach her again and was surprised that she answered this time. I'd become so used to getting the voice-mail that it caught me off guard.

"Where have you been? Didn't you get my messages?"

"Hello to you, too. Yes, I got all fifty of them. But yesterday was Sunday, JP. I know you wouldn't know anything about this, since you worked for GNZ, where the assistants have assistants, but I'm the whole show at the *Gazette*. I write it, edit it, and on Sunday's I *deliver it*."

"I was worried about you, so sue me. You said you'd call me back when I talked to you Saturday night. I hadn't heard from you in thirty-six hours. And what the hell were you thinking going out on the lake with that monster?"

"I couldn't talk, JP. I was in the middle of getting proposed to."

My stomach sank. That, or it was just seasickness. Either way, I suddenly didn't feel well. "Did you accept?"

I'm sure she was tempted to tell me she had, but I think she felt the urgency in my voice. "I told him I wasn't ready and he didn't take it well. He got all bent out of shape and we returned to Rockfield that night. Haven't heard from him since."

"I'm not sure you need to follow Jones anymore. I figured out who he is, and his motivation. The next step is to find evidence to put him away."

"Are you going to let me in on this or are you going to try to out scoop me, as usual?"

She obviously hadn't checked the latest mark on my personal growth chart. "I can't go into the details right now. I'll tell you all about it when I get back to Rockfield. In the meantime, research a man named Grady Benson. Be sure to take a look at his Air Force photo, I'll email it to you."

"Have you left Charleston yet?"

"I'm in Ocracoke to pick up Carter. We should be home early tomorrow."

Maybe it was the lack of sleep, or that I never think straight when I'm talking to Gwen. But it wasn't until I heard the deathly silence from her end that I knew I made a major oops.

"What is Carter doing in Ocracoke?"

I got the feeling that she had a pretty good idea what the answer was. Just because she had the evidence didn't mean she didn't want to hear a confession.

"Well ... um ... well ..."

"I thought we were going to trust each other ... like partners. I can't believe you sent your bodyguard to spy on me."

"The only person who can't be trusted is Jones."

"You're the one with trust issues, JP."

"I was worried about you."

"The only person you were worried about was yourself!"

Click.

I couldn't help but to smile. Not only was I relieved that she was safe, but it was nice to know I could still get under her skin.

The ferry arrived on Ocracoke exactly forty minutes after it left the Hatteras dock. I then drove the Humvee onto the sandy roads of NC-12—my injured leg throbbed with pain and I felt a little naked without my cane. The initial adrenaline of the Grady Benson discovery had worn off and I now stood at the crossroads where hope and reality collided.

I used the lighthouse to guide me to the village. That's where most of the island life resided, so I was sure I'd find Carter there. He was genetically programmed to seek out a crowd.

I searched bars, restaurants, stores, and beaches—no sign of him.

I continued to search in vain for hours, before deciding to go right to the source—Jones/Benson's house on the island. I called Christina and followed her directions to a remote sandy road on the north shore of Silver Lake.

Just like the owner, the house was unremarkable. A weathered structure balancing on wooden stilts. A red pickup truck with an attached sailboat was parked underneath. I decided to go the breaking-and-entering route once again.

I studied the house, noticing an open window on the second floor. I was in no condition to scale a wall, but gritted my teeth and managed to use crevices in the exterior to climb to the window, wincing the entire way.

Once inside, I began searching each room, emptying drawers one by one, and investigating every nook and cranny. The place was clean. No Carter. Nothing incriminating. Then I almost jumped out of my skin, startled by the ringing of my cell. It was Gwen, and her tone had completely changed.

"JP, I just received an anonymous letter from someone who claims to have Carter, and says if we don't back off he will be killed."

I racked my brain. I ruled out almost all of our enemies, including Az Zahir and his buddies. There was only one true suspect.

"It's got to be Jones."

"You mean Grady Benson?"

"You got my email, I see."

"I have the photo on my laptop right now," she said, her voice quivering. "But if Carter was in Ocracoke like you say, and I was with Kyle … I mean Grady, the whole time. Then who …"

I continued to stand in the master bedroom, suddenly feeling a little paranoid. "Was there any point during the day that you were not with him?"

"There was only about a ten minute period when we were changing to go out on the boat. I found it strange it took so long after he was so eager to launch the boat before dark. I got the feeling that he was hiding something in his bedroom."

"I'm in there right now," I said. I could tell Gwen was surprised I'd broken in. I don't know why, she'd known me since we were five.

I searched the entire room again, including under the bed and in the closet, finding nothing. If Grady Benson was smart enough to maintain an alternate identity all these years, he surely wasn't stupid enough to leave a trail at any of his homes. What was clear, was that I needed to return to Rockfield—I knew that was where the next battle was to take place.

But before leaving, I decided that if Benson was sending messages, it wouldn't be polite not to return the favor. I tossed all his clothing on the floor and threw a chair through the sliding glass door. I departed through the gaping hole and down the front steps.

It made me feel good. I finally realized it's better to get things out into the open. Keeping things inside just builds resentment and hard feelings.

CHAPTER 64

I drove to the airfield, where I was told no flights were available. When I offered a pilot a couple of grand for a trip, with my vehicle to be used as collateral, suddenly a flight opened up. Funny how that works.

I arrived at Oxford Airport two hours later, a small, private airport near Rockfield. Gwen greeted me with a long hug that surprised me. When we finally pulled away from the embrace, she capped off the intimate moment by letting me know that I didn't smell good. She had a point—I hadn't changed clothes or showered since Friday morning.

As we walked toward her van, I breathed in the cool air of New England autumn. A sharp contrast from the mild Carolina temperatures.

"Where is your cane?" she asked

"I decided I didn't need it anymore, so I gave it to Byron."

"Did your doctor also decide that?"

My silence answered her question, and she shook her head as if I was a lost cause.

Once in the van, Gwen handed me the typed letter. It didn't shed any new light on the situation.

"Do you think Benson knows we're onto him? Because if he did—then why let me return? Why not push me over the side of the boat and claim an accident?"

I think I started having stroke-like symptoms. What if she hadn't answered my call? I couldn't go there right now, so I put forth a different theory, "Perhaps he isn't sure about our involvement and is trying to test us by seeing how we react to the letter."

Her expression said she wasn't buying it. And she was right. Benson knew by going after Carter he was going nuclear. This move was not meant to be subtle. We were getting too close and he was the first to blink.

I was never short on theories. "He's sending a message, but think back to Casey Leeds and the fires, where he covered his tracks with an alibi. Perhaps he's doing the same thing here. So he can lure us, eliminate us both, and nobody could connect him to taking Carter."

"I still don't know how he was able to do it. Do you think he has a partner?"

"I doubt it," I said. I hadn't thought about the partner angle until Christina brought it up. I was quick to dismiss it at the time, but with the current situation I felt it required further review.

But I ruled it out again. "He's working alone."

"How can you be so sure?"

"Ever hear of the fable of the Fox and the Hedgehog?"

"I think you're forgetting that any class you passed in school was with my help."

"Then I'm sure you remember that the Greek poet Archilochus used the fox and hedgehog as a metaphor to support his belief that human beings are categorized into two types. The hedgehog is symbolic of those who have one central vision of reality. Their existence is completely shaped by that vision."

"And a fox has a sense that reality is too complex to try fit it into one central vision. What does this have to do with anything?"

"Benson is a hedgehog. His central vision is that it's his destiny to eradicate the ills of drunk driving—he has a messianic view of himself. And most people I've met with such a divine sense of their work, tend not to like to share the credit. No partner."

"Then where do you think the real Kyle Jones is?"

My look turned grim.

"I thought so, too," she replied in a soft voice.

Our destination was the small building on Main Street that housed the *Rockfield Gazette*. The only employee present on the late Monday afternoon was Murray. As usual, he was typing away on his 1950s black typewriter, writing his weekly editorial.

Murray was all business, and didn't spare anything beyond a pleasant greeting. Gwen and I went to her office—a desk adjacent to the one where Murray typed away. This was not the *New York Globe* by any stretch of the imagination. She moved to a dry erase board tacked to the wall behind her desk and began scribbling. We were the foxes, filled with complex questions, but not a lot of definite answers.

As if our mentor was sending subliminal reminders from across the room, we first went back to the beginning to try to decipher the ending. To the best of our knowledge, it began when a drunk driver killed Grady Benson's parents in 1989. We didn't have the name of the driver, due to state laws protecting juveniles, but we researched suspicious deaths in the Redmond, Washington area on Benson's preferred holiday for killing. One that caught my interest occurred on July 4, 1991, when a Phillip "Flip" Tompkins mowed down five college students at a cul-de-sac party, in what was thought to be an accident. All victims were reportedly acquaintances, and all were intoxicated at the time of the accident. But what most interested me was that they all would have been juveniles when Benson's parents were killed.

But we had no evidence that linked Benson. In fact, we had no real connection between him and any suspicious death until July 4, 1996, when Leonard Harris drowned at Lake Havasu. And the only link was that he was there, as were a hundred others. Not exactly incriminating evidence.

We were confident that Benson killed the real Kyle Jones around May of 1998. The next month, Benson bought the beach house in Ocracoke using Jones' identity. But then our trail went dry until he arrived in Rockfield.

Gwen studied the board. "Okay, let's leave the real Jones out of it for now. The common thread is that all were involved in alcohol related incidents, resulting in death, and in each case the perpetrator received a light sentence."

She thought for a second, before adding, "He seems to have a thing for July 4, the anniversary of his parents' accident. But Noah's murder throws a wrench into that theory."

"It was an anniversary though—it was two years to the day of the accident." I let out a frustrated sigh. "But we can't tie any of these killings to Benson, because we can't even prove that any of them were murders. Leonard Harris' death was listed as accidental. Noah committed suicide, and the police shot Leeds. And there was no foul play suspected in the Tompkins accident."

Gwen looked equally frustrated. Our earlier hopefulness now seemed premature. The most we had on the guy was identity theft.

Murray finished his typing and started for the door. "Good night, fellow journalists."

We came up for air to wish him a pleasant evening. He mentioned that he was in a hurry, hoping not to be late for his great-granddaughter's dance recital.

Murray did have one piece of advice for us, "If you don't mind my butting in, I think you need to answer why he came to Rockfield. His killings are symbolic, so there must be a symbol here. The alcohol related incidents of Noah and Casey Leeds occurred after his arrival, so they couldn't be the reason he graced us with his presence. And while they are both tragic, neither case seems to fulfill his visions of grandeur. He strikes me as a big game hunter, and there must be a very large critter in Rockfield that he wants to hang over his mantle.

"But once you decipher his reason for coming, don't get stuck trying to understand his past. You can't bring Noah or anyone else back, but you can stop the next one. Too many dwell on the past, and they get stuck there. Always look toward the future, my fellow journalists."

With that pearl of wisdom, Murray smiled, placed his fedora on his head, and left for the evening.

Gwen and I looked at each other. He could have just as easily been talking about our relationship. Maybe he was.

When the door closed behind him, Gwen looked at me strangely. "What are you smiling at?"

"He called me a journalist."

"He's getting old. Sometimes he gets confused."

I kept smiling as I glanced at my watch. "I better go. I have an early start tomorrow."

"What are you talking about?"

"I'm flying to Arizona. I plan to talk to the police chief in Gilbert, along with anyone who might have been on that boat the night Leonard Harris died. Then I'm going to Seattle to find out about Benson's parents, and see if it's connected to the Tompkins accident."

I was surprised she didn't declare that she was coming with me. I kind of hoped she would. To keep her safe, of course. "I will trail Benson while you're gone. My guess is that he'll lead me to Carter," she replied, catching me off guard.

"Oh no you don't. Do you know how dangerous that is, Gwen?"

"Thank you for your concern, Dad, but why don't you quit while you're only slightly behind."

I knew I wasn't going to win the battle—again—so I decided to take her advice … for now. But despite the tough front, I could tell that the Carter letter had affected her. I noticed her hands shaking.

"Why don't you stop by tonight and let me make you dinner. Knowing you, you'll be so focused on the task at hand that you'll forget to eat. And besides, Dad and Tommy would love to see you," she offered.

She left out the part about feeling safer with someone else there, especially with her father not in peak physical condition. But it didn't take away from the fact that those were the words I'd been waiting to hear for so many years.

Just because I'm difficult, I acted like it would be a hardship to rearrange my schedule, before finally agreeing. We then locked up the office and headed back to the past, but looking toward the future.

CHAPTER 65

Gwen stirred a spattering tomato sauce with the help of Tommy, who stood on a stool, wearing an apron that was about five times too big for him. After an overdue hot shower, I changed into a *Delaney Construction* T-shirt and a pair of jeans, borrowed from her father.

The four of us then ate dinner together at the kitchen table. Everybody knew this was the way it should have been, but nobody brought it up. The adults were quiet, while Tommy made loud sucking sounds as he slurped the spaghetti into his mouth.

After dinner, a group effort of cleaning dishes took place, in which, predictably, I was the only one to break a plate. Soon after, Mr. Delaney ordered Tommy to his room to do his homework. Then a half hour after Tommy's departure, Mr. Delaney called it a day for himself, leaving Gwen and I to struggle with the awkward alone time.

We sat at the table with a bottle of Pinot and a lot of memories. I noticed her hands were still shaking as she lifted her wine glass.

"It's going to be okay, Gwen."

She forced a smile. When I peered into her beautiful green eyes, I saw a look I hadn't seen in a long time. She'd let down the wall, exposing a fragility, but also her firm resolve. It reminded me of the pleasant past.

She poured me another glass of wine. In doing so, she got close enough for me to become intoxicated by her perfume. It sent my memories back to prom night. Dancing to our song—"Never Say Goodbye" by Bon Jovi. I was just glad we never had the opportunity to say goodbye.

"It's going to be okay," I said again, this time with more conviction.

Gwen didn't seem so sure. She took another gulp of wine and looked across the table at me.

"Something on your mind?" I asked.

"When you took the full-time job at GNZ, you told me if you ever got my call in the middle of the night you'd be right by my side, no matter where you were in the world. It took you a while, but you kept your word, JP Warner."

I smiled, then took a glance at the clock in the kitchen. "I should be going."

"You better stay a little while longer—with all the wine we've had, I don't want Officer *Grady Benson* to lock you up and throw away the key."

I shook my head at the absurdity of the whole thing. With all the dangerous places I'd traveled to throughout the world, I couldn't believe the irony of meeting up with such danger in quaint Rockfield. In our teenage years we used to constantly whine, *"I can't wait to get out of this town—it's so boring! There is nothing to do!"*

"I only had one glass. You're the one drinking like there's no tomorrow."

Bad choice of words.

I thanked her for dinner, stood, and leaned down to kiss her on the cheek.

As I began to walk away, Gwen grabbed me by the shoulder and pulled me around. Then she kissed me.

My mouth engulfed hers. We slammed up against a wall, knocking a family photo to the floor. I pulled away and tried to catch my breath. "I'm not sure this is a good idea."

"JP, I know eventually you're going to leave. I'm okay with it. I'm not concerned with the future anymore. Nobody's guaranteed tomorrow."

Instinct took over and lips locked again. We crashed into another wall.

"I'm not going to leave, Gwen."

I knew she didn't believe me, but didn't seem to care. "Will you please shut up JP?"

Good enough for me. First, off came her sweatshirt. My T-shirt was next. She reached up to the waist of my jeans, and began to unbuckle them. After a struggle that briefly turned comical, they came off and she threw them onto the coffee table, knocking over a remaining glass of wine.

We swept through the living room and into her bedroom.

Gwen pushed me onto the bed and then climbed on top. She looked down at me intently and said, "Because he wasn't you."

"What?"

"You've been dying to ask me why my marriage broke up. I finally decided to answer you."

There was nothing left to say, so for once we didn't.

I would not get the rest I sought for my trip. I didn't want to go to sleep, worried that I might wake to find it was a dream. I barely got an hour, but being intertwined with Gwen's body made it the best sleep I'd had in years. I woke to streaming sunlight coming through the small crack in the shades. I kissed her and she woke with a smile. It was not a dream.

I was sure of this, because in no dream I'd ever had about this moment was Tommy Delaney standing in the open doorway that we forgot to close in our haste. "Gwen and Mr. JP sitting in a tree *K-I-S-S-I-N-G*," he sung out gleefully.

Mr. Delaney arrived, not looking the least bit shocked. He smiled at us as he pulled Tommy away from his sightseeing, and shut the door.

After we dressed, and I ate a plate of leftover spaghetti for breakfast, Gwen drove me home so I could pack. We kissed again before I exited the van, and I pleaded with her to be careful when she followed Jones. I'd given up on trying to stop her.

I walked into the house, whistling, and was surprised to see my mother. I suddenly felt like a teenager again—Mom waiting up for me as I tried to sneak in.

She inspected me as I came through the door. "Well, look what the cat dragged in."

It was nice to see the peaceful smile on her face. I walked over to where she was sitting on the floor and took a seat beside her.

"You aren't using your cane," she observed.

I'd almost forgotten. "After seeing Byron in his wheelchair, it made my problems seem as if they weren't problems."

"It's nice to see you smiling again. It's been a while. That wouldn't have anything to do with that pretty girl that drove you home this morning?"

There was no way to fool Mom. "She is pretty great, huh?"

"It took you long enough to figure that out, John Pierpont."

"I figured it out a long time ago, but things were just a little complicated. They still are."

"Yeah, it's called life. But when you find a way to be with the one you should be with, it sure makes things seem less complicated."

My eyes wandered toward the cardboard box she'd been sifting through, realizing it contained Noah's old junk. I noticed a high school yearbook, assorted photos of Noah and Lisa, and some sort of ugly contraption he'd made for a school project. I thought it was an ashtray, but my mother contended it was a paperweight. Noah had always claimed it was a key-chain holder.

I joined her in the sifting. I came across a second-grade paper with the topic being who Noah wanted to be like when he grew up. When I read it, I felt my eyes well-up with tears.

"He never wanted you to see that. He was afraid you wouldn't think he was cool with all the mushy stuff he wrote about you."

"I wish I'd lived up to his expectations."

She looked shocked. "Noah was so proud of you, JP. You should have heard him talk about you, and I'm sure he is especially proud of what you are doing for him right now."

"What do you mean?"

"JP, I wouldn't feel the same sense of peace if I believed Noah took his own life. I want you to nail that bastard, Jones."

"I plan on it. In fact, that's where I'm headed right now. Do you think Dad could take me to the airport? I'm kind of in a hurry."

"I'm sorry, your father is bailing your brother Ethan out of jail this morning."

I'd awoken in an alternate universe. "Ethan's in jail?"

"I guess some loud mouth at Main Street Tavern said some not-so-nice things about his brother and Ethan socked him in the nose," she added casually like it was some ho-hum event. After what she'd been through the last few years, maybe it was.

"They were saying bad things about Noah?" I asked.

"No JP. He was defending *you*."

CHAPTER 66

Gilbert, Arizona

October 4

I arrived at Phoenix Sky Harbor Airport at just before noon. My mood was aglow, my thoughts still focused on the previous night with Gwen.

I rented a Taurus and headed for the Phoenix suburb of Gilbert. I walked in the police station demanding to see Chief Dahl "right now!" as if I owned the joint. My leg was killing me. Too much driving and sex in the last week—not that I was complaining.

Almost an hour later, I was escorted into his office.

I expected a rigid looking, mustached cop with a straight brimmed hat and a surly attitude. But quite the contrary, Chief Dahl appeared more like an aging surfer.

His attitude was laid back. I hated laid back. Dahl's feet were up on his desk like he'd just awoken from a nap, and the remnants of the salad he ate for lunch were strewn over his desk—not the doughnut or artery-clogging meat sandwich I'd expected.

"Can I help you?" he greeted me with nonchalance.

"My name is JP Warner and ..."

He cut me off, which irritated me. "I know who you are, Mr. Warner. If you're here to uncover some sort of police corruption, I can assure you that you've come to the wrong police department. Let's start again—can I help you?"

"I'm here to talk about a police officer who once worked here."

"Since I'm fairly certain you're the anonymous reporter who phoned me last month to discuss Kyle Jones, I'm going to assume that's who you're referring to."

His street smarts impressed me and I confessed to making the call.

"If I recall, you mentioned an award he received back east. He's a good man and I'm glad to see he's doing well. Is that why you're here?"

"I wish I could say that," I said, my voice darkening.

"Then why are you here?"

"It's my belief that Kyle Jones is dead. It's also my contention he was killed here in Gilbert back in 1998. I believe his body is buried in the backyard of a house he rented at 52 Ash Street."

Dahl glanced at his desk calendar like he was checking to see if it was April Fools' Day. "Well, if that were true, Mr. Warner, how do you explain the reference I gave for Kyle to get a police job in Connecticut?"

I reached into my overnight bag and pulled out the newspaper from the day Jones was given the award at the fair. A photo of Officer Kyle Jones accompanied the article.

I tossed it onto Dahl's desk and pointed to the article in the lower right corner. I got the impression he knew who the man in the photo really was. I thought he might.

"Do you recognize him?" I asked impatiently.

He nodded. "It's Kyle's old roommate—Grady something." He tapped his hand on his desk as if it would help him think.

"Grady Benson," I tried to speed up the process. "I want you to dig up the yard on Ash Street."

"You've made quite a leap from stolen identity to murder. Do you have any evidence that Kyle is even missing?"

"With all due respect, Chief Dahl, you know as well as I do that Jones had no family, and his friends were the people he worked with at any given time. I don't think it's a coincidence that Benson picked him to prey on."

"I'll take that as a no on the evidence."

"If you don't take some action, then I'll go over there and dig it up myself."

"If you think being held captive by terrorists was bad, I can guarantee you, Mr. Warner, it will seem like Club Med compared to an Arizona prison."

A stare-down followed. He wasn't the pushover I'd suspected—I could hear my mother's warnings about judging books by covers. My eyes wandered to some of the framed photos on the wall behind his desk— numerous shots of Dahl, posing with other police officers and state officials. What I found most interesting was that a few of them featured the real Kyle Jones. For Kyle to make the wall of fame, they must have been close, and hopefully had formed an emotional bond that I could tap into.

"Listen, I understand your hands are tied. But if you can't do something as a police officer, can I at least get your word that you will look into this as Kyle's friend?"

Dahl saw right through my act. "I met Grady Benson on a few occasions. He was your typical hanger-on. Maybe he saw stealing Kyle's identity as an opportunity for a new life. It would make sense that he landed in an obscure small town in Connecticut, where he would likely never be questioned. I'll contact the Rockfield Police Department and present them with the possibility that the Kyle Jones they know may be impersonating an officer. That's the best I can do."

"Your best isn't good enough."

Dahl studied me, before asking, "This is personal, isn't it?"

"Grady Benson killed my brother."

"I'm sorry."

"I don't need you to be sorry, I need you to do something about it. You should take it personally—he killed your friend!"

"You don't know that."

"Don't you find it strange that you never heard from him again once he left here. And you're a smart guy, so you now realize that those emails you received from Kyle Jones were actually from Grady Benson, as were the Christmas cards."

"Kyle was a loner. He's probably living in some remote section of Alaska, or saving some rainforest halfway around the globe. To be honest with you, I never really expected to hear much from him again, unless he needed a reference."

"You obviously aren't willing to accept the truth. Can you at least give me the name of Kyle's former girlfriend? In our earlier conversation you said it was Lucy, but cut me off before I got a last name. Maybe she still cares what happened to Kyle."

"I'm not at liberty to give out information to someone looking to serve up some vigilante justice."

"Vigilante justice?" *Oh, the irony.*

"What else would you call it? Despite your preconceived notions, Mr. Warner, Arizona isn't the Wild West with shootouts at the OK-Corral. But there's a good Wyatt Earp Museum about two hours south of here if you're interested."

"I'm talking about justice and you are talking about bad Costner movies." I boiled over. "Grady Benson is the only vigilante here!"

"It's been fun. I believe you have a great future writing fiction, Mr. Warner." He stood and reached across the desk to shake my hand.

Fire shot through my veins. I rose and pointed at him. "Grady Benson's parents were killed by a drunk driver in Redmond, Washington on July 4, 1989. It sent him on a two-decade killing spree to exact revenge on drunk drivers. One of the cases I've been able to link him to is right here in Arizona—Leonard Harris, who you might remember was the drunk driver who took the lives of two college students. Benson worked so closely with him that Harris considered him his spiritual adviser."

"Leonard Harris was a high profile case here in Arizona, and nationally. If there was some foul play, and Benson was involved, then I'm sure it would have been discovered."

I would not be deterred. "Upon moving to Rockfield, using the identity of Kyle Jones, Benson was involved in two suspicious deaths. One was a man named Casey Leeds and the other was my brother, Noah. Both men were connected to alcohol related deaths. And in each case, Benson was present at their death. Do you really think all this is a coincidence, Chief Dahl?"

He sat back down in his chair where he remained silent for moments. He seemed to be debating whether he should open a smelly can of worms.

"There was an incident a few years back that Kyle mentioned to me," he finally said.

I was all ears.

"It was Labor Day weekend and we had our usual department picnic. Afterward, my wife and I went out with Kyle and Lucy, along with a few other couples from the department. Kyle had a little too much to drink. I offered to take him home, and looking back on it, I shouldn't have taken no for an answer. It went against every oath we took. The next day I called him in my office and we both agreed we were in the wrong. That's when he told me what happened."

"Which was?"

"When he came home, Benson physically attacked Kyle and Lucy. He said he thought the source of the rage was that Benson's parents had been killed by a drunk driver."

"Dig up the yard."

"Even if I wanted to, I would need more to get a warrant."

"What *can* you do?"

He took out a business card and wrote the name *Lucy Enriquez-Hayes*, followed by an address and phone number.

CHAPTER 67

I arrived at the city limits of Glendale, greeted by a sign promoting it as the home of the Arizona Cardinals. It made me think of Leonard Harris, which set my mind off on a wild tangent that eventually led to the image of Jones tossing Noah's lifeless body over Samerauk Bridge. I pounded the steering wheel, shooting pain through my hand.

I was mad at myself for not thinking to check any Lucys who might have worked with Jones on the police force. The workplace has always been the ultimate dating service, even if most of them ended badly—Lauren Bowden came to mind—but I hoped to find someone who still cared for the real Kyle Jones. She must have seen Jones and Benson together at the house on Ash.

Lucy lived in a modest Spanish Colonial style home in a planned subdivision. When I arrived, she had her head tucked into the hatchback of a station-wagon type SUV, pulling out bags of groceries. She stood barely five-foot tall with dark curly hair. She wore a floral colored dress with sandals. The dress was a maternity dress. I was no pregnancy expert, but she appeared as if she could give birth at any moment. So I had better make it quick.

I parked the Taurus by the curb and like a knight in shining armor, or a kiss-ass reporter trying to get some information, I rushed to help Lucy with the groceries.

"I'm JP Warner," I introduced myself.

"I know who you are," she said, handing the bags to me. "Chief Dahl called to warn me you might be stopping by."

Lucy moved to the back door of the driver's side. She opened it and removed a child from her car seat. I was then introduced to six-year-old Dani Hayes. She looked like a clone of her mother.

"He told me you want to talk about Kyle Jones."

"That's right," I said, but decided to hold off on the murder portion of the story until Dani's ears were at a safe distance.

When we entered the house, Dani anxiously begged her mother to let her go swimming. When given approval, the little girl excitedly went to change. Lucy poured two glasses of pink lemonade and we moved to the backyard. I followed her lead and took a seat at an umbrella-covered table that provided shade. Dani soon appeared, wearing floatation devices on every appendage of her body and a nose clip, and dove into the in-ground pool.

"Chief Dahl tells me you have some wild theories about Kyle."

"My guess is if he really thought they were so wild, he wouldn't have sent me over here to talk to you." I felt rushed for time, so I reached into my bag and handed Lucy the newspaper.

"Grady Benson," she replied without hesitation. She handed me back the paper like she wanted no part of it. "I always told Kyle to stay away from that loser."

"Sounds like you weren't a fan of Benson."

"He was totally living off Kyle. He couldn't hang onto a job, claiming he had Gulf War sickness. Kyle was a nice guy and Benson took advantage of it. He played on his emotions about their bond of war, and the fact they both tragically lost their parents."

"Don't you find it strange that you've never heard from Kyle since he left Arizona?"

"Not really … are you in contact with all your ex-girlfriends?"

Good point.

"And I did hear from Kyle about two years ago when he was in town."

This surprised me. "That's impossible."

"And why is that?"

"Because I believe that Grady Benson murdered Kyle Jones, long before two years ago."

"You believe? Either he's dead or he isn't," Lucy asked and patted her pregnant stomach to make a point. "You can't be half pregnant … or half dead."

"That's why I need you to help me convince Chief Dahl to dig up the yard at the home he shared with Benson. I *know* Kyle Jones is buried under there. My guess is you never saw Kyle two years ago, or heard his voice when he contacted you. Email?"

"I hate to burst your bubble, but when I was still on the Gilbert PD, I got a call to a domestic dispute at the house on Ash, a few years after Kyle left. I noticed that the new owners had put a pool in the backyard. If there was a dead body buried back there it would have been found."

I tried to act like I wasn't even fazed that my theory just got completely blown out of the water.

I asked her about the Labor Day incident in which Benson attacked her and Jones after they'd allegedly driven drunk. She provided a similar account as Chief Dahl, but with the detail of an eyewitness.

"He apologized to me a few days later," she added.

"What was your reaction?"

"I was furious. It was just another play to keep his free rent." She became more and more worked-up as she talked about it. "So Grady took me aside one day and gave me a lame excuse for his behavior."

"What was his explanation?"

"He told me he was watching a news program earlier in the night about some judge who let off drunk drivers. He claimed it brought back the bad memories of his parents' death, and when combined with our actions that night, made him temporarily lose his mind."

"Did you believe him?"

"It didn't make a difference. His behavior was unacceptable, regardless. We were wrong to drink and drive, no doubt, but who appointed him judge and jury? Kyle, of course, felt empathy for him and kept procrastinating about kicking him out, as he'd promised me. Their relationship caused a big split with us, and we broke up a few months later. It wasn't the only reason, but it did play a role."

"So you weren't around when Benson took Leonard Harris under his wing?"

Lucy snickered. "I just know it was some nonsense about being his spiritual adviser. It was typical Grady Benson—using people's emotions to get himself a free ride."

At that point, Dani rose from the pool and sprinted toward our table. Lucy wrapped a towel around her and headed for the house. I gathered the half-empty lemonade glasses and pitcher, and followed.

When the little girl entered her room to change, Lucy said, "What you tell me is disconcerting, to say the least. I am no fan of Grady Benson and wouldn't put anything past him. So I'll help you find Kyle. But everything you tell me is at best circumstantial. You need a lot more proof."

"But you would agree it's within the realm of possibility that Grady Benson could have killed Kyle Jones?"

Her voice cracked, "I'm sure of it."

I was surprised by the resolute response. She had no reason to stick her toe back in the troubled waters of the past.

"Based on Benson's pattern, I'm glad he never got to you," I said.

Lucy looked down the hallway, staring at Dani's room, probably thinking of when someone calling themselves Kyle Jones contacted her two years ago. She then surprised me by opening up a kitchen drawer and pulling out a handgun. "I will do anything to protect my family, Mr. Warner."

Point taken. And loaded.

A loud male voice filled the room, causing me to turn quickly. "Is everything okay in here?" said a very large man.

But there were no shots fired. It was her husband, Larry, who just returned from a long day at his pool cleaning business. She went to him and wrapped around him in an emotional hug. It made me think of Gwen.

I found Larry to be surprisingly calm, considering a strange man was in the kitchen with his wife, and she was holding a firearm.

"Everything is fine, honey. I'd like you to meet JP Warner."

Larry and I shook hands, and he affably offered me a beer. But it was time for me to leave and take the troubling past with me. When Dani ran to the kitchen, shouting "Daddy, you're home!" my presence officially became an afterthought. So I slipped out of the house without anyone noticing.

Once I got to the car, I called Christina. She wasn't home and didn't answer her cell, but I left a message to check on television news programs the Sunday before Labor Day in 1995. Especially one about a judge with a habit of giving light sentences to drunk drivers.

CHAPTER 68

I headed for Lake Havasu City. The ride would be over two hundred miles and I wanted to make it there before dark. I originally planned to do some digging at Luke Air Force Base—Benson and Jones' old stomping grounds—but scrapped the idea. JP Warner was the last person anyone in the US military would be divulging information to.

I was driving through the town of Parker, situated on the northern corner of the Colorado River, nestled between the Sonora desert and rugged mountains, when Christina called.

"Do you have the information I asked for?" I greeted her.

"Sure do, boss."

"Let's hear it."

"You know that glass table in the living room?"

"Yes," I said, not liking where this was headed.

"Do you *really* like it?"

"What happened to my table?"

"It's not important JP. What's important is that nobody got hurt."

I sighed. "Just make sure it's fixed when I get back. So did you find the news program I asked for, or not?"

"I did, but I was surprised you needed to ask me for it. You would think you would've remembered it."

"Why is that?"

"Because it was your report. On the Sunday before Labor Day in 1995, GNZ and their *dashing* young reporter did a segment about a Judge Raymond Buford from North Carolina. Buford was from the school of 'drinking and driving is only a problem when you spill your drink.' Nobody really noticed until a guy named Craig Steele, a repeat offender whom Buford kept sending away with a light tap on the wrist, killed an entire family that was traveling on vacation."

The report was starting to come back to me, but the details were a little hazy. But what was very clear, was that it had set Benson off.

"It gets better," Christina continued. "Buford owned a home on Ocracoke Island just down the street from … guess who?"

"How did Buford die?"

Christina began to chuckle. "Let's just say the judge had an accident."

"What kind of accident?"

"I would say an embarrassing one. Ever hear of auto-erotic asphyxia?"

I thought for a moment, wondering if it was a name of one of those crazy bands she listens to. "Doesn't ring a bell, no."

"Well, it's a solo sex act where the participant constricts air flow to heighten the pleasure during orgasm. But I'm guessing the fact that Judge Buford accidentally hung himself made it less pleasurable."

I remained puzzled. "How could that heighten the pleasure?"

"I have no idea. All I know is those things you guys carry around make you do some strange things."

I got back on track. "What was the date Buford died?"

"This is where the plot thickens a little. All the others were on Benson's favorite holiday—the one with the fireworks—but the judge died on October 10, 1998."

I tried to think of any significance of the date. "Was Steele the only one who caused a fatality after Buford let them off?"

"As far as I can tell, yes."

"Was his accident on October 10?"

"Nope—April. He only received a six month suspended sentence and probation for killing the family, thanks to a clean record that was helped by Buford continually letting him plead to lesser traffic violations. He moved to Panama City, but must not have been able to kick the habit because he crashed into a telephone pole on July 4, 1998. The police report indicated they thought it was a suicide because there were no skid marks, but after they saw the blood work, they decided he had passed out behind the wheel due to alcohol consumption."

"Good work. Anything else?"

"I was able to obtain a copy of the sealed documents from the settlement Kyle Jones received for his parents' death."

"Since Jones is no longer a suspect, and likely a victim himself, I'm not sure how that would help."

"I thought it might add some insight into the Benson/Jones relationship. Just got it like two minutes ago, so I haven't had time to even look at it yet. If I find anything interesting I'll email you the PDFs."

I found a receipt from my fast-food lunch and jotted down Benson's 1998 timeline. He likely killed the real Kyle Jones in May, moved to Ocracoke, took care of Steele on his favorite holiday, and finally his new neighbor, Judge Buford, on October 10. It was a busy year.

"Anything else before you hang up on me?" Christina asked.

"Yeah, keep trying to find a connection to October 10."

CHAPTER 69

When I arrived in Lake Havasu, I went directly to the office of Kelly Dumas, the deputy sheriff who worked the Leonard Harris case. Luckily for me, it seemed that nobody in Arizona ever changed jobs.

Kelly stood to greet me. She was a plain but pretty woman with a boyish bowl cut. But what caught my attention was her height.

We exchanged pleasantries, but I could tell she was less than enthused by my visit, especially at this late hour. I took a seat facing her cluttered desk and noticed a bumper sticker push-pinned to a cork bulletin-board behind her: *I know I'm tall—please don't ask me if I play basketball.* I saw my icebreaker.

"So do you play basketball?" I asked with a smile

"As a matter of fact I played for Northern Arizona University. Three time all Big Sky Conference."

"I'm impressed."

My niceties didn't fool her. "Did you come here to discuss my basketball career? Because there's usually only two issues the national media is interested in talking to me about. So is it MTV Spring Break or Leonard Harris?"

"MTV Spring Break? I can't watch that crap—it makes me feel two hundred years old," I replied with another smile.

"So what do you want to know about Mr. Harris' death?"

"I would like to know why your department called it an accident when it was a homicide?"

She looked annoyed. "Unless you have some evidence I wasn't privileged to see, that's a baseless claim. And you're wasting my time."

She opened a file drawer and pulled out the folders from the Harris case. The fact that they were so accessible after all these years told me that it must come up often.

I scanned through the reports. The folder was littered with pictures of Harris' corpse that made my stomach queasy. It also contained sworn statements from the many witnesses. I searched until I found the statement given by Grady Benson and skimmed it.

"I notice you weren't present at the crime scene."

"Mr. Warner, it's late, so I'll make this fast. It was the Fourth of July and there was only one of me. I usually traveled to an incident with the dive team, but it was impossible that night. The only thing out of the ordinary in this case was that one of the persons who died was a famous athlete. Besides that, it was a textbook carbon monoxide poisoning. And if you read further into the reports, you'll see that the coroner backed up the finding at the scene." She let out an exasperated sigh. "A UNLV student died on a houseboat in the same manner last year and nobody shows up here to discuss it."

"How can you be so sure no foul play was involved?"

"First of all, the way Mr. Harris and Ms. McCarron died—she was also a victim, but people seem to forget that—the bodies were in the semi-fetal position with legs loosely drawn up. Their arms were pulled close to the chest with hands limp and palms down. Do you know what that means?"

I felt like I was in eighth grade math class and forgot to do my homework. "Um ... no."

"It means it was a textbook accidental drowning. And when the toxicology tests came back, we found that Harris had a gas content in his body of fifty-nine percent, while Candi McCarron's was fifty-two."

"Is that high?"

"It's a hundred percent fatal."

"So he and Candi would have died regardless, even if they were on dry land?"

"The gas likely made them woozy, or pass out, which led to their drowning. The water was the final nail in their coffins."

"But how did they know this at the scene? My guess is this thing is rare."

Kelly shook her head. "I wish you were right, but over the last two decades there has been an epidemic of carbon monoxide poisonings on houseboats. Nine people have died here and six up at Lake Powell in the last seven years. That doesn't include the many who had to be hospitalized."

I'd never heard of anything like this. But I had a feeling that Grady Benson was well aware of it.

Kelly held up the photographs of Leonard Harris and Candi McCarron's naked bodies. "Notice the blood around their mouths and dripping from their noses. And how their skin is splotched a cherry red color—it's classic carbon monoxide poisoning. Our divers knew the minute they found them."

I picked up the photos and was drawn to the before-and-after pictures of Candi McCarron, whom I'd never seen before. The "before" showed stunning beauty, looking like a stereotypical California blonde. The one taken after her trip to the bottom of the lake was equally stunning, but not very beautiful. I made a mental note to research any connection she might have to a drunk driving fatality.

I found a copy of the rental agreement in the file folder, and as expected, Grady Benson's signature was on it. His spiritual adviser had rented the boat for the party.

"Would it be possible for me to talk to the lead diver in this case? The one who was first on the scene," I asked.

The vibrating sound of Kelly Dumas' phone stole her attention. She looked at it and cringed.

"Looks like you'll get your chance, Mr. Warner."

CHAPTER 70

The situation centered on Copper Canyon, a secluded cove that was a favorite spot of houseboaters. A father and two young children took a ski boat out over two hours ago and hadn't been seen since.

Either they had some sort of mechanical trouble and were floating around the lake, or this exercise would be about body recovery. There was no time to waste, and in what seemed like microseconds, I was standing in front of a dive locker in the marina, putting on a black wet suit.

Jerry Sidwell headed the dive team. A tall, fit man who looked like he lived in a gym, despite being in his late fifties. The pace was hurried, but I didn't notice any panic. I helped with what I could, loading their dive tanks, buoyancy compensators, and vests. Once the entire crew was on board, the boat sprinted from the dock, hopping over the dark, choppy water.

I was surprised that Sidwell took time out of his duties to approach me. "Kelly told me that you had questions about the Leonard Harris drowning."

"I do, but are you sure you don't want to discuss it later?"

"I've been doing this for twenty-five years. I know every inch of this lake and what we're up against. I need something to take my mind off what we might find tonight. So what do you want to know?"

"Anything you can remember might be helpful."

"I recall that it was a worst-case scenario that night from our standpoint. We couldn't use the helicopter because of the lightning. Plus, it was Fourth of July, so we were short on manpower."

"Would it have made a difference?"

"Nope. The minute I heard the call I knew it was the generators. Harris and the girl were already gone."

"So you arrived at the scene with a pre-conceived notion of the outcome? Is it possible that you didn't investigate all angles of the death because, in your mind, you already knew what happened?"

"No," the self-assured Sidwell replied. He peered out into the black water, maybe seeing the ghosts of rescues past.

"Kelly was telling me about this carbon monoxide problem on these houseboats. Is that what you mean by generators?"

The body language of the divers turned tense—I realized they were nearing their target. Sidwell and I were the only ones still talking.

"There's a place beneath the swimming deck on many of the old houseboats where swimmers often like to play. It's also the place where many of these boats vent their exhaust. We call it the death zone."

"So that's where you think Leonard Harris and the girl were?"

Sidwell nodded grimly. "Witnesses said Harris came up for air and attempted to yell for help, but then he was sucked down like an anchor. The witnesses on the boat thought he was joking around. But it was no joke. It was very typical of these tragedies.

"The girl never made it out. Makes sense, since he was much bigger and stronger. He could absorb more fumes. That area with the fumes is usually a private area where couples like to go to be alone. My guess is that they were likely in the heat of passion and didn't even know they were dying."

"So if someone knew about this 'death zone,' they could theoretically lead a victim there if they wanted to kill them, and make it seem like an accident."

"It's possible, I guess."

"So how come nobody has done anything about this problem?"

"I thought a high-profile death such as Leonard Harris would bring some attention to it. But nothing has changed. The owners complained about the cost to upgrade. And even when I offered to test the CM levels in houseboats at no charge, most declined because it was an inconvenience. Everything happens to somebody else."

"I know it was a long time ago, but do you remember a man named Grady Benson? He was one of the people on the boat the night Harris drowned."

The name grabbed his attention, which surprised me. I had thought it was a major long-shot. "Yeah, I know him—he was friends with Harris. After the accident he wanted to become an advocate to make houseboats safer. We worked together in many cases."

"You worked with Grady Benson?"

"Sure did, even went to Lake Cumberland with him to put on a safety clinic. The kid could really put emotion into a speech. Never a dry eye in the house when he talked about Leonard. There was no doubt there was a connection there."

"What's the deal with Lake Cumberland?"

"It's in Kentucky—known as the houseboat capital of the world. They have a convention each year. Benson and I put on a safety demonstration." He thought for a quick moment. "What's your interest in Benson?"

"He killed my brother."

Sidwell flashed me a curious look, filled with many questions he didn't have time to ask.

"Over there," he suddenly shouted, his attention diverted. We sped toward a docked houseboat. A woman, presumably the mother, stood on the deck waving her hands frantically.

The dive team boarded the vessel like pirates, and obtained all the information they could out of the hysterical woman. Then like precision, we were off again. Sidwell was in full control as we jetted into the dark night, using radar and global-positioning satellite signals to plot the course. I sat alone, no longer thinking of Officer Jones, Noah, Leonard Harris, or even Gwen. The moment was compelling. I hoped for the best, but I'd seen too many bad endings to be overly optimistic.

A half-hour passed and radio calls were made requesting reinforcements. The mood was tense and the water was silent. The eerie quiet of death.

But just when the search appeared hopeless, Sidwell pointed at a silhouette on the water that would have surely been missed by the untrained eye. A floodlight flashed on the area and I could make out a small ski boat that containing a man. Next to him were two young boys. They were trapped on a sandbar.

The knot in my stomach slowly untied. I saw relief plastered on Sidwell's face. There would be one less nightmare for him.

I left the jubilant divers around midnight and checked into a local motel. I was still on an adrenaline rush that made sleep impossible. So I checked my email and found the files that Christina sent about the settlement in the death of Kyle Jones' parents.

His parents died in a boating accident. The boating manufacturer that was potentially liable for the accident, quietly settled out of court with the Jones' only heir, Kyle Jones.

The cause of death was carbon monoxide poisoning on a houseboat in Lake Cumberland, Kentucky.

CHAPTER 71

Ocracoke Island

October 5

The rain pelted down in sheets. If it was raining cats and dogs, then they were mountain lions and Saint Bernards. To Gwen, it appeared to be shooting horizontally, as she did her best to follow Grady Benson in her rented minivan.

She'd tracked Benson for the past few days. Her sources at the Rockfield PD told her that Officer Jones had been acting jumpy and agitated. He'd taken personal days for Wednesday through Friday, using the excuse of needing to secure his North Carolina home, facing the expectation that Hurricane Ava would hit the Outer Banks by the weekend. Benson booked a flight for Wednesday morning, but heavy rains in the Carolinas canceled all air traffic. So he scrambled to rent a car. Even though his response was logical, Gwen was suspicious of the urgency. She believed it had everything to do with Jeff Carter.

The rain began lightly when she hit the Pennsylvania Turnpike. By the time she passed by the nation's capital it was a downpour of biblical proportions. And the constant struggle for visibility, while keeping a safe distance from Benson's vehicle, gave her a splitting headache. He drove straight through, only stopping for gas and bathroom breaks at rest-stops outside of Scranton and Fredericksburg.

After twenty hours on the road, Gwen arrived at a deserted Cape Hatteras. Huge signs featuring skull and crossbones warned that Wednesday would be the final day of ferry transportation. The locals were evacuating in large numbers, but the atmosphere didn't appear to be fraught with fear or panic. Hurricanes were not uncommon in these parts.

Gwen let Benson take the first ferry, choosing to wait the half-hour to catch the next one. Once arriving on the island, she made the journey to the north shore. The heavy wind created a sandstorm effect and the waves crashed ashore like they were angry. The noon skies were as black as midnight. She jumped with every crash of thunder.

She parked the minivan at a deserted home down the street, and entered the elements. A cold wind whipped and she felt like a hose was spraying precipitation into her face. Trees swayed, to the point that they appeared on the verge of being ripped out of the ground.

She found a hiding spot behind a sand dune that provided a direct view of Benson's house. His vehicle was parked underneath.

The only thing keeping her warm was thoughts of her night with JP. And then as if he were reading her thoughts, her phone rang.

"I miss you," she shouted over the relentless whipping of wind.

"Not as much as I miss you," he said back, always competitive. He seemed to be having equal trouble hearing her over the roar of voices.

"Where are you, JP ... the airport?" Gwen asked, never taking her eyes off Benson's house.

"Actually, I'm in a bar called Cransky's."

"Very nice. I'm squatting in a sand dune in the middle of a hurricane and you are out enjoying yourself!"

"Hurricane? Where are you, Gwen?"

"I followed Kyle, or Grady, or whatever his name is, to Ocracoke."

"Gwen, this is no time to be a hero. You should hear some of the stuff I've learned about this guy. Please get out of there."

Loving JP and letting JP get the last word were two separate issues. "You should have seen how desperate he was to get here. I know he has Carter trapped somewhere down here. I can't leave now."

"Are you crazy? Did you alert anyone that you're even there?"

"I just told you. Now tell me what you learned on your trip, I know you're dying to impress me."

He let out a frustrated sigh. "According to police reports, Cransky's is the last place that Flip Tompkins was seen. I've talked to a couple of regulars who were here that day. Timothy Kent, one of the guys Tompkins hit with the car, was the one who had killed Benson's parents. The records might be sealed, but the local gossip wasn't. They remembered Tompkins leaving with a mystery man that nobody had seen in the bar, before or since. They couldn't give a really good description after twenty-some years, other than he was rather nondescript. But one guy did remember that he wore a US Air Force shirt."

"I'm impressed. I guess you are doing a little work in between beers. Did you learn anything in Arizona?"

"I met the mysterious Lucy. She'd worked with Jones on the Gilbert PD. She basically confirmed that Benson was a psycho who once assaulted her when he discovered that she and Jones had driven home drunk one night. She also told me that Benson was set off by a GNZ report I did on a judge named Raymond Buford, who was known for letting drunk drivers off the hook."

"That doesn't sound like good news for the judge."

"Let's just say that Benson didn't let him off the hook. Like usual, it was made to look like an accident, but it doesn't fit into our anniversary theory."

"Although, it does fit our pattern of not being able to prove anything."

"Maybe so, but I can prove *where* Buford died."

"Why does the location of his death matter?" she shouted over a loud crackle of thunder.

"You're on Benson's street, right?"

"Yes, I'm across the street from his house."

"Well, look down about three houses from Benson's. That was Buford's home."

She gasped, suddenly feeling that they were in way over their heads.

He continued, "I traveled to Lake Havasu yesterday, to look into Leonard Harris' death. I learned that there's a section of some houseboats where exhaust fumes gather that the experts call the 'death zone.' Benson rented the boat—it wasn't a coincidence. He sent Harris to his death."

"And you can prove that?"

"No, but Kyle Jones' parents retired in Lake Cumberland, Kentucky, which happens to be the houseboat capital of the United States. Christina was able to get at the court documents, and learned that they died in the exact same way as Leonard Harris. That's how Benson learned of the tactic."

This news sent a shiver down Gwen's spine. As if on cue, Benson exited the beach house, got into his rental car and drove off. She knew she had to get some hard evidence.

"He just left ... I'm going in."

JP began screaming at her, but eventually saw it her way. Mainly because there was nothing he could do about it from Seattle.

"I'll be careful. Is there anything else you want to tell me before I go?" she asked, while struggling to climb over the wet sand of the dune.

"I helped save a missing family last night on Lake Havasu."

"Well aren't you special," Gwen said, no longer listening, all her focus on Benson's house.

"Just be careful," he warned.

CHAPTER 72

Gwen stumbled through the wind and rain, which was so fierce it knocked her off balance. She splashed through puddles that were turning into small lakes. She hurried across the marshy ground, falling twice, before reaching the beach house. After making sure the coast was clear, she climbed the stairs, holding tightly to the slippery railing.

Her naiveté in thinking she could actually walk through the front door worked in her favor. The sliding glass door was smashed in. She didn't know what to make of this development, but entered the house through the large hole. Her best guess was that Benson had left in search of supplies to fix it, and would be back soon. But for all she knew, he could have been off to kill a drunk driver. Regardless, she didn't have a moment to lose.

She pulled out her dripping cell phone from her poncho, surprised it still worked, and re-dialed. "JP, someone must have broken in or out of here, the glass door is bashed in. Maybe this is where he was holding Carter, but he was able to get out," she said, excited by the possibility.

He tempered her enthusiasm, "I broke it during my own search. I also emptied all his drawers when searching for evidence. There's nothing in there."

Gwen urgently moved from room to room. "He must have cleaned up because everything is back in place."

"Hurry up and get out of there!"

Gwen ignored, but kept him on the phone. His voice made her feel safer. "I know there's something going on in his bedroom."

She searched the room and then checked the closet. When she parted the hanging clothes, she noticed a piece of the paneling slightly peeling off the wall. It might have gone unnoticed if she wasn't looking for something. When she yanked on it, it came off, exposing a hidden door with a combination lock. She knew it!

She began fiddling with the combination lock with no luck, and finally settled on the tactic of banging on the thick steel door and shouting, "Carter are you in there!?" Not very effective.

"Can you please just get out of there, Gwen? I just can't deal with the thought of losing you again," JP pleaded.

Gwen took his words with a smile.

Then she screamed.

A strong hand strapped around her neck. The other hand covered her mouth, muffling her screams.

Her phone fell to the ground.

CHAPTER 73

Once again Grady Benson swallowed the bitter taste of betrayal. When his necklace signaled an intruder, he had hoped it was a looter, but deep down he knew he'd find Gwen Delaney.

Even though he knew she'd plotted against him, he still held out some hope she would mend her ways. No woman had ever made him feel like she did. But now he saw that she was nothing more than a test. And it was one he was going to pass.

He kept a firm hand over her mouth, while reaching down to pick up the phone. He listened for a moment, hearing Warner's pleas, as if it would help. He unceremoniously hung up on him.

He first secured the prisoner with a pair of Rockfield PD handcuffs, and placed masking tape over her mouth. It was bad enough she betrayed him, but he didn't have to listen to her refer to him as a "sick bastard" and tell him over and over again he wouldn't "get away with it."

He spun the combination lock and proudly informed her the combination was *74891010.* The first part was the date of his parents' murder, while the other was the date that would live in infamy.

He tore off her hood and baseball cap. He grabbed a chunk of her hair and walked her into the secure room. When he tossed her on the floor, she landed right next to the unconscious Carter.

"You very much disappoint me, Gwen."

She couldn't respond, which suited him fine. "You were supposed to be a journalist, to report the story without prejudice. But instead you used your platform to support an enabler of evil like JP Warner. He was once a courageous truth-teller who exposed Buford, but like Kyle, he chose the dark side. And look what he's done to you—he turned you into a common criminal, willing to break into a private home to support your agenda of lies."

He noticed her eyes casing the room, viewing the pictures on the wall. Many that she was very familiar with. He took pleasure in the shock on her face when she viewed the one remaining photo without an **X**. She knew he was next. Too bad she wouldn't be around to see it.

He took out a bag of candy bars and tossed them on the floor. "Don't fret, Gwen, you are a prisoner of war. A prisoner of a just and morally correct war. Therefore, you and your friend will be treated with the policies outlined in the Geneva Convention. You are too important to the final outcome for me to let you starve to death."

He tore the masking tape off so hard he first thought he tore her lips right off her face. "I will leave the keys to your handcuffs over here. You are very resourceful, I'm sure you'll find a way to remove them. It won't matter, since you will never be able to escape this room."

He viewed the trepidation on her face. "Don't be afraid. This room is designed to withstand winds up to three-hundred-miles-per-hour. The rest of the house may fall apart, but your final resting place will be stable."

He used the remainder of the afternoon to eat a light lunch and board-up the sliding glass door. He penned a chapter in his journal as the rain pounded on the roof and the wind howled. Before leaving, he returned to the storm-room with a large mixing bowl filled with water. He figured it would keep his prisoners alive for the precious few days he needed from them. Then he locked them in.

He secured the residence, in case of looters, or JP Warner, whom he was convinced was responsible for the previous damage. He then left the island.

But before heading back to Connecticut, he decided that he needed to make a stop in Raleigh.

On the ferry ride back to Cape Hatteras, he threw Gwen's cell phone as far as he could and watched it plop into the turbulent waters.

PART SIX -

BRIDGING THE GAP

CHAPTER 74

Cape Hatteras, North Carolina

October 6—present

The minute Gwen's phone went dead I made a beeline to North Carolina. No flights were landing in the area, so I had to fly to Norfolk, Virginia and drive. The irony didn't escape me that it was the same city I landed in on my return from Germany, convinced that my life was about to take a turn for the better, or at least would be calmer.

My calls to the authorities went nowhere—the local police in the Outer Banks were too busy with hurricane evacuation, while the FBI has a standing policy against taking my calls. I did get in touch with the state police, but they hung up on me after I started talking crazy stuff about stolen identities, kidnapped wrestlers, and vigilante killers.

I rented an SUV with four-wheel drive that seemed like my best bet with the looming hurricane. But what I really needed was my Humvee, which was still docked at the Ocracoke Air Field as a security deposit on my last trip home. At least I hoped it was still there.

The hurricane evacuation had turned the road heading out of town into a virtual parking lot. But working in my favor was that I was the only moron heading toward the storm, so traffic was clear my way. I took US-158 and then crossed over the Wright Memorial Bridge into Kitty Hawk. I wound through the center of Roanoke Island until I reached Whalebone Junction in Nags Head.

When I reached Hatteras, I received some bad news—no more ferries were traveling to the island. I was left to face the reality that the only way to reach the island was a twenty-mile swim. I actually thought about it for a moment, before realizing I couldn't even walk five miles in perfect weather in my condition. I retreated to Sloopy Joe's in need of a new plan ... and a drink.

The only person present was Joe himself, and since I was his lone customer, I received the VIP service. Joe was a slim older man with a matter of fact style that was softened by his gentlemanly, southern charm. As I nursed a Killian's Red, the past few months suddenly rose up like a tidal wave. Gwen and Carter were likely captured, my brother was dead, and another loyal friend was paralyzed. And I was no closer to stopping Benson. I'd never felt so helpless in my life.

Probably feeling sorry for me, Joe brought another beer for his only customer, on the house. My only other request was if he would change the Weather Channel to the news. I was hoping to hear some good news on the Gwen and Carter front, but the reality was that they hadn't even been reported missing and nobody was actively searching for them.

Joe obliged, clicking the remote until he landed on GNZ. Close enough.

Lauren Bowden appeared on the screen and I instantly regretted my request. I was about to ask Joe to change to some other form of newsertainment when Lauren announced, "GNZ was the first to report to you earlier this morning that there has been a break in the murder case of Senator Craig Kingsbury."

This was news to me. And seemed to grab Joe's attention also because he raised the volume.

"Ron Culver, a member of the North Carolina State Police, committed suicide last night in his Raleigh apartment, leaving behind a note in which he confessed to the murder of Senator Kingsbury. Culver was originally ruled out as a suspect, but the speculation now is that the Kingsbury family had created the alibi to avoid potentially embarrassing facts coming out about the relationship between Culver and Senator Kingsbury, which might have hurt him in the upcoming election. The suicide note cited the romantic relationship between the two, and how Culver's jealousy drove him to the crime."

Lauren continued on, "As many of you know, Lamar Thompson has been an exclusive guest of GNZ many times during this fascinating investigation … and Mr. Thompson joins us again."

Lamar appeared on a split screen from his current residence in Kitty Hawk. He looked very much like the man I remembered from twenty years ago, but his face was scarred with the lines of a hard life. The ones I could spot when I looked into the mirror.

"Lady, can we hurry this up—I got to get back to my job."

Lauren faked a smile. "We at GNZ are thrilled to hear you are now employed and making a useful contribution to society. Can you tell our audience what you now do for a living, Mr. Thompson?"

I took a swig of my beer, unable to decide if she was more condescending or patronizing.

"I'm a tour guide at the Wright Brother Museum here in Kitty Hawk. But I ain't gonna have no job for long if I don't get back to it! Can we get on with this?"

Lauren smiled again. She would've had the same reaction if he said he was the head of an international terrorist organization. "Mr. Thompson, with the admission by Ron Culver that he murdered Senator Kingsbury, do you feel vindicated?"

Lamar's face creased with anger. "Vindicated for what? The reason I gave you the interview in the first place was to set the record straight that

Craig Kingsbury was the one driving the car that night when we hit Mrs. Lacey."

"But it must be a relief not to be a suspect anymore?"

"I was never a suspect."

"Maybe not in a court of law, but I think in the all-important court of public opinion you were."

His already short patience had run out. "We've already been over this—I had an alibi that day. Nobody in their right mind thought I was a suspect. And as for this court of public opinion, nobody sees me nothin' more than a washed-up druggie who never lived up to his potential. Way I see it, I got nowhere to go but up."

"So you're sticking to your story that Senator Kingsbury was the unidentified juvenile in the car that night?"

"For the last time—Kingsbury wasn't listed in the police report! They kept him out of it. Brad was dead, so they used the juvie kid to testify against me. It was my word against his."

"I am not that easily fooled, Mr. Thompson. GNZ has secured the police report you speak of, and the unidentified person in the car was referred to as 'Weasel Suit' to protect his identity. I know that the Secret Service gives code names to presidents, and candidates for the office. For example, Ronald Reagan was codenamed Rawhide, while Bill Clinton was Eagle. So the fact that the unidentified passenger was being protected by a similar code leads me to believe it was indeed Senator Kingsbury."

Lamar shook his head, exasperated. "He wasn't a candidate twenty years ago. Weasel Suit was just a stupid nickname we used for the kid—Brad Lynch was a big wrestling fan, so he gave us all names based on his favorite wrestlers. Brad was the Mouth of the South because he never shut up, and I was Andre the Giant, since I was so tall."

"If that's the case, what was Weasel Suit's real name?"

"The lawyers told me I couldn't bring up his name or they'd sue my ass. I don't got much, but I don't wanna lose what I got."

"That's very convenient, Mr. Thompson."

"Believe whatever you want, lady ... I need to get back to work!"

Lauren then used her savvy interview skills to segue to the next topic. "As reported first by GNZ, sources tell us the murder of Senator Kingsbury may have been motivated by a homosexual love triangle that included the accused, Ron Culver. Would you still vote for Senator Kingsbury if he was found to be gay?"

Lamar looked around like he was trying to see if he was on *Candid Camera*. "First of all, I can't vote because thanks to the lies of Kingsbury family, I'm a convicted felon. But the biggest reason I wouldn't vote for him ... is he's dead!"

Lauren regained her look of superiority. "I hate to disagree, Mr. Thompson, but our latest GNZ Internet poll contradicts you. 72% of those polled said they would still vote for Senator Kingsbury even if he were gay."

Lamar ripped his microphone off and stormed off camera. I really liked this guy. The camera panned back to Lauren who didn't seem affected by the early departure.

Joe shook his head. "She sure ain't the brightest bulb in the bunch. I'm sure there's a guy out there somewhere she's making miserable."

Not anymore, I thought, before turning my attention back to the television.

"If you are just joining us ..." Lauren flashed her most serious look into the camera. "There has been a thrilling conclusion this morning in the murder of former North Carolina Senator, Craig Kingsbury. His alleged lover, Ron Culver, admitted to the crime in a guilt-filled suicide note. Sources within the state police have confirmed that Culver was in charge of an undercover security escort for the Kingsburys that night. The case has taken many twist and turns, but has remained unsolved since it occurred on July 4 of this year."

For once I was focused on something Lauren said.

Fourth of July.

CHAPTER 75

I had to get to Lamar Thompson.

The northward evacuation traffic was as bad as the weather and it took over two hours to get to Kitty Hawk, which according to Joe, was normally a twenty-minute drive.

Kitty Hawk looked much like the other Outer Banks villages I'd passed. Endless rental homes, clapboard cottages and fishing boats. The museum stood on the grounds of the Wright Brothers National Memorial.

Lamar was dressed in a beige park-ranger-type uniform and he was hunched over with bad posture that made him appear shorter than he was. His head was shaved bald and he walked with a limp. Besides myself, the only other folks taking the tour were a senior citizen couple who must not have had access to a weather report.

Lamar appeared a little nervous, and spoke mechanically on the tour. But the charisma I remembered from years ago would occasionally appear. And as a bonus, I learned more about the Wright Brothers, Orville and Wilbur, and their first flight, than I ever thought possible.

Following the tour, I introduced myself to Lamar, and informed him that I had a few questions for him. He didn't look happy to see me.

"I'm done with all you reporters. That crazy blonde lady told me she'd pay me five hundred bucks to come on, and how much of that do you think

I've seen? It was supposed to be one time, then it was until they solve the case ... I'm sure it'll be something else now." He limped away as fast as he could.

It didn't surprise me that Lauren would offer money for interviews—a definite no-no. Or at least it used to be.

When I caught up to him, I pleaded, "Lamar, I don't work for GNZ anymore. I don't want to do a story with you, I just have a few questions."

"I don't got time for this, man. I gotta get home to see if I still got one."

"I'll buy you dinner," I desperately offered.

Thompson stopped. When you spend your teenage years being the most highly recruited high school basketball player in the country, you get used to free stuff. He looked nostalgic ... and hungry. I could tell he was up for a free dinner; I guessed it had been a while.

We didn't go to a fancy restaurant, rather, the coffee shop in the museum. Thompson splurged with an order of roasted chicken and a cheeseburger on the side. He ate like he hadn't eaten in a month.

"So how's the new job going?" I asked.

"You saw me out there, what you think?" he replied, flashing the smile that was once splashed on the cover of *Sports Illustrated.*

"I thought you were good," I answered as I bit into my greasy Salisbury steak sandwich. I was pretty hungry myself. "I learned a lot about the Wright Brothers."

He laughed. "Yeah, an airplane is the only way a couple of white boys like Orville and Wilba could get off the ground."

I laughed back, finding his straightforwardness refreshing. We had a lot in common—two limping guys who wanted the truth ... and to avoid Lauren Bowden at all costs.

"Lamar, you mentioned that the Kingsbury family lied during your trial. I also believe that a deal was cut with the judge in the case."

He looked relieved that someone finally believed him. "The not-so-Honorable Raymond Buford. I'll never forget that sumbitch as long as I live."

The thing was, Buford and the others who knew about the cover-up didn't live that long. And I was convinced that this was because Benson got to the judge, and got him to spill the beans, probably while he was begging for his life on that hook.

"I need to know the name of the kid you called Weasel Suit. The one who got paid by the Kingsburys to lie on the stand. It's very important, Lamar." I was sure I knew who it was, but needed confirmation.

"Like I told the blonde lady, the lawyers ..."

"It's okay, Lamar—this will just be between us."

I was sure he'd heard that one before. He thought for a moment, but I could sense when a source felt a trust between us. He just needed to be nudged across the finish line. "The Kingsburys are dead, Lamar. The nightmare is almost over. If you give me this name, I can put an end to it."

Thompson thought for a moment. "Things are better for me now. Not what I thought life would be, but better than yesterday. I don't want to go back there."

"It's important, Lamar."

"He was this rich white kid who lived down the hall from me. I didn't even know him that good. Brad was the one who asked him to come that night. He used to wear a suit and tie to class like he was some sort of businessman. And he would blast U2 music from his room. I told him once if he didn't turn it down, the only Bloody Sunday he was going to witness was when I introduced my fist to his face."

"Did he?"

He smiled confidently. "I could always spot an opponent with no spine."

"Like a weasel ... I need a name, Lamar."

His smile vanished. He rubbed his temples, as if he were having an internal debate. His face scrunched like he was feeling physical pain. But I could see he'd passed the moment of no return. The volcano was bubbling over with twenty years of pain ... and then it erupted, "His name was Bobby ... Bobby 'The Weasel' Maloney. If I ever get my hands on that sumbitch I will ..."

I was already scrambling through my overnight bag. I removed a bunch of objects, including my cell phone, and placed them on the table. Finally, I found the copy of the newspaper I was looking for. On the front page was a picture of Maloney giving the *Lisa Spargo Memorial Award* to Kyle Jones at the Rockfield Fair.

"Is that him?" I asked, shoving the paper in his face. "Is this the Bobby Maloney who sold you out?"

Lamar studied the photo. Years had gone by, but a person never forgets the man who sent him to prison. He simply said, "Sumbitch."

Having spent countless hours with Coldblooded Carter, I'd become quite knowledgeable on the history of professional wrestling and it's cast of characters. At the center of many of Carter's stories was a wrestling manager named Bobby Heenan, who was known derisively in many quarters as Bobby the Weasel. He was infamous for talking tough at his opponent, but then cowering when confronted. This led to a famed match in 1988 against the Ultimate Warrior, in which the loser had to wear a weasel suit.

When Lamar mentioned the wrestling nickname to Lauren, it clicked for me. I first thought of Carter's Bobby Heenan stories, but then my mind wandered to weasels I knew named Bobby, including one who used to wear his weasel suit to school to impress the teachers. Before that moment I hadn't connected that Maloney had also attended UNC, and would have been a freshman at the time of the accident—having been pushed up a grade in elementary school, he was not yet eighteen at the time of the accident. I now understood why Grady Benson moved to Rockfield. There was just one more key piece of information.

"What was the date of the accident?"

He flashed ten fingers. Then he did it a second time. "The day that ruined my life."

10/10

I thanked Lamar like he just saved my life, and rushed out of the museum into the torrential downpour. I climbed into my rental and headed north toward the airport. I went to call Christina to pick me up and realized I left my phone in the cafeteria. It was too late to go back.

I now knew Officer Jones' next move, and I had the date marked on my calendar.

CHAPTER 76

Rockfield

October 7

All flights were canceled on Thursday night due to Hurricane Ava. This was not good news for the woman who had the misfortune of working the ticket counter. Dealing with JP Warner was not discussed in the job manual.

I thought of driving, but the reality was that I would arrive in Rockfield no earlier than Friday morning, no matter what I did. So I gritted my teeth and took the first flight the next morning.

When I finally arrived, I purchased a new cell phone. I then tried to get in touch with Christina, but she was nowhere to be found ... or more likely, wasn't answering. So I was forced to call my mother for a ride, which made me feel like I was twelve years old. She sent Ethan instead. It was an obvious attempt by Mom to get the two bickering brothers together.

"Nice shiner," I greeted Ethan.

"You should see the other guy," Ethan replied, stealing my line. We climbed into his minivan, which was filled with a strange combination of dolls and football equipment. I saw it as another sign that I should never have children.

"I really appreciate what you did for me."

"It was nothing. Although, I'm not sure the school board sees it as such a noble act."

"What did they say?"

"I can coach the rest of the regular season. But I will be suspended for the league championship game and state playoffs."

Guilt churned in my stomach. "That's total BS! They purposely took you out at the pinnacle of your career to make a point that they wouldn't play any favors because Dad's on the board."

"The pinnacle of my career is every day when I wake up and get to do something I love for a living. I'm lucky they didn't fire me."

"It really doesn't bother you they are taking away your chance to win your first state championship? This year was your best shot."

"It's not *my* championship, JP … it's the kids' championship."

I took a moment to let it sink in. Just more proof that we were from different planets. "You really are about the story and not the glory."

"Huh?"

I smiled. "It's just that I always wanted to be like my older brother. I guess the more things change the more they stay the same."

"Try living with three screaming kids, and busting your rear to make the next mortgage payment, then tell me you still want to be like me."

"I wish I could have been a better role model for Noah."

Ethan patted me on the shoulder. "If Noah knew what you were doing for him he'd be proud. Did you find anything new about Jones on your trip?"

I was too tired to go through the whole convoluted story. "Nothing I can prove. Is there anything positive we can talk about?"

"The Rockfield High football team is undefeated—are you coming to the game tonight?"

"Now *that's* positive. I wouldn't miss it for the world. Keep the good vibes going."

"Mom tells me that you and Gwen might be getting back together."

That didn't last long. My face slumped. "There's a problem."

"I'm sure whatever it is you two will work it out. You're meant for each other."

"It's a big problem."

"Another man?"

"Kind of."

"What does that mean?"

"Jones is holding her captive."

Ethan slammed the breaks in the middle of the I-84, almost causing a thirty-car pile-up. "You're sure?"

"Yes."

At least I hoped she was a captive. The alternative was too dismal to even think about. I was banking on the fact that Benson was intelligent, and the smart move would be to keep her as an insurance policy.

"Then what are we waiting for? Let's go to the cops."

I shook my head. "The only way to get her back is to lure him out. If we scare him we might never see her or Carter again."

"He has Carter, too?"

I nodded.

"Do you have a plan?" Ethan asked.

"I need you to take me to Town Hall."

CHAPTER 77

I was told that Maloney was in a meeting with Rich Tolland. I took that as a cue to barge into his office.

Bobby the Weasel first looked stunned, but quickly regained enough composure to snarl at me, "We are in a meeting, Warner." He called for his secretary to remove me.

Rich stood, looking intimidating. "What is it now, JP?"

"I just wanted to tell both of you that Kyle Jones didn't kill my brother, and I wanted to apologize."

"We know that, Warner. I'm glad you came to your senses," Maloney said. "Apology accepted, now please let yourself out before I have someone do it for you."

"The name of the person who killed my brother is Grady Benson. His parents were killed by a drunk driver way back in 1989, and since then has been performing his brand of vigilante justice across the country. Some names of his victims include pro football star Leonard Harris and former US Senator Craig Kingsbury."

A tense silence hung over the room, until Maloney responded, "What size straightjacket do you wear, Warner?"

Rich concurred, "You're wasting our time here, JP."

I kept my attention on Maloney. "Do you know how Benson found out about Craig Kingsbury being involved in a drunk driving fatality, Bobby?"

"Probably from that lunatic Lamar Thompson spouting off on TV," he said. "And I thought I told you to call me Robert."

"I'm sorry, Bobby, I was just feeling a little nostalgic. Thinking back to when we were simple college students—me at Columbia, you at UNC. I think you were there at the same time as Craig Kingsbury, right?"

"What are you getting at, Warner?"

"I was just curious if you'd heard any talk on campus. You see, my sources tell me that Kingsbury was driving and Lynch was in the passenger seat. I also know Lamar Thompson was in the backseat on the driver's side. But for the life of me, I can't figure out who that other kid was in the car. I just thought you might have some inside knowledge, going to school there at the same time and all."

I took a long look at him. I would have smirked, but there was nothing funny about this. He nervously fidgeted with his silk tie. It reminded me of a sweater that had begun to unravel. The first loose string looks so innocent, but soon it leads to another, and before you know it you can't stop the demise.

"I don't know, Warner. Maybe you can consult one of your great sources. I have work to do," he said and sat down behind his desk.

"I did, and do you know what I learned?"

"I couldn't care less." His words were still firm, but the tone had turned hesitant. He knew he was entering a minefield.

"George Kingsbury arranged a deal with a crooked judge named Raymond Buford. They paid off the fourth kid in the car, the juvenile, for false testimony to make it all disappear for his son. It worked well, that is, until Grady Benson found out about it. Craig Kingsbury and his father are dead, along with Buford. And now Benson is coming after the last piece of the puzzle. Are you *sure* you don't know who he is, Bobby?"

He stood and pointed angrily to the door. "Get out!"

Rich stepped in. "JP, I'm not sure where this is going. Is there a point in there, or do you just like to hear yourself talk?"

"Trust me, Rich. I'm as sick of myself as you are. So I'll shut my fat trap and let Bobby tell you what my point is. I think he knows what it is."

"You've lost your mind, Warner," Maloney said.

A grown man having a mental breakdown was not a pretty sight.

"Tell him, Bobby."

"Get out!"

I reached across the desk and grabbed Maloney by his pricey tie and pulled him close enough to my face to feel my stubble. "I said tell Chief Tolland who the fourth person in the car was."

Rich physically separated us with a very recognizable look. It was the "I've had all the JP Warner I can stand for the rest of my life" look. I got that a lot.

I began to nonchalantly walk out of the office. "I'm a little hurt, Bobby. I was just trying to save your life."

"Freeze!" Rich's voice echoed throughout the room. He knew I was up to something.

I stopped and turned.

"Spill it, JP," he said. It was an order.

I walked back to Maloney's desk. I reached into my overnight bag and pulled out a glossy black-and-white US Air Force photo of Grady Benson and tossed it on the desk. It fell right beside framed pictures of Maloney's perfect family. Even with the passing of years, there wasn't any reasonable doubt who they were looking at.

Rich stared hypnotically at the photo. Maloney looked like he was about to throw up.

"By the way, Benson loves to kill on anniversaries. Just ask Noah. What was the date of the Lamar Thompson accident?"

"October tenth," Maloney mumbled.

"Well, at least that gives you a couple days to say your good-byes and to get your will updated. Did I mention that October 10 this year is the 20th anniversary of the accident? I'm guessing that Benson might be planning a reunion for that day."

I began strutting toward the door

"Please come back," he uttered feebly.

"Excuse me?"

"Please come back," he said, this time louder.

I turned to face him, and he bowed his head in shame. If he thought the sympathy card would work he had the wrong jury.

"I was a kid. George Kingsbury was a powerful man. They promised me that my name would never be released. Not a day goes by that I don't think about that Lacey woman. But it's not like I was the one driving the car."

I walked behind the desk, lifted Maloney's sulking head, and drove my fist into his nose.

"That's for Lamar Thompson. And if it weren't for you, Benson would have never come here. So I'm holding you responsible for what he's done since he arrived. If it weren't for you ... my brother would be alive. If it weren't for you ... Gwen wouldn't be his hostage right now!"

Rich pulled me away from Maloney before a murder occurred. He wasn't overreacting. His expression then changed to confusion. "Did you say Gwen is being held hostage?"

I pointed at Rich in the way my mother taught me not to point at people. "That's why I'm in charge now. That is, unless you want the world to know you enabled a mass murderer. And covered up that video of 'Officer Jones' assaulting Carter."

Rich stood motionless, his bulky arms crossed across his massive chest. Maloney's head was tilted back with a rag over his nose, trying to stop the bleeding.

I had the floor. I began with Benson's parents being killed by the speeding car of Timothy Kent. And then walked them through each disturbing step that led us to this day.

The story was insane, but nobody in the room could doubt it.

Rich added, "That's all circumstantial. I can't arrest him just on innuendo. My only option is to charge him with impersonating an officer. That will at least get him off the street if he has plans of doing something on the anniversary of the accident."

"If you arrest him I will never see Gwen again."

"Then what do you propose we do?"

"I have a plan. Go set up a press conference for tomorrow morning, Bobby. You have a big announcement to make."

CHAPTER 78

Friday night was idyllic for football. Heavy rains were predicted, but held off. Temperatures were October brisk, just a shade below fifty for the game between the undefeated Rockfield Mountain Lions and Newtown High.

The onslaught began immediately, with Rockfield returning the opening kickoff for a touchdown. Midway through the second quarter, Ethan's troops had a twenty-one to nothing lead and were closing in on more.

I took in the sights and sounds. I noticed my father working the crowd like it were Election Day, in his first public appearance since Noah's funeral. My mother was more subdued, huddled under a blanket in the bleachers, chatting with old friends. The band struck up a catchy fight song, drowning out the obnoxious shouts coming from the parents in the crowd. When my eyes got to the cheerleaders, I thought of Gwen, and how stunning she used to look in her cheerleader uniform back in the day. Come to think of it, she'd still probably look pretty good in that uniform.

The thought sobered me. I knew I had one shot to get her back. This had to work. The stakes were Gwen's life, which meant it might as well have been my own life. The plan was based on Benson's weakness—his heroic view of himself. You take my girl, I take your glory.

But I wasn't naïve enough to think that Benson didn't have the upper hand. It no longer mattered if we were onto him—he held the ultimate equalizer in Gwen. He knew it, and I knew it. All I wanted to do was to level the playing field.

Halftime came with Rockfield being cheered off the field, owning a commanding four-touchdown lead. I made my way to the snack bar and shamelessly used my celebrity status to cut in line. It wasn't that I was so hungry, or on an ego trip—I was just strapped for time. The first step in the plan should be arriving in just moments.

On the way back to my position, I saw him. Working security detail for the game in his light gray police uniform was Grady Benson, or as he was known in these parts, Officer Jones. I held my stare on him, and could tell it made him feel momentarily uncomfortable. I was skilled at causing discomfort in others, which normally worked as an effective weapon in keeping people from sitting next to me on the subway. Benson turned and went on his way, diligently carrying out his police duties. I smiled at winning a small battle.

I returned to the meeting spot and waited. She showed up wearing a long black leather coat. It came down just above her high-heeled shoes, giving her a flasher look. Her big blonde hair shone so brightly it could have been used to light the field.

I cringed when I heard her voice, "Hello, John Peter."

CHAPTER 79

"You look radiant as usual," I greeted Lauren.

"Don't try to butter me up, John Peter. If you invited me here because you want me to interview you, well, you are a dollar late and a day short."

"Actually, I wanted both you and Cliff to come. Where is he?" I asked, letting the butchered saying pass without comment.

"He's parking the car. Before he gets here, I just want to say that it's very obvious the reason you asked us here was to beg for your job back. So I want you to know that I'm a team player, and I won't stand in your way. I will do my best not to think less of you when I'm your boss."

I began to choke on my hot dog. "I'm sure any man would be honored to be under you. And I'm sure many have been."

"Your smarty-pants comments don't work on me anymore, John Peter. The fact is, you thought GNZ would crumble without you. Between my reporting on the Kingsbury case, and our new edgier shows this fall, not only did we not miss a beat, but we found that old guys like you were making us stale."

"I caught Todd Scott's edgier show, the Todd Squad for Truth. Where'd you guys find him, the Mental Health Channel?"

"Make fun all you want, John Peter, but Todd is a revolutionary."

"Sort of like Castro was."

"You are just jealous that he's not afraid to feed America the answers it starves for."

"I guess if you can't report the news, you might as well make it up."

"You wouldn't know cutting edge if it hit you in the head."

She might've had a point, but to be fair, I often did want a sharp cutting edge to stick in my eye when I was with her. I thought that should count for something.

Our stimulating conversation was interrupted by Cliff Sutcliffe, also stylishly overdressed for a high school football game. I was getting worried that he'd dropped Lauren off and hightailed it back to the city. Not that I could argue against the strategy, but I needed him here.

We shook hands like we were long lost friends. Lauren excused herself so that she could use the "ladies room." Her acting hadn't improved since the last time I'd seen her.

When she was safely out of earshot, Cliff began his spiel, "JP, I need you back. Even MSNBC has passed us in the ratings."

"Ratings are overrated." I said with a smug grin.

"You drive a hard bargain, but I'll double the offer from last time."

"I'm not coming back, Cliff."

His face slumped. "Then why was it so urgent for us to trek out to the wilderness tonight?"

"I started working at GNZ when I was seventeen. The place will always be part of me, and I hate to see it struggle. So I wanted to give you a scoop about something big going down here in Rockfield."

"What big event could possibly take place in this Podunk town?"

"You mean like the brother of a certain celebrity journalist dying in a tragic accident last month?"

"I'm sorry, JP, I forgot to mention to you how sorry we at GNZ are for your loss."

"The only thing you'll be sorry about is if you don't follow up on the lead I'm about to give you. Here's the scoop—Noah's death wasn't a suicide. Do you remember those terrorists who put a bounty on me last year?"

His eyes grew wide behind his spectacles. "You're telling me that Al Muttahedah killed your brother in an act of revenge?" he asked with a little too much excitement.

"No, what I was going to tell you is that when it's revealed who was behind Noah's death, it will be bigger than that."

Right on schedule, Lauren returned. "So have you come to your senses, John Peter, and decided to come back to work for me at GNZ?"

When she realized that the answer was no, her face flushed with anger.

But before the tongue lashing commenced, Cliff spoke, "JP won't be re-joining us at this time, but he offered us a lead on a big story."

Her pouty look perked up. "How big?"

"Huge," I said. I'd broken so many big stories over the years that they couldn't completely dismiss me. "There will be a press conference here at Rockfield Town Hall first thing tomorrow morning, at which the police will announce the arrest of the man who killed my brother. And when the name is released, it will be the biggest story of the year, I promise you. I took the liberty of booking you both rooms at the Hastings Inn here in town, so you can be there bright eyed and bushy tailed."

Sutcliffe didn't need convincing. Lauren appeared visibly intoxicated. This was too easy—like shooting fish in a barrel. Although, I once watched Carter try to do that and it wasn't really that easy.

The game ended with Rockfield winning 52-6. "You want an interview tonight?" I asked.

"Of course, John Peter," Lauren could barely contain herself.

I led them onto the field and introduced them to my brother Ethan, who was sporting the smile of a victorious coach.

Lauren looked indignant. "I thought you wanted me to interview you, John Peter—your first official interview since being captured. Why would I interview *him?*"

I shrugged. "Because he's the winning coach. They always interview the winning coach."

I guess she wasn't interested because she stormed off, muttering to herself. Sutcliffe followed, but gave me a thumbs-up to indicate they'd be at the press conference.

I congratulated Ethan on the win, and he predictably gave credit to the players.

On my way out, I again made eye contact with the man claiming to be Officer Jones. I smiled at him, which seemed to momentarily confuse him. I might not be cutting edge, but this old dog still had a couple tricks up his sleeve.

CHAPTER 80

Rockfield Town Hall

October 8

Rain fell steadily on Saturday morning. A group of reporters gathered under the dark skies outside the Rockfield Town Hall, holding umbrellas and wearing rain-slickers.

For those who claimed I'd inevitably return to the life of chasing the big story, I guess they were right, because even though I stood off to the side as an observer, I was directly in the eye of the storm.

Just as I suspected, and was counting on, Lauren was unable to keep her yapper shut. Which explained how everyone from NBC to CNN showed up to provide national coverage of the arrest of Grady Benson. He always wanted his story to be grandiose. The lesson: be careful what you wish for ... you just might get it.

Lauren flashed me a dirty look across the press row, unhappy that word of the press conference spread to other networks—oblivious that she was the one responsible for the leak.

Most of the reporters on hand looked as if they'd just graduated college. It used to be that when word leaked of GNZ covering a story, everyone would follow them with their 'A' team. That wasn't the case anymore, which I took into account. With the JV on the story, I wasn't sure they'd ask the right questions, so I planted Christina in the crowd with a list of questions I wanted answered.

At exactly nine o'clock, Maloney burst through the front doors of Town Hall, wearing a dark pinstriped, three-button Tasmanian wool suit. If this didn't work out, he could very well be buried in the same suit in a few days' time. He walked in front of the reporters in an informal style, trailed by two uniformed Rockfield police officers. One was Chief Rich Tolland, and to my delight, the other was Officer Jones, aka the real Grady Benson.

Maloney looked nervous, which seemed reasonable, considering his life was on the line. I was more interested in Gwen's life and encouraged him to "get on with it" with an impatient nod of my head. I figured once the lies started flowing off his tongue, he would find his comfort zone.

His voice was confident, but muffled by the click of flashbulbs and the pitter-patter of rain on umbrellas, "Thank you all for coming. I know the conditions are not the best, but I have an important announcement to make. We're here to announce an arrest in the death of Noah Warner.

"Original reports of a suicide were premature, and we have continued to explore all possibilities this past month. Last night, a local drifter named Grady Benson was picked up for questioning and subsequently arrested for the murder."

I examined Benson's face. He remained stoic, but watchful.

Maloney went on, "Without provocation, Mr. Benson confessed to the crime. The police were initially skeptical, but the bullet found in Noah Warner matched the weapon we found in possession of Mr. Benson."

Christina shouted over the buzzing reporters, "Mr. First Selectman, if you knew about the gunshot, why was it originally listed as a suicide?"

Maloney introduced Chief Rich Tolland as someone more qualified to answer. Unlike his cohort, he wasn't a very good liar so he spoke in a nervous tone. "Our strategy was to make the guilty party feel comfortable.

Our investigation never stopped treating Noah's death as a homicide, and the family was informed about our investigation. They understood that the killer could have slipped out of town if he felt threatened."

Maloney introduced Kyle Jones as the police officer on the scene. Only Gwen's precarious situation kept me from breaking into a big grin.

"Is it true that Officer Jones didn't hear the gunshots that night, and the bullet was discovered later?" Christina again bullied the rest of the national media to get her question out. She had a future in this.

Rich stepped forward once again. "That is correct. Officer Jones attempted to convince Mr. Warner to get down from a position on top of Samerauk Bridge, trying to prevent him from harming himself. That's where his focus was, and should have been. There was also loud thunder present on the night in question, making it hard to hear. It was logical that Officer Jones believed Noah Warner's fall was intentional, as we all did at first."

The still-too-young-to-be-cynical press clapped for Officer Jones. I held back any applause for the man who killed my bother. But I did wish I could have been a fly on the wall when Maloney and Rich Tolland informed the real Grady Benson of the arrest.

"Was there a silencer used?" asked a young female reporter from CNN. They were catching up quick.

"I can't get into the specifics of the investigation at this time," Rich stated.

"Where was the gunshot wound?" followed up the same reporter.

"Back of the head, but that's all I can say," Rich said.

Christina aggressively jumped back in. "My sources tell me that while in custody, Grady Benson confessed to numerous high profile murders. I was also told he passed two separate lie detector tests. Can you comment on the validity of the report?"

"I can't comment on that at this time."

Christina pushed, "So are you denying that Benson confessed to murdering former NFL football player Leonard Harris, along with US Senator Craig Kingsbury?"

The other reporters gasped. A buzz in the air was palpable. They were starting to realize they were in the middle of catching their first big break in the business. Sort of.

"The only arrest concerning our department is for the murder of Noah Warner. These other so called 'high profile' confessions will be turned over to the FBI for a full investigation. We will cooperate with them in any way we can."

I kept sneaking peeks at the guest of honor, who stood like a statue. I tried to gauge the thoughts in his psychotic mind. I doubted he was very happy that his life's work was being hijacked right before his eyes.

Lauren was not holding her anger well. "Lauren Bowden ... GNZ ... this is ridiculous. The case of Craig Kingsbury has already been solved. As first reported on GNZ, Ron Culver confessed to the murder in his suicide note."

"Like I said before, ma'am, the only arrest we are making at this time is for the murder of Noah Warner. Any additional charges against Mr. Benson will be determined only after an FBI investigation—it's out of our jurisdiction."

Rich took another question from Christina. "What was Mr. Benson's motivation for killing Noah Warner?"

After looking at Maloney, as if to get permission, Rich answered, "As the First Selectman stated earlier, we are in the early stages of this investigation. But what's clear is that Mr. Benson was affected greatly by his parents being killed by a drunk driver. All the victims Mr. Benson confessed to killing had some link to a drunk driving fatality, including Noah Warner."

Lauren was still not satisfied. "Do you have any evidence, besides the confession of this homeless guy, that he was involved in any way in the murder of Senator Kingsbury? How would a homeless guy get to North Carolina? Don't you see how ludicrous this is?"

Rich just shrugged his shoulders. Welcome to my world, Chief. I flashed Maloney a look to indicate he needed to stop mugging for the national cameras and wrap this thing up.

"I just want the people of Rockfield to know they are safe and always have been. And with dedicated servants like Chief Tolland and Officer Jones behind me, they will continue to be. Grady Benson never targeted average citizens—he specifically chose his victims based on their past actions." A satisfied look formed on his face and I thought for a moment he might take a bow. He was probably already strategizing how he was going to ride this all the way to the governor's mansion.

At that point, Rich announced that they were going to hand out the latest photo of Grady Benson to the media members present. He had Officer Jones assist him in this endeavor—awkward. The picture was of Christina's friend, and Fordham theater major, Damon, who was getting his big acting break. Sort of. With the help of make-up he looked twenty years older, which would coincide with Benson's current age.

A young JP Warner would have done his due diligence and found an old photo of Benson. He would have been fascinated by how much he looked like Officer Jones and dug deeper, but that type of detail is no longer prevalent in the rapid pace of the modern 24-hour news cycle. So I doubted any connection would be made.

Lauren gave me a dirty look on her way out, but Chuck smiled at me. He knew I'd delivered him a big story. Little did he know that I'd completely gone to the dark side and finally embraced the modern cable news mantra of: if you don't like the news, make up your own. I once thought that newsertainment would be the end of me, but now I realized it might be the one chance to save my life.

CHAPTER 81

Sunday October 9

I drove the van to the *Gazette* headquarters to get the first edition. I sat at Gwen's desk, drinking coffee that Murray had brought, along with a bag of jelly-filled doughnuts.

The headline read: *Local Drifter Arrested in Noah Warner Murder Case*.

I read the front-page story that I wrote under Gwen's name. It wasn't too bad, considering I hadn't written for a newspaper since college, but it didn't compare to Gwen's work, and I knew it.

I moved on to the more important, and much better written, full-page editorial. As only Murray can do, he turned Benson into a heroic figure, lashing out at the epidemic of drunk driving that took approximately eleven-thousand lives last year, more than triple the number of lives lost in 9/11. Where is the outrage? he asked. He compared Benson's actions to everyone from Robin Hood to New York subway vigilante Bernie Goetz. And of course, Batman.

He used his endless connections to get the editorial run in most major newspapers around the country. The article sparked debate, much to Murray's delight. He always was a firm believer in the accuracy of news stories, but the editorial page was the playground for his contrarian nature. The "Hero vs. Vigilante" question was being argued on the Sunday morning news shows, and trending on the Internet. Grady Benson was getting his headlines.

Murray put on his fedora and headed toward the door. Before leaving, he turned back to me. "I'm off to church, John Pierpont. Hopefully nobody will decide to hang me on one of those many crosses they like to decorate the walls with."

"Thanks for everything, Murray."

"We'll get our girl back, don't worry."

He didn't have any sources to back it up, but his words made me feel a lot better. When he exited, I skimmed through the rest of the paper. A fake opinion poll said 75% of all citizens in the area believe Benson performed heroic deeds and shouldn't be prosecuted. Fake letters to the editor vociferously praised Benson. We were turning him into the heroic figure he craved to be. The only problem for him was that he was no longer Grady Benson. Two can play that game.

I leaned back in my chair and ran my hands through my hair. I thought about the beautiful editor who the letters were addressed to.

CHAPTER 82

Ocracoke Island

Monday October 10

Gwen sat on the concrete floor, shivering in her wet clothes. She was angry and drained.

There was no possible escape. For a man who built a whole life on lies, Benson sure picked a great time to start telling the truth. She could hear pieces of wood ripping away from the house, along with cracking tree branches. The whistling of the wind was so loud that it was hard for her to think. But the room was holding up against Hurricane Ava. She didn't know if that was a good thing or not.

She wasn't sure what day it was, but had narrowed it down to either Sunday or Monday. It took her days to get out of the handcuffs. A torturous experience of trying to maneuver her fingers in ways they shouldn't bend, in order to get the key into the small hole. She did all this without being able to see her cuffed hands behind her. It was like trying to put her contact lenses in without hands.

The food and water had dwindled. It took a lot of willpower to ration it when she wanted to gulp the entire bowl. Her mouth was as dry as the Sahara, with lips chapped to the point they were bleeding.

Carter remained unconscious. She wiped the sweat off his head, and the stubble felt like sandpaper. She noticed a big gash where Benson had knocked him out. The blood, mixed with the sweat, trickled down his face like wet paint. Gwen guessed he was in some sort of body trauma or shock. She knew he needed a doctor soon or he would die.

With all the free time, she was able to catch up on her reading. But Benson's journal entries were so disturbing that they made her never want to read again.

A sharp noise jolted her. It was Carter—the giant was awakening.

"Did somebody get the license plate of that truck that hit me?" he grumbled as he tried to sit up. He didn't make it, and laid back down.

Gwen felt relief. "Carter, are you okay? How do you feel?"

"Are you an angel?"

"I'm JP's friend, Gwen—you've been out for days."

"I figured I'd only see a piece of ass like you in heaven," he said, before going on a long tangent about some guy named Jimmy Snuka, who was something called a super fly, and one time jumped off a top rope in a wrestling match and caught him with an elbow that put him in a coma for a week. He was definitely delirious.

On his second attempt, Carter managed to sit up against the concrete wall. He took a whiff of himself and made a face of displeasure. "What the hell happened?"

"If you remember, you were following me like you shouldn't have been. Now we're being held hostage at Jones' beach house."

He rubbed his hand over the gash on his head and nodded like it was all coming back to him. "The pictures—I remember looking at them before I got whacked."

A large crash shook the room.

"What the …?" Carter almost leaped to his feet.

"There's a major hurricane hitting North Carolina."

"There's no way out of here?"

"I've searched every possibility."

"What about these handcuffs?"

"I tried the key. It only worked on mine."

Carter smiled.

"What's so funny?" Gwen asked.

"I'm locked in a room with a hot chick and handcuffs, but I'm trying to get out. That hit on the head really musta effed me up." He tried to laugh and it looked like it was painful.

"You make one move and a headache will be the least of your worries."

He smiled. "I see why JP's so crazy about you. You're one tough broad."

"Is that a compliment?"

"Let's just say, I've known JP Warner for most of our nine lives, and in all that time you've been the only one to get entry into his heart."

Gwen shot him a crooked look.

Carter shrugged. "Hey, I didn't say there haven't been others that got entry into other places ... actually there have been a lot of ..."

"Okay, okay, I get your point."

"When you spend time in the places that we have, you learn what makes someone tick. I always thought he was just a prick, but turns out he was a guy with a broken heart, and you're the only one who can fix it."

Gwen wasn't so sure. "If you understand him so well, then you'd know he's programmed to always leave in the end. There's always a next story."

"The only thing I know about JP is that he's honest to a fault. A fault that has gotten that cute nose of his broken a few times. If he says he's stayin', he's stayin'."

"I'll believe it when I see it." Gwen wanted to have faith, but there was just too much historical evidence working against her. But if they didn't find a way out, and quick, it would be a moot point.

Carter's eyes swept the room. "I've seen a lot of sick bastards in my time, but this guy takes the cake."

Gwen looked up from the journal. It was filled with stories that rivaled Stephen King for pure horror. "Each one of those photos on the wall represents someone he's murdered. He described each depraved act in this journal."

Carter viewed the photos. "A US senator? This guy has some set of nads, I'll give him that."

"You're complimenting our captor?"

"It's only half a compliment. You need nads *and* brains. But what happens with these psychos is they get hooked on the arrogance drug and their brains turn to mush. Taping your victim's pictures to a wall in your house comes to mind."

Gwen began to lay out the case against Benson like a prosecutor. Unfortunately, this tomb was likely the only place that the case would be tried. She'd put together what she and JP had discovered, along with what she'd learned the last few days from the journals. She brought Carter back to the beginning, where Benson's parents were killed by a drunk driver, and then took him step by step through each sick act up until the present, including his transformation from Benson to Jones.

It was Benson's glimpse into the future that scared her most. He wrote of a "final" climactic event to take place in Rockfield, in which he didn't believe he'd survive.

He planned to "eliminate" Bobby Maloney, who had been a key figure in the Kingsbury cover-up, and the reason that Benson went to Rockfield in the first place. And most distressing was that he also planned to use JP to complete his "mission," by using Gwen as the bait. It was to take place on the tenth of October.

Carter's face scrunched—it wasn't a pretty sight. "What's today?"

Gwen sighed. "I think today is the day."

As if it was the last straw, she began to break down. First a sniffle and then a single tear. When the floodgates opened, she began to sob uncontrollably.

Carter struggled to raise his massive body off the floor. He wobbled with dizziness, and the handcuffs made it near impossible for him to push up off the floor. But he made it to Gwen. She wrapped her arms around his large frame.

"Is it something I said, or that I smell like piss?"

"It's hopeless. We're going to die here like rats. There's no way out!"

Gwen held on for dear life. She really needed JP, but Carter reminded her of the oversized teddy bear she would grip onto as a child when she was upset.

Suddenly he pulled away. He looked around the room as if he were searching for a lost set of keys. Then he flashed a big grin, which confused Gwen.

"We are going to get out of here," he stated confidently.

"There's no way you'll be able to bust the door down."

Carter pointed to a black object that looked like a lunch box. It was neatly placed next to the bookshelf where Benson kept his journal.

"What is that thing?" she asked with a hopeful sniffle—she had tried to open the box earlier, hoping it might contain food or a tool that might help them pry their way out of there. But she couldn't open it.

"It's called a videophone, and it's our ticket out of here."

CHAPTER 83

Rockfield

October 10

When I awoke this morning, I knew today would be the most memorable day in the history of Rockfield. I just wasn't sure if it would be recorded as a triumph or a disaster.

Our Saturday press conference had played to rave reviews, except from the FBI, who stormed in later that day like the cavalry. An agent named Hawkins made it clear he was in charge, and would be handing out our punishment. The severity of which would be based on our level of cooperation.

The rest of the crew consisted of an African-American woman agent named Clarisse Johnson, who appeared to be second in command. A bearded agent named Hendrickson who looked like Shaggy from Scooby Doo, and seemed to be a little nuts, which might not be a bad thing in our predicament. And two young agents, looking as if they were late for their high school geometry class. One was named Ellsworth, while the other was Agent Justice, which I thought sounded like the name of a cheesy 1970s detective show.

Rich Tolland took the brunt of Hawkins' wrath. He focused on falsified arrests, public spectacles, and endangering the life of a college theater major. I insisted that the fake arrest was a hundred percent my idea. They ignored me at first, but I remained adamant, to the point that Hawkins eventually shifted all blame and anger in my direction. But with the business of 10/10 at hand, a temporary cease-fire was called.

I played nice enough so that I wasn't completely banished from the operation. And as an offer of goodwill, I secured my mother's historical society building to use as a makeshift command post. Hendrickson, posing as a maintenance man, fitted the town hall with hidden cameras that would show a closed circuit video back to the historical society. Ellsworth and Justice took turns tailing Benson for most of the day, but he showed no signs of having done anything out of his normal routine.

Maloney was fitted with a wiretap. The first option was to bug Benson's squad car, but Hendrickson thought it would be too risky. It would be up to Maloney to get Benson to confess his "heroic" tale. When he provided enough to make it an open and shut case for a federal prosecutor, the FBI would move in, arrest Benson, and use threats of the electric chair to leverage the location of Gwen and Carter. It sounded good in theory, but I was skeptical.

What they didn't take into account was Benson's planning and creativity. The murder of Kingsbury was probably years in the making. And there was no specific pattern to his murders—he killed Leonard Harris and Casey Leeds in public spots full of potential witnesses. But he acted covertly when it came to Noah, Buford, and the Kingsburys. And now that we put all the cards on the table with the fake arrest, we had turned him into a cornered animal. Would that change how he operated? And was it possible that he knew the ballgame was over and he'd decide to go out in a blaze of glory, perhaps just walking into Maloney's office and shooting him? Since Maloney was already an emotional disaster, and we needed him to pull this off, I kept these questions to myself. Not that anyone was listening to me at this point, anyway.

I was told that I couldn't be involved from this point on. A proclamation that led to a lot of yelling on my part—I was more invested in this than anyone, I argued. But they cited an FBI policy of not allowing civilians in operations such as this, particularly crazed ones like myself. When I declared that this was America, and they couldn't stop me, they informed me that they were the FBI, and yes they could. And just to be sure, I was left with a babysitting task force made up of Ellsworth, Justice, and Officer Williams from the Rockfield PD.

As dusk descended, the FBI agents and Rich Tolland moved to their position in the surveillance van. The van was white with *Martinez Painting* inscribed on the side. Until today, it had been the *Rockfield Gazette* van.

At 8:32 pm, my babysitters and I watched on the video surveillance as Benson parked Kyle Jones' patrol car in front of Rockfield Town Hall. The only light came from the office of First Selectman Maloney, who was presumably burning the midnight oil.

Benson walked methodically through the corridors of the deserted building, in full police uniform, including the straight brimmed hat. It was eerily quiet, except for the rhythmic clicking of his heels. He knocked on the heavy oak door that read *First Selectman Robert J. Maloney* in silver engraving.

A meek voice on the other side uttered, "Come in please."

CHAPTER 84

Maloney hid behind his large desk, wearing a brown suit over a crisp white shirt and a fashionable wiretap. He noticed the gun attached to Benson's belt and swallowed hard. He rose to his feet, his legs feeling like jelly. He didn't think they'd hold him upright very long.

"Can I help you, Officer Jones?"

"I think we need to go for a ride," Benson responded coldly.

"I'm very busy. Can you tell me why?"

"I think it would be in your best interest to come with me."

He doubted it would be. Benson tapped on the gun holstered at his waist to make his point. Maloney took a quick look down at his desk calendar that read October 10. It made it seem too real.

The two men walked into the dimly lit parking lot. Benson showed the first signs of aggression by grabbing Maloney's elbow and forcing him into the passenger side of his squad car. He drove out of the complex onto Main Street.

"What is this about?" Maloney asked again.

"I think you know," Benson replied, his eyes never leaving the dark country road as they sped by the village store.

"I demand you tell me right now what is going on," Maloney attempted to be stern, but he knew he wasn't convincing. He lived as a coward and now it was obvious to him that he was going to die as one.

"On the anniversary of this day, twenty years ago, you, along with Craig Kingsbury, Lamar Thompson, and Brad Lynch, made a conscious choice to toss a dummy resembling a human onto an oncoming car, giving the driver the perception of striking a human being."

"It was just a college prank," Maloney defended. He always knew that night would come back to haunt him. "We never meant for any of this to transpire."

"Everybody is sorry after the fact."

"Did you kill Noah Warner?" Maloney asked, hoping he would say yes, then the feds could pounce and end his misery.

Benson smiled cryptically. "I think there's a good chance you may have arrested the wrong man in that case."

"What do you mean the wrong man?"

"I think we both know the man they have in custody is an imposter. He's as fake as that testimony you gave in Judge Buford's court."

"I was forced to say those things—I had no choice," Maloney pleaded. "Please, I have children. It wouldn't be fair for them to grow up without a father."

"Fair?" Benson asked incredulously. "Was it fair for Marilyn Lacey's children? They lost their mother, while Kingsbury walked away, thanks to you taking their blood money. Did that judge make you do naughty things to get your money, Bobby?"

"They twisted my words."

"I have your taped conversations with Buford, along with your deposition that the judge kept in a safe in his home, ironically, to protect himself. He kept his records in very neat order."

"How did you get those? Did you kill him?"

Benson laughed. "Buford died from an accident, resulting from his hedonism. I was his neighbor, and he provided the records to me in case something happened to him. Sort of an insurance policy."

Maloney realized that Benson was much better trained for this fight, and was going to win it. He was the judge and jury, so Maloney threw himself on the mercy of the court. "I was just a kid. I'm a different person now. Nothing we do can bring back Mrs. Lacey or Brad. I never meant for..."

"It doesn't matter what your intentions were. Your bad choices led to death and misery and it's now time for you to pay for your sins."

"I wasn't driving—Kingsbury was."

Benson began to respond, but stopped when he noticed something in the rear-view mirror. In a flash, he reached across the seat and ripped open Maloney's sweat-drenched shirt, exposing the wiretap. He tore the wires off, ripping off patches of chest hair.

With steely determination, Benson picked up his speed along Main Street. And now that their conversation had gone wireless, he spoke freely, "You want to know who really killed Senator Kingsbury? You did! By covering up his actions you sentenced him to death. Just like everyone else involved in your 'prank.' They are all gone now, and I'm here to deliver justice to the last remaining murderer."

Maloney was fairly certain that by justice, Benson wasn't referring to a long trial with an expensive lawyer and a consultant to pick the most sympathetic jury. He shouted desperately, "The FBI is following right behind us in a van—you will never get away with this."

"Neither of us is getting away. We're going to die together, Bobby. We will die just feet away from each other, but our legacies will be miles apart."

Benson picked up the receiver of the police radio and squeezed. "For those of you listening in the van, you have failed."

"Kyle, this is Chief Tolland. I implore you to stop your vehicle so we can discuss this."

Benson clicked the radio again and responded, "I will only negotiate with JP Warner. I know he's in your vehicle."

CHAPTER 85

The young FBI agents looked at each other with confusion—Benson's surprise request wasn't in the manual. I was sure the same blank looks were going on in the van. So I did what I always do—I took the initiative.

I limped to the police radio in the command center and picked up. "Yeah, I'm here, Jones."

I visualized the angry look on Hawkins' face, but I didn't care. Some two-bit bureaucrat wasn't going to be able to save Gwen. It would take someone willing to put his life on the line for her. That person wasn't Agent Hawkins.

"If you ever want to see Gwen Delaney again, I suggest you keep the van at a safe distance."

"If you harm one hair on her head, I will break every bone in your body. Then I'll wait for them to heal and break them again."

"I think you are overrating your negotiating leverage. Now back off the van."

I stood and kicked a row of historical books in disgust, spilling them to the ground in a clutter of dust. But when I observed the feed of the surveillance camera being shot from the front of the van, I noticed that they were actually getting closer.

Benson must have noticed the same thing, because he lashed out, "I said back it off or you will never see her again."

I scrambled for my phone, but came up empty. I'd left my phone in North Carolina. And then Agent Hawkins had confiscated the new one I'd purchased as part of the babysitting guidelines. So I went to Plan-B. I turned to Officer Williams, who seemed like a better option than the two feds, and demanded his cell. He surprisingly handed it to me.

I panic-dialed Rich Tolland, who answered on the second ring. "Back the van off!" I shouted into the phone and ended the call.

Silence filled the airwaves, before Benson responded, "I'm glad to see you are being sensible, Warner."

They had backed off. I felt relief.

The cat and mouse game was all well and good, but I had to get into the fight. I demanded Officer Williams give me the keys to his police cruiser. He didn't look as willing this time. And on top of it, the two young agents stepped in and announced that their orders were to not let me out of their sight.

I didn't have time for this, so I apologized to Williams. Before he could ask why, I punched him across the face. I struck him clean and a fountain of blood spilled over my mother's carpet. I was never going to hear the end of that. I scooped up his gun and aimed it at Ellsworth. I held it on his temple and shouted at Williams, "Give me the keys or the kid dies."

Nobody ever confused me with Jack Bauer. Within seconds, Agent Justice performed some wrestling move on me that Carter would have been proud of, and snatched my gun.

Desperate times called for desperate measures. So I pulled a new technique from the Sutcliffe bag of tricks—begging. "Please, we don't have time. Gwen's life is at stake!"

I could tell they were paralyzed by a moral dilemma. Which was more than I expected. Williams finally relented and tossed his keys to me.

Justice lowered his gun, and before anyone could change their mind, I once again ran toward the danger.

CHAPTER 86

Charleston, South Carolina

The videophone connection was poor, but it couldn't wipe the smile off Byron Jasper's face. He'd been sick with worry since hearing the news of the disappearance of Gwen and Big Ugly.

After the initial excitement of the video reunion, reality began to set in. Figuring a way to get Gwen and Carter safely out of that house, before they succumbed to Benson, hunger, the hurricane, or some combination, would be no easy task. The island had been evacuated and all transportation was cut off, including emergency response.

Gwen made it clear the top priority should be to reach JP as soon as possible, and let him know that Benson was planning to use her to lure him into his web. So Byron kept the hostages on the videophone while he dialed JP's cell.

"Who dis?" came an annoyed greeting from someone who definitely wasn't JP Warner.

"I think the better question would be *who are you?*"

"The name's Lamar Thompson. I got a tour to give, so I got no time for your games. This ain't even my phone, so make it quick."

Byron was confused. "I'm sorry, I was looking for JP Warner." But then something clicked. "Is this the Lamar Thompson who was the greatest basketball player I've ever seen?"

"That was a long time ago, man. And I already told you people, no more interviews. Especially that crazy blonde lady."

"Lamar, what are you doing with JP's phone?"

"He came here, bought me lunch, and then left like a bat out of hell. I didn't steal no cell phone."

"I didn't say you did. I was just trying to get in touch with JP. My name is Byron, I'm a friend of his. It's very important that I talk to him."

"Then why you calling me?"

There was no time to explain, reason, or argue. "Lamar, I need your help ... where are you located?"

"Kitty Hawk, North Carolina. First in flight, last in avoiding hurricanes."

"The best flight I ever saw was when you took off from behind the foul line to dunk on Charleston High. I remember they jammed so many people in there to see you that night, the game almost got shut down for violating the fire code."

"Like I said, that was a long time ago, man. It was nice talking to a fellow Carolina guy, but I gotta go."

Byron needed to keep him on the line, and kept laying it on thick. "Maybe so, Lamar, but once a clutch player, always a clutch player. I need a clutch player to help me right now."

"Man, the only clutch I got now is in my car. And even that don't work no more."

"You're talking crazy—greatness is for life, you don't lose it. I need your help, Lamar," Byron pleaded.

Lamar sighed. "Listen, man, I'll get this JP dude his phone back, okay? My word is good. It better be, it's all I got left."

"If you don't help me, Lamar, people are going to die."

"Now who's talkin' crazy?"

"People I know are trapped in a house on Ocracoke Island. You are my last shot to get them out alive."

"I don't got no time for this."

Byron had no choice but to play dirty. "It's not a coincidence that you ended up with JP's phone. This is your chance to make up for the death of Marilyn Lacey. I know you've been waiting to make up for that for years, Lamar. Now is your chance—are you going to let it just slip away?"

"There's a hurricane doing something fierce down here. Even if I wanted to, the island's been evacuated … not even the police can go there."

"Lamar, people are going to die if you don't act now!"

He went silent—he was thinking about it. "Why don't *you* go?" he finally asked

"I would, but I'm in a wheelchair."

One thing Byron had learned from a few months in the chair was how guilt could be used as an advantage. And he would need every advantage he could in order to get Lamar to Ocracoke.

It was clear that Lamar Thompson was Gwen and Carter's only chance—a man nobody believed in for twenty years, and worse still, didn't believe in himself.

CHAPTER 87

Rockfield

I tore out of the parking lot in Officer Williams' squad car. I took the radio receiver into my hand and squeezed so hard that I thought I might crush it. "You wanted me, Jones, now you've got me. Your move."

I visualized Benson doing his psycho-stare out at the dark country road with Maloney trembling beside him.

Benson's all-too-familiar voice emerged from the crackling static of the radio, "I said to back the van off. This is your last chance, Warner."

Benson believing I was in the van was my lone advantage, but the fact that I couldn't control the van minimized it. I clicked the receiver. "I am sorry. We *will* back the van off."

I dialed Rich Tolland's phone—he picked up on the first ring. "JP, we ..."

The voice at the other end changed. This was not good news. "I'm in charge of this investigation, Warner, and don't you forget it. We will back off the van when I give the order, and only then," Hawkins stated.

I couldn't believe this guy was more concerned with protecting his turf than saving Gwen's life. But on second thought, sadly, I could.

"Perhaps you haven't been paying attention, but Benson is in control. Now back off the van!"

"You are on a short rope, Warner. One more outburst like that ..."

"You are now officially out of the loop, Hawkins. I'm done with you—put Agent Johnson on the phone before you get my friends killed."

I continued to speed down Main Street with nothing but silence coming from the other end, thinking I'd made a big mistake. His ego wouldn't allow him to give in to my demands. I held my breath.

"Agent Johnson here," she said at last, and I let out a sigh of relief. But I had no time to waste.

"First of all, Agent Johnson, I need you to back the van off the suspect."

"Hendrickson—back off the van," she called out.

"The next thing I need is your location. I have no idea if I'm even going in the right direction."

I heard her ask Rich Tolland for assistance on the local geography, before telling me, "He's still driving north on Main Street. Just about to pass Skyview. His speed is around fifty."

"I'm going to keep this line open. I'll be the only one to speak to Benson on the radio. I need you to give me constant updates of his movements. I will be speaking to him as if I'm in the van—it's imperative that he continues to think that I am."

"We will follow your lead, JP. You better know what you're doing."

If I were thinking clearly I would have realized how much they were putting their collective asses on the line, including my friend Hawkins. If something went wrong, allowing a television reporter to call the shots would be catastrophic when guys like the old J-News started asking the tough questions. But when it came to Gwen, I hadn't thought clearly since we were five.

Benson's voice filled the airwaves once again, "That's better, Warner. Keep the van at that distance and I won't have to put a bullet into Maloney's pretty face."

"I think you're overrating my level of concern for Maloney."

"What *do* you care about, Warner?"

"All I care about is justice for my brother."

"The brother you never cared about when he was alive? The brother who murdered that innocent girl?"

I bit my lip so hard I tasted blood. But I couldn't let him bait me. "This is between you and me, Jones. Let Maloney go. Toss him out the door and let him bounce a couple times on the asphalt. A few broken bones never killed anyone—I'm living proof."

I continued my juggling act, alternating between getting updates on the phone from Agent Johnson, and then responding to Benson on the radio. He was still going north on Main, passing the cemetery where Noah and Lisa were laid to rest. I continued gaining speed, making a dangerous pass of a slow moving station wagon, and barely swerving away from the on-coming headlights of a truck.

"This has nothing to do with that murderer you call your brother. We both know this is about you being jealous about my relationship with Gwen."

"I gave you my word that I'd back off the van, now I need your word that she's okay."

"She won't be for long if you don't start cooperating. She's tucked away in a place you'll never find in a million years. You'll need me to take you to her."

He held all the cards, and he knew it. I had an idea as to why he wanted my cooperation, but I was still curious where this was all headed. What was his end game?

A short silence filled the airwaves. I used the brief moment to make a decision. Should I stay the course on Main and try to catch him from behind, or take Zycko and try to head him off at the pass? I chose Psycho Hill. I had to beat him. It was my only chance.

"So what do you need from me to finish the job? Some unmarked bills and a free trip to Argentina? That's where all the Nazis went after World

War II. I think it would be a good fit for you," I tried to spark him to action. We were running out of time, and I've learned that you can't get to resolution without conflict.

"You would think being the son of a historian that you would have a better knowledge of history. The obvious difference being that the Nazis took millions of innocent lives, while I am saving future lives. So much of how history is viewed depends on the scribes who record it. They have the power to glorify or demonize."

Which was why I was here. I was JP Warner, one of the most trusted reporters of this generation, and with the unique power to write Benson's chapter—Murray always said journalists write the first drafts of history. Benson needed me. His mission wouldn't be completed until his "noble deeds" were embedded in the history books. And he knew my J-News size ego wouldn't allow me to not tell it. He was wrong about the J-News part, but it was his lucky day, because the resurrected journalist in my blood wouldn't allow me to leave his story untold.

I sped around a hairpin curve where a kid back in high school named Sharkey ended up with brain damage after going head on with a large oak tree. My police cruiser hit soft sand and began to fishtail, but I held it steady and accelerated into the night.

I was faced with another interview at gunpoint to spew hateful propaganda. Once again, I wanted no part of it, but as long as Benson had Gwen, I had no choice. Visions of Qwaui and Zahir filled my mind. I remembered their unwavering belief that their acts of terror were derived from a higher calling. And suddenly I knew where I'd seen Jones' eyes before.

They were the same as Qwaui's eyes.

The eyes of the zealot.

CHAPTER 88

In preparation for the most important interview of my life, I flashed back to my high school journalism class.

Murray Brown was teaching the five W's and one H of journalism—*Who? What? Where? When? Why? How?*

I squeezed the receiver and asked my first questions. *Who?*

"Your true identity is not Kyle Jones. Who are you and when did you begin this quest?"

"My name is Grady Benson," he stated. "My parents were murdered by a drunk driver on July 4, 1989. I didn't know it at the time, but it was for a bigger purpose. A purpose not chosen by me, but by a higher power."

"So you're saying that you're not the Grady Benson who was arrested on Saturday?"

"Since you set that whole charade up, Warner, I believe you know the answer to your question." His tone turned from philosophical to angry in a heartbeat, again reminding me of my captors.

When? "You were responsible for the death of Timothy Kent—the man who killed your parents—on the anniversary of their murder. Was that when your quest began?"

"It is not my quest, nor did I choose it's beginning or end. I am just a simple servant of justice. Whenever it began, it wasn't soon enough to save my parents, or that innocent girl that your brother murdered."

I had almost bitten completely through my lip. "You seem to have a pattern of applying your brand of justice on the anniversary of your parents' death. Anniversaries are very important to you."

"It is a day that needs to be remembered and honored. Just like tonight—October 10—to most it's just a regular autumn day, but it is the anniversary of one of the most heinous crimes and cover-ups in history. One in which Bobby Maloney is the last remaining criminal left to pay for his actions."

What? "What is this 'heinous crime' you speak of? What makes it stand out above the others in your mind?"

"October 10, twenty years ago to the day, Craig Kingsbury spearheaded the murder of Marilyn Lacey, a loving mother who was returning home to her family. In itself, it was a devious act. But the Kingsbury family used power and influence to cover up the murder, with the help of the crooked judge named Raymond Buford, and the testimony of our friend Maloney. Those who had the power to cover up those atrocities, yet willfully continued the cycle of pain, are the worst kind of evil."

"With his high profile, I am assuming that you would consider Senator Kingsbury to be the biggest victory in your battle."

"Your focus is too narrow. Kingsbury might be the most visible symbol, but he's just one in a long line of powerful people who have committed atrocities against the innocent, and then used their influence to save themselves. I just do my best to dry the tears of those who weep at the sword of injustice, as I was called to do. No one life is more important than another."

He already covered the *why?* Sparked by his parents' death, called by a higher being, et-cetera. For someone who didn't think one life was more important than the next, he sure had a superior vision of himself.

I moved on to the *how?* "My focus might be too narrow, but I'm a reporter at heart, I can't help it. I'm fascinated how you were able to get access to a US senator. And Leonard Harris—sounds like you got the houseboat idea from Kyle Jones."

"The means are irrelevant, as long as the ends were achieved."

"Who do you think you're dealing with here? You brought me here for a reason—you've been following my work at least since you saw my report about Judge Buford—you know I'm all about digging under the surface."

"We don't have time at the moment to go into it. But you will receive a complete interpretation in my journals, including a thorough account of how the symbols were eliminated. It will be an important part of your story, and you have my permission to publish them."

"Where will I find these journals?"

"You will be provided those details when we are finished here. It is mutually beneficial to both of us that you do."

"Is that where Gwen is—with your journals?"

No answer. I took that as a yes. I visualized her chained in a dungeon like the "Bat Cave" in his Rockfield house, and I almost put my foot through the accelerator..

I continued up the curvy Zycko. The speedometer rose, as did the danger. I hated the feeling of not being in control, so I decided it was time to retake it.

Clarisse Johnson shouted into the cell phone, "JP, he is really picking up speed. Do you want us to get closer?"

Benson had provided them enough ammunition to take him down, so I was surprised they were continuing to listen to me, and hadn't made a hard charge—one that I feared would get people killed, namely Maloney and Gwen.

"Stay where you are," I demanded.

I was whipping around sharp curves like I was maneuvering a bobsled course. It was the same route Noah and Lisa took that fateful night. I overloaded with emotions.

I passed The Natty where Noah asked for Lisa's hand in marriage. I went to wipe away tears, but found it was just sweat.

I wasn't sad.

I was pissed off.

CHAPTER 89

Grady Benson was in Batman mode now, as he flew his final mission. Maloney was hardly a suitable replacement for Kyle. Thoughts of his former wingman flashed him back to the trip they took to Seattle. They had drove out to Mount St. Helens, where Kyle spread his parents' ashes. He'd never felt so close to anyone as he did at that moment, and they vowed to fight, so others wouldn't have to feel the same pain.

But there was no time for sentiment. He knew the clock was ticking and he needed to act fast. It was time for his final summation. He reached for the radio receiver.

"I'm just one man, and my accomplishments are nothing more than a start. But I am confident that many others will pick up where I left off." He paused for a moment, trying to check his emotions, but this time he couldn't contain them. "I never want someone else to have to go through what I did."

"What about the real Kyle Jones ... did he deserve to die?"

"Kyle was anything but innocent. Like me, he was granted the opportunity to protect lives, yet he chose to hide behind a wall of closure, and even accepted blood money from his parents' killers. By doing so, he was responsible for enabling more families being torn apart. And the ironic thing was, while he remained silent, I was the one who spoke out about houseboat safety."

"Only after you used it as a tactic to kill Leonard Harris. I think your concern was more about covering your own tracks."

"Who was going to get justice for those girls that Harris murdered in cold blood? The police, who were too busy looking the other way when one of their own like Kyle Jones was caught driving drunk? Or maybe the judge who let Harris off with just probation?"

"The church of Grady Benson doesn't seem to believe in redemption or forgiveness. I know Noah did, and he had dedicated his life to making up for past mistakes. And from what I've learned, so did Leonard Harris. Perhaps they could have been assets in your fight, but you were too focused on revenge."

"It's so typical of the media to shift the focus away from the victims. Where is your empathy for Lisa Spargo? How come there are no questions about Marilyn Lacey?"

Batman felt his nerves straining, but he fought to stay focused. He knew Warner was just trying to distract him from the task at hand, as many had tried to do along his journey. But he needed to complete his story, and JP Warner was a necessary evil to make it happen.

His attention was stolen away by the vibrating medallion around his neck. He filled with paranoia, visualizing an escape at the beach house. But he realized that there was no way out, and figured it was just a piece of wood dislodged during the hurricane.

He used Gwen to lure Warner to this final confrontation. And now that his story was almost complete, he had no use for her. He had kept her alive to use her as a bargaining chip, but any thoughts that the FBI would cut a deal with him in exchange for Gwen Delaney was ludicrous. It couldn't be trusted, even if offered. He would die today.

But his tale would live beyond his life. A smile came over his face as he visualized Warner finding the bodies of Gwen and Carter, when the authorities searched the beach house. The storm that had protected the island from outside forces, and kept any possibility of discovering their whereabouts before he completed his final mission, was another helping hand from above. It might be days before anyone would be allowed back on the island. The storm room would protect them from the hurricane, but he only left enough water to survive for a couple of days. Just like him, they were running out of time. If they hadn't already.

But his journal would survive. A collection of stories about how one man doing his small part could change the world for the better. He felt at peace, confident that driven by Warner's thirst for revenge following the discovery of Gwen's death, he would go to great lengths to condemn Grady Benson, and in doing so, bring attention to his story. But Warner's hate would backfire, and in the end, people would rally around the triumphant stories.

Batman sped toward the bridge, knowing the guardrail couldn't hold his police cruiser that was traveling at over ninety miles-an-hour. He would not allow the enemy to capture him—his message would be crushed by their propaganda, which would label him as a ranting lunatic. He was in control of the ending.

He looked at the whimpering Maloney, slumped in the passenger seat. His face was ashen and paralyzed with fear. In his last moments he should have been thinking of those whose lives he helped destroy, but in the end he only begged for his own life.

Batman took one final glance into the mirror. He noticed the FBI van gaining speed. But he knew they would never catch him.

CHAPTER 90

My speedometer hit triple digits—everything was a blur. I'd driven Zycko hundreds of times in my life, but I'd never seen it in fast-forward. My familiarity with every nook and cranny was the only thing keeping me alive.

"I thought I told you to back off."

By the irritation in Benson's voice, I knew the moment of truth was upon us. The intrusion of the van into his plan had struck a nerve.

"For Gwen to live, you need me, Warner—so you better come to your senses *real* quick," he warned.

But there was something different about the answer. Every previous response was measured and scripted. But this one was different. It was as if he were improvising. And then it hit me—he was stalling for time, just as I was doing. And I knew why. He needed time to end this on his own terms. I pressed on the accelerator.

Hawkins shouted into my phone, "We have everything we need now to take Benson down. I'm moving the van forward and going in. Consider me back in charge."

I set down the phone, ignoring Hawkins. No threat of his could match Benson's threat to Gwen's life.

"Where is she? Tell me where Gwen is," I demanded.

"Back the van off. I see you getting closer."

Clarisse regained control of the phone. "JP, he's headed for the bridge. He's going too fast—we'll never catch him. I think he's going over the edge!"

Benson ended our interview, "I bid you farewell. I'm sorry, Warner. I lied about giving you Gwen's location—but don't worry, she won't die alone. Your enabler Jeff Carter will die with her."

"You're a sick bastard."

"History will be the judge of that. And since you will be the one writing the final story, it will be up to you how I'm portrayed. My only hope is that you mention that Noah was the most satisfying, because his crime was not against a stranger, but against someone he claimed to love—someone who trusted him, yet he betrayed that trust."

Benson shut off his radio. The silence on the other end was the worst sound I'd ever heard.

Samerauk Bridge was now in my sights. As I sped toward it, I pictured Noah falling on the rocks below. I was tempted to let Benson go over with Maloney.

Benson's police car entered my radar, speeding in the opposite direction, and careening for the guardrail. I thought of my mother telling me it was just a matter of time for me. I thought of the bedroom she kept the same, knowing her son would certainly die a premature death. I thought of Gwen, and was glad we got one last chance to make things right.

But most of all, I couldn't believe I was about to sacrifice my life to try to save Bobby Maloney's sorry ass. I turned my headlights off and shot toward the bridge.

I heard Agent Johnson's voice in the cell phone, "He's really going to do it, JP—he's going over the side!

I made a mad dash across the bridge and beat Benson to the spot like a player taking a charge in a basketball game. Metal smashed on high-speed metal. I had spent a career avoiding gunfire and car bombs, but as Carter always said, the last one always hits you.

My luck had run out.

CHAPTER 91

When Benson's car hit mine, it took off like a plane and shot over my vehicle, flipping in the air. My car hit the road with a thud, skidded over the bridge, and shooting sparks everywhere. It came to a stop about two hundred feet down the road, sounding like a train wreck. Maybe looking worse than one.

I checked myself to make sure I was still of the living. It was inconclusive. But if I was dead, death sure was painful. I pushed the airbag out of the way and climbed out of a hole that was ripped in the side of the car.

My adrenaline pulled me toward Benson, but my body was not cooperating. I fell to the ground, unable to put weight on my leg. It wouldn't stop me—I was going to get to Benson or die trying. If I had two minutes left on the planet, I would use every remaining second to find Gwen.

The Martinez Painting van showed up seconds later. They looked stunned to see me still alive, and trying to crawl across the bridge. I was just as shocked.

Clarisse Johnson met me. The other agents ran guns blazing toward what was left of Benson's squad car.

"Lie still," she instructed.

Taking orders wasn't really my thing. I tried to get to my feet again, before falling down and coughing up blood. I was not a pretty sight.

"JP, I need you to remain still so I can check you out."

Out of the corner of my eye, I saw the other agents surrounding Benson's demolished car. He was now out of the mangled steel and holding a gun at the head of his hostage—Bobby Maloney. We were right back where we started, except for a few additional broken bones and hurt feelings.

"I'm fine," I lied.

"That's what Noah's girlfriend thought," Agent Johnson tried to sober me. It worked, but didn't stop me.

The whole thing was happening in slow motion. "Help me to him. Hawkins will get Maloney killed," I said. And more importantly ... Gwen.

I must have been really convincing, because she agreed to assist my insanity. I draped one arm around her shoulders and hopped on my one remaining good leg.

"Get him out of here," Hawkins yelled at the first sight of me.

"Warner stays or Maloney dies," Benson shouted out, and we momentarily became teammates. Benson looked even more surprised to be alive than I was. But unlike myself, he looked like he didn't want to be.

I knew Benson wasn't stupid enough to think holding Maloney would keep him from an onslaught of FBI bullets. I had to get to Benson before he killed himself, or got himself killed ... whichever came first.

Rich Tolland met me with concern. "Are you okay, JP?"

I repaid him by stealing the gun from his holster. Before he could try to regain it from me, I was aiming it at Benson's face, ready to fire. "Where is Gwen!?"

"Put the gun down or I kill Maloney," Benson fired back.

"Shoot him and get it over with. This is between you and me, Benson, and he's getting in the way."

The FBI agents all looked at each other—not sure what to do. They didn't teach JP Warner at Quantico.

Maloney met the statement by throwing up. It was always harder to die the second time in a night.

"Where is, Gwen?" I asked again.

Benson just smiled. It worried me.

Time was running out. I had to do something, so I fired the gun. The blast echoed off the river below, and also pierced Benson's right shoulder. The surprising shot caused mass confusion, allowing Maloney to get out of his clutches.

Benson screamed out in agony. He attempted to fire back, but his gun feebly dropped to the pavement.

"Wrong answer, where is she? I know she's alive."

"You're crazy," Benson said to me, clutching his wounded shoulder.

I didn't have time to ponder the irony of the statement. I broke away from Agent Johnson, but my legs couldn't support my weight. I screamed out in pain and dropped to my knees. Before anyone could figure out what I was about to do, I slithered to Benson and stuck my gun in his mouth.

"Where is she?"

The FBI shouted for me to back off, and I could feel their weapons pointed at my head.

"Don't do it, JP," Agent Johnson exclaimed.

"Put the gun down, Warner," Hawkins said firmly, with gun drawn.

"He killed my brother. He wants justice and now he's gonna get it, old-school style, unless he tells me where Gwen is!"

I shoved the gun to the back of his throat and he began to gag.

Rich Tolland spoke up, "JP, if you shoot him then you become as bad as he is."

"Why should I let him live? So he can have a trial where he would try to garner support for his sick acts?"

"Drop the gun or I'll shoot you, Warner," Hawkins reiterated. I didn't doubt him. In fact, I thought he might enjoy it.

Benson turned a shade of purple as my gun tickled his tonsils. I shoved deeper.

But when I looked deep into his bulging, psychotic eyes, I realized that Rich was right—I didn't want to be like him. And more importantly, I knew that a dead Benson equaled a dead Gwen. I tossed the gun on the pavement. I raised my hands in the air as the agents moved in on me like I was the mass murderer.

Benson shouted, "Either let me go or you never see Gwen again. Do you understand?" It was the last card he had to play.

The ringing of a phone temporarily froze everyone. The agents instinctively checked their pockets, but the phone didn't belong to any of them. Agent Johnson and I simultaneously located it—on the ground beside Benson's mangled police car. It was *his* phone.

I tried to speed-crawl for it, but had no chance to beat Agent Johnson. She scooped it up and answered with the casual greeting of "hello" like it was her home phone. She listened intently while nodding. She then walked toward Benson and tossed it toward him. "It's for you."

He reached up to catch it, but couldn't raise his bullet-punctured shoulder. The phone fell to the ground in front of him.

With an arsenal of FBI firepower still pointed at him, Benson picked up the phone with his left arm. When he listened to the caller, the life ran out of his face. He tossed it on the ground in my direction.

I picked up the phone and I got my answer. I smiled as wide as I ever had.

"Are you causing trouble, JP Warner?"

"Are you calling your boyfriend's cell phone?"

"I would have called yours, but being absentminded like you are, you left it with Lamar Thompson."

I was full of questions. The journalist in me had returned. Gwen answered my rambling questions with a simple, "Long story." Then I felt another huge relief shoot through my body. The voice of Jeff Carter boomed into the phone, "I thought retirement was supposed to be less dangerous. What's all this commotion about?"

I kept smiling as I watched the FBI take Grady Benson, aka Officer Jones, away in handcuffs.

"I guess it's just who I am," I said with a shrug.

EPILOGUE -

SUNDAY BLOODY SUNDAY

CHAPTER 92

Rockfield

Sunday October 16

Gwen reached into the backseat of what was once the *Rockfield Gazette* van. Anyone who thought the FBI would gladly pick up the bill to fix their paint job has never worked with the FBI.

She reached back into a sea of bagged newspapers and grabbed one. When the driveway came into sight, she whipped her arm and sent the paper flying. It bounced onto the driveway.

I looked up from the copy of today's paper that I'd been skimming in the passenger seat. I was again struck by the volatility Gwen had shown all morning, but wrote it off as one of those womanly things I wasn't evolved enough to understand. I went back to trying to decide what was more beautiful—the multicolored fall foliage of the New England countryside or Gwen Delaney. Even in her Sunday morning look of Columbia sweatshirt, no make up, hair in a ponytail, and scowl on her face, Gwen won by a first round knockout. No contest. But for some reason, she didn't seem to be sharing my poetic view of our relationship this morning.

"Are you okay?" I bravely asked again. It was exactly an hour since the last time I attempted such foolery and almost got my head bitten off. Miraculously, the collision with Benson hadn't led to further broken bones, but I wasn't as confident I'd survive this Sunday drive.

"I'm fine—what makes you think something's wrong?" she snapped back at me.

I took it as a cue to return to the paper, focusing on the front page. It was the exclusive interview Gwen had done with my brother before his death. One particular section drew my attention as I read Noah's words.

Nothing good ever comes from looking back they tell me, but looking back is the only way for me to see Lisa. The first year after the accident I didn't want to do anything but kill myself. Then, for the first time in a year, I heard her voice in my head. I used to always hear her voice, especially when I was about to do something stupid, but after the accident I only heard her scream. On the one-year anniversary I was on top of Samerauk Bridge ready to end it and I heard her voice again. It told me to live.

I looked up, tears blurring my vision. "This is an amazing article, Gwen."

She flicked another paper. "I'm glad Noah's story could be told. But he's the one who told it—I just wrote it down."

"Stop being so modest, you brought his story to life."

"I said it was nothing," she snarled at me. I shrugged, returning to the safety of the sports page, as Gwen whipped another paper.

The awkward silence was broken by the ring of my phone, which had been returned by Lamar Thompson. I gave him my Humvee for his help in saving Gwen and Carter. Seemed like a fair trade to me. It was Lauren Bowden, so I let it go to voice mail.

Gwen pulled the van safely into home base—it was five minutes past seven. We'd started at four. It was hard enough to get up at that hour, but my father couldn't resist the urge to wake me even earlier, to inform me that the school board voted to rescind Ethan's suspension. The wake-up was not necessary, since this was not news to either of us—my father was the one who twisted the necessary arms to make the deal happen.

We entered the creaky colonial that housed the *Gazette*. In the three hours of newspaper delivery, I tallied Gwen's words to me as less than fifteen.

Murray was already present, in his formal church attire, including his trademark bow tie. He'd brewed a pot of coffee and brought an assortment of doughnuts.

Earlier in the week, following the arrest, I lamented the attention being given nationally to the man who'd killed my brother, with his media-savvy lawyer feeding the flame. I believed that Benson was going to get his wish to have his story told after all, and part of me regretted not shooting him on the spot.

But Murray set me straight. "John Pierpont, the news moves at such a rapid pace these days that Grady Benson will be in the battle of his life to remain relevant beyond this week. I'd stake my reputation upon it."

That was a big reputation, and as usual, he was right. On Wednesday, Benson became old news locally when Maloney stepped down as First Selectman, claiming that the hostage incident had sparked a re-evaluation of his life, and he wanted to spend more time with his family. Peter Warner would serve in the interim, until a full time replacement was in place.

On Thursday, Grady Benson became old news nationally. Peace talks broke down between the US and North Korea. Tensions were at an all-time high, and two-hundred-thousand US troops had landed in Seoul on Friday morning.

After our arrival, the old teacher critiqued the Sunday writings of the current issue. He called Gwen's interview with Noah "compelling" and "a perfect mixture of fact and emotion." She seemed to be saving her unpleasant demeanor for me, as she smiled at Murray and cheerily replied, "Thank you, Murray. Coming from you it means a lot."

Murray described my article about Ethan's suspension being lifted as "improved" and "coming along." Not exactly beaming praise, but I took what I could get at this point.

A visitor entered the office. She kissed Murray on the cheek, to which he replied, "Congratulations on becoming the First Lady of Rockfield once again, Sandra." They both smiled at each other. She then greeted her son and should-have-been daughter-in-law with hugs.

My mother brought with her a large framed object that appeared to be a painting. She turned it around to display a framed copy of the *Rockfield Gazette* front page, which detailed the events of October 10.

"We are going to hang it in the historical society, but first I hoped to get the three of you to autograph it."

Gwen and I both signed. But before completing the trilogy of autographs, Murray read the article aloud.

Local Policeman Charged in Murder Spree
By Gwen Delaney and JP Warner

Rockfield police officer Kyle Jones was arrested and charged with multiple murders spanning over decades. The latest of which was longtime Rockfield resident Noah Warner, 25, on Labor Day weekend of this year.

It was later revealed that Jones' true identity was that of Grady Benson, originally from San Diego, California. The arrest of Benson followed a daring car chase along Main Street, in which Benson was holding former Rockfield First Selectman Robert Maloney hostage. Maloney was too shaken for a formal interview, but issued a statement thanking everyone for all the good wishes he has received.

According to sources within the FBI, the alleged arrest of a man named Grady Benson on October 8, was part of a strategy to lure the real Benson into the open. Agent Hawkins, in charge of the FBI investigation, said it's not a common tactic, but "this was a case with special circumstances that required cooperation between departments. I would like to thank Chief Tolland and the Rockfield Police, along with Robert Maloney and his office."

The same sources within the FBI have told the Rockfield Gazette that a search warrant has been issued and performed for a home that Benson owns in Ocracoke Island, North Carolina. The FBI has no official comment on evidence seized, but the Gazette has learned the contents tell the clear story of a vigilante serial killer, including details of the murder of Kyle Jones, the man whose identity he'd assumed. When asked the nature of the evidence, the source stated, "The moron actually wrote every detail down in a journal."

The journals told the story of a man distraught over his parents' death at the hands of a drunk driver on July 4, 1989. Benson's first recorded murder in the journal was that of Timothy Kent, the man convicted of killing his parents, on the anniversary of their death in 1991.

The killing spree resumed in Arizona in 1996 when Benson allegedly murdered former NFL football player Leonard Harris. Harris, like all Benson's alleged victims, had a connection to a drunken driving fatality. His former teammate Byron Jasper commented yesterday from his home in South Carolina. "Leonard Harris was a man who learned the value of life the hard way. He worked daily to become a better person. Benson in no way helped the two girls who died in the accident. All he did was add to the misery, and I'm glad that justice has finally been served in this case."

The highest profile of any of Benson's alleged victims was US Senator Craig Kingsbury. The Kingsbury family released a statement calling George and Craig Kingsbury patriots, and added, "The Kingsbury family has always been the strongest advocates of the law and the judicial system. We have full belief that justice will be served in this case. We also categorically deny any involvement by Craig Kingsbury in the untimely death of Marilyn Lacey, and find any allegations in that case both slanderous and insensitive to a grieving family."

Concerning the deaths that touched closest to Rockfield's heart, Casey Leeds' family had no comment, but regulars at Main Street Tavern plan to celebrate their friend's death this upcoming Sunday by watching football and drinking beer, just as "Casey would have wanted it." The families of Noah Warner and Lisa Spargo released a joint statement. "We are happy that justice has been served. Taking Noah's life could never have brought Lisa back or stopped our grieving for her, which will last for the rest of our lives. Our hope is that the two of them are together again in a better place. All Grady Benson accomplished was taking another child away from another mother."

Benson has hired renowned defense attorney Barney Cook, who issued the following statement, "Grady Benson has an important story to tell. He looks forward to his day in court." Benson's arraignment will take place on Thursday in federal court.

CHAPTER 93

"Just perfect," Murray beamed. "I'm sure somewhere out there Woodward and Bernstein are wallowing in envy. It would have been very easy for you to slant the article based on your very understandable emotions and biases, or incorporate yourselves into the story. I'm also proud you didn't focus on the celebrity of Senator Kingsbury, like the national media did. Kingsbury was just a small part of a bigger story, which you captured the true essence of."

Murray completed his autograph and made eye contact with the still strangely quiet Gwen, who was munching on a doughnut with Hannibal Lecter-like intensity. She was starting to scare me.

He then turned to me and said, "I really think you are returning to your journalistic roots, John Pierpont. What would you say about working for the *Gazette* full time? I can't offer you top pay, but I promise you honest and fulfilling work."

When I scanned the room, I noticed my mother smiling with pride, while Murray looked at me with anticipation. Gwen, on the other hand, was still brooding.

"I appreciate the offer, Murray, but at the moment I have some other commitments I have to attend to," I said.

"Why not, JP? It sounds like a perfect opportunity," my mother said, sounding disappointed.

Gwen walked slowly to the office answering machine. No high-tech voice-mail system for the *Gazette*. Like a lawyer dropping a bombshell in a courtroom drama, she pushed the "play" button and coldly said, "Maybe because of this."

"John Peter, it's Lauren. I'm calling to congratulate you on returning to the GNZ family. I'm glad to hear that you finally were able to put your ego aside, and see that working for me is best for you."

Click. Rewind.

Gwen stared at me so hard I thought I was going to catch on fire. "I always knew you'd leave again. All that talk about staying was just that, *all talk!*"

She covered her mouth and turned her back to me. It hurt to watch, but at least I now understood the drastic mood swing—I shouldn't have underestimated what a great reporter she was.

"You promised that you were done with that life, JP," my mother said.

The glares grew intense. I cleared my throat and offered an explanation that I hoped would get me out of here alive, "Yes, it's true I'm going to do some work for GNZ, but it's not what you think. I've agreed to do six features a year on domestic problems that I feel need more attention. I already have the first year lined up—what can be done to curb drunk-driving fatalities. Another to expose the generator death traps of house boats."

I smiled, hoping that I avoided the bloody mutiny for a few more moments. "My first feature will be about finding cures for paralysis and the work the Rubber-Band Foundation plans on doing to make sure it happens. I'm excited about this. Plus, the travel will be minor, and a lot less dangerous … at least if I can avoid flying coach."

No laughs. Tough room.

Murray and my mother looked on with pride, seemingly buying the answer. Gwen was still a holdout. She turned to face me.

The ringing of the historic landline phone on her desk cut off whatever she was about to say to me. Nobody answered.

The machine clicked on. Following a professional message from Gwen and a loud beep, a message projected for the whole room to hear.

"JP, it's Christina," she started off, sounding annoyed. "Pick up if you're there. C'mon, JP—pick up the phone, you lazy ass."

After some more choice words for me, she finally gave up. "Well, I guess you really aren't there. I just wanted to let you know my train just got into New Haven. I am taking a cab to Rockfield, which I hope you know will be expensed on your dime. I want to hook up so I can say goodbye to you ... with the plane to North Korea leaving tonight, and all."

"She's just mad I gave her Humvee to Lamar Thompson," I attempted humor.

Still no laughs. Just the deadly silence of the lynch mob. No wonder they have those drink minimums at comedy clubs.

Gwen pointed an angry finger at me. "You lying ..."

She held back, sucking in an extended deep breath, then slowly decompressed. "I don't know what I'm upset about—I always knew you would go back. You just needed a warm body while you were stuck in this one-horse town. It's not what you do—it's who you are. It was pretty arrogant of me to think I could change that. Enjoy North Korea—send me a postcard ... and remember to duck."

She started to throw the answering machine at me, but held back at the last moment. We just stood there and stared at each other for what seemed like an hour. I let her win the battle of wills. I looked at my watch, as if I were late for something, before turning toward the door.

When my face was safely out of Gwen's view, I smiled. I chose not to tell her that part of my deal with Sutcliffe included an agreement that GNZ would hire, young, aggressive, and talented field reporters as the core lifeblood of the news organization. Less style, more substance. One of those new reporters would be Christina, who was headed to North Korea as a rookie correspondent. Not me.

I could feel Gwen's eyes boring a hole in my back as I began walking toward the door. When I reached it, I looked back and flashed her my smuggest of smiles. The one that has annoyed people on all seven continents at one time or another.

"I'll be back in a couple of hours. I have a meeting with a realtor—I'm looking into buying a farm."

ACKNOWLEDGMENTS

Finding someone to "edit" a book is easy, but finding someone who understands the story like you do and cares for it like it's there own is a not. So I want to thank Charlotte Brown once again for helping to mold the pile of clay called a manuscript into a flowing story. I've also found (often the hard way) that it takes a village to proofread a book. So I want to thank all those who volunteered, especially Sandra Simpson for her meticulous work and going above and beyond. And to many of the readers of the advanced copies, who made some great suggestions, including Ramin, Ralph, Don, Kelly, and Bob.

Another great cover from Carl Graves. And thanks to Curt Ciccone once again for his ebook formatting. If I had to rely on my tech ability to do this, the book would have been out sometime around the year 2046.

One of the things I enjoyed about writing this book was that it took me back to my time growing up in a small town of Bridgewater, Connecticut, where I lived until I was ten. We had 16 kids in my entire class at school, and yes, there was a fair in town every year. There wasn't much to do, but it sure was a great place to shape an imagination.

I hope you enjoyed "Officer Jones," and found it a fun read. But under all the twists and turns, and JP's antics, there is the very real message of the dangers of drinking and driving. Thanks to awareness and tougher laws, the fatality rate has fallen in half since Grady Benson began his fictional rampage in the early 1990s, but there were still something like eleven-thousand deaths in the US in 2011 related to d&d, or some crazy number like that. We all like an occasional cocktail, but be sure to call a cab when you do.

Excerpt from Kristmas Collins

CHAPTER ONE -

Sunday December 22

Christmas in Connecticut—

Was the name of a campy 1940's comedy starring Barbara Stanwyck. But there was nothing funny about the modern version I was living out this afternoon—a horror film that made me want to return to the safety of prison.

My cab passed through the electronic gates and drove up the Belgian-block lined driveway. We passed rolling, snow-covered lawns, before coming to a stop in a circular drop-off area in front of the ivy-draped English manor. I was here for the Wainwright holiday party, held every year on the Sunday prior to Christmas. I was unable to attend the past three years, and I would have pushed the streak to four if not for some business that needed attending to.

I secured the envelopes that contained my gifts, placing them in the pocket of my suit coat, and grabbed the pastry dish that I'd purchased at a bakery along the way. I then stepped out into the late afternoon—the sky was a dreary gray, and a light snow had begun to fall.

I was met by a portly man in an elf costume. I didn't recognize this particular greeter/security-guard from my previous times on the property, going back to when I used to live here with my ex-wife, Libby, during our first years of marriage. This surprised me, since the Wainwrights always made it a point to surround themselves with loyal soldiers, even if loyalty had never been a two-way street for them. Perhaps they had added extra security this year since a convicted felon was on the guest list—their favorite former son-in-law.

I started to walk in the opposite direction. This predictably upset Buddy the Elf. "Sir, the party's this way," he commanded.

"I'm going to take a shortcut," I replied without looking at him.

I braced, expecting to be wrestled to the ground and kicked with the curled-up tips of his elf shoes. But as luck would have it, I noticed a longtime Wainwright security guard named Lonnie—windbreaker, winter hat, no elf costume—who nodded at Buddy, instructing him to back off. Lonnie knew from firsthand experience that Kris Collins was capable of creating a scene on a moment's notice, and the last thing the Wainwrights wanted to do was to call attention to my presence.

I ventured over a slate path, which was lined with sculpted boxwood and ornamental trees that were decorated for the season. In the summer, the formal landscape of the estate was breathtaking, filled with magnolia trees and kiwifruit arbors. But for the party it had been transformed into a world of Christmas fantasy.

Music was being pumped out through speakers—"Winter Wonderland" was currently playing. *The weather outside is frightful,* the lyrics informed me. And while I would agree that it was a tad on the frosty side, I found it downright delightful compared to what was awaiting me inside.

I walked past elaborate ice sculptures, then an empty tennis court and pool house, before I began to smell the real party. I trudged through another frozen acre until I arrived at the Lake House.

It actually sat next to a pond, not a lake, and it would be more accurately described as a mansion. Like most things on this property, it was more about perception than reality. As a former attorney, who was once known as the "lawyer to the stars," I understood the concept of "perception over truth." And now it was likely the only thing keeping me alive.

Outside of the Lake House, sitting in lawn chairs on a brick patio, and enjoying the warmth of a fireplace, were the self-proclaimed Amigos—Tomás, Gustavo, and Berto—spending their final Christmas on the Wainwright property.

Alexander Wainwright had always referred to them as "the Mexicans"—his name for all those of Spanish descent—but they actually emigrated from Peru as children. And what I've learned over the years about these Peruvian house parties, called *tonos,* is that you don't arrive *manos vacias*—empty handed. So after exchanging warm greetings with the Amigos' wives and large extended family, I handed over a panettone cake to Tomás' wife, Mia.

I then moved to the patio area, and attempted to spread more holiday cheer. I handed each of the Amigos an envelope that contained a Christmas card. Inside the card, besides a sappy holiday greeting, was the final information regarding a project of mine—one that the Amigos had agreed to lend their considerable talents to. I'd been plotting it since my time in prison, and now we were just days away from the big moment.

Tomás motioned for me to take a seat and join them.

"I don't have much time," I cautioned. "I need to make an appearance at the big-boy party. Then I have a few more rounds to make tonight."

"Just like Santa Claus," Gustavo said with a chuckle.

"If that's the case, you're going to need a drink," Tomás added. He got up and poured me our traditional Christmas drink—Mountain Dew and tequila, hopefully heavy on the latter.

Berto brought me a plate from the barbecue, what Gustavo referred to as a "Peruvian specialty." I was fairly certain that a cheeseburger and tater tots wouldn't qualify as Peruvian or a specialty, but I wasn't about to argue.

"I'm surprised you didn't get an invite to the party ... sort of a going away present," I said between bites, but wasn't really. The Amigos hadn't been invited in the thirty years they'd lived here.

"We didn't fit the 'white Christmas' theme they got going this year," Gustavo said with a grin.

"Same theme as every year ... the Wainwrights are traditionalists," Berto chimed in.

The volume of the surrounding festivities muffled our voices, which made this the ideal place to go over the final preparations. Children were ice-skating on the pond, while the teenagers were shooting off fireworks like it was the Fourth of July. Gustavo's college-age son, Angel—a dead ringer for his father—headed up a salsa band that had attracted a group of dancers on an adjoining patio. Many of them were attractive girls in outfits that didn't appear to be weather-appropriate.

I pointed at the envelopes. "The disc inside the card contains a complete route of all the houses and their floor-plans." As much as technology had advanced communication, it also left proof, which is why this old-school drop and chat was the still the best way to transfer information.

I viewed the large house in the backdrop, along with all their friends and family who were reveling in the holiday spirit. Things had changed a lot since they'd first arrived here. "I'll understand if you don't want to go through with it. You have a lot more to lose these days."

"What's the point of having our gifts, if we can't share with others. Tis the season of giving," Gustavo responded with another sly grin. The others nodded.

The gift he spoke of was the ability to break into houses like few who'd come before them. And not just any houses—the biggest and wealthiest estates in the area. That was, until Alexander Wainwright's security team apprehended them. But luckily for the Amigos, eleven-year-old Libby Wainwright was convinced that there was good in all people, and just as importantly, she had her father wrapped around her finger. She convinced him not to turn them over to the police. Instead, a compromise was reached in which they would live on the Wainwright property and pay for their crimes by living as indentured servants—performing tasks ranging from keeping up the fourteen acres, to serving as the Wainwrights' personal chauffeur.

I'm an admitted skeptic of most things Wainwright, so I've always had my doubts that this agreement was completely about granting a daughter's wish, or saving a few bucks on lawn care. It would be very convenient for an institution like Wainwright & Lennox to have access to the Amigos' talents, if they were in need of gaining private information from their competitors.

But their working agreement with the Wainwrights took an unexpected turn this year. They were being kicked to the curb so that the Lake House could be sold off. This was supposedly related to W&L's 600 million dollar loss in a business deal gone wrong with Kerstman Publishing a few years back.

This was not news to me, since I was the one who represented Diedrich Kerstman at his trial. This didn't sit well with the general public, as Kerstman had become the poster-child for corporate greed, and it went over even worse with my former father-in-law. When the smoke cleared my client was dead, I was in jail, and Alexander Wainwright was still out over half a billion dollars. So it went without saying that I was surprised to receive an invitation to this year's Christmas party. Although, I was starting to get the feeling that the case was still pending … and I was the one on trial.